A Gentleman in the Street

Alisha Rai

Dear Karen:
So good to
meet you! Happy
reading. ☺ #long live romance
Alisha
Rai

Copyright © 2014 by Alisha Rai
http://www.alisharai.com

Edited by Sasha Knight
Cover by Kanaxa

ISBN-13: 978-1514616956
ISBN-10: 1514616955

For a certain group of authors who are truly "awesome."
Thanks for keeping me sane.

CHAPTER 1

Akira Mori was partial to a certain kind of man: the kind you fucked raw and dirty until your voice was hoarse and your skin slick with sweat. The location wasn't important—up against a brick wall, in the back of a car, on a kitchen island…

Jacob Campbell is not that kind of man.

Bullshit. Every man could be that kind of man. Or at least that was what she wanted to believe, when she was currently eyeing a delightfully sweaty and half-naked Jacob.

The late-afternoon sun flirted with smooth, tan skin. Muscles flexed and danced as he raised an ax and brought it down in a rhythmic cadence. Wide shoulders tapered to a narrow waist. His abs were flat and ridged with muscle, his chest powerful and shiny with sweat. Worn jeans hung low on his hips, revealing a thin line of paler skin.

Had she ever seen him without a shirt? No, she didn't think so. Thank God for small favors or she would have forgotten long ago their contentious relationship didn't allow for tracing that tan line below his hipbones with her tongue.

If he came out to the sticks to bare it all like this regularly, she would happily sacrifice the two-thousand-dollar high heels currently sinking into the dirt to play voyeur.

In theory, at least. She shifted, conscious of the mud clinging to her precious babies.

He won't thank you for your appreciation.

She pushed the thought aside. Tight-lipped disapproval would come soon enough. Akira leaned back against the tree behind her, the better to settle in for the show.

How did he get an ass like that sitting around writing books? She had a desk job too. Even with her predisposition to slimness and inability to sit still, she had to work out like a fiend not to succumb to office spread.

He brought the ax down with a loud thwack and left it there, leaning over to pick up a bottle of water from a nearby stump. He turned, and she was treated to a view of his profile. Too-long dark brown hair tangled around his face. His throat worked as he swallowed the water. He'd grown a beard since she'd last seen him. She hated stubble burn, but he looked so good with facial hair she could not imagine minding some scrapes on her inner thighs.

She must have made some sort of noise; his head lifted. There was too much distance between them, but she knew his hazel eyes would darken to the same color as the leaves on the trees the instant he caught sight of her.

It always took her a second to collect herself when he turned his stare on her, a brief instant to remember what role she needed to play. She assured herself time and again he would never spot that smidgen of vulnerability. No one could.

Better she laugh and taunt and outrageously flirt to the point of irritation. Better he think her an empty-headed, useless, sex-crazed twit than guess the mortifying truth: she'd wanted this man for over a dozen years.

He was the first to end their staring contest and move, capping the water bottle. She clenched her hands behind her as he walked toward her, letting the rough bark scrape her sensitive knuckles.

Get ready. Shields in place. Ice ran through her veins and steel grafted to her spine.

He stopped a foot away from her. It was rare for her to find a man taller than her, especially when she was wearing her high heels, but Jacob easily topped her. If she extended her arm, she'd be able to touch him, run her fingers over his deliciously muscular stomach.

She worked up her most blinding smile, the one that could stop traffic and launch a thousand ships, that could destroy a man or make him feel a thousand feet tall. "Hello, Brother Jacob."

CHAPTER 2

$\mathcal{J}$acob stared at her for a long minute. She refused to fidget or quail. The bark of the tree was harsh and unrelenting. The action hidden from his sight, she dug her hands harder against it, welcoming the shot of pain.

When he finally spoke, his voice was low and gravelly, as if he hadn't used it for a while. "I've told you not to call me that."

"I apologize. Though it hurts when you rebuff my filial overtures. You are so difficult, Jacob."

A muscle under his eye twitched. She couldn't even utter his given name without paining him, but he would sound crazy and unreasonable if he snapped at her about that. And crazy was *her* role to play.

Without another word, he walked away. She checked herself from hurrying to keep up with his long strides, partially because Akira Mori hurried after no man, and partially because she was physically incapable of hurrying anywhere in her high heels and pencil skirt.

She ran her gaze over his naked, muscular back, his tight ass. Besides, the view was pretty good from here.

He spoke over his shoulder. "My father was married to your mother for three minutes over fourteen years ago. Doesn't make me your brother."

What a logical man. She delighted in twisting logic. "A year, brother. They were married a year. But can you put a time limit on the bonds of family?"

Was that a pile of crap on the ground? Ew. Distracted, she didn't realize he had stopped until she ran smack into him. For an instant, she inhaled clean, warm male. Her hands went to his narrow hips in an automatic move to steady herself.

Before she could make contact, he pivoted and recoiled. "Don't...touch me."

Ice. Steel. The desire froze where it started. "Don't flatter yourself," she responded, every word razor sharp.

"I never do." With that cryptic mutter, he dismissed her, his giant strides eating the distance to his cabin. His heavy boots thudded on the plank steps before he disappeared inside.

This isn't worth it.

Akira looked around the clearing filled with nature and birds and trees and crap, and considered abandoning her mission. What was the point, really? This was a long shot, and her eyes were gritty from lack of sleep.

She'd been forced to put in a surprise-but-totally-planned appearance at her Vegas club the night before in light of some dipping numbers. An appearance, in her line of work, took a lot of fucking energy. It meant four-inch heels, a dress so short she had to keep a constant eye out for inadvertently flashing paparazzo (purposeful flashing was okay), and fake drinking shot after shot so she could ensure patrons had a good time and buzz was generated while she kept a clear head. Partying all night and hopping a flight in the wee hours of the morning had been far easier in her twenties.

She should be working right now to make up for the time she'd missed yesterday. Or better yet, curled up in front of a fire while the gloomy San Francisco fog rolled in. Or best, curled around a guy who *wanted* to touch her.

She didn't need to be in the middle of fucking nowhere with a man who hated her, who had never been able to linger long in her presence. Hadn't she endured enough of that attitude from her real family?

Well. Most of her family.

She gritted her teeth. There it was. The reason there would be no bed or fire or fiery bedmate for her, not until she'd chased down every lead in her hunt for her grandmother's lost legacy. Uttering a vicious curse under her breath, she made her way to the porch, keeping a wary eye on the ground for surprises.

"Yoo-hoo," she called out, putting as much annoying cheer into her greeting as she could muster. *Play your role.* "If you're naked, put your pants on." She finished on a mutter, letting the screen door shut behind her, "Or don't."

Maybe he was naked—the sound of running water came from the other room. Mmm. If half-naked Jacob made her lightheaded, what would the full monty do to her? She allowed herself a moment to linger over that image before shaking her head.

The cabin was tiny, with one slightly ajar door presumably leading to a bedroom and bathroom. Everything else was laid out in front of her: a bare-bones kitchen, a sagging couch, and a two-person breakfast table tucked away in the corner.

No television, but a shiny, thin laptop sat on the linoleum counter.

Tall piles of newspapers sat in a corner. Who on earth read the newspaper anymore? Jacob, that's who. She kept a twenty-four-hour news station on mute all day at work, and checked her tweet stream for the latest goings-on.

The place was clean and well-maintained, but she had to suppress a shudder. The closest she'd come to camping was when she'd organized a corporate retreat at a glamping site, which mostly consisted of creatively built structures that allowed tenants to feel like they were enjoying nature while still appreciating the comforts of home.

She loved nature. Except it had so many creepy-crawlies and animals and things that made her sneeze. Peering out at it from a fully equipped yurt was far preferable to wallowing in it. You got WiFi in the yurt.

"I like your couch," she commented. "Orange is my favorite color."

No response.

At a loss for entertainment, she prowled the room until she came to the bookshelf, which was crammed tight with mystery and horror novels. None of Jacob's books lined the shelves. Made sense. He was far too perfect and humble to have them displayed all over the place. She bet they were properly tucked away in his home office.

Idly, she pulled a novel off the shelf and perused the back of it. The water in the other room shut off. "I didn't realize you knew how to chop wood," she said, pitching her voice so he could hear her through the thin walls. "You know, I bet if there's a zombie apocalypse, you would do really well with that ax and all. I bet you have a whole host of survival skills up your sleeve." She pushed the book back in and ran her finger along the dust-free shelf, until she came to a framed photo. A younger but still solemn Jacob in the center, his arms around two smiling teens and a pigtailed little girl.

Jacob had been twenty-two when their parents had united for their brief marriage. He was older in this photo, maybe twenty-four? Yes, that was about how old he had been when his father had died and he'd taken custody of his siblings. She remembered, because she'd been regaled with the news of Jacob's sense of responsibility when she called her mother to tell her she was posing for *Playboy*.

Akira cleared her throat and put the frame back, adjusting it so it sat at the same angle as when she'd found it. "I doubt I'd do so well. In a zombie apocalypse, I mean. No weapons and no survival skills. Though I imagine I would be excellent at looting." She paused. "I can't guarantee I would only loot necessities, especially when every store would be open and mine for the taking. But proper footwear is important. I could be a ninja with the right pair of shoes." Too bad he wasn't in the room, so she could shift and draw his attention to her legs in the navy heels she was wearing. She didn't consider her legs her finest feature, but she made the best of what she'd been given.

As if he would be swayed by something as simple as a pair of nice gams. Moron.

Suck it up, buttercup.

"I assume I can come running to you for help when—" Her words cut off when he reentered the room pulling a white T-shirt over his head in that sexy way a guy men sexily pulled T-shirts on. He wore the same jeans, but he had washed up even if he hadn't showered; his hair was damp at the ends.

He glided to the kitchen, surprisingly quiet for such a large man. "What do you want, Akira?"

The way Jacob said her name...well, it almost made her forget she hated it with the passion of a thousand suns.

"What makes you think I want something?" she hedged. "Can't I come see my favorite brother?"

His shoulders tightened, and he reached for the coffee maker, his motions economical. Like a sexy robot. "Call me your brother one more time," he said quietly, "and I will carry you to your car and put you inside it."

No, that wasn't a seductive threat *at all*. Not when it was delivered in that measured, deliberate way.

She really wasn't imagining he'd sound the same when he was threatening to spank her.

Nope.

Her fingers itched to rip those casual clothes off him and see how long he remained in control when she was trailing her lips down his belly. She curled her fingers into her palm. "Relax, Jacob."

He grunted. "How did you find me here?"

An easier question. "I went to your house. Kati pointed me in the right direction."

His brow furrowed. He measured grounds into the coffee maker. Hesitated. Measured out more. "You talked to Kati?"

"Yeah." He was overprotective of all his siblings, but he had raised Kati since she was five. He was particularly over-bearing when it came to his little girl.

Not that the scowling, surly seventeen-year-old who had answered his door a few hours ago needed much protection, Akira thought. That girl would make it just fine on her own.

"Relax. I only exchanged a few sentences with her. There was hardly any time to corrupt her with foul language or my vast sexual experience."

He closed the coffee tin harder than it warranted. "She's supposed to be at a friend's house this weekend. It's why I'm here. I wouldn't leave her alone."

Oops. Sorry, Kati. She hoped the kid had some cover story in place, if she was pulling one over on her guardian. "I'm sure she has a good reason for being there," she said lamely.

Jacob drew out a cell phone and glanced at the display. "I'll have to go down the road to catch a signal." The coffee perked in the pot while Jacob's scowl grew darker.

Privately, Akira thought seventeen was plenty old enough to be left alone at home, but it wasn't like she'd had a healthy adolescence for any kind of frame of reference. At seventeen, she'd pretty much been on her own for years. "I didn't hear any kind of raucous party going on, if it helps."

"She's not the type to throw a party."

She's not the type. *She's not like you,* was what he meant. Men, so dumb. So consumed with classifying women into types to satisfy their own sense of comfort.

Suddenly, Akira hoped young Kati was engaging in all sorts of debauchery this weekend with her brother gone. *Don't be a type, girl.*

"Maybe she was delayed," she offered.

"Maybe." A frown played over his face.

She sighed and reached into her purse for the lifeline she was rarely without. A quick peek at the display reassured her she had one weak bar for a signal. "Here. You can try mine. It gets reception everywhere."

Jacob paused. "Oh. Okay. Thanks." Their fingers brushed

when he accepted the phone. An electric zing traveled up her arm.

He seemed oblivious, already moving a few steps away and punching in a number. He shot her a quick look over his shoulder, and she pretended great interest in the coffeepot.

His voice dropped two octaves. "Kati-cat."

Kati-cat? Oh, poor child.

"Did something happen? Why are you still at the house?"

This super kind, caressing tone had definitely never been directed her way. Not that she was jealous of his sister. That would be weird, given all the non-sisterly feelings she harbored toward him.

The coffee maker sputtered, and she eyed it warily. She had a restaurant-quality espresso maker at home, but she employed people to operate it.

It's a pot with liquid in it. She could manage this.

"Mm-hmm. So when is Kristen picking you up then?"

There were only three overhead cupboards, so she located the collection of chipped mugs quickly. She withdrew a sufficiently manly blue mug, and then eyed a fetching pink one with daisies on it.

Hell, he'd made enough for both of them.

"I don't know, sweetheart. Maybe I should come home."

Out of his sight with her head poked into the fridge, she rolled her eyes. Poor, poor child. She grabbed the gallon of milk and plunked it on the counter next to the mugs.

"Okay, okay. Ah. No. I don't have a signal. It's Akira's phone."

The burst of excited chatter on the other end of the line was loud enough for Akira to hear. She raised an eyebrow as he cast her a discomfited glance and moved into the other room, shutting the door.

Good thing the walls were so thin in these cheaply made cabins. She only had to tiptoe over and plaster herself against the door to eavesdrop, and his muffled words came through loud and clear. "Kati, calm down. No, I don't know why she's here. No. No."

Silence. Then, "Well, why did you tell her where the cabin is?"

More quiet. A long-suffering sigh. "She's smart. I'm sure that's all she needed to figure it out."

At least he acknowledged she was smart. She would ignore the sigh.

"Relax. You don't need to worry about me. I can handle Akira."

The hell he could. Akira sniffed. Men didn't *handle* her.

There was no warning before the door opened. Startled, she pitched forward, steadied by a strong grip on her biceps. His eyes grew wide before he hastily righted her, his surprise morphing into discontent. "Of course she's not here to cause trouble."

She raised an eyebrow at him. She would happily cause trouble. However, there was a fine line she needed to walk right now between pissing him off so much he kicked her out and maintaining the arm's-length distance that kept him safely away from her squishiest parts.

It would be easier to keep him at arm's length if his hand hadn't remained wrapped around her arm. Why had she not worn long sleeves?

He spoke into the phone, but his gaze burned into Akira. "Have fun at Kristen's, and I want you to contact me immediately if anything changes. I'll go down the road and check my messages every couple of hours." He hung up and glared at her. "Are you eavesdropping?"

"That's kind of a dumb question," she pointed out. "What else would I have been doing, checking for termites?"

Another gusty sigh left him. They were getting annoying.

He sidestepped her, heading back to the kitchenette.

"Um." She glanced pointedly at her upper arm. "As much as I enjoy being dragged around, could you maybe lighten your grip a little?"

He looked down and pulled away as if she'd scalded him, backpedaling until he bumped against the counter. His cheeks flushed a dull red. "Sorry. I'm, uh. I didn't realize."

She massaged her arm. It tingled where he'd touched her.

"Here." He handed her the phone. There was no brushing of fingers this time. "Thanks."

"No problem."

He hesitated before speaking, every word dragged out of him. "Do you…want some coffee?"

Ask him what you came to ask him and leave.

But she was the one who had pulled out two mugs. A pink mug no less. "Sure. Black."

He poured the coffee and passed it over the counter. Akira grabbed the mug and took a bracing sip, her eye twitching at the hit of caffeine. Did Jacob ever sleep?

"Too strong for you?"

His tone was carefully neutral, but damned if she'd give him a single reason to feel superior. Trying to hide her grimace, she placed the mug on the counter. "Nope. I—Wait, is that skim milk? I didn't realize. I love skim milk in my coffee."

"Do you?"

"It's my favorite." She poured in a dollop of watery milk, until the liquid turned creamy brown. "Kati okay?" she asked when it was clear he wasn't going to be forthcoming.

He gave a terse nod. "She had a change of plans. Going to another friends tonight, but she won't be picked up until much later."

Yeah, right, Akira thought cynically. "See? Told you there was a good reason."

"She also said she didn't tell you where this place was."

"She didn't. Don't blame the kid for my superior deductive reasoning skills."

"You said she told you."

"She said you were on a writing retreat at your cabin. You've mentioned in interviews the general location of your cabin. It took about an hour to search the property records, and another hour to drive out here." She tsked. "Really, you ought to be more careful. Bad enough you don't write under a pen name. Any overzealous fan could find you." Or an overzealous socialite turned businesswoman.

"I'll keep that in mind." He drank his coffee, and she did the same, though the milk hadn't helped the taste of the drink much. The silence stretched between them.

"So."

"So."

He rolled his shoulders. "It's been a while."

Akira eyed him warily. They weren't adept at small talk. Thrust with a cutting remark, parry with a cold comment, duck heavy silence. That was their MO.

What the hell. "Yeah. Six months, right?" Six months and eight days since her mother's funeral. She vaguely remembered Jacob and his siblings attending, but she'd been out of it.

She and the Campbells had been the closest thing to family her mother had had left, but there'd been lots of friends and acquaintances to pack the church. Akira's father hadn't come, because Akira'd refused to allow entrance to the camera crew hovering around him 24/7. Even without the cameras, she didn't think she would have permitted him to show up. The woman deserved to not have her first husband, a man she'd utterly despised, at her funeral.

Before that, Akira hadn't seen Jacob in well over a year, since she had decided to stop inflicting her presence on her mother. So it had been a while.

"Sounds right." He shifted. "It's strange without Mei. I didn't realize she was such a big part of my family's life until she was gone."

Akira nodded, though she couldn't quite empathize. Mei had lived a comparatively quiet life after she'd divorced Akira's father, but she had enjoyed socializing with non-Moris. Though Mei and Jacob's father, Harvey, had divorced quickly, their parting had been mutual and surprisingly non-acrimonious. The Campbell siblings had been welcome guests on most holidays and special occasions. Occasions for which Akira's presence had been demanded but begrudged.

Did she miss her mother? Akira hadn't known her well enough to miss her, and at the end, being around the woman had only led to sadness and guilt. She'd missed her chance at any degree of closure, though. She'd missed the chance to request absolution for being so fucking unlovable.

Jacob's eyes shifted to stare at a point to the right of her head. "The funeral was beautiful."

The funeral had been little more than a blur, coming a

mere four days after her mother's unexpected death. Unexpected to her, that is. She hadn't known Mei had suffered a series of small strokes in the months leading up to her last days.

Jacob, on the other hand, had visited her mother regularly on her sickbed.

"Thanks. She planned it all before she died."

His lips softened. "I thought it was very tasteful."

Akira's funeral wouldn't be tasteful. There would be firecrackers and alcohol and beautiful men weeping. "Incredibly tasteful."

Jacob placed his half-full mug on the counter. His dark lashes hid his eyes. "I was going to call or something at some point. See how you were doing. But it's been so crazy with Kati's senior year and the boys launching their new business…"

Startled, her mouth dropped open. Jacob had considered checking in on her? As if she were some normal person who might be affected by her mother's death and not the sociopath he probably considered her to be? "Oh. No. I mean, that's fine. I wouldn't have expected that from you."

His lips twisted. "I figured. But, you know, I should have, since…"

"Since you're such a good brother?" she retorted, before she could catch herself. Wincing, she raised her hand to stave off the storm cloud gathering on his face. His beautiful, beautiful face. "Sorry. Sorry." She was sorry. It had been instinct to counteract the unexpected kindness of his intention to check in on her with a verbal shove.

"What brings you here?"

There. He was back to being Mr. Stiff. *Happy?*

No.

But this was better. It had gotten a little too touchy-feely there, and with all this talk about her mother…well, she needed a wall between them. It protected all her softest parts.

Suddenly weary, she massaged the back of her neck. "This is, actually, about my mother. And a gift she may have given you."

"The bequest?"

Akira had been expecting her mother to leave the Campbell family a sizable sum, but her will had only bequeathed a hundred thousand dollars to be split between the four siblings. Mei Mori hadn't been born rich, but at eighteen she'd had the distinct misfortune to stumble directly into the path of Hiro Mori, who, smitten, had not signed a prenup. Mei could have taken the sizable fortune she received in the divorce settlement and sat on it, but the woman had been a crafty investor and had more than doubled it over her lifetime. In light of the rest of her estate, a hundred grand was a drop in the bucket.

Then again, Akira bet Mei knew Jacob would balk at a huge sum of money. Her mother had once proudly told her Jacob was determined to make it on his own, though she had offered to help them more than once.

This information had been imparted, of course, to imply Akira had done nothing but take advantage of the silver spoon she'd been born with.

"No, not the bequest." Most of her mother's estate had gone to charity, with the remainder to Akira.

Akira had wanted only one thing. "We finished cataloging her possessions this week, and there's one item missing. It was last seen seven months before her death. Six months before her death, she started refusing to see everyone except her household staff and a few select friends." She paused for a beat. "You and your siblings were part of that small group."

It took a few seconds for realization to dawn. He straightened, and suddenly the kitchen felt even tinier. "Are you asking if I took something from a dying woman?"

"No, of course not." Please, Jacob would never steal. The man didn't know how to deviate from the straight-and-narrow path. He was physically incapable of sin.

What a miserable existence.

"I was there in the capacity of friendship," he said coldly. "She was lonely at the end. Not to manipulate her into…what, handing over her jewels?"

Lonely because her own daughter didn't visit her. No, she refused to feel guilty about that. Her presence would have only made Mei more miserable. "I'm not implying there was a single element of coercion." She raised her hands. "Look. I didn't come here to fight or ogle your ass—"

Jacob's head snapped back. "Ogle my…"

"Oh, shut up," she retorted, out of patience. "You know very well it's a first-class ass. What do you do, do squats all day? Never mind, don't answer."

"Trust me," he said grimly, "I wasn't planning to."

"I came because the item looks like nothing more than a wood box. Well crafted, about a foot square. A design on the sides. No one would steal it, and it's probably the only gift she could give you that you would take because it doesn't look expensive."

"You think she gave me a box?"

Akira sighed. Her feet hurt. Her head ached. She was sleep deprived and tired, and his wide, steady shoulders were right there.

It took every ounce of energy for her to continue speaking. She was unable to think anymore, perilously close to dropping her shields. "It was my grandmother's. There is no price I wouldn't pay to get it back." There. She'd handed him every single ounce of bargaining power.

Jacob had stilled, and he watched her far too carefully for her peace of mind. His tone was quiet when he spoke. "Mei didn't give me anything."

"What about your siblings?"

"I would know. They would tell me. We're close."

Akira flinched from the last two words, though she knew he didn't intend it as a dig about her lack of closeness with her own family.

She had developed a sense to recognize when people were lying to her, a skill that served her well when negotiating with men who assumed she was an empty-headed doll. Truth. It rang in every syllable of those sentences.

Defeat tasted like ashes in her mouth.

The rage she had managed to control for too many years rose inside of her. Her damned mother. Holding Hana's box over her head like a carrot since her grandmother had died unexpectedly. *Behave, and I'll give you the box. Behave, and I'll give you your legacy.*

You should have behaved.

Well, she hadn't. And the hope she'd had, that finally, finally she could recover it, was dashed, because there was no place left to look.

It was gone.

If she opened her mouth, she would cry or wail, and Akira Mori did not break down. Not ever.

She inclined her head and carefully placed her half-full coffee mug on the counter. She managed to make it to the exit, barely registering Jacob's presence behind her until a heavy palm shut the door she had opened a crack. "Akira. Are you okay?"

He was so big and warm behind her. All she had to do was lean back, and she could absorb his heat into her. She craved it.

That's why you can't have it. It was dangerous to lust after someone so fruitlessly. Hadn't she learned all about wanting the unattainable with her family? Constant rejection took its toll. It chipped away at your soul, made you doubt yourself. It hurt. "Yes, I'm fine."

He had to lean down to catch her breathy answer. His beard scraped her temple. "You don't look well. I don't know if you should drive."

She suppressed a shudder. Brother Jacob. So good. So honorable to everyone, even a woman he found repugnant.

She could snap her fingers and have anything she wanted in the world. But she couldn't have her legacy. She couldn't have her mother, eager to forgive her and love her. And she couldn't have him.

Funny how they were the things she wanted the most.

Dangerous. This was far too dangerous.

So get rid of him.

That she was adept at. And if she stole a little something for herself in the process, he would never know.

She placed her hand on the arm he had extended in front of her, trapping her in the cabin with him. Coarse dark hair sprinkled his forearm, scraping her knuckles, which were raw from the tree bark earlier. "So eager to keep me here?"

"Don't twist my words."

Pure, perfect Jacob. "I wouldn't mind staying." Her fingers smoothed over the curve of his massive biceps. She tended to gravitate toward slender, elegantly lean men. In comparison, Jacob was a brute who could snap her in two. "Especially if you promise to entertain me."

He had stiffened behind her. "Akira—"

The warning in his voice only made her bolder, desperate to gain control. "We could go back outside, and you can take off your shirt. I liked watching you chop wood." She leaned back until she was cradled against his chest. His thick thighs surrounded hers.

She couldn't quell the shudder that went through her. In all the long years they had been acquaintances, this was the most physical contact they had ever shared. Immediately, she knew she had made a terrible miscalculation.

Because this was delicious.

She wanted to stay like this forever. But he would shove her away. Any second now. So she would enjoy it for the few short moments she was going to get.

Jacob exhaled, long and low, shifting behind her so his cock nestled directly against her ass, sending a thrill up her spine. Was it possible Jacob was semihard for her? Unable to help herself, she moved her hips, rocking back against that tantalizingly thick bulge.

He started to curse but cut himself off. She wanted him to curse. She wanted him to be bad, as bad as her. She wanted to corrupt him, stain his pure soul, stamp the imprint of her nastiness on him.

"Yeah," she murmured. "Let's go outside. It would be nice, wouldn't it? I could show you all the things I was thinking about doing to you when I was watching you. All the ways I would touch and lick every part of you." Akira squeezed his biceps. Her other hand went behind her and grasped his hip, which gave an imperceptible jerk, grinding his semihard cock into her ass. "You like that?" She slid her hand down his big thigh. "I could start at the top and work my way down. Or maybe…maybe you'd prefer I started at the bottom."

His chest expanded behind her, and she gave a grim smile of victory, stroking his thigh down and then up again. Letting him imagine how it would feel if it were his cock. "I think you would. Maybe I should get on my knees so I can be thorough."

They stood in silence for a charged minute, during which Akira thought maybe…maybe…

"Stop it." His voice was harsh, furious. Though she had been prepared for it, the rejection sliced through her, leaving a bloody wound. Jacob's hand fell away from the door. There was a tug on her scalp as he jerked away, her hair caught in the bristle of his beard.

Her lips twisted, and she spoke through the haze of lust, fatigue and anger clouding her brain as she opened the door. "See you around, Brother Jacob."

CHAPTER 3

There were seven hundred and forty-eight atrocious pink roses on the wallpaper spanning Jacob's home office.

He cocked his head and contemplated the north wall. The rest of his family's home had been slowly renovated during the five years they had lived here, but since he was the only one who used this attic room, it had been shoved to the back burner.

Maybe this weekend he could tackle it. He mentally reviewed his calendar and scratched that thought. Kati had a soccer game on Saturday, which would monopolize most of his day. Since he had fallen behind in his word-count goals, he would have to spend Sunday confronting the blinking cursor on his half-finished manuscript. He was already dreading it.

The trip to the cabin should have revitalized him, but after two days he'd returned to his home exhausted, unable to think of anything but *her* and the clawing sexual need inside of him.

She had felt so good.

His eyes slitted, the roses blurring. Over all the years Akira had flitted around him, he'd always been so careful to avoid touching her, fearful a single brush would be like a match dropped on dry kindling.

His suspicions had been right. Simply verbally sparring with her left him hot and bothered. The instant she'd plastered her body against his, a wildfire had exploded. No amount of taking himself in his hand could douse it.

His cock stirred. *Think of something else. Think of anyone else.*

Impossible.

That slim, angular body had fit against his perfectly, her toned bottom resting in the cradle of his hips. He could have cupped her breasts, peeled off the semi-sheer shell she wore to reveal the darker bra beneath. Stripped her of the narrow gray skirt and her underwear, until she stood facing his doorway in nothing but those completely impractical blue high heels.

Impractical for roughing it. Completely practical if they were hooked over his shoulders as he drove into her.

Jacob swallowed, his mouth dry.

In his fantasies, after he got Akira naked, his imagination traveled two smutty paths. One in which he tenderly laid her down on a soft surface and made love to her, as he had made love to other women in the past.

One in which he did bad, bad things to her.

Unable to stand the pressure of his cock against his jeans, he squeezed the thickness, wincing at the rough fabric rubbing his sensitive flesh. What deviant scenario could he conjure up this time?

Slipping his cock into her mouth while another man fucked her? Holding her still as a woman licked her between her legs? All while she sobbed in pleasure...

Now you've done it.

His teeth sank into his lower lip, and he squeezed his cock harder through his jeans. He'd made the mistake of reading an article a couple of years ago filled with heavy insinuations regarding the secretive house parties she regularly threw. Orgies. Since then, the thought of multiple hands running over her silken flesh had taken over his dreams.

Not this time. They'd been alone at his cabin, isolated. There would be no audience in this fantasy, no other participants, just the two of them.

I could show you all the things I was thinking about doing to you when I was watching you.

She'd been taunting him, but those words had struck him mute and frozen, unable to react when she'd pressed herself against him.

Because he knew she was only spouting nonsense, but that hadn't quelled his erection. She didn't know—couldn't know—what visions had danced through *his* mind when he'd caught her standing against the tree, watching him with that hot black gaze.

Stripped to the waist, her bare breasts exposed to the sun, nipples tight from the cool air and her arousal.

He squeezed his penis again, but it wasn't enough. After a quick guilty glance around his empty office, he unfastened his jeans, silently groaning at the relief of pressure.

The instant his palm closed around his cock, his spine tingled, his balls drawing up tight. He was raw from fucking his own fist over the last couple days, but that was what he expected whenever he saw Akira. She made him insatiable, his fantasies spinning out of control, the recovery time between the orgasms he gave himself to work her out of his system abnormally short.

Disgust and lust swirled through him as he followed the perverted path of his desires.

No words were exchanged between them. Her slender wrists were bound with rope and tied to the tree branch above her, her back arched, as if she were presenting her breasts for his perusal. He came closer, and she licked her lips. His hand stroked down her flank, the skin smooth and delicate. So flawless. He pressed his fingers hard against her skin, raising red marks to decorate the pale expanse of her belly.

The zipper of her skirt magically parted, loosening the material so it could fall to the dirty ground. No panties underneath. Just a hot, wet, lickable pussy waiting for him.

Jacob had seen Akira's breasts before, when she had been drunk and flashed him at his father's wedding. Though it was years ago, he had an indelible image of those round, firm mounds burned into his brain. Her pussy, he had to use his imagination.

He had a really good imagination. He swallowed, wishing he could wet his dry throat with her juices. Drops of precome seeped from the head of his cock, and he used it to lubricate his palm, so it could slip easier over the steel-hard surface, twisting upward at the sensitive tip.

His hands went to her waist and turned her around, the rope encircling her wrists having enough give to let her face the tree. He brushed her long black hair aside, the silky strands clinging to his fingers, and placed a hot kiss on the side of her neck. When he bit the spot he had just licked, her hips bucked in his hands, grinding back against him. He bit her harder, using his teeth to hold her steady as he undid his jeans and drove into her tight, wet heat, her firm ass cushioning his body as he thrust again and again...

Jacob's abs tightened and he crunched up, grabbing a handful of tissues from the box on his desk in the nick of time to capture the messy evidence of his filthy fuck-toy fantasy.

His chest worked as if he had run a marathon, each breath bringing with it a healthy dose of guilt and self-disgust. Hands fumbling, he cleaned up and tucked himself back inside his jeans. Like he could hide what he had just done.

He was still semihard.

Gritting his teeth, he launched himself out of his chair, pacing to the window and back. He should go running, he thought desperately. Or go work out.

He couldn't do this anymore. He couldn't think about those things. Especially not with her. Never with her.

There was no doubt Akira was the most beautiful woman he had ever seen, but that wasn't the only quality that spurred his near-obsessive interest. A palpable energy hummed around her. The air crackled when she came into a room. People looked up, paid attention, became nervous. She was charismatic and engaging, dramatic and flirtatious.

Not to mention, the most sexual creature he had ever met.

He wasn't a virgin. The sex he'd enjoyed in the past had been satisfying and pleasant, if not mind-blowing. It didn't need to be mind-blowing, because it was safe. The women were perfectly nice human beings who didn't threaten to make him forget every other thing in his life. He walked away from those encounters with his heart and his head intact.

If he ever became one of Akira's conquests, he didn't think he would be able to crawl away. He would lie at her feet, starving for even the tiniest morsel of attention.

The danger of that thought titillated him as much as it alarmed him.

There was no risk of that, though. If she genuinely found him at all desirable, he would be shocked. Teasing and flirting with him was a game to her, a way to prick his temper. He'd watched her employ the same strategies on other people for years.

Let her think he was an uptight prig. She didn't know that every time she called him "brother" he wanted to put her over his knee and paddle her delicious bottom before he demonstrated all the unbrotherly thoughts in his head.

She had no idea he employed every defensive strategy in his arsenal to not go around on his hands and knees after her, begging for a taste.

I could start at the top and work my way down. Or may-be...maybe you'd prefer I started at the bottom.

If she only knew.

She could never know.

The front door opened and slammed shut, and he jolted at the noise, spinning around as if he'd been caught with his hand in the cookie jar. "Jacob?" His sister's high-pitched voice came from downstairs. "You home already?"

And that was why he didn't have the luxury of indulging his desires. Not when the fallout could affect someone else.

Jacob yelled down, "Yeah. Be right there."

His desire had been doused the instant he'd heard the kid's voice, but he lingered a couple of minutes before making his way down the steep stairs.

He found his baby sister in the kitchen, rummaging in the fridge. As usual, a smile touched his lips at the sight of

Kati, fondness and anxiety warring within him. When had she grown up? Sometimes he half-expected to turn the corner and have a tiny blonde six-year-old run into his knees, not this slender teenager.

Unlike her three brothers, Kati was petite. Her mother had been short too. Jacob mentally shied away, never eager to dwell on Jane. He preserved her memory for Kati and encouraged his sister to have a relationship with the woman who had left for the East Coast shortly after she was born. That was as much as he could manage without dredging up his own demons. "Hey, Kati-cat."

She didn't turn around, but the breath she exhaled made it clear she was probably rolling her eyes at the childhood nickname.

"How was Kristen's?"

Kati pulled out a carton of almond milk from the fridge and slammed it shut with her hip, her short hair swinging around her pixie face. She'd gone platinum this week, which he was grateful for. The puke green had made him wince. "Great."

"Did you go biking?"

"Yup."

"Stay up late?"

"Yeah."

"Break into her father's wine cabinet and get drunk?"

This time, Kati did roll her eyes. "Jacob. Please."

He forced a smile to hide his genuine concern. He worried about all his siblings, but Kati most of all. Not because she was the only girl, but she was so…small. And breakable.

Thankfully, she was a good kid, so he hadn't had to deal with any huge issues beyond the occasional teenage sulks and non-responsiveness. Maddening, but not enough to inspire fear she was huffing paint.

Did kids even huff paint anymore? Jacob made a mental note to Google that later.

"Sorry I worried you on Friday. Did you get a lot of writing done this weekend?"

No. None. "Some."

"Phew." She wrinkled her nose. It made her look like an annoyed fairy. "I was worried when you said *that Akira* stopped by to bug you."

That Akira. He'd heard Akira's mother use the phrase more than once. Jacob frowned, discomfort niggling through him. Nothing was wrong with it, on the surface, but he hadn't liked it coming out of the older woman's mouth, and he definitely didn't like it coming out of Kati's.

"I swear, all I said was you were writing at our cabin all weekend and didn't have cell service, and I only told her that much because I was so surprised to see her." Kati poured cereal into a bowl.

"I guess you don't need addresses when you're as clever as Akira." Damn, he really shouldn't have mentioned even the general location of his cabin in interviews. Not like he expected anyone to come Misery him, but there were crazies in the world, and he had Kati to worry about.

Kati added milk and took a healthy bite. "I had no idea she would come track you out there."

"Don't talk with your mouth full," he said automatically. "And that's fine."

Kati swallowed. "What did she want anyway?"

He leaned against the counter. For some reason, he was reluctant to discuss his dealings with Akira with anyone else, even his sister. They were his, damn it. "It was nothing. She wanted to ask me about some box she thought Mei might have given me."

If he hadn't been watching Kati, he would have missed the slight tensing of her body. Her eyes dropped to her bowl, studying it far more intensely than granola deserved.

He straightened. Surely Kati wouldn't have accepted a gift from the dying woman without telling him. Mei had attempted to give them money more than once over the years. He had declined each time. This was his little family. He would provide for them.

But it was possible Mei had managed to manipulate Kati. While Mei hadn't paid much attention to any of the kids for the short period of time she'd been a stepmother, she had shown his sister increasing warmth over the past couple of years. Kati had gone over to visit her unsupervised more than once after school during those final months.

"Akira said the box belonged to her grandmother," he continued more slowly, watching his sister. "It holds a lot of sentimental value for her." She hadn't said the second part, but there had been heavy emotion in her voice when she had spoken about her grandmother. Plus, Akira, who was known as a smart and savvy negotiator, wouldn't have essentially handed him a blank check to get the box back if she wasn't running on feelings.

Kati hunched her shoulders. A light flush darkened her fair Irish skin. "Huh."

"Kati."

Vulnerable green eyes met his, and Jacob could read the truth in there. He groaned and dropped his head in his hands. "No. Tell me you don't have it."

"Jacob—"

"Kati." He dug his palms into his eye sockets. "I told her I didn't know what she was talking about. I berated her for even thinking we would be so greedy as to take something, a family heirloom, from a sick, dying woman to whom we share no legal or familial tie. Tell me you don't have it."

"Jacob…"

He pointed in the general direction of her room, his incredulity making him immune to her quivering lip. "Go get it. Right. Now."

Head hanging, she turned on one blue Converse sneaker and left the room. Jacob pinched his nose, imagining the scene when he brought the box to Akira. Would she gloat? She would gloat, wouldn't she? Maybe he deserved that, after piously informing her he wouldn't have dared take something from Mei.

And, God. How sick was it a part of him was glad Kati had whatever thing Akira was looking for? Because now he had an excuse to see her again.

Kati returned with a wooden box decorated with beautiful inlaid geometric patterns on the sides. "Where were you keeping that?" He was in and out of her room with laundry and random chores. He would have noticed a foot-long box sitting on her desk.

She averted her eyes. "Under my bed."

Hidden under her bed. Because she had known he would be displeased. He accepted the box and turned it over in his hand. At first glance, he had thought it was a jewelry box, but it was unlike any other one he had ever seen. Four of the six sides had odd, narrow panels on them, but there was no discernible opening.

"You can't open it. Well, you can, but it's like a puzzle or something," Kati volunteered.

He glanced at her sharply. "Mei did give it to you, right? You didn't take this?"

Kati's eyes widened. "Jeez, of course not! I'm not a thief."

"No, but you are a sneak." Grimly, he laid the box on the kitchen counter. "You couldn't tell me she gave this to you?"

"Mei told me not to." Accurately interpreting his stormy expression, Kati quickly continued. "She said you wouldn't accept it. That's why she couldn't leave us a lot of money in her will, either."

"If you knew I wouldn't take it, why would you take it?"

She tucked her hands into the sleeves of her sweater. "Mei said there was probably something expensive inside. Once I broke it open, I could use it to make sure my college tuition was taken care of."

"Jesus, Kati. Between your scholarships and what I earn, we have college covered." He didn't want any of his siblings burdened with student-loan debt. His brothers had both gone to state schools with scholarships, but Kati had her heart set on Stanford, and she'd been accepted. She'd have it, even if he had to work around the clock to make it happen.

Kati laid her hand on his sleeve. "Mei was tired of seeing you work so hard. So am I."

He placed his hand over hers, struggling not to get sucked into her beseeching eyes. "Kid, don't get me wrong. I would love to win the lottery someday. But this isn't how we do things. This isn't right."

Her rounded chin came up. "I don't see what's so wrong about it, I guess. *That Akira* has more money than she knows what to do with, and it's not like she didn't inherit every other thing her mom owned. Even if this thing has gold bars inside, it's nothing compared to all her other money."

Patience. For all her posturing, Kati was still little more than a child. "I told you, it was her grandmother's. Even if it weren't, it doesn't matter. It's wrong for us to have this because we're not Mei's family. Akira is."

"Mei said if she and Dad had been married when he died, we would have been her stepkids. She would have raised me, not you."

Jacob raised an eyebrow. Was that why Mei had been so kind to them over the years? Had she felt guilt over the timing of his father's death? As if it had cheated them out of some sort of life of wealth and privilege?

His dad had been a firmly middle-class physician before he met Mei at a charity fundraiser and recklessly married her a month later. At that point, Jacob had already been out of the house, so he hadn't experienced living in Mei's world the way the three younger Campbells had.

The marriage hadn't lasted long, a surprise to no one who was familiar with Harvey Campbell's flightiness. Jacob hadn't thought Ben, Connor or Kati had particularly hungered for luxury after it was over, but maybe they had.

Privately, Jacob doubted anything would have changed, even if Mei and his dad had been married when the old man had died of a sudden heart attack. While Ben and Connor had been older at the time—fifteen and sixteen respectively— Kati had been a baby who Jacob had sheltered since she was born. He wouldn't have been able to tolerate someone else raising her, especially since he had barely known Mei. He wasn't his father, ready to entrust his charges to a relative stranger.

"That's possible, but it's not what happened. As her daughter, family heirlooms belong to Akira."

Kati's lower lip pouted. "Mei didn't even like Akira, and Akira never visited her like we did. Did you see what she wore to Mei's funeral? That slutty dress didn't scream mourning to me."

Jacob's eyebrows snapped together. He didn't recall what Akira had been wearing at her mother's funeral, because he'd been too busy searching her face for a sign of life. For the first time since he had known her, there had been no sarcastic quip on the tip of her tongue, no mocking tilt to her head as she skewered him. She had looked pale and muted, limply taking his hand and staring right through him as if she barely noticed him.

She had looked grief-stricken.

And why not? He had been heartbroken when his mother died not long after Ben was born. He'd had his differences with his flighty father, but Jacob had been sorrowful at Harvey's death. Akira's strange and antagonistic relationship with her parents didn't preclude the possibility she loved them. That she could love someone, other than herself.

She's not a monster.

No. But she was…alone. An island. An entity unto herself.

At the funeral, the sexual tug he always felt toward her had been subsumed by something larger. Something strange and frightening had urged him to pull her close and get her away from the conservatively decorated service and the nosy mourners.

Instead, he had mumbled his condolences and sat in the back of the church with his family. Leaving her in the front row on her own, her profile stony.

Maybe he should have elbowed in and made sure she was okay. If it had been someone else, he might have. But he was certain she didn't particularly like him, so inflicting himself on her would probably have been the last thing she wanted. That was what he'd continued to tell himself when he occasionally considered seeking her out after the funeral, to ensure she was holding up okay. The Akira he had thought he knew would have been fine…but the Akira he had seen at the funeral? She had needed someone.

Now that he thought about it…the air of brittleness she'd carried at the funeral remained around her, hadn't it? Maybe she'd lost weight too. She'd seemed somehow diminished, less robust standing in his cabin.

He shook his head. *Not your concern.*

No, but his sister and her words were.

"Judging her isn't your place," he said quietly. "Plus, she could have been naked, and it wouldn't give you an excuse to call her slutty."

Kati's eye roll was epic this time. "Ugh, don't get all saintly on me. Even Mei used to call Akira a slut."

His stomach tightened. Not in his presence, she hadn't.

It was silly to feel any kind of sympathy for Akira, because he had the feeling she would take it and fling it in his face, but it bloomed regardless. What mother would say that to her child, no matter the problems they might have? How had Akira managed to take that sort of abuse? "I don't care what Mei said. I have never," he said, biting off each word, "called any woman a slut, let alone Akira. And I didn't raise anyone in this family to do so either."

Her sigh made her bangs flutter. "Okay, okay. Sorry. I

don't see what the big deal is, but I won't call *that Akira* a slut again."

His rage was usually a slow-boiling thing, but it was explosive when prodded. Red covered his vision, and he thrust out his hand. "Give me your phone."

Kati scowled. "What, why?"

Normally, he was careful about his size around his little sister, but now he straightened to his full height, uncaring that he loomed over her. "Give it to me."

Apprehensive, she dug into her pocket and pulled out a pink, bejeweled phone. He tightened his fist around it, easing up only when the plastic gave a threatening crack.

It was a struggle to speak coherently past his anger. "When Ben and Connor were younger than you are now, I told them if I ever heard them call a woman a whore or a slut, I would be the first in line to smack some sense into them. Clearly, I was remiss with you. Since you don't understand what the issue is, I'm taking your phone. Maybe that'll help you figure out what the big deal is."

Her eyes widened with dismayed alarm. "What? You can't do that! How am I going to call you if I need something?"

Actually, a valid point. Kati had been amongst the first of her peers to have a cell phone, not because he was so cool, but because his overactive imagination couldn't help but play all the ways she could be hurt and in need when she was away from him. "I'll give you my old flip phone," he improvised. Since he was pissed, he continued. "It has no texting capabilities."

Frustrated tears filled her eyes. "You're being so mean right now. You're not my dad, Jacob."

Jacob had to control his flinch. Talk about rubbing salt

into a wound. Kati had ripped his raw spot open, stuck a splinter in it, and then dipped it in kerosene.

If she had slapped him, it would've hurt less. "That may be true," he rasped. "But it's still my job to raise you into a decent human being."

A tear slipped down her face. "I am a decent human being."

"Then act like it." He gestured to the box. "Keeping this from me. Being so disrespectful to a person you barely know. Think, and once you understand what you did wrong, maybe you can get your phone back."

Looking nothing like the almost adult she was, Kati choked out a small scream. "You hate her anyway! I don't understand why you're taking her side." She ran out of the kitchen before he could respond. Her feet thudded up the stairs, and a door crashed shut.

Jacob gave a humorless laugh and massaged his neck. Hate her? Please.

He couldn't hate her if he tried. She was going to make the return of this heirloom of hers painful, and he couldn't work up concern over that because the reckless, insane part of him he could never quite silence was excited. Excited over the prospect of seeing her legs, her eyes, her cynical smirk, the languid way she moved. The husky way she laughed when she was teasing him.

No. Hating her wasn't his problem. Figuring out how to resist her if she put her hands on him again? There was the problem.

CHAPTER 4

A. M. Enterprises owned and operated high-end bars and nightclubs in some of the most sophisticated places in the world: London, Dubai, New York, Miami. Little surprise had been expressed when Akira had set up headquarters in San Francisco—her flagship establishment, a thriving rooftop bar, was near Union Square.

People expected her office space to be as sleek and swanky as her bars, and to a lesser extent, her family's old business. The London headquarters of her father's former business, the Mori Corporation, had defined high-tech and impersonal. She could well remember sitting quietly in her father's office while he ignored her, unable to get comfortable on the piece of modern art doubling as his sofa.

Since she both enjoyed crushing expectations and being nothing like her father, Akira had found an old mansion in lower Pacific Heights that had been restored to its turn-of-the-century charm. The grand staircase, European stained glass and intricate woodwork gave her a sense of history, while the marble floors and HVAC system catered to her and her staff's comfort.

She strode through the double doors of her office, each step soothing the raw, vulnerable part of her that so rarely managed to break free of the defenses she'd built to hold it in. *Mine. I built this.* Built it with her brain and her ambition and yes, her body, because her body was a part of her. No shame. This was who she was.

Jacob could go fuck himself if he didn't like it.

Everyone, she corrected herself hastily. Everyone could go fuck themselves if they didn't like it. Jacob didn't need to be singled out for fucking.

Actually…

Releasing a low growl under her breath, she struggled to retain the zen-like pleasure her business gave her.

It was too early for her assistant to be in; too early for most of her staff, actually. She loved the hours before the normal workday started. She could deal with East Coast and European markets in peace.

She sat down in her large desk chair and gave it a second. A second for the zing of pleasure, for the sense of purpose to take over and tell her whether she would reach for the phone or boot up her computer. To tell her how she could make the world dance and shift.

Her mother had sneered at her profession. It didn't matter that Akira's bars and clubs were expensive, exclusive venues. They would always be dens of sin. Akira would always be a useless, partying slut.

Stop thinking about her.

Easier said than done. Akira cranked her head on her shoulders, the nagging restlessness that had ridden her all weekend settling over her like an unwanted mantle. Running hadn't gotten rid of it. Neither had furiously reverse alphabetizing and then alphabetizing her extensive book collection.

Work called. She was in the process of acquiring a chain of a hundred pubs and bars in Europe, which would take her business to the next level. A purchase of this magnitude was huge for her, and she needed to ensure everything was going smoothly.

Right...now.

Now?

Now.

She scratched at a small stain on her desk.

Damn it.

She should have called a friend this weekend. How long had it been since she'd enjoyed an athletic, sweaty bout between the sheets? Between her mother's death and the issues with her estate, as well as her preoccupation with finding her grandmother's legacy, too long. Maybe that was why she'd been ready to climb Jacob like a tree. Maybe that was why she hadn't been able to get his ass out of her dreams.

Yeah, sure. It wasn't because she'd spent a good chunk of her life battling her attraction to the man. And the man's ass.

Nope, this was old-fashioned sexual frustration, something remedied as easily as dialing a number. Ready to do just that, Akira pulled out her cell phone and scrolled through the list of available candidates. Models, actors, socialites, politicians, businessmen and women, lawyers, doctors, even a lumberjack or two from when she'd gone through her outdoorsmen phase.

Oh, yes. A lumberjack might be nice. She had a sudden and inexplicable hankering for a nice, thick beard.

Did she know any green-eyed lumberjacks?

Akira snarled and tossed her cell on the desk. Heaven help

her.

It's because you have so much on your mind.

She snorted, too viciously honest to lie even to herself. Multitasking was her life's blood. She was capable of feeling raw and juggling a multibillion-dollar business. Unless, it seemed, she added her unwanted attraction to a man who despised her to the mix. Then, you know, everything went to shit.

The phone rang, shrill and loud, interrupting her thoughts. Distraction! Not checking the display, she snatched it up on the second ring. "Akira Mori."

"Akira! My love. You are a hard woman to get a hold of."

Ice spread through her veins, chilling her. That would teach her not to pay attention. "Father." The single word was mocking. Over the years, she'd made an art form out of paternal annoyance, rivaled only by her aptitude at maternal rage. "That should tell you something. I'm busy."

"Too busy for your own father?"

"Too busy for the cameras following my father around."

Her dad gave a chuckle, roughened from years of smoking. She knew he was probably tucked away in his lavish Calabasas home this early in the morning, his new family sound asleep from whatever late-night escapade they'd enjoyed the evening before.

Thank God the Mori Corporation had been dissolved long ago, the great hotels once bearing her family name now Hiltons and Marriotts and God knows what else. Granted, the move had probably made her paternal grandfather turn over in his grave, but his son had been an inept idiot when it came to business. Anyway, her father was far too busy to run a hotel empire now, since he was busy running his second family. Or, more accurately, letting them run him.

"Speaking of cameras..." She swiveled in her seat and stared out the window. She had a view of a lush green park not far away. A child was playing there, running behind a ball. "Take me off of speakerphone. And tell the film crew to leave."

A pause lasted a fraction of a beat too long. "What do you mean, my love?"

"You know I have attorneys," she said quietly. "And I'm not afraid to use them."

There was a click on the other end, and then the muffled sound of her father speaking to someone. A second later, he was back, much of the manufactured warmth amazingly leached from his voice. "They're gone."

"What do you want?" Because, without a doubt, her father wanted something. He had no use for his only biological child otherwise.

Without an audience to thrill, her father didn't bother to beat around the bush. "We want you to be on the show."

The freak show. Who would have thought the American public would embrace the wild exploits of a rich ex-hotelier, a washed-up actress, and her five insane asshole children?

Oh. Everyone. Four years later, it was still a ratings powerhouse.

And would forever be the bane of Akira's existence. Her family had been in the public eye prior to this show, but never quite like this. "I've already told you. No."

"We were thinking of doing a family dinner, Akira. Wouldn't that be nice?"

Whatever part of her soul had craved family dinners with her father had died long ago. If it had ever existed. "No."

"Akira, it would be a great angle. My daughter and Chloe's kids, all at a table together?"

It would be a great angle, until she clawed someone's eyes out. Not that she had a problem with clawing eyes out, but she wasn't keen on getting the clawing on tape. Terrible for legal reasons. "You know the last time I saw him, your precious stepson Brandon called me his little china doll?"

"What? Were we filming?"

She closed her eyes. "Goodbye."

"But it would be amazing." Her father paused for dramatic effect. "A real yours, mine, and ours moment."

Oh, fuck. Fuck, fuck, fuck, shit, fuck. Her lips barely moved. "What are you saying?"

"I wanted to wait to announce it at the dinner, but I suppose you have the right to know…Chloe and I are pregnant."

She clenched her hand around the phone receiver, wishing it was her father's neck. Did he think she would be overcome with sisterly affection for the fetus? That she would show up at the set of their show to support her new half-brother or -sister?

Jacob's caressing voice, when he spoke to his half-sister, popped into her mind. No, this wasn't the same at all. Her involvement with the unborn kid could be dealt with later. Only one thing was important right now. "Does she want it?"

"What?"

"Chloe. Does she want it?"

"What a silly question. Of course she wants it."

"No," she bit off. "It's not a silly question. Not with you."

There was a long pause. "I don't know what you're talking about. And neither do you." The words were low and threatening. Akira almost laughed. Like her father could threaten her with anything. A person had to care to feel a threat, and she made damn certain no one knew where her affections lay.

Bitterness rose in her throat, choking her. "You're fucking ancient. Isn't your sperm dead by now?"

"Watch your language." Akira could visualize his hands clenching around the phone, his face turning red. Age was a sore spot for the man, which was probably why he tended to go for women half his age. Chloe was forty-eight to his almost seventy. Akira's own mother had been eighteen when he'd snapped her up, well into his mid-thirties.

Grab them young, that was Daddy's motto. The better to manipulate them.

"Sorry. I didn't mean to singe your virgin ears with my unladylike language. I'm just expressing my surprise you can get it up, let alone have any swimmers."

"You..."

"What?" she asked, sweet as pie. "Bitch? Whore? Maybe you should bring the cameras back in so we can film you spewing your pet names for me. Such a wonderful moment we're having, when you announce new spawn. I'm sure it will be as big a dick as all of Chloe's other kids."

"You will show her respect."

"Uh, no. I don't think I will, Father. Congratulations, by the way. I hope it's yours and not that hot young tennis instructor Chloe hired."

Her father's voice was loud, a sure sign she had struck a nerve. "How do you know about the tennis instructor?"

"There's always a tennis instructor. At least the instructor is employed, right?" *That's right, Daddy. Remember I succeeded where you failed. Remember if I had inherited the precious Mori empire, it would have thrived.*

"You fucking bitch."

Bitch. Cunt. Whore. She should thank her parents, really. By the time she had become an adult, those words had lost all power to hurt her.

She injected a note of false cheer into her voice. "This has been fun. I'll call you on Father's Day. Maybe we can go to brunch. Toodles, Daddy." She ended the call with a quiet click, loath to give the fucking asshole dick the satisfaction of her slamming the phone down on him.

Akira didn't have to wonder if the birth of the newest Mori would be televised. The ratings would skyrocket, and her father could milk the pregnancy and birth and first year for at least three or four seasons. That was something the kid could look back on, a televised scrapbook of dysfunction. *And these are my parents and siblings showing their asses on cable TV.*

She massaged the back of her neck. Of course, when the pregnancy became public knowledge, reporters would come swarming around, as they always did when something dramatic happened on the show. Poking at her private life, smirking over her house parties, waiting outside her home to ask her what she thought about her father's "leaked" sex tape or her dearest stepmother's alleged affairs or the ancient history that made up her parents' acrimonious divorce when she was a baby.

Being the center of attention was fine, but not when her dad was the cause of it.

A knock on the door startled her. She smoothed her hair and straightened her jacket before rapping out, "Yes."

The door opened almost instantly, and a small dark-haired woman stepped in. Akira frowned at her. This was not her assistant. "Who are you? You're not Kim. Where's Kim?"

Big brown eyes blinked at her. "Um, she's on maternity leave, ma'am. I'm her replacement, Tammy? We met last week."

Maternity leave. Of course. Babies were in the air, obviously.

Her assistant was in her late forties, and this was her first child, so of course Akira had encouraged her to listen to her doctor and not work up to the day before her due date, as the dedicated woman might have done. Between flying about the country and chasing down gorgeous aloof authors, Akira had completely forgotten the date.

Akira struggled to contain her irrational dismay. She didn't want this Tammy, who, while competent, wasn't her assistant.

Or her friend. "How long will you be working for me?"

"The full length of the maternity leave, ma'am. Four months."

Four months hadn't seemed so long when she and Kim had discussed it. *Put on your big-girl panties.* Her employees were absolutely allowed to have families. "I ought to send her something," she mused, half to herself.

"I believe Kim already scheduled a floral and gift basket delivery from you and A.M. Enterprises, ma'am."

Akira almost smiled. "If there's anything remaining on her baby registry, buy it." She hesitated as an impulsive thought popped into her brain and her innate selfishness struggled with her good business sense. Selfishness lost. Damn it. "And arrange it so she can take an additional two months, if she wishes. Paid."

Tammy's professional mien slipped. "Um, ma'am?"

Akira glanced over her shoulder at the park. The child had left, but another had taken his place. "Have you ever passed a watermelon through your vagina?"

A choking noise came from her substitute assistant. "No, ma'am. I have not."

"I'm not an expert, but that's what birth sounds like to me. I should have told her earlier, to take some extra time. In fact, schedule a call with HR so we can look at our maternity-leave policies across the board."

When Tammy said nothing, she looked at the other woman. The assistant's face was nonplussed. "Is there a problem?" Akira inquired.

"No, ma'am. That is…very kind of you, is all."

Hardly. "I like hiring good, competent women. It's not our fault parasites can grow inside our wombs and wreck our bodies and imbalance our hormones."

"Um…"

"I mean, it's not our fault delightful gifts from God bless our lives. And everything else."

"Ah." Tammy licked her lips. "Okay."

Akira clasped her hands on the table. "Since you and I will be working together for the next four to six months, let's get a couple of things straight, okay?" Akira raised her hand. "First, I'm a bitch. Judging by how startled you are that I'm okay with my assistant taking some extra time to recover from popping out a screaming infant, you've heard that already."

The poor girl's mouth had dropped open, horror making her eyes big. "Ms. Mori, I would never—"

Akira waved her hand, cutting her off. "I don't care. You can call me a bitch to my face, if you like. However, you now directly represent me, which means I basically expect you to destroy anyone else who talks shit about me within your earshot. I pay for loyalty, and I think I pay well for it."

Tammy swallowed. "Yes, ma'am."

"Second, my father is a complete and utter asshole. I don't care if you have a Team Hiro shirt or have slept in his hotels or watch his show or own his sex tape. He's an asshole. The next time he or his production company calls, I want you to grab that call and tell them all to go fuck themselves. Or each other. I don't care who they're fucking as long as I don't have to talk to them. Ever. Clear?"

"Yes, ma'am."

"Good." Adrenaline sang through her veins, revitalizing her. She had shit to do, and she was doing it. She would be fine. With or without her grandmother's box. With or without Jacob's body on top of hers, ever. "That's all for now."

"Yes, ma'am."

Akira sighed. "I don't like to be called ma'am. You can call me Akira."

"Yes, ma'am—Akira." Tammy practically curtseyed as she backed away. "Please let me know if you need anything. I'll be at my desk."

"Great."

Tammy hesitated. "If I may speak frankly, Akira. I have watched exactly one episode of your father's show, while on a treadmill at the gym, and it made me want to weep for humanity."

Akira cracked out a laugh. "Good. Maybe we can manage to get along then."

Tammy made her way to the door, only to pivot around in a flurry. "Oh my goodness. I am so sorry. I forgot why I came in here. A Mr. Jacob Campbell is downstairs asking to see you."

CHAPTER 5

*P*oof. That was the sound of all Akira's lovely resolve and focus going up in smoke.

Akira swiveled away from her computer. "What?"

"He said he's an acquaintance? But he isn't on the list of approved visitors."

Aw. How very like serious, sober Jacob to not even be able to lie and upgrade their status to friends to gain entrance to her office. Hell, "Facebook friends" would have been warmer than "acquaintances."

"Shall I tell security you aren't available?"

Tempting. The call with her father had abraded her raw nerves, and she'd learned a lesson about sparring with Jacob when her shields were low. It had been a close thing, there in that cabin. There were dangers in permitting an adversary to see weakness, and she wasn't in fighting shape right now.

If you refuse to see him, you'll look wussy.

Steel grafted to your spine. Ice in your veins.

More like Play-Doh and lukewarm milk.

But why was he here? This wasn't their dynamic. She was the one who always went barging, unwelcome, into whatever space he occupied, be it a holiday party or his cabin or her mother's home. Before today, she would've assumed he had no idea where her office was even located.

Damn it, her curiosity had been piqued, and Akira's curiosity often trumped her good sense.

She could do this. He would be on guard from their last encounter, ready to shove her away the second she came near. All she had to do was make it absolutely clear she didn't care about a damn thing he did or said to her.

"Akira?"

Indecisiveness was a foreign emotion for her. "Send him in." She regretted the words the instant they emerged, but efficient Tammy had already ducked out.

Akira licked her lips, glancing around the office. Anxiety had her seeking out every nook and cranny, uncertain what she was looking for.

The office itself was warm and inviting, with gleaming, restored oak floors and plush furnishings and rugs. Other than framed art consisting of shots of all of her establishments' locations on the wall and a photo of her grandmother on her desk, there was nothing personal in this space. Nothing that could reveal any weakness.

Meeting him was for the best. She could have hardly faced herself in the mirror if she'd cowered in here from Jacob, of all people. She would see what he wanted, and then send him on his way. No doubt, he was probably on some sort of saintly errand.

Was it a little bright in here? Taking care not to hurry, she rose from her chair and pushed the button that would lower the shades on her windows to mid height.

She thought of the fine lines around her eyes. Lowered

them some more.

There. Better.

Her hands automatically smoothed invisible wrinkles from her skirt before she stopped herself. Hell if she needed to primp for anyone.

Walking swiftly back to her desk, she rested her hand on her chair and picked up a stack of paper at random just as the knock came on the door.

Staring blindly at the report in her hand, she raised her voice. "Come in."

She counted off a few beats after she heard the door open before she glanced up. "Oh. Hello—" Something caught in her throat, and she had to clear it. It was like the forest had stepped inside. Jacob was far too big and too wild for her fussy Aubusson rug and damask curtains.

Not shirtless this time, alas, but he was dressed in another pair of those delightful jeans, worn and faded at the crotch and knees. The soft green cotton T-shirt hinted at the muscles beneath. His brown leather jacket was a concession to the spring chill outside. His hair was curling and disheveled, as if he'd been running his fingers through it.

Was it soft? She bet it was soft. Her fingers itched. Now that she had touched him once, her body craved more.

The door clicked as Tammy closed it behind him. Jacob turned at the noise, his torso twisting and his shirt tightening over his abs.

No place to run. You're all sealed up in here with me.

She coughed, attempting to regain her powers of speech. "Jacob." She placed the file she held as a prop on the desk. "This is a surprise."

He shifted the reusable shopping bag he carried from one

hand to the other. His gaze bounced around her office. She resisted the urge to follow it, to confirm the space did not, indeed, reveal anything about her she didn't want this man to know.

Did this small glimpse into her world intimidate him? Surprise him? She couldn't tell. His face was impassive.

He finally focused on her, probably realizing he hadn't responded to her greeting. "I apologize for barging in. I know you're a busy woman. I should have called first."

"You don't have my number." Was her tone too plaintive? She didn't have his number either. They were hardly going to stay up late, twirling phone cords and gossiping.

"I do, actually."

The strange flare of excitement those words brought was quickly squelched when he continued. "Since I used your phone to call Kati."

Ah. Made sense. So much more sense than him simply having the means to contact her because he might one day want to talk to her. Without someone holding a gun to his head. "Of course. And how is young Kati? Survived a weekend without you?"

He rolled his big shoulders. "Yeah. She did just fine without me."

Was that a note of bitterness she heard? "Aw. Is Papa Bear's nest feeling preemptively empty without his little Kati-cat?"

It may have been a trick of the light, but she could have sworn a slight flush darkened his cheeks. "Don't worry about Kati. It's family stuff."

Family stuff rarely had anything to do with her. Never her, unless a parent needed to score some ratings or keep up appearances. She lifted a shoulder. "I rarely worry over things that don't concern me. Trying to keep the Botox fairy away as long as possible, you know." *Get this over with.* "So what brings you here?" She strode around the desk so nothing was between them, perching against the solid surface. She stretched her rather nice bare legs in front of her, mentally pouting when he kept his gaze fixed on hers. "Did you decide to take me up on my offer?" The words were light, though she felt anything but.

I could show you all the things I was thinking about doing to you when I was watching you. All the ways I would touch and lick every part of you.

"Can you please be serious?"

"I'm deadly serious." She gave him her best elevator eyes, traveling down his body and back up. "There's no lumber to chop here, but I'm certain we can improvise."

Irritation made storm clouds gather on his face. "Look, this is hard enough, and I haven't slept much, so I'm not really in the mood for this…whatever it is we do."

"Maybe I didn't sleep well, either," she said, and then started. There it was again. That bleating, plaintive tone. More obvious this time, so obvious he stilled, a confused look on his face.

Why shouldn't he be confused? She kept changing their script left and right. Only she wasn't doing it deliberately. *Get a grip on yourself.* There was no way in hell she would unravel in front of this guy.

She shook her head, her mouth firming. "What do you want?" The words were sharper than she intended, displaying her unease.

He cleared his throat and held out the bag in his hand. "I,

uh… I wanted to give you this."

She rose from the desk, his hesitation unnerving her.

"Most men don't bring me presents in grocery bags."

"I didn't want it to get wet if it rained."

She accepted the bag, eyeing the store name. "What is it? Cookie butter and artisanal marmalade?"

"What's cookie butter?"

Shaking her head, she placed the bag on her desk and reached inside. "Tell me, Jacob, is your life utterly devoid of all joy and pleasu—?" Her fingers brushed against something wooden, and she froze, unable to do anything but stare at the man in front of her. Unable to hope.

He shoved his hands into his back pockets. "I didn't know about it when you came to see me. Mei gave it to Kati." His lips twisted. "Told her to keep it a secret from me and use what was inside to pay for her education."

Of course her mother had given the box to Kati. A final *fuck you* to Akira. *You weren't good. You don't get what you want.*

The worst part was Akira was certain her mother didn't fancy Kati as the daughter she should have had. The woman had been fond of the Campbell family, that might be true, because of her nostalgic memories of their father and because they were quiet and humble and respectable, but she'd never particularly wanted any children. No, this had been a convenient gesture, a way to screw around with Akira without having to leave her sickbed. All she'd had to do was target the weakest link.

Had her mother handed Kati the contents of her entire safe, Akira wouldn't have quibbled. Hell, Mei had earned every penny of wealth she had extracted from Hiro Mori as his wife of three years. She reserved the right to leave it, and the larger fortune it had grown into, to whomever she wished.

But this box had been Hana's. It should have been Akira's the second Hana passed away, as her grandmother had intended. It would have been hers, if the elderly woman had had a will. If her mother hadn't snatched the box away and hidden it. If Akira hadn't been a dumb nineteen-year-old and used a better attorney than her mother's when she'd tried to get it back from her.

The ifs had run around in her brain far too long. Time to end them.

She pulled out a mahogany box decorated on each side with dozens of narrow, inch-long panels in varying shades of brown. She nudged one panel, and it moved, though stiffly. The box was heavy and sturdy, the wood warm, as if it were capable of retaining the heat of those who had previously touched it.

Jacob shifted. "I didn't open it... I don't really know how it opens. You can check, if you want, to make sure whatever's in it is still there."

"I can't open it. Not yet," she said absently. There was something inside. She could hear it when she tilted the box.

I got it, Ba-chan. It's mine now, finally.

Her grandmother had been dead for fifteen years. She was never going to pat Akira on the back the way she used to, with her soft hands.

However, those hands had curled around this box. They had shown it to a fascinated young Akira, adeptly manipulated the panels on the sides.

Akira ran her fingers lightly over the panels. Two hundred and twenty-six. Two hundred and twenty-six moves until she could get inside. Her eyes stung, and her nostrils flared. She knew it looked weird, but she lifted the box to her nose and inhaled. Surely she imagined a hint of baby powder clung to the item?

"Are you crying?"

What? No, she was not crying.

Don't do it. Not in front of Jacob. She would rather the man find her disgusting than pity her.

Distantly, she was aware her legs had weakened, that Jacob was suddenly at her side, his hand lighting on her arm, steadying her none-too-graceful slide to the floor. The softness of her expensive rug cushioned her butt.

"Akira." Jacob crouched in front of her. "Talk to me. Are you okay?"

Yes. Her mouth moved. She was certain of it. But nothing came out.

A vertical line formed between his dark eyebrows. The hand on her biceps grew more sure, smoothing down her arm to touch her fingers, which were wrapped tight around the wood. He tugged at the box and eased it from her grip, setting it to the side before his much larger digits returned to curl around hers. "You're like ice. I don't like this."

Too bad.

She was like ice. It was in her veins. Ice in her veins. Steel in her...

His arm slipped around her, and he adjusted her with no discernable effort, arranging her so her bottom was now resting against his lap instead of the rug.

He was...hugging her.

Akira didn't really seek out hugs from anyone, though she didn't shove away embraces from people she liked.

But Jacob hugging her was a whole other kettle of fish. This was crazy and dumb and fraught with peril.

His big hand skated up her back, subtly massaging her spine.

His concern slipped over her like liquid warmth, and she closed her eyes, her head coming to rest on his shoulder, swaying into the seductiveness of the moment. In a second. She would pull away in a second.

A second passed. A minute ticked by, and then another, and another. Later, she wouldn't be able to remember how long they sat there, wrapped in each other and cloaked in silence.

Her eyelashes fluttered open when he shifted, and she stiffened. Jesus. He probably had places to be and things to do. So did she. Yet she was just sitting here like an idiot, wrapped up in his big, solid arms.

"I apologize for this scene," she whispered.

"A scene is swimming naked in an Italian fountain."

"I've done that."

"I know."

She would have called that a dig, but he was speaking softly, his hand still making subtle patterns over her back.

A joke. Was he joking with her? Cranky, scowling Jacob was joking with her?

She was so startled she leaned back, unable to get far due to his hold on her. He looked down at her, his ever-present disapproval gone, replaced by something strange and soft. "Akira."

He'd never said her name like that.

She licked her lips. "What?"

He frowned, but it was more perplexed than angry. "I

have to..." His hand came up and touched her cheek. The fresh calluses on his palm rasped her skin as he clumsily brushed away the damnable wetness. "There," he said. He spoke so low, she had to duck her head closer to hear him. "Better."

His task was finished, but he didn't leave her. His thumb remained, moving an infinitesimal amount. Stroking her flesh.

Her world narrowed to focus on every point of contact they shared, his intent gaze burning a hole into her. The fine hairs on the back of her neck rose when his index finger grazed her jaw.

Her head turned toward the subtle pressure. Not much. Enough so his thumb could bump the corner of her lips. Dark lust flashed through his gaze, his lids falling to half-mast.

He was the one who twitched, his finger gliding over her lower lip, coming to a rest against the center. Acting on instinct, her tongue flicked out, making contact with his skin. It was a tease, not nearly enough to gain any kind of grasp of his taste. She could retain plausible deniability when he jerked away and dumped her off his lap.

He didn't chastise her or shove her off for daring to corrupt his offering of platonic comfort. Instead, his thumb remained against the cushion of her lower lip.

And then exerted the smallest amount of pressure.

His fingers were on her mouth, not her clit, but her thighs clenched, arousal making her wet and squirmy. Her mouth opened, puffs of breaths warming his finger.

He gave a wordless exclamation when she sucked him in. She couldn't break their gaze. There was too much going on in those expressive eyes: shock, nervousness, heat. Yet...not an ounce of disgust.

She grasped his wrist and sucked his finger like she would suck his cock, hungry for at least this piece of him. Her head bobbed, pulling him in all the way, again and again, until he was shifting beneath her, his face tight and distressed. A hardness had grown against her ass, but her position was too awkward for her to fully experience it.

Disappointment assailed her when he jerked his finger out of her, her suction so tight, there was a pop of noise. She supposed she would never get to explore his cock now. Or really, any of him, because if this didn't chase him away forever, she'd be stunned. Akira struggled to regain her usual attitude, make it clear she was entirely unaffected. "Don't you know? You have to kiss it to make it better—"

His lips slammed down on hers and cut off her words.

For a split second, she could only sit, stunned, as his mouth moved on hers. What. The. Fuck.

Had she ever been kissed like this? Had he ever kissed like this? Because he kissed like he hadn't tasted a woman in forty years, like she was the last woman on earth. He kissed like there would be no beginning or end without her.

He kissed her like he...wanted her.

Fucking. Hot.

All of the stress of the day, of the morning, of the last six months converged until nothing existed except for his big body, his lips and tongue, his calloused hands, and the scent of him wrapped around her.

So long. She'd waited so long for this.

You weren't good. You don't get what you want.

She shoved the annoying, smug voice away and concentrated on the moment, twining her arms around his neck and throwing herself into this kiss that was somehow sexier than full-on fucking.

His tongue thrust into her mouth, rubbing against hers, exploring her. His beard was surprisingly soft against her skin. She had imagined he would be gentle and hesitant, but his hands were as greedy and grasping as his mouth as they roved over her back, tugging and coaxing and pulling her until she was straddling him, his palms cradling her ass.

The position was awkward, her snug skirt constricting her. Jacob was a master problem-solver, breaking their kiss to run his hand down her legs and then back up, forcing the fabric up to her waist. Breathing hard, she took in his saliva-slick lips, his focused concentration, the pants making his chest rise and fall. She had to reassure herself she was indeed kissing *Jacob*, and she hadn't wandered into some strange wonderland where bearded giants stormed her office to fuck her.

Not that they were fucking.

Yet.

His eyes skated down her body, and she followed his gaze to where her black panties were revealed by her hiked-up skirt. He guided her up, and they both groaned as his jeans-clad dick notched against her pussy. Had she thought he was large before? No, that must have been before he was fully erect.

Jackpot.

Gone. She wanted the barriers between them removed. Nothing was more important at the moment than getting his cock inside her and getting off. She ground down on him, his cock forcing her wet panties against her folds.

"Akira…"

No, she didn't want them to talk. Talking would bring reality, and she wasn't prepared for that. She captured his lower lip between her teeth, biting it hard enough to bring a growl from his chest.

Her hands went to his fly, but before she could unbutton him he launched up, spilling her to her back.

She rose on her elbows, ready to fight for what she wanted so badly. Feeling small and delicate was an unusual thing for her, but he was massive as he loomed over her, his arms bracketing her body. His gaze met hers, and the dark, fierce intensity of his arousal stunned her.

Her lips parted. "Don't stop." That wasn't her, surely. She didn't beg anyone to fuck her.

He shook his head once, but didn't respond. His fingers went to the neckline of her blouse. She expected him to undo the buttons, opening her slowly to his gaze.

The silk of her blouse disintegrated, ripped off with a few hard tugs. Startled, she let out a squeal and slapped her hand over her mouth.

He didn't notice. All of his attention was on her breasts. Her bra fared a bit better than her shirt, because he only shoved the material down until her tits were propped on the shelf of her bra.

His head lowered, and he licked a circle around her areola before he sucked the nipple in, drawing on it hard. A cry fell from her lips when he backed off, but it was only to lick his way to her other nipple, giving it the same treatment.

She planted one foot on the floor and twined the other leg around his waist, arching up in a desperate effort to relieve the pressure building inside her.

His hand steadied her hips, holding her still. "Shh."

"I need…"

"I know what you need. I'll give it to you."

She stopped straining, stunned by the way her body instantly responded to the certainty in his voice. His hot mouth traveled over her breasts and down her belly, biting the flesh above her navel when she shifted. Halting, she tipped her head back and stared at the ceiling. *What the hell is happening?*

Even when she permitted a man to treat her roughly or she played at being submissive, she was in charge, not him. She was the one initiating and directing the action.

She just needed relief so badly. That was all. Everything would go back to normal once she came.

His hand brushed over the gusset of her panties. One thick knuckle pushed inside of her, rasping the silk over her clit, wetting the fabric. She whimpered, spreading her legs wider in an effort to tempt him into touching her deeper. He grasped the waistband of her underwear.

Rip it.

She suppressed a smidgen of disappointment he didn't go into barbarian mode on the panties, but instead worked them down. The second they cleared her ankles, he tossed them aside before using his grip on her inner thighs to push her legs open farther.

His dark head was level with her cunt, his wet lips so close she could feel every breath he exhaled. His focus was where she needed it to be, on her pussy.

His gaze flashed up to hers, giving her a much-needed reassurance she wasn't the only one of them who wasn't acting like themselves. Gone was the controlled, distant man she had known for so long, the man who wouldn't commit a fleshly sin even if his life depended on it. His eyes were hot, filled with passion and longing and need. Bearded and wild-haired, every trapping of civilization had disappeared.

He slipped two digits over her pussy, finding her as wet as she'd ever been. His fingers widened into a V, opening her up to him. "Don't let anyone hear you."

His rough, agile tongue rasped over her pussy in a long lick. Whatever thoughts and concerns she had in her brain vaporized into mist as he settled in to feast on her cunt, his tongue fucking into her. She'd been eaten out before, but never like this. He wasn't an expert, but he was so damn enthusiastic he could be forgiven minor technical errors.

Of course, she wasn't averse to helping him correct his form. She tangled one hand in his hair, tugging him away from her pussy. He snarled at her, an animalistic noise, like a dog denied a treat. "My clit," she gasped. "Lick it. Suck it."

He obeyed instantly, two fingers plunging inside to re-place his tongue while he licked and sucked and toyed with her clit. She had to swallow her cry when he shifted and inadvertently rasped his beard over her sensitive flesh. He paused, as if gauging her reaction, and did it again. And again, directing that roughness right over her hard clit.

A fast learner. God bless him.

His motions grew less refined as he became more aroused, somehow turning her on more than the most choreographed cunnilingus. He groaned, long and low, and the vibration against her cunt tipped her over the ledge, her leg wrapping around his back, a silent scream emerging from her throat. He kept his fingers tight inside her, filling her while his lips delivered soft kisses over her labia.

Her chest was working like she'd run a marathon, her

limbs loose and ready to sink into the carpet. Usually sex revved her up, brought all her senses to laser sharpness, but right now all she wanted to do was curl up and take a nap.

Correction: all she wanted to do was curl up next to Jacob's big body, take a nap, and have him wake her up with his more-than-talented tongue in the morning.

Her lips tilted up, and she let out an airy chuckle. She felt light enough to float away, something strange and large expanding within her chest. "My God," she said, unable to think of anything else to say. "You could make a fortune off your tongue."

At her words, his scratchy face rose from where it rested on her thigh, and even without looking at him, she could pinpoint with sickening dread the second he came to his senses.

Closing her eyes didn't help. It couldn't stop him. Each gesture of withdrawal—his fingers pulling out of her, his body heat leaving hers—shattered something inside her.

The lightness vanished, a cold weight taking its place. She counted to ten before she opened her eyes, not cowardly enough to hide away. He had moved a solid foot away, his body language hunched over and unwelcoming.

Her legs were still spread lewdly open. For the sake of principle, she took her time closing them, but didn't bother to shove her skirt down. When she rose to balance herself on her elbows, her ruined shirt gaped over her breasts.

He looked up from his contemplation of the rug, his gaze flying over her exposed body. She wanted to cover up. Which was exactly why she didn't.

Thankfully, she had braced herself, so she managed not to reel from the horror clearly written all over him. "My God," he echoed.

Jacob scrubbed his hand over his mouth, before pulling it away and staring down at it as if he'd been singed.

She smirked. Her juices were all over his face. She hoped they set him on fire. She hoped she was imprinted on him forever.

"This shouldn't have... This can't happen again."

You didn't deserve to have this happen. Not a muscle twitched in her face. She made sure of it. "You started it," she reminded him. Mild. Uninterested. Like he hadn't just blown her mind.

He raked his hands through his hair and launched to his feet. "I know. I'm sorry. I don't know... I have no idea what I was thinking."

"Probably not with your brain." She was proud of herself. *Just get through this. Get rid of him.* "Don't worry," she said, her tone as dry as she could make it. "I won't take this little incident as a sign you like me or anything."

The look of anguish he gave her cut her to the quick. This was that painful for him? Really? "It's not you—" he started to say, his vocal cords rough.

"Shut up." God, she couldn't, wouldn't sit here and listen to him tell her that inane, blatantly false platitude. Of course it was her. It was always her. "Just. Shut. Up."

"I'm sorry. It can't...It won't happen again. Please, just...forget it." He backed away as he spoke, looking everywhere but directly at her. His hand groped behind him, and he found the door handle. "Goodbye."

The door shut behind his hasty exit. Aldra stared at the door, aware she needed to rise, clean up, change into the spare clothes she kept in the office.

But all she could do was sit there, in the wreckage of her garments, her defenses stripped, simultaneously satisfied and hungry for more. Hungry for him. Even when he made it perfectly clear how disgusting he found her.

Underneath the frozen layer of calm she had adopted as a stopgap measure to keep him from guessing her true emotions, a small, hot kernel of rage bloomed.

CHAPTER 6

*H*e should have stayed home.

One of the joys of Jacob's career—other than wearing sweatpants to work—was that he rarely needed to interact with humans unless it was absolutely required. Parties and socializing could be kept to a minimum.

It wasn't that he hated people. Jacob rolled his shoulders, the bow tie around his neck foreign and uncomfortable. He simply didn't like most of them as much as he enjoyed his own company.

And when he'd spent the better part of a week turned inside out thanks to a certain beautiful woman and certain explosive events that had happened on the rug in her office, the last thing he wanted to do was put on a tux and mingle with people he barely knew.

However, he had committed to this particular dinner months ago. After his father had died of a sudden heart attack, he'd started contributing his time to this heart disease prevention charity. Stephen King he wasn't, but Jacob supposed he had become something of a public figure in the past couple of years as his books grew in popularity.

He settled himself against the wall, a watered-down scotch in his hands. He had made some halfhearted bids in the silent auction and greeted the organizers. Once he finished this second drink, he would slip out and head home.

His lips twisted. Home, where he could deal with Kati's continued silent treatment and try not to wallow in guilt and self-disgust over his lapse in control five days ago.

Like that was possible. If he wasn't kicking himself for kissing Akira in the first place, he was tearing himself apart over how he had run out on her like his ass was on fire.

After multiple sleepless nights dissecting the encounter down to its guts, he still didn't know what had possessed him to take her in his arms. At the time, he'd had some vague notion he had to fix the pain bringing Akira to her knees. Seeing her stripped of her sass and strength was wrong. He hadn't thought before he'd gathered her up, desperate to restore balance to his universe.

As to why he'd kissed her and all the rest...he didn't know. He'd only had platonic intentions, until her tongue had flicked his thumb. And then all of the willpower he'd employed for over fourteen long years had gone up in smoke.

Should never have touched her. He gave a humorless laugh. No shit.

He ought to apologize, his guilty conscience whispered. He already had, during his stumbled rush out the door, but it wasn't enough.

But she was far too dangerous for him to seek out, even to apologize. He now had a proven disastrous track record around her.

"Jacob?"

Disturbed from his introspection, he started, relaxing

when he recognized the statuesque blonde woman a couple feet away. "Elizabeth."

"Oh my God," she said. "It is you. I thought surely the hermit hadn't left his house."

His smile was genuine. Elizabeth and he had dated casually for a couple months a few years ago. Their relationship had fizzled, and their breakup had been amicable. Jacob's breakups were always amicable.

That was a good thing, idiot.

"The hermit pokes his head out when he's paying hundreds of dollars a head for rubbery chicken. Take a picture, these sightings are rare."

She chuckled. "Aw. There's the deadpan sense of humor I loved. It's so good to see you." They exchanged a quick embrace. She smelled like lavender. Familiar.

"Good to see you too."

"You look great." Her blue eyes were admiring.

He should be returning her regard. She was beautiful and smart, and they had enjoyed a spark once before. If he was clever, that was exactly what he would do. "You too. Can I get you a drink?"

"Nah. I'm here representing the firm tonight, and I'm saving my allotted glass of wine for dinner so I can numb the pain when one of our senior partners starts to canoodle with his wife." She cocked her head. "I actually have an extra seat next to me, if you'd like to enjoy your rubbery chicken at my table."

He should accept. Any other man would.

The fact that a larger part of him would still rather go home and sit alone in his house didn't bode well for their prospects, though.

He opened his mouth to politely decline and make a smooth exit, but a flash of red in his peripheral vision caught his attention. Was that...? No, it couldn't be. She couldn't be here.

But it was. Akira's blue-black hair shone under the light of the dozen chandeliers. Amidst the sea of women wearing floor-length gowns in muted colors, Akira's bright red strapless satin dress was like a crimson flag. The slippery material was cut low in the back, hugged her breasts and small waist, and only came as far as mid-thigh.

Her jewelry was minimal, not that she needed any more adornment. She was already packaged like the perfect present. Hell, her fancy fuck-me shoes even had little bows wrapped around her ankles.

What he wouldn't give to pull those satin bows free with his teeth. Or trace the delicate bumps of her spine with his tongue. Between her bare arms, legs and back, there was too much Akira on display for his sanity.

Light flashed off the diamond studs in her ears as she turned slightly. Black eyes met his.

Jacob didn't need a mirror to know he was probably staring at her agog. In stark contrast, there was zero shock on her face.

A corner of her red-painted mouth kicked up. While his heart pounded triple-time, she treated him to a languorous study before giving him a mocking salute.

The man at her side leaned in to whisper something to her, and her attention shifted. God damn it, who was that man? Her date?

She had never brought an escort to any of her mother's parties—strange, since that would have been an ideal way to annoy the other woman—but she had often found companionship when she got there. He'd become an expert at finding excuses to leave the room or avert his gaze when she sidled close to someone, an intimate look in her eyes.

It stirred too much inside him to watch her trail her fingers over another man's arm or face. Envy, because of the man's right to stand so close to her, to touch her and be touched. Lust, over thoughts of what she would do to the stranger when she got him alone. Greed, because he wanted to both be the object of her desire and have a front row seat to it.

He felt all those things now when the man's perfect face pressed far too close to Akira's. But he couldn't look away. Not this time.

Not even when she offered the man a blinding smile and pressed her body against his. Or when she snaked her hand through the crook of his arm.

They slipped away from the crowd surrounding them as if they were accustomed to sneaking off on their own. Just before they disappeared through a doorway, Akira turned her head, the tips of her hair brushing over her spine, and made eye contact. She lifted her hand languidly.

And crooked a finger at him.

With a sultry smile, she disappeared.

"Jacob?"

Spell broken, he jerked, startled, and looked at Elizabeth, who was studying him with curiosity.

He should forget about Akira and her bizarre beckoning. He should spend the evening with proper, safe Elizabeth, and wipe Akira from his mind entirely.

He had done it before, all those other times she had disappeared with some other man. He'd buried his desire down deep and soldiered on.

Not tonight.

The thought came unexpectedly, but once it took hold in his brain, he couldn't shake it off. He couldn't march away like a good boy. This time, he was going to feed all those emotions swirling in his chest.

"Excuse me," he said to Elizabeth, aware he was a shade too abrupt, but unable to correct his behavior. "I'm sorry. I have to go."

She patted him on the shoulder and said something to him. Perhaps he agreed to see her later. He couldn't quite recall.

He was too intent on finding his prey.

A deserted hallway lay beyond the door Akira and her man had exited through. Like Akira's office building, this place was another converted mansion, used for events instead of offices. As he moved down the hallway, the sounds of the party became muted, assisted by the thick carpeting and solid walls.

There was nothing, in fact, to disguise the noise that made him stop in his tracks, his muscles locking.

Surely she wouldn't...

He took another couple of steps and heard it again, a feminine gasp followed quickly by a man's sigh.

Moth to a flame, a magnet to metal...there was nothing that could prevent him from following that sound. The door was ajar. He only had to nudge it open so he could peek inside. Bare and plain, the room beyond was an unremarkable storage closet.

What made it remarkable was the woman leaning against

the shelf. Dark eyes clashed with his, daring him to…do something. What, he wasn't sure. He was fairly certain he had no blood left in his brain to manage any sort of cognitive functions.

Akira's dress was peeled down to her waist, her small, firm breasts propped up on the shelf of her black corset. The dim light from the bare bulb hanging from the ceiling gleamed on her date's head as he sucked one long brown nipple into his mouth, his cheeks hollowing with each motion.

Red-tipped fingers tightened on the fine fabric of the tux covering the man's shoulders. "If you're going to watch, come in and shut the door," she drawled.

Shameless. That's what she was.

The man lifted his head at Akira's words.

Good. Yes, Akira's date would stop this madness. Order Jacob out. Or better yet, leave himself.

But there was nothing but amusement in the blue eyes meeting Jacob's. Elegant and lean, with a perfectly formed face, the man looked like a male model. Dismissing him quickly, the man returned to burying his face in those magnificent breasts.

No help from that quarter.

A drop of sweat rolled down Jacob's temple. He ought to be outraged. Or disgusted. Maybe writhing with jealousy. His cock shouldn't be so hard it ached as he watched another man suck on the woman he lusted after. It shouldn't grow harder at the thought of watching the other man fuck the woman he wanted to fuck.

Shameless. That's what she made him.

It was the only explanation for why he stepped inside.

He relished the flash of confusion and surprise on her face

as the door clicked shut behind him. What did she think, he would become flustered and run away? Actually, given his track record, that wasn't a crazy expectation.

Running wasn't an option when it meant he'd be missing the sight of Akira's nipples hardening and tightening as someone else toyed with them.

"Fine, then," she breathed, recovering from her shock. "Stay. Remy and I don't mind, do you, darling?"

The man—Remy, what kind of fucking name was that?—bit down on her nipple and tugged so the flesh was even more elongated. He released her when Akira gave a sharp cry and trailed his lips up to her neck. He groaned into the skin there. "I don't care if this place burns down, as long as I don't have to stop."

Akira stroked a forefinger over her nipple, wet from Remy's saliva. Jacob clenched his hands into fists and leaned against the door, striving to appear nonchalant when the reality was he couldn't support his own weight.

"No need to stop. Right, Jacob?"

He was barely capable of shaking his head, once.

Akira stretched and gripped the shelf above her, the movement lifting her breasts and arching her back.

"What do you want?" Remy asked her. He licked her ear. Her dress pooled over his arm as he slid his hand farther up her thigh, the red a harsh contrast to his black jacket.

She arched her back. Showing off. "Since Jacob's the guest, he should get to pick."

Jacob jerked. What?

Remy's chuckle was low. "Fine by me." The dull light shone on his shaved head as he glanced at Jacob again. "What do you want me to do to her?" His hand moved down her leg, his fingers hooked in a scrap of black lace.

"I can suck Remy off. Or he can eat me." A sly smile crossed her beautiful face, and he wondered if she was remembering the moment Jacob had slipped his tongue inside her sweet cunt.

He wet his lips. His palm made contact with the door-knob behind him, hesitated there, as she continued in a whisper. "Or he can fuck me while you watch."

Jacob's hand fell away from the knob. He was barely conscious of taking the six steps separating them, until he was close enough to Akira to count each breath she took. Close enough to Remy to see the droplet of sweat trickling down the man's neck and the thick outline of his cock against his tuxedo pants.

"What do you want, Jacob?" she murmured, challenge in every word.

He lifted his hand, unsurprised to find it shaking, and touched his fingertip to her cheek. What did he want?

Everything.

"Fuck her." The words were so guttural, it hurt when he uttered them.

Akira's mouth parted in a wordless exhale of air. Because he was watching her, Jacob caught the subtle nod she gave Remy. Distantly, he was aware of the other man moving—the rasp of a zipper, the crinkling foil of a condom being opened—but Jacob's eyes were on Akira and the flush coating her face and skin.

He had missed this, when he'd taken her roughly with his mouth on her office floor. He wanted to press the pause button and catalogue every single sign of her arousal, from her dilated eyes to the way her toes curled in sexy black high-heeled sandals as Remy ran his hands over her ass and hoisted her up the wall.

She let out a small cry when Remy sank inside her with a single thrust. Jacob ran his finger over her cheek and traced her open lips. Hot breaths puffed against his skin.

She bit the fleshy part of his forefinger when Remy thrust inside her again, and Jacob welcomed the pain. It echoed the throbbing of his cock. Punishment for all the years he'd lusted after her. Punishment for loving this moment as much as he did.

When she closed her eyes after a particularly deep thrust, Jacob grasped her chin and shook her head. "No," he ordered, unable to fathom how he was able to speak at all. "You look at me."

Remy gave a half-laugh as she opened lust-dazed eyes. "She could look at me too." He inserted his hand between their bodies. Akira's feet flexed, the sexy satin bows wrapping around her ankles bouncing as Remy shafted her deeper.

"There's the spot I like," Remy murmured.

Remy's cock was large and thick as it thrust in and out of her, her copious arousal making the condom shiny. Jacob had felt her pussy clamping on his tongue and fingers. How would he survive if that was his penis fucking into her?

He could take a single step closer and change his relatively innocent touch on her face to something more depraved. He could run his hand down her body, finger those swollen pussy lips stretched around Remy's cock. His knuckles might rub against the other man's erection.

"This is what you love, then? Watching?" Her breaths came in increasing pants.

Jacob was silent for a moment, fascinated by the way her

pussy clung to Remy's cock on withdrawal, the controlled brutality of the other man as he shoved himself back in.

"Jacob."

Jacob looked her in the eyes. "I love watching," he confessed. "You."

Her teeth clenched. "Harder."

Remy's next thrust rattled the shelves. "Hard enough for you?"

Jacob bit the inside of his cheek until he almost broke skin.

Eyes locked on Jacob's, Akira shook her head and squirmed on the cock impaling her. "No. Harder."

Greedy. He didn't mean to say the word, but his lips formed it, a silent judgment. Or praise, he wasn't sure.

She caught it, a fierce smile crossing her face. "I am greedy," she purred.

Remy laughed, out of breath and clearly nearing his own orgasm. "The greediest bitch I know." He ground his hips.

"Yes. Yes." Akira arched her back, her hungry pussy straining to keep him in. "That deep."

Remy's hand settled on her clit. "You need to come, you greedy little slut."

That word, the one he despised on principle, the one he had punished his sister for using, shouldn't make his arousal ratchet higher. But then, he shouldn't be aroused by Akira being held open for another man's cock.

If this was to be a night for firsts, he may as well go all the way.

Akira's hips jerked. "I do need it."

"Then take it." Remy pinched her clit hard. Akira stiffened in his arms, her breasts trembling. Shivers racked her, and she came, a small, keening cry leaving her.

Jacob clamped his palm over her mouth. "Shh," he heard himself say. Her lips were wet and soft under his hand.

Remy grunted and shoved deep, heat pouring off him as he came inside Akira.

Akira's cries subsided to soft whimpers, and Jacob eased his hand off her mouth and stumbled a step away, his cock so erect it was a vicious pain. There was no helping the condition, not with Akira standing there, bare breasts heaving. Her skirt had drifted down to cover her pussy. She steadied herself against the wall as Remy turned his back.

Ice ran down his spine. Sick. This was sick. And so dangerous. What had he done?

It didn't matter that he hadn't come. It didn't matter that Akira had invited him in. He had stayed.

The self-disgust kept him frozen in place as Akira pulled up the bodice of her dress and twitched her skirt into place. Remy said something—Jacob wasn't in any kind of condition to pay attention—and slipped out of the room, leaving them alone. She stopped on her way out and rose on her tiptoes. Her breath brushed across his ear as she whispered, "Now we can forget it. Well. You can try."

AKIRA WAS PROUD OF HERSELF FOR TOSSING OUT THE SASSY final words, though her legs were shaking and her head spinning from one of the most intense orgasms she'd ever had.

Time to make your exit.

Easier said then done, when her triumphant march was interrupted by Jacob reaching above her head and slamming the door shut in front of her, keeping her trapped inside. Her nose twitched. Damn his long arms.

His fingers wrapped around her shoulder and swung her around, pushing her against the thick wood. The dull overhead light highlighted the sweat trickling over Jacob's flushed face.

She'd had no set plans when she'd spotted Jacob across the ballroom floor, beyond some vague, half-formed idea of revenge.

Please, just...forget it.

Forget it? He meant forget her, and she'd decided long ago no one would ever fucking forget her. Eating her out would be a memory he took to his grave, because God knew it would get some extra screen time on her own recap of life. She couldn't, wouldn't be the only one.

When Remy had whispered a naughty invitation to accompany him to the storage room he'd scoped out, it had seemed like fate. She hadn't honestly expected Jacob to follow her, even after she'd beckoned him. At best, she'd hoped he'd be tormented with images of what she might be up to.

But then she'd found him framed in the doorway, face flushed, eyes hot, not a trace of disgust clinging to him. So she'd thrown out the invitation.

And he had taken it.

As expert a lover as Remy was, she couldn't ascribe her most-excellent orgasm to his talent alone. Without Jacob here watching her, wanting her, she doubted she would have flown so high.

Akira licked her lips, tasting the sweat from the hand he'd placed over her mouth to stifle her cries. Could she keep his taste on her lips forever?

He leaned in close, massive arms bracketing her head, palms flat on the door. He loomed over her, but she wasn't scared.

"I think we're finished," she said, struggling to be cool. It was a challenge, though she had gotten both her orgasm and her revenge.

"No."

She raised an eyebrow. "Oh, yes. Very much yes."

"Why did you do that?"

Though she realized the words were dipped in agony, they made her bristle. He had no right to question anything she did. Uncaring that he was so much larger than her, she took a step closer, her heels helping her to get up in his face. "Why did you stay, darling?"

No answer.

Her lips curved in a bitter smile. "I mean, it couldn't have been the same reason you kissed me on Monday."

A muscle jumped in his jaw. "You don't know why I kissed you on Monday."

"Of course I do. The blubbering I did probably brought out all your protective manly instincts. Turned you on."

"I'm not turned on by weakness."

She snorted. "Yeah. Sure."

"I'm not."

Lies. Maybe it was the Molotov cocktail of emotions inside of her, but she needed to push him. Force him to admit the truth. "Yeah, it's a coincidence after almost a decade and a half of knowing each other, your face wound up in my vagina the one time I cried in front of you?"

He flinched at the word vagina, which only made her want to say it again and again, like a snotty teenage boy.

Shoulda said cunt.

"It didn't happen because you were crying."

"Oh, was it the fetal position I was in then?"

"No." The single word was low and held a warning.

"A glimpse of my softer side because I held my grand-mother's—"

"It happened because I touched you."

She froze. For a normal person, that would have been a forceful declaration. For usually quiet Jacob, it was a roar. Shock chased across his face, as if he had been unprepared to make that announcement.

Akira blinked. "What?"

"We don't... We've never touched."

Not before she'd made the not-too-strategic move in pressing herself against him at his cabin. Because there was only so much contact she could manage with the man before her mask was in danger of cracking, before she showed him how she really felt about him.

Can't let him see.

He shook his head. "I knew if I touched you, if you gave the slightest hint you were..." A deep breath. "I wouldn't want to stop."

"You're not making any sense." The world had tilted on its axis. Up was down, right was left, and the sky was green. She spoke slowly, as if she were trying to make a small child understand a basic truth. "You can't even stand to be in the same room as me."

His teeth clenched. "Not because I hate you."

"Then why?" she shot back. Comprehension was coming, and with it a cold anger, but she wanted it perfectly articulated. Damned if she'd ever let him complain she misunderstood him.

Visibly discomfited, Jacob ran a hand through his hair. "I just can't look at you without...without wanting you."

"You—" She choked. "You want me. All these years, you've lusted after me."

He closed his eyes briefly, as if she were a cross to bear. As if the thought of wanting her pained him so much.

The light bulb clicked on, and with it came an icy rage. Rage hot enough to eclipse the mortification of being abandoned half-naked, post-orgasm on her office floor.

She would show him pain.

"But let me guess the problem. You don't want to want me."

He winced. "No."

She would show him *all* the pain. "Oh," she drawled. "I get it. I'm not the *type* of girl you should want, right? I'm so soiled, of course a decent guy like you couldn't just enjoy being attracted to me." Someone like her. Unnatural slut. Whore. Bitch.

"What?" His brow furrowed. "No."

"Yes." Fine, maybe she had been a dick to him over the years, deliberately poking him. Because she didn't want him to know the extent of her vulnerability. Not because she was grossed out that he made her body sit up and take notice.

It was nice when a man you desired reciprocated the attraction, but not when that man was otherwise repelled by you. Her voice was a hoarse whisper. "You made me think you despised me for fourteen years, and now I find out it was because I committed the cardinal sin of attracting your lust."

"Akira—"

"Guess what? I reserve the right to not be punished for

your desires." She tugged at her skirt until every wrinkle was gone, her latest indiscretion vanished.

His fists flattened on the door, and he leaned closer. "What we just did was dirty. It was wrong."

"Which part? The part where you followed me for what was obviously an indiscreet assignation? Or when you stayed to watch? Or when you stood so close you could have fingered me while another man fucked me?"

"Stop."

"I wish you would have," she continued in a throaty purr. "You only touched my cheek, my lips. You had the chance. You should have sucked on my tits. Or rubbed my clit."

"Akira."

Uh-oh. She was turning herself on again anew, but she couldn't. Shut. Up. "Did it make you feel good?" Taking advantage of his proximity, she dropped her hand to his cock, the width and length of it making her feel empty and unfulfilled. She craved this, wanted to hold it, lick it, suck it, fuck it.

His hips jerked at her touch, but he was silent.

"I guess it didn't make you feel good enough." She stroked his dick through the fine fabric of his tuxedo pants. He had shaved his beard off for the night, but a dark shadow was already creeping over his square jawline. He might be dressed up, but he would never look civilized. "You're so hard." She released him when he shuddered, her lips kicking up in a humorless smile. "You must be so ashamed about—" She cut herself off, his expression slicing through her anger.

She considered herself an expert in reading people. It was part of what made her successful. How had she missed this?

She answered herself almost immediately: she'd been too

busy wrestling with her own emotions where this man was concerned.

Shame. It was there, in his words, the way he held his body, the flush over his face, the way his eyes burned. Not because he was ashamed of her. He was ashamed of himself.

"I don't hate you," he said again. There was a slight tremor to his voice.

"Oh, Jacob," she murmured. "Maybe you do and maybe you don't. But either way, I think you hate yourself far more than you could ever hate me."

The shuddery, pain-filled breath he released told her she had guessed right. He looked as though he had dropped ten pounds in the last ten minutes, the skin of his face stretching tight over his cheekbones.

Despite her lingering anger, pity moved in her chest. She lifted a hand to his cheek. He exhaled and imperceptibly leaned into her touch. "I'm sorry for you," she said very clearly, not relishing his flinch. "But you still had no right to treat me like you have."

He didn't stop her when she ducked under his arm and left the room. The hallway remained deserted, and she skirted through the busy ballroom to make her way to the cloakroom.

There was no description for the emotions roiling inside her, so she didn't bother to try. Restless, her fingers drummed against the counter as she waited for the coat-check girl to find her wrap.

"I should have known you were up to something when you asked to be my plus-one." Remy reached past her and placed a tip into the jar when the girl returned with her cloak.

"I don't know what you're talking about." She accepted

the cloak and allowed Remy to assist her with donning it. He placed a hand on the small of her back as they walked out of the mansion into the chilly night air. "I donate to many charities."

"Yeah, I know. Generously. But anonymously. You only attended these events when your mother summoned you."

Because Mei wanted to maintain her image as the perfect, beleaguered mother in front of her fellow philanthropists. "I love raising my profile in the community."

Remy snorted, the sound out of place on the otherwise elegant man. "Please. Who was that guy? I would assume an ex, but you don't do relationships long enough to have an ex."

"I do relationships."

"Trust me, you don't. Or we'd be married by now."

She clutched her wrap closer and managed a small smile. She had met Remy a few years ago at a friend's house. The younger man wasn't, as many people assumed, a fashion model. He was an escort. A damn good one too, and amply compensated by his clients. "The hell we would. You wouldn't last two days as my husband."

Remy gave an injured sniff but didn't argue with her assessment. "Come on, sweetheart. You didn't show up here out of the goodness of your heart."

She shrugged as he handed his ticket to the valet.

"I'm never going to believe—"

"Remy, just drop it."

He clammed up and stared at her, surprise written all over him. Unable to look at him, she turned and stared at the driveway, willing their car to arrive faster.

"Akira. Is everything okay?"

"Everything's fine. Thanks."

Her short answer did not satisfy him. "You haven't been the same since your mother died."

She gave a harsh laugh. "I'm hardly mourning my mother, darling. You know what she was like."

"Yeah, but death affects us—"

She made a sharp gesture with her hand. "Please stop. If I wanted you to treat me like one of your clients, I would pay for your services."

Remy pursed his lips, considering her. "Okay," he finally said. "If you want to talk, I'm here."

She didn't want to talk. She wanted to go home and brood over Jacob and lick her wounds in peace. Was that too much for a woman to ask?

Akira uttered a sigh of relief when Remy's sleek Porsche came into view. She slid inside the passenger seat and relaxed inside the buttery-soft leather. Only to stiffen when she made the mistake of glancing out the window, catching Jacob frozen in the act of donning his coat.

So she wasn't the only one who had lost the partying mood.

Jacob shrugged his light coat on slowly and stood on the top step of the mansion, staring down at her. The moonless night cast too many shadows on his face for her to decipher his expression. His hands pushed into his pockets, and he took a single step down the stairs.

She swallowed and turned her head deliberately to look forward, though it took a massive force of will, hating the taste of grief and anger in her mouth. "Let's go."

CHAPTER 7

*J*acob spun the bottle of beer around, watching the condensation ring on the table become larger. The music from the bar was white noise, the clatter of plates and glasses a cacophony he was able to tune out.

The beer was his favorite, an IPA from a local brewery, but it was bitter and disgusting on his tongue today. His taste buds were ruined for everything. He swallowed, but it didn't help.

"…up with you?"

"I think he's brooding."

"This seems a bit intense, even for him."

"These artist types, man. Yo, Jacob!"

Jacob jerked his head up, startled at the sound of his name. His brothers stared back at him, equal amounts perplexed and amused. "You aren't even paying attention to us," Ben, his youngest brother, complained.

"Ah. Sorry, guys. I'm, uh, not good company."

"Is it your book? I know you have a deadline." Ever mindful of obligations, Ben cocked his head. "How's that going?"

"Great," he lied, attempting not to think about the manuscript languishing on his hard drive. Like he'd been able to write a single word today after last night. Shell-shocked and sleep-deprived, he had spent the day in a stupor, too many thoughts shooting through his brain for him to focus on any one.

"You don't look great." Ben frowned. "Is something wrong?"

What was wrong was that he was a stupid asshole. He couldn't eat, he couldn't sleep, and he had barely managed to look at himself in the mirror this morning when he was brushing his teeth.

A bit of beer spilled on the table. Absentmindedly, he wiped it with a napkin. "Nah, it's fine."

"Really?"

"Yeah, really. I'm just kind of tired. You know."

"Man, tell me about it. You didn't tell us how hard running our own business is," Connor said. Ben and Connor were Irish twins, with Connor older by only eleven months, but they looked enough alike to pass for identical. All the Campbell brothers looked similar, actually, big and broad and dark haired. Kati was the only oddball, with her blondness and petite frame.

"I actually told you exactly that, before you started." Jacob frowned, his attention suddenly diverted from his own troubles. "What's wrong? Is it going poorly?"

"Nah. Business is picking up," Ben replied. "We're finally moving past mowing lawns."

Connor grinned, his smile looking so much like their late mother's, Jacob felt a pang in his chest. "Got a huge new client last week. Out of town, has eight properties here they want to completely redo." Without even looking at each other, the boys high-fived. "It's gonna be great."

Jacob's smile was weak, but it was there. "Good. I'm happy for you guys."

"Maybe he'll like us so much we can get a deal on rent in one of those properties," Ben mused. "It would be nice to have running hot water. I've taken more cold showers…" He cut himself off.

Connor made an annoyed sound. "Damn it. Finish that sentence."

"Not a chance. I know you already have some smartass remark ready."

Deprived of a prime teasing opportunity, Connor's full lips turned down.

"Your landlord still hasn't fixed your water? I can come over and take a look," Jacob offered, ignoring their antics.

"Nah. We can handle it."

"I told you two, you could move back home until the business gets off the ground."

"Yeah, I'm sure that'll drive all the chicks crazy." Connor's smile was sardonic. "Your place or…my brother's?"

"And trust me, too many of those girls will choose your place, Jacob. We practically have a revolving door in our apartment for all Connor's women."

"Not true…"

Jacob raised an eyebrow. "Boys," he said mildly, gratified when both men shut up and sat a little straighter. Ben and Connor might be as big as him, twenty-six and twenty-seven respectively, and business owners, but they'd always be his younger brothers.

Wait a minute. Jacob directed a frown at Connor. "What

women?"

His brother returned his gaze steadily with the light blue eyes he had inherited from their mother, but Jacob caught Connor's Adam's apple bobbing as he swallowed. "I'm seeing a couple of girls. No one serious enough to bring around."

"They know about each other?"

"Jesus, Jacob." Connor ran his finger under the collar of his shirt with an annoyed jerk. The boy had always been good-looking, and Connor wallowed in the attention of females, lapping it up.

Jacob knew his brother was a decent guy and didn't expect him to be a virgin or even puritanical, but he didn't think it hurt to reinforce the lessons he'd spent a lifetime teaching the kid. "I don't care what you do or who you do it with. As long as you're honest and careful with the girls."

"What do you think I am? Of course they know it's nothing serious."

Ben grinned irrepressibly. "Tell me you're going to lecture him about condoms next."

Connor shot their little brother an annoyed glance. "You know what, Jacob? It would be really nice, just once, if you wouldn't play Dad."

You're not my dad. Jacob stilled, his wound still too fresh. "What?"

"You know. You're our brother. I know you're old, but for God's sake. Just be our brother."

He was not old. He was older. There was a difference. "I am your brother."

Connor sighed. "Never mind. Forget it."

Jacob shifted, more aware of his creaky knee than ever. He didn't want to forget it. He wanted to snarl at the ungrateful runt, flip the table, and stomp out.

But that wasn't what responsible, caring adults did. So he sat there and struggled to swallow another sip of his beer before putting it down. "Maybe we should call it a night."

"But we haven't had a family dinner in weeks," Ben protested.

Which was why, no matter how out of it Jacob had felt, how eager he had been to hole up and lick the wounds Akira had inflicted and ponder her words, he'd forced himself to shower and drag himself out tonight. Family first.

Even if they did chastise him for being old and fatherly.

Connor selected a mozzarella stick and bit into it. "Are you going to tell us why a quarter of this family is a no-show? I mean, I'm glad we got to order junk food and beer instead of tofu and sprouts, but I wanted to see the squirt."

Kati had become a full-fledged health food advocate since she had started high school. It was annoying as hell for all three of them, but Jacob didn't think his brothers had any room to complain. Ben and Connor lived together halfway across town—he was the one who had to sneak cheeseburgers and buy expensive, unfathomable staples for the pantry.

Jacob scraped at the corner of the label on the beer bottle. "She's a little upset with me."

"Uh-oh." Ben pulled a sympathetic face. "What happened?"

Jacob didn't particularly want to talk about anything so closely related to Akira.

Yet, his brothers were watching him expectantly, so he swallowed his own distaste and quickly sketched out the story about Mei and the mysterious, unopenable box she had handed over to Kati.

Connor whistled when Jacob was done, a flash of avarice glinting in his eyes. "How much do you think it—or whatever's inside it—is worth?"

He thought of Akira curled on the rug, weeping, the smallest and weakest he'd ever seen her. *Probably brought out all your protective manly instincts. Turned you on.* She couldn't have been more wrong.

"Doesn't matter how much it's worth. It belonged in Akira's family, not ours." He paused, a thought occurring to him. "Mei didn't give you guys anything, right?"

"If Connor was given some expensive bauble, it would be long gone by now. Liquidated and the money in some offshore account in the Bahamas," Ben replied.

"Shows how much you know. I would never do the Bahamas. The Swiss are the way to go." Connor held up his hand when he caught Jacob's frown. "I kid. Of course Mei didn't give us anything. Though we didn't visit her nearly as much as you and Kati did. I think she thought I was an asshole."

"Smart lady." Ben poked over the chicken wings and selected one laden with barbecue sauce. "Yeah, she didn't give me anything either. Except for what was in the will, that is."

"Which is doing pretty well, if I may say so," Connor interjected.

Jacob only nodded. Connor was a whiz with numbers, so it had made sense to entrust him with investing the bequest. Jacob had no plans to touch his portion. He only wanted it to do well so his siblings could enjoy it.

Ben cleared his throat. "You know, you said Mei told Kati to sell off the box to pay for her education. But Connor and I have been talking, and with the scholarships Kati has, there's enough in the principal Mei willed to us to cover a lot of expenses."

Jacob was already shaking his head before Ben could finish speaking. "That money will come in handy for your business." A refrain he had been repeating since he had heard of the bequest.

"We're on track to breaking even this year, and maybe being in the black," Connor said. "We save a ton by living together. We were planning on talking to you about this before we got the bequest. It's dumb for you to shoulder her whole expense when we're finally in a position to pitch in."

"Kati's our sister too, Jacob. Taking care of her shouldn't only be on your plate."

Jacob peeled the label off his bottle. "Guys. Really. This is sweet, but I have this."

Connor's lips compressed. "This is exactly what I'm talking about. For God's sake, Jacob—"

Ben rested his hand on his brother's arm. "Not now." To Jacob, he said, "Is Kati sulking 'cause you took the box away? That doesn't seem like her. She's a reasonable kid."

Jacob winced at Ben's question. He didn't think his reaction or the punishment he'd meted out to Kati had been out of line, but he didn't particularly enjoy being a hard-ass. "She's sulking because I yelled at her and took her phone away last week. And haven't given it back." He wouldn't give it back until Kati was able to comprehend what she had done and said was wrong. Since they were currently not speaking to one another, that might take a while.

Connor gave a soundless whistle and helped himself to another portion of sliders and mozzarella sticks. "Her phone? Harsh."

"Not to question your parenting skills, big brother, but I think you could have calmly explained about the box not belonging to us, and she probably would have gotten it," Ben pointed out.

"I didn't yell at her about the box. I mean, I expressed disappointment she kept it from me. But I wouldn't have punished her for that alone."

"What else then?"

Jacob toyed with a French fry. "She called Akira a slut."

Connor winced. Ben's eyes grew big. "To your face?"

Jacob dipped the French fry in ketchup and took a bite, though he wasn't hungry. "Yeah."

Connor pursed his lips. "She's lucky all you did was take her phone away. If that had been either of us, you would have kicked our asses."

"Deservedly," Ben said, in a rare moment of seriousness.

Jacob warmed at their instant agreement.

Hypocrite. You didn't storm out when Remy called Akira a slut.

That had been...different. Completely different. Still, Jacob internally squirmed, immediately throwing up a mental block on last night's events. If he thought about it at all, he would be utterly useless.

"She said Mei called Akira names often enough." He hesitated. "Did either of you hear her talk about her daughter like that?"

He was gratified when Ben and Connor instantly responded in the negative. "But, you know, they had a contentious relationship. You could tell Mei wasn't very fond of her," Ben mused. "Mei tried to keep up appearances, but she was so cold to her in public, I can't imagine she was much kinder to her in private."

Connor's eyes warmed with appreciation. "At least Akira didn't take any shit. I kind of loved how she would bait Mei."

"What do you mean?"

"The act she would put on. Mei would walk into a room, and Akira would just slip into it. Like every word she uttered was designed to annoy the woman." Connor shrugged. "Hell, it's kind of how she treats you, right?"

Jacob dropped his half-eaten French fry, struck by the words. "What do you mean?" he repeated.

Ben and Connor glanced at each other. The two were so close, despite their bickering, sometimes it seemed like they shared a brain. Jacob had nurtured that bond, but now it only annoyed him.

"Uh," Ben stalled.

"Answer me." All of the jumbled chaos rioting around in his mind suddenly calmed, his thought processes crystal clear.

You made me think you despised me for fourteen years, and now I find out it was because I committed the cardinal sin of attracting your lust. I reserve the right to not be punished for your desires. Absolutely right. She didn't deserve to be punished for his wants.

He'd told himself repeatedly today she was wrong. He had never told her he hated her or found her disgusting, or even that he disapproved of her lifestyle. For fourteen years, he'd simply avoided her. He hadn't sought her out or tried to bait her.

But a little voice in the back of his head had been unconvinced. And now that voice had come roaring back with a vengeance.

"I think the two of you have a complicated relationship,"

Connor said diplomatically.

"What do you mean?"

"It means it's okay for two people to not get along."

"Akira has always been perfectly nice to us, though we don't see her that often," Ben admitted. "But we like her. Maybe she picks up on the fact...you don't."

The blood rushed in Jacob's ears.

"I don't think you would ever be as vocal about your dislike as Mei was. But she's astute, Jacob."

"You guys think I hate her?" he said roughly.

His stomach caved when both his brothers nodded, Ben more reluctantly. "Especially after you killed her in *Shield of Sorrows*."

Jacob stared at his brothers. "What are you talking about?" *Shield of Sorrows* had been his first book, published when he was the tender age of twenty-six, and had launched his series about CIA Agent James Talent, a rogue operative frequently called on to save the world.

"Lidia was Akira, right?"

"No." Even as he denied it, a sinking sensation came to the pit of his stomach. "She wasn't anything like Akira."

"She might have been Korean-American, not Japanese-American, but..." Ben ticked off the points on his hand. "She was rich, sexy, mouthy, beautiful, and the heir to a fortune."

Also, utterly shallow and all-around unlikeable, a femme fatale luring the hero to his doom. In the book, she had been killed execution style by the shadowy villain, the final death before the stalwart James had taken the man down. Lidia hadn't been designed to be a character anyone would mourn.

"It was weird when we read it. We didn't think you even knew Akira well enough to dislike her personally." Connor made a face. "But the other option was that you just disliked her on principle. And you're not the type to insta-hate someone."

"I'm not," he said, numb. He would never condemn Akira for living whatever life she damned well pleased.

How could he, a small, truthful voice whispered, when he knew the only thing keeping him from doing the same was his obligations to his family? How could he despise a woman for acting on her basc instincts? If there was no one in his life who would suffer for his decisions...

Naked limbs, sweat, grunting, growling, biting, his hard cock sinking into a tight pussy, a wet mouth.

He shuddered, slamming the mental brakes on the Pandora's box of fantasies he had kept contained in his brain for the majority of his adult life. On the fantasy she had brought to life for him last night. *Not for you. Never for you.*

Jacob wiped his hand over his mouth, but it couldn't rid himself of the bad taste left there. He prided himself on being a good man, a progressive man. He felt like the lowest of the low. "I don't hate her," he confessed. Both men leaned forward, and he realized he was close to whispering. "There was no history. I didn't want to be like Dad... I had you guys and Kati to think of and take care of..." Every word Akira had hurled at him last night came flinging back at him. "I wanted her. I didn't want to want her. My response must have seemed like disapproval. But it wasn't directed at her."

There was silence for a moment before Connor spoke. "You aren't Dad. You could never be like that fucker."

Jacob's hand tightened on his beer, the reflexive defense of their father popping out of his lips. "Dad was—"

Connor held up his hand, stalling him. His mouth twisted cynically. "I'm not Kati. I was old enough, Jacob. I remember what Dad was like."

"He was ill-equipped to have children," Ben said quietly, somberness stamped into his face. "Far too irresponsible."

"He tried," Jacob faltered. "He had…problems." Despite all his flaws, Jacob had loved his father. And unlike his brothers, who had been one and two when their mother had died, he remembered a different man. A man who had been less troubled and more balanced. The memories were why he had stuck so close to home, long past the time he should have become independent.

"He did. That doesn't excuse him." Connor looked away, his gaze distant. "You're not him. Even if you hooked up with Akira, hell, with a hundred women, you could never be like him."

He couldn't speak. In the ensuing silence, Ben straightened from his slouched position. "Holy shit."

"Jacob," Connor said slowly. "Did you and Akira…?"

He shook his head. "This—Nothing much happened."

"But something did." Connor propped his chin in his hand and stared at Jacob like he'd never seen him before. "With Akira? Wow."

Ben cleared his throat. "You don't have to give us details, Jacob, but, uh. We won't turn you away if you do."

"There will be no details." He pinched his nose. *I'm sorry for you. But you still had no right to treat me like you have.*

No. He had no right.

He could posture about disapproving of Mei calling her daughter a slut. He could take away all of Kati's electronics. But at the end of the day, was he really much better? He may not have said the derogatory words, but his aloofness could easily have been taken as disapproval. It didn't matter he hadn't intended it. What mattered was how he had made her feel. "How could I treat a woman like this?"

"Because you're not God," Connor snapped. "You're allowed to make mistakes."

His lips twisted. "My mistakes affect three people." His daily reminder, the thing keeping him on the straight and narrow path for so many years.

"Really?" Connor responded. "Because as far as I can tell, this mistake? This affected you. And a completely innocent woman."

Ben nodded. "Do you think we're happy you sacrificed her to spare us…what? The knowledge our brother is human and has sex or feels desire or something? Come on. You're allowed to be selfish."

He suppressed a shudder, unable to think about selfishness and not relive those moments on the soft red rug in Akira's office. It had been everything he'd thought it could be. For that period in time, he'd forgotten everything else in his life. His world had been reduced to him, and her, and satisfying their most basic needs.

Wrong. Dangerous. The path to destruction.

So why had it felt so right? The only thing that felt wrong about this scenario was the way he had treated Akira for all these years. He'd hurt her. He shoved his now-lukewarm beer away. "I just didn't want you guys to be hurt." The excuse felt dumb and stupid on his lips.

But then, his brothers didn't know everything about him and their father, the secret he would probably take to his grave.

"Wake up, Jacob." Uncharacteristic impatience colored

Ben's voice. "We're all grown up. So is Kati."

"What are you going to do when Kati leaves for college in a few months?" Connor asked with brutal honesty. "Be alone? Seal yourself up in your house with your books and your computer and never come out again? Why don't you try living for yourself for a little while? You might like it."

Live for himself. Do whatever he wanted, and damn the consequences.

What an utterly terrifying yet exhilarating possibility.

He glanced up at his brothers, stunned at the emotion written all over their faces. Worry. Worry for...him?

No, that was crazy. He was the one who had to worry for his siblings. Not the other way around.

"If you had a 'nothing much' going on with Akira...you should crawl back to her and turn that into something," Connor said. "You'd be dumb as a rock not to."

Ben nudged his brother. "Akira may be jumping into the deep end of the wild side," he cautioned. "Maybe have a one-night stand first."

"If he's going to have a wild night with someone, it should be someone who knows what they're doing."

Jacob held up his hand to stop the absurd argument. There was truth in what his brothers were saying, but he needed some time to get there. After a lifetime of self-denial and responsibility, he couldn't imagine rushing out and grabbing something for himself.

But you want to.

God, how he wanted to. Forget the universe and get down on his hands and knees between her legs and...

Jacob swallowed. At the very least, he had to make things up to the woman he'd inadvertently stomped upon.

"I don't know if Akira's ever going to talk to me again." Jacob's voice was low. "But if nothing else, I have to somehow make up for being an asshole."

His brothers quieted, thinking. "Jewelry? Sweets?" Ben suggested.

"Food." Connor nodded knowingly. "All those people who talk about a man's heart being through his stomach are idiots. It's the other way around. Cook a woman a nice dinner or bring her coffee in the morning, and she's yours. I think it's the effort."

Jacob squinted. "Effort."

"Yeah. Women like to know you put time and energy into pleasing them, especially when you're trying to apologize to them."

"I doubt she'll be happy to see me," Jacob pointed out.

Ben pondered that. "Maybe she doesn't need to see you."

Jacob scrubbed his hand over his stubble, something stirring inside him. It was much like the stirring he felt when he was pulling together a new plot, thinking of all the characters and the actions and reactions and consequences to follow.

He had to fix this. He had to make things up to Akira.

Plot achieved. Now, he just had to figure out the details.

Connor motioned to the bartender and held up three fingers. "You need to refresh your drink," he said to Jacob when he protested. "And we're going to be here a while."

Ben nodded. "You've come to the right place. Connor's been apologizing for being an asshole for way longer than fourteen years."

Without even looking his way, Connor reached out and slapped Ben on the side of his head. Hard. "Ow!"

Jacob squinted. Dear Lord. He was screwed, but his resources were limited. "Boys."

"Sorry."

"Sorry."

CHAPTER 8

Contrary to popular rumors, Akira's bedroom ceiling was not bedecked with mirrors, dirty etchings, and crystal chandeliers. Though, on nights like these, when she spent most every minute contemplating the damn thing, it might be nice to have something to look at. It would take her attention from the thought of Jacob's hot gaze on her body in that storage closet, the heavy weight of his palm over her mouth, capturing her cries as Remy drove into her, the regret and pain dripping off him after...

Akira's phone chimed a text alert on her bedside table, startling her. Almost six a.m. Though it was still dark out, by this time of day she would usually already be awake and raring to go.

Grateful for the distraction, she rolled over and grabbed the device, the simple movement painful. Boiling emotions made for a potent cocktail. Whiskey had never given her a pounding headache quite like this.

So sorry I missed your call a couple days ago!! Wyatt and I were at a party. Am awake now, call me when you want.

Warmth leached through her exhaustion. In the wake of

the devastating charity dinner two nights ago, she'd forgotten she had left a message for Tatiana. Her circle of friends was deliberately small, and since she had crossed paths with the jewelry designer at a flea market years ago, Tatiana Belikov had quickly been elevated to the ranks of those she trusted.

Now a successful artist who commanded high prices for her art, Tatiana spent a good deal of her time in Vegas with her new husband. The distance hadn't affected their friendship. Eager to have something else to concentrate on, Akira quickly initiated a video call.

The phone only rang twice before the connection was established, and she caught the petite blonde mid-yawn. "Why are we awake? It is too fucking early for decent people to be awake," she greeted Akira.

"You texted me."

"Yeah, I know. I've got meetings with vendors all day, and I wanted to get some work time in." Tatiana took a bracing gulp from the mug she held. Despite her complaining, her gaze was alert, which told Akira this was probably her friend's second cup of coffee. "I figured you might already be at the office. I don't know how you do this every morning." Tatiana eyed her. "But since you're naked, I'm guessing you're still at home."

Akira sat up against the mound of pillows. Only the upper slopes of her breasts were visible to Tatiana. Not like she would be terribly upset if more was revealed. The other woman had been to her house parties, and they had shared a few adventures together. "I'm still in bed. Of course I'm naked."

Tatiana's rosebud lips pursed. "Wyatt's going to be sad you called after he left."

Akira half-smiled. "How is your sexy husband? I heard he had a less-than-stellar last quarter."

"Damn, you really can't stand me having someone richer than you in my life, can you?"

Akira stroked a strand of her hair. "Just making conversation."

"My husband is doing fine, thanks, despite his financial woes." A secret smile curved Tatiana's lips. Probably because she was still tickled to call the man her "husband".

A pang of something foreign and unwelcome shot through Akira's system. She wasn't jealous of the other woman, Akira assured herself. As much as she had grown to like Wyatt, she didn't crave him for herself. She could see herself with that kind of cold, dominant man for a night or two—any more and she would slit his throat and leave him in a ditch somewhere.

Maybe it was simply wistfulness she was experiencing at how happy Tatiana appeared. She identified with Tatiana—neither of them fit the mold the world considered appropriate for women. Neither of them particularly cared.

It was rare, in Akira's experience, to find people who understood and accepted women like them as they were. To find one you would want to tie yourself to for life? Tatiana had discovered a needle in a haystack. "You know you can back out still, if you're worried about his financial solvency," Akira responded. "I'm sure a Vegas divorce is as easy to obtain as a Vegas marriage certificate."

Tatiana snorted. "Please. As if I married him for his money."

A person only had to look at Tatiana and Wyatt together to know why they had married. Even to a cynic like her, their love was practically an incandescent entity.

Akira shifted, inadvertently flashing Tatiana with her breast. The other woman sighed. "Wyatt's going to be so sad he missed this call."

"If he gets his financials back up, he could get back to playing instead of working."

"I'll be sure to pass that message along." Tatiana paused to take another sip of her coffee. "Now, what's up with you?"

Akira curled her legs beneath her, the silk of her sheets rasping against her shaved legs. "I found the box."

Tatiana's loud squeal came through the connection. "Get out. Can I see?"

Since she had been loath to be separated from it, the thing was sitting on her nightstand. She leaned over and picked it up, holding it so Tatiana could view it.

Tatiana was silent for a moment and then sighed. "That is some fine craftsmanship. I've never seen a puzzle box so intricate before. How many moves?"

"Two hundred and twenty-six." The panels on the sides of the box slid back and forth and had to be manipulated in a certain sequence in order to get inside. Better than a diary with a lock and key.

Akira had been careful not to mention her grandmother's box to many people. However, Tatiana could be trusted. Plus, she was an artist and had contacts Akira had been aware might come in handy.

"When did you find it?"

She recalled that glorious instant she had realized what she'd held, dressed down in Jacob's mundane shopping bag. "Last week."

"And you waited until now to tell me?"

"I've been busy. Sorry."

"If you want to send me photos of it, I have a couple of colleagues in Japan who might be able to help you track down the company that made that box, if it's still in business," Tatiana offered, affirming Akira's decision to bring the other woman into her confidence. "I mean, I'm sure you have resources there too, but…"

"Actually, I don't. None in this particular sector." Except for her paternal grandmother, whom she had never met, Akira's parents and grandparents had all been born and raised outside of Japan—her father's side in Europe, her mother's in the United States. If she had relatives remaining in Japan, she didn't know them.

She had established a nightclub in Tokyo, but her contacts through that were limited to others in the nightlife and hospitality industries. "I'd appreciate your help. Though I have no idea if it was a company or a solo craftsman that made it, or when. My great-grandfather gave it to my grandma when she was young." She turned it over in her hand, the sound of the contents tumbling inside oddly comforting her. "As far as I can tell, there's no craftsman mark."

"Hmm. Well, send me the photos anyway. Do you know what's inside?"

"No. My grandma knew how to open it, but whenever I would try to grab it, she'd laugh and tell me it was a secret. She'd tell me only when she was older, so I would be able to open it after she died." Akira paused. Her poor grandmother had been wholly unaware she would suffer a fatal stroke when Akira was nineteen, leaving the box in ignorant hands. "I have fiddled with it a little, wondering if I could get it open."

"I wouldn't have the patience," Tatiana said dryly. "I'd

probably get frustrated and smash it after a day or so."

As much as Akira wanted to claim she would be capable of calmly manipulating the panels forever until she found the proper sequence of moves, she knew that was a lie. Sitting still had never been her forte.

Tatiana frowned. "When I traveled to Japan, I saw these boxes in a couple of high-end stores, so someone is still making them. Maybe any manufacturer can give you some pointers, or if you send them the box, they can open it for you. That way you don't have to resort to the hammer."

Something within Akira shied away from the thought of someone far away handling her grandmother's treasure. The box itself was as important as what was inside it. "I'll send you the pictures," she said. "Let's start there. In the meantime, I'll keep poking at it."

"I'll keep an eye out for them. Where'd you find it, anyway? I thought you searched your mother's house from top to bottom."

Akira tensed, Jacob's stupid, sexy face rushing right back to the forefront of her brain. It appeared she would have no peace from the man. "My mother had given it to her ex-stepchild before she died. He returned it to me after I went to see him." Speaking of which, she would have to come up with some way to compensate the Campbells. Jacob could take the high and mighty, saintlike road all he wanted, blathering on about who had a moral right to the box. Legally, Kati Campbell had a proper claim. Akira refused to be beholden to Jacob in any way.

"Uh-oh." Tatiana raised a honey-brown eyebrow. "I sense a story there."

Akira shook her head, unwilling to discuss the anger, resentment, pity, and desire making up her feelings toward that man.

The last emotion was the most annoying. Now that she had discovered the truth about Jacob's issues with her, nothing could ever come of it, which was a damn shame given his talented tongue. She demanded respect from her sexual partners, and she respected them in turn. As much as she lusted after Jacob, and as much as he might lust after her, he didn't like her. Or want to want her. That was something that couldn't be changed.

You have kind of been a dick to him over the years too, an unassailably honest part of her whispered.

It had been in self-defense, she assured herself. Driving people crazy was her time-honored way of dealing with those who disapproved of her. Give them exactly what they were looking for and they would never look any deeper.

She forced a smile for Tatiana. "No story."

"I'm happy for you, Akira. You must feel relieved to have found this."

She should. After all, she'd won. Recovered her grandmother's possession.

So why did she still feel so damn itchy and off-kilter?

"I do feel great," she lied to Tatiana. "I'll be in touch. I owe you one."

"Next time I'm in town, I expect a house party in my honor."

"Already done and planned, love."

They made plans to speak next week, and Akira hung up. She sat for a moment, pulling together the will to haul herself off the bed. Yesterday had been difficult. Marching herself off to work, putting on her cool, collected face, pretending nothing was wrong, when all the while she wanted to curl up under her covers and eat ice cream. Today would be easier. It had to get easier, right?

How much power will you give this one, insignificant man?

She showered and dressed in record time, aware that if she dawdled, she might be tempted to return to her large bed. Makeup was essential to cover the dark shadows under her eyes, but that didn't take long either. While she might give the impression of high maintenance, she had learned long ago the value of efficiency with regards to her personal hygiene. She could probably make up her face in the time it took most women to select a lip color.

She was fastening her watch as she strode down the stairs, directly to the front door. Since she had gotten a late start, she would grab some coffee and a bagel on the way to work.

Akira almost stepped on the package on her doorstep, the crinkle of paper beneath her heel startling her into pulling back.

On the front stoop lay a large bouquet of wildflowers, simply wrapped in brown butcher paper and tied with twine. Curious, she leaned down and picked up the offering. It wasn't unusual for flowers to be delivered to her door, but the sunny mix of orange and yellow wildflowers, the ends unevenly cut, was out of the ordinary. Plus, it was early, far too early for a floral delivery, and this—she held up her fingers, where a stray bit of dirt clung to her skin—didn't look like it had come from the local high-end florist.

A small piece of yellow paper peeked out from the brown paper. She pulled it out. AKIRA, it spelled out in scrawled block letters. She flipped it over. Nothing. No florist she knew of would use a Post-It for a card.

She shifted her bag and the bouquet to one arm and buried her face in the blooms, inhaling the sunshine.

Orange is my favorite color.

She shook her head. As if Jacob had trekked out here to leave her these.

High heels clicking on the flagstone, she went back into the house. Only one member of her staff stayed on premises—the rest would come in much later in the day. She pressed the intercom next to the door. "Harris?"

Her butler/housekeeper appeared almost before she finished the word. Harris had come highly recommended by a friend of a friend. In the six years he'd worked for Akira, she had never regretted her decision to hire the small, always impeccably dressed man. Dour, discreet, loyal, and unflappable, he was the perfect person to man her household, barely blinking at even her most outrageous requests. She was certain he didn't miss a thing, including the flowers in her arms.

"Yes, Ms. Akira. Good morning," he intoned, as if it were perfectly normal to find the mistress of the house clutching a clumsily wrapped bouquet in the early morning.

Akira hefted the weight of the bouquet. "Good morning. This was on the front stoop. It has my name on it. Do you know anything about it?"

The permanent frown lines on his face deepening, Harris looked at the bouquet with genuine puzzlement. "No, Miss. I have been in the kitchen since I came downstairs."

"Is anyone else from the staff here yet?"

"No, Miss."

There was a privacy fence around her house, but the only gate was at the driveway around the side. It wouldn't be a hardship for anyone to walk up to her door and leave her the gift. Obviously thinking the same thing, Harris scowled. "I shall review the security footage. Here, let me take those. You should not be handling any suspicious packages."

She hesitated a beat before handing him the bouquet, which he treated as gingerly as a bomb. "Let's look at the footage right now."

Harris's bald head shone in the morning light as he inclined it. "Yes, Miss."

She followed Harris through the kitchen, where he placed the bouquet on a counter, and into a small pantry she had converted into a security office. Three flat screens showed split video of all of the cameras, both inside and outside the house. Harris leaned over the keyboard and typed a series of commands. The middle screen changed, displaying the front door and the gate. Harris played the footage at double speed, until a dark blur had him pausing. He backtracked a bit.

Three a.m. A large figure came up the walkway, bold as anything, and carefully placed the bouquet on the stoop. Though the exterior lights didn't shine directly on the man's face, they didn't need to. Akira stiffened. Oh. My. God. She would recognize the way that man moved anywhere.

Jacob had left her flowers in the middle of the night? Jacob? Straight-and-narrow, felt-ashamed-to-get-a-boner-for-her Jacob?

"Hmm. Rather late to leave flowers. Suspiciously late. Shall I call the police?"

Yes. Call them. Have this man arrested for delivering flowers and reminding me he exists. Here, I can give you his address.

"No." Damn it.

"Miss?"

"No, Harris. I can handle this." She spoke through her teeth, wishing she could be cold enough to shuffle her ex-stepbrother and ex-moment-of-madness-lover to the big house.

"I've told you before, you should consider around-the-clock security," Harris fretted.

She had an alarm system and excellent locks on her doors. Generally, she only employed security when it was absolutely necessary. Her father had insisted on personal bodyguards because he'd liked how important they made him feel—she'd had enough of people following her around when she was growing up. "No. This is no one to be concerned with." Maybe he had suffered momentary insanity, resulting in a floral delivery. Of course Jacob had to be exceptional even when he went insane.

She could call him and chew him out, or visit his house. The bolt of anticipation shooting through her at those ideas immediately nixed them. Hadn't she decided just last night she didn't need his brand of crazy? Her life was volatile enough on a good day.

"All the same, you never know—"

"Trust me. I know. This man isn't unstable." She glanced at the screen and muttered under her breath, "Just annoying as hell."

Harris bowed in that way he had that managed to look neither mocking nor ridiculous. "Yes, Miss."

She almost made it to the exit of the kitchen before she had to halt, her body quivering. Muttering a curse, she stomped to the counter, picked up the bouquet, and glared at the fragrant sunshine.

She thought of the tidy home she had visited a couple of

weeks ago, where she'd found Jacob's sister instead of him. There had been no room in front, but perhaps Jacob had a flower garden behind his house filled with the sunflowers and daffodils and other various blooms making up this bouquet.

Don't you dare be charmed. Don't you dare find the thought of a massive Jacob lumbering through flowers and snipping them for you the slightest bit adorable.

Oh God, what if he had arranged this bouquet?

Control yourself, woman.

What was she supposed to do with these? What was this anyway? Weeds to serve as a sop to his conscience?

They were a pretty sop, though…

She stiffened, her spine straightening. Fuck this weird, vague offering. And fuck him.

She marched over to the trash can and held the bouquet over the bin. For some strange reason, her fingers wouldn't uncurl enough to drop the blooms into the basket.

Finally calling herself a weakling, she laid the flowers on the counter as Harris joined her in the kitchen. "Put these in water, please," she said, not caring that she sounded more than a little grumpy. "You can leave them in my bedroom."

She didn't wait for a reply. If the scent of sunshine and spring followed her out the door and all the way to her office, she'd never admit it out loud.

CHAPTER 9

*A*kira managed to keep Jacob out of her mind until noon, due to a fire at one of her Houston locations. Thankfully, the bar hadn't yet opened for the day when the wiring in the walls had sparked, so no one was hurt. Still, the damage meant the place would be out of commission for a few weeks, at least, and she was kept busy dealing with the fallout.

The media was the biggest hassle. She understood she was an easy target since a lot of people would love to see her fail, and implying her venues were unsafe or dangerous was a favorite pastime, but it was annoying as hell to have to grit her teeth and calmly instruct her PR department on how to proceed.

Not for the first time, she cursed the arrogance of her youth that had dictated the name of her business. She should have gone for something anonymous, placed a no-name figurehead at the helm, and faded into the background as a faux-silent partner. Thanks to her father, this fucking name of hers practically painted a bull's-eye on her company.

She was not in the best of moods when Tammy came in carrying the salad Akira had ordered from the deli down the street. "Bless your heart. I'm starving."

Tammy set the familiar plastic takeout box on her desk and placed a brown bag next to it. Akira cast her a questioning look at the latter. "What's that?"

"It was waiting for you at the security desk downstairs. I told them to send it up with your lunch order. I figured you ordered something else?"

Akira studied the innocuous bag, her morning flower delivery popping into her brain. "No. Just my salad."

"Do you want me to…?"

"No." Akira waved her away. "I know who it's from. Thanks." She waited for Tammy to leave. The second the door closed behind the other woman, she snatched the bag closer. The name emblazoned on the front was familiar, though she hadn't seen the swirling script in a while. Davide. She traced her finger over the simple black lettering. How on earth had Jacob known…?

Akira stiffened. Ah. Yes. How long ago had that been? Five years? Leaving her mother's house on a brittle New Year's Eve, she had encountered the woman gushing to Jacob where he stood on the stoop, ready to leave, his coat draped over his arm. "The clock hasn't even struck midnight yet, Jacob."

Jacob had responded, but Akira hadn't been concentrating on his words. So rarely did she get to hear the low rumble of his voice, she wallowed in it when she did.

"Well, give Kati and the boys my regards. I'll drop by your house tomorrow. With Davide's of course."

A pang of hurt had wormed through the champagne Akira had been drinking all night to make the evening at her mother's home bearable. It wasn't enough Mei showed Jacob and his siblings more warmth at these parties than she did Akira. She also stopped by their homes the day after? With treats from one of the most expensive bakeries in San Francisco?

This time, she heard Jacob's response. "Kati's looking forward to it. She loves those scones you bring."

She sneered at the exact moment Jacob's eyes shifted to her standing behind her mother. His easy smile froze.

It took a second for her to banish the outward signs of emotion, but she managed it by the time Mei glanced over her shoulder, her shiny black bob swinging. Disdain replaced the affection. "Are you leaving?" There was no entreaty to stay, as Jacob had received.

She hadn't planned on going. It was barely ten. There was a stockbroker lingering in the ballroom she'd been working on seducing all night. She always tried for at least one conquest at each of these parties.

Hell, she needed to eke some pleasure out of the experience. And her mother's angry attention was better than no attention at all.

But suddenly, facing this matching wall of disapproval, she lost her stomach for courting even that. "Yes. I have a hot date waiting for me at home," she lied. She stepped around her mother and through the door, her hurt insulating her from the cold breeze brushing over her bare arms. She hadn't worn a coat, the better to shock her mom upon arrival with her short slip of a dress.

Jacob took two hasty steps back as she descended the stairs. Annoyance over his retreat, combined with the alcohol in her system, made her toss her next words over her shoulder. "I'll try to clear my, um, friend out tomorrow in time for our traditional New Year's lunch, Mother."

"Don't rush on my account, dear," her mother said smoothly, both of them aware they were playing a game. "I know how you like your fun."

That was her. Fun.

Jacob's eyes shifted warily between her and her mother. "I have to get going. The kids are waiting for me."

Mei softened. "Of course. Good night, Jacob."

"See you tomorrow, Mei. Akira." Jacob gave her a curt nod and turned on his heel, heading down the path to the valet.

"That man is a saint," her mother murmured behind her. "As kind as his father, but far more responsible."

Akira struggled not to shiver. "Yes. A regular saint. I suppose I'll see you at Easter."

"Valentine's. I'm having a fundraiser requiring your presence. Try to behave. Important people will be in attendance."

She merely looked at her mother standing framed in the door. "I show up." Appearances were met. In society's eyes, her mother was the poor, kind mother with the slutty, useless daughter.

"And I should be grateful for that?" Her mother's narrow nostrils flared, but she was forestalled from speaking further when a burst of laughter came from behind her and she had to turn to speak with more departing guests.

She gave her mother a wave. "Bye, Ma."

Her mother grimaced in response.

She found Jacob waiting for his car at the valet stand. He didn't look her way, but the tap of her heels must have announced her presence because he stiffened. They rarely spoke to each other at these parties anymore. Or rather, he did his best to avoid her, and she did her best to pretend she didn't care.

"You're worthy of Davide's, hmm?" she asked, hating the silence. Hating him a little bit. "That means a lot, coming from my mother." And, thanks to the damn champagne, she continued bitterly, "She's never even taken me there." Akira had gone on her own, curious as to why her mother liked the small bakery so much. But it wasn't the same.

He didn't respond for a second, before a gruffly uttered, "I'm sorry."

Mustn't reveal too much. She lifted her chin. "Don't be. It's better that way. I have to keep my figure."

He gave her a short once-over, and though she was certain he didn't intend it, his gaze burned over her bare legs. "You look fine."

She had been told she looked amazing, delicious, riveting, gorgeous, and once, from a sexy Scot, "bonny." So it was silly to draw Jacob's "fine" close to her breast, as if it were the greatest of compliments.

"Cold, though." He started to shrug out of his coat. "Do you want my coat?"

She eyed the battered leather hungrily. Yes, she wanted it. She wanted to steal it and wrap herself up in it and never give it back. So tempting.

He was merely being polite, the same way he'd offer his coat to a chilly old woman or a small girl. "No. Thanks, Brother Jacob."

A muscle in his jaw ticked. He settled the outerwear back on his shoulders with a jerk as the valet drove a small, sensible sedan up to them. "Enjoy your evening."

There was nothing but innocent meaning in Jacob's words, but she gave him a bright, lascivious smile. "Trust me,

I will. Night, Jacob." She didn't have to try to make her voice husky. That was automatic.

His gaze dropped to her lips for an instant before he got in his car and sped away.

Akira bit her lip, the memory making her chest ache all these years later. She edged open the bag, the scent of peaches and warm bread filling her nostrils. The scone inside was huge, the size of her entire hand. Peaches and cream.

Delicious. Her mouth watered, but a ball of melancholy had lodged in her throat. Jesus, but that encounter had been characteristic of all their encounters at her mother's place, hadn't it? She was the interloper, he the welcomed guest. She was the one who limped away wounded, while he sailed off, heart and soul intact.

A sane person might wonder why she had spent her life coming whenever her mother summoned her. There was no rational answer. Akira had told herself at the time it was an opportunity to annoy the woman to no end with her antics. Maybe a part of her hoped Mei would reward her attendance and hand over her grandmother's legacy, but the chances of that were slim. Despite showing up, Akira never behaved the way her mother intended when she used the box as a carrot.

Akira guessed she simply liked the feeling Mei needed her for this small thing. And a tiny, weak part of her had been resistant to closing down the single chance she had to be around the woman. Because if she was around her mother, maybe one day her mother would...love her.

Akira released a shaky sigh. Damn Jacob. Dredging up all these memories. He was so closely entwined with her mother in her mind, it was difficult to think of one without thinking of the other. Pain either way.

Call him. End this. If she coldly told him to knock it off, he would.

She didn't reach for the phone.

Would he send her something else? Would he do it today? Tonight? The eagerness with which she anticipated that worried her so much she placed the scone on top of the bag and shoved it aside. Attempted to turn her attention to the salad she had longed for not ten minutes ago.

The lettuce and grilled chicken tasted like sand in her mouth. Her gaze kept skating back to that scone, the scent of peaches making her dizzy. After choking down a few more bites of greens, her hand moved. Her pinky picked up a fallen crumb. She brought it to her mouth, savoring the burst of sweetness.

It was a slippery slope from crumb to scone. She pulled out a napkin from the bag to catch the crumbs as she brought the dense, chewy treat to her mouth. The rich taste of fruit and bread exploded against her tongue, the bakery's treats as heavenly as she recalled from the couple of solitary forays she had made to the shop, curious as to her mother's preferences.

She caught sight of the script on the napkin, and she held it up to read it. More of Jacob's blunt, no-frills handwriting.

I don't really like sweets, so I never understood why this place was so amazing, but your mom should have taken you there. Or I should have taken you there.

She swallowed, sweetness lingering on her tongue. So he had remembered that encounter. This wasn't merely a coincidence. "How I despise a clever man," she murmured.

The problem was, she realized as she ignored the healthy salad staring at her in favor of finishing the calorie bomb in her hand, she actually didn't.

CHAPTER 10

When Tammy knocked on the door at half past five and promptly carried in a large brown bag, Akira heaved a silent sigh. Finally. Fuck work. About seventy percent of her attention during the afternoon had been on whether Jacob would send anything more.

"This came for you," Tammy announced brightly.

For a moment, Akira missed her usual assistant. Kim would have teased her about her mysterious deliveries. Tammy was still too scared of her to dare.

The dangers of having a group of amazing friends and employees and no family. When push came to shove, those friends would always put their own families first.

Which is as it should be. Anyway, you were the one who gave Kim extra time off. Which was the right thing to do, since a newborn was maybe a bit needier than Akira. Maybe. Not as exciting, though.

Tammy placed the bag on the desk. Thanks to her unexpected lunchtime dessert, Akira wasn't hungry yet, but her stomach nonetheless rumbled at the scent emanating from the delivery. When she finally went home at whatever hour, there would be a frozen meal waiting for her, prepared by the personal chef who came in twice a week to make her custom dinners, as dictated by her nutritionist. They were good meals, but they never smelled as delicious as this.

Akira inhaled. Chinese, if she wasn't mistaken. She couldn't recall the last time she had bitten into an egg roll.

Tammy lay something else on the desk. "This was delivered with it."

The lush red rose was a harsh contrast to the plain simplicity of the bag, a familiar Post-It attached to the stem with a pink ribbon tied in a messy bow. Anticipation zinged through her. This time she didn't suppress it.

"Get me the number for Jacob Campbell. I have his sister's. His may be on the same account." Akira rattled off Kati's number, her eidetic memory having captured it from her phone. Tammy produced a pen and pad from thin air and jotted it down. "Use the PI if you need to."

"Yes, Akira."

That didn't mean she would call Jacob, she assured herself. She only wanted to have the option to call him. She picked up the flower and brought it to her nose, inhaling the scent of the fragrant bloom. She had never cared for roses when they were tight and closed up. She preferred them as this one was, at the end of its lifespan—fully blown open, every secret and flaw revealed. Her finger traced a petal, strangely loath to open the note and read what it said. Maybe the words would ruin whatever perverse enjoyment she was getting out of these weird, cryptic gifts.

And she was enjoying them. After all, when had a man ever sent her flowers, a scone, and Chinese food in the same day?

She could keep the rose and throw away the note, avoid any potential unpleasantness. The gifts would stop eventually. Probably after she gained a dozen pounds, but eventually.

Sadly, avoidance had never been a personality trait she laid claim to. She wasn't about to start now. She tugged open the note.

I'm sorry.

Akira closed the paper before opening it again, as if the words might change.

Nope.

I'm sorry.

Sorry?

Akira ran her forefinger over the word, her nail resting on the period. She tapped that period. Once. Twice.

She bit the inside of her cheek, a warmth settling in her chest.

I'm sorry.

The warmth spread through her, until her cheeks heated. She twirled the rose in her fingers, appreciating that the thorns had been thoughtfully removed.

The petals looked so soft. To test that theory, she ran the velvety rose over her arm.

A knock on her door had her jerking, dropping the rose on her desk as if it were on fire. "What?" she asked, too sharply.

Tammy poked her head in. "I emailed the number to you."

Akira raised an eyebrow in bemused exasperation. That had been easier than she thought. She supposed she ought to be grateful Jacob had such flagrant disregard for safeguarding his privacy. It was working in her favor so far. "Thanks. Why don't you head home?"

Tammy murmured her thanks and closed the door.

In her experience, apologies were rarely as unvarnished as *I'm sorry*. It was always *I'm sorry, but,* or *I'm sorry, however,* or the classic, *I'm sorry you feel that way but...* and then everything would be ruined again, and she'd be forced to destroy him.

That would be messy.

Messier than things already are?

She reached for the phone. Drew her hand back and curled it into a fist.

This was ridiculous, she chided herself. She regularly faced rich, powerful and/or beautiful individuals all over the world, and she persuaded them to come to heel. She refused to be intimidated by a mild-mannered goody-goody author, no matter how nicely defined his abs were.

Avoidance still wasn't a character trait she was interested in possessing. Akira turned off the sound on her computer so she wouldn't be distracted by new email alerts, and grimly dialed the number Tammy had provided.

It rang twice before he answered. "This is Jacob." His voice was raspy, as if he hadn't used it much recently. A bolt of lust shook her, and her hand tightened on the phone. Was this what he sounded like right after he woke up in the morning? When he was still in bed, tangled in a mess of sheets?

Maybe he *was* in bed. His nocturnal floral deliveries of late had probably wreaked havoc on his sleep cycle.

"Hello?"

We're done. Go away. Stop sending me presents. Your tongue wasn't that amazing.

That last lie would have been impossible to choke out, but there were a million other words she could've lobbed at him. Instead, she found herself saying, "Why Chinese food?"

There was a long pause.

"Akira."

Her fingers curled into a fist in her lap. Had he ever said her name quite like that? Caressing every syllable? Because if she had loved the way he spoke it before, this thrilled her to her toes.

"Yes." Committed to the question now, she shifted. "I get the orange flowers. I get the scone. Why the Chinese food?"

He was silent for a long minute before he spoke. "Can I come up?"

She drew back and looked at the phone before putting it to her ear. "Come up?"

"I'm outside your building. Do you mind if we do this in person?"

She glanced at her windows, but she was in the back corner, with no view of the street. "Super creepy, Campbell."

"I know. The Chinese place I like won't deliver out this far."

So pragmatic. "Are you holding a boom box in your hands?"

"No, but I can get one if it'll get me upstairs."

She bit the inside of her cheek, refusing to be charmed. "It's probably not a good idea."

"It's probably a worse idea to talk about this where people can hear me."

Good point. Reporters weren't often a problem for her, unless her father was up to some shenanigans. Still, a lifetime of carefully controlling the image she portrayed to the world wouldn't permit her to have anyone eavesdrop on even half of their conversation. "Fine. Come up."

It took a second to alert the guard downstairs and place Jacob on the visitor list. Eager to give her hands something to do, she fished out the cartons of food from the bag while she waited for him. The rose she pushed to the corner of her desk, unwilling to let him see she'd been fondling it.

When he knocked on the slightly ajar door, she jerked and clasped her hands together to hide their slight trembling. "Come in."

His heavy footfalls were swallowed by the thick carpet as he walked inside. Though Tammy was gone and there was no one in the outer office, he closed the door with a solid click and faced her.

They stared at each other for a long minute. His face was somber, wiped clean of the heavy mix of lust and panic that had characterized it the last time she had seen him.

She licked her lips. Again, there were a million things she wanted to ask him. *What is wrong with you* and *why do you treat me like this* and *did you go home and jerk off, thinking about that storage closet?* All important questions. "Why the Chinese food?"

He shoved his hands into his pockets. She had always preferred a man in a tux over casual clothes, but not Jacob. No, she liked him as he was, barely tamed, with stubble growing on his jaw. Another pair of those old, comfortable jeans sat low on his hips. The blue long-sleeved Henley was snug enough to display his muscles but loose enough so he didn't look like a showoff.

He wrapped his hand around the strap of the brown messenger bag slung across his body. "It's your favorite," he said quietly.

Her eyes narrowed. Not true. She didn't really have a favorite food. Food was fuel, enabling her to get from point A to point B as efficiently as possible. Her preferences didn't come into play when she inhaled a protein shake or a salad. "Where'd you get that idea?"

"At the wedding."

"What wedding?"

"Our parents."

She thought back. It had been a small affair, limited to the immediate Campbell family, Akira, and those friends of both sides who hadn't disapproved of the couple's headlong rush into marriage one month after the pair had met at a golf tournament.

Angry and young—God, so young—Akira had still been prone to hurt feelings over not being invited to the ceremony, only the reception, so she had sashayed in once she'd pregamed with shots of vodka in the back of a limo.

She couldn't recall the food, but she was certain it had been exquisitely catered. Tasteful hors d'oeuvres, specially prepared entrees, sumptuous desserts. Her mother wouldn't have had it any differently, even if she was celebrating her uncharacteristically tacky rushed marriage.

There hadn't been any Chinese food, for sure. "I don't remember," she admitted.

"Think back to the first time you and I met."

She drew in a breath, the moment coming back to her in crystal clarity. Even drunk, she could remember the instant she caught sight of gangly, awkwardly large Jacob. He had been standing near his family, but somehow apart, half his attention on ensuring his snickering teen brothers didn't commit a social faux pas in the luxurious setting they were obviously unaccustomed to, the other half on politely declining the handful of women on the prowl who had been sucked in by his messy hair, green eyes, and loosened tie.

Women like her. She had glided up to him, exaggerating her drunkenness because she was certain her mother was keeping an eagle eye on her. "Hello," she slurred. "You must be one of my new brothers."

"Uh. I'm Harvey's oldest." His big paw stuck out between them. "Jacob."

"Akira." She had taken his hand limply. At that age she hadn't quite mastered a strong handshake.

He grasped it, and a zing traveled through her arm, shocking her into dropping contact with him. His head snapped back, and he looked at her, really looked at her. Took in the inappropriate wedding outfit she wore of a halter top, miniskirt, and stilettos—clothes she would normally never wear unless she was busy aggravating her mother or going to a club. His gaze dipped down over her legs and arms and breasts, and then he came back to her face.

He had frowned. Such a simple facial expression, a matter of fine muscles contracting. In that frown, even tipsy, she had been able to read it all, didn't need to speak to him anymore to understand how disappointed he was, how he disliked her, how he had examined her and found her wanting.

Out of the corner of her eye she had caught a flash of blue silk. Her mother. Acting on evil impulse, she'd stroked her hand up his arm, to his shoulder. Squeezed his strong, young flesh and leaned in, until she could breathe in his mild cologne. "Let's get out of here, Brother Jacob. I know a great Chinese restaurant not far from here. We can grab some takeout. Head back to my place. Get to know each other."

She hadn't heard his response because her mother had taken a hold of her and led her away. The rest of the evening was a blur. She might have flashed the party at some point.

Akira squinted. Nope, she had definitely flashed the party.

She couldn't remember what had prompted partial nudity. But she could distinctly recall the exact expression on Jacob's face when he had weighed and judged her.

Her breath was coming faster. She swiveled in her chair and stared out the window, the distant view of the lush park in the setting sun, the happy families milling about, not calming her in the slightest. "You looked at me like she did."

"Like who?"

"Like my mother."

The sharp inhale from behind her was her only response.

It was easier to speak when she wasn't staring at him. "That's how you've always looked at me. Judging me. Like I'm some weak, worthless person. An intrusion."

"I never thought you were worthless, or weak." His quiet voice carried so much conviction, she almost believed him. "I'm sorry I treated you the way your mother did. She wasn't right to do that."

The blunt criticism of Mei was unexpected but not unwelcome. Since the woman had died, she had listened to countless stories of Mei's grace and wisdom and love, qualities she had never shown her only daughter.

It was sick she needed someone to corroborate the dead's unkindness, but she'd long since been accustomed to being sick. *Tell me my mother was in the wrong. Tell me I'm worthy of all the things she didn't give me.*

"You should have taken me up on my offer," she murmured now, half to herself.

His response was immediate. "Yes."

She set her teeth, as if that might keep the plaintive words lodged there. No luck. "Why didn't you?"

A long beat. A pressure was exerted at the top of her chair and it turned around. He dropped to his knees so his face was on level with hers, his familiar serious expression almost grave, his skin drawn tight, as if he had lost weight...or was grieving. "I don't know. I was...scared." The word was low, like he didn't enjoy admitting it.

Appropriate, because she hated hearing it. So scary, she was. So terrifying to all the poor little men. When she'd been young, maybe sixteen or seventeen, she'd confessed to a girlfriend that she didn't understand why men found her difficult to be around. "They're just intimidated by you," her friend had consoled.

Like that was supposed to make things better?

She'd decided not long after that men needed to either nut the fuck up or leave her be. Her hand clenched tight over the arms of her chair. "Of me," she spat, with disdain.

"No."

Liar. Her nostrils flared. "Then what?"

"Of me," he finally said.

She studied him, struck by the words. They were in line with the determination she had come to yesterday, but still confusing. What kind of hang-ups could this guy possibly have that made him so incapable of indulging his desires?

"Why?" When it looked like he wasn't going to respond, she pushed him. "I have a right to know."

"You aren't the only one," he whispered, his voice barely a

sound, "whose parents saddled them with baggage."

Her brow furrowed. Her mother had despised her and her father only wanted her when he could pimp her out to television viewers. What problems could Jacob have had with his parents?

Granted, she didn't know much about his earlier years. His mother had died when he was young, his brothers barely babies. She hadn't interacted with Harvey Campbell much in the two years she had known him before his death, but he had seemed like a kind, friendly, mild-mannered physician. "I don't understand."

His lips tightened. "Everyone marveled when your mother married my dad after a month. No one who knew my dad was surprised." His laugh was without humor. "That was entirely within character for him, throwing everything aside to run off and do something new and exciting. Get-rich-quick schemes, women, business—there was nothing my father liked more than the thrill of risk."

Jacob wasn't a verbose man, but as he spoke now, his words came faster, as if he had to get them out before the spigot shut off. "Once when the boys were about three and four—I must have been twelve, maybe—he straight up did not come home for three days." Jacob's lips twisted. "I was scared, but more scared of social services, so I didn't ask for help or call anyone. I just kept the kids in our nice, tidy, middle-class house, and fed them Cheetos and Doritos when we ran out of cereal."

"Where was he?"

"Vegas," he responded succinctly. "He went with a colleague after work and got on a hot streak. He didn't mean to be gone so long. He hadn't even thought to tell me he was going. Or wondered if he should leave a bunch of kids on their own at all.

"When my mom was alive, I think she managed to keep him balanced. Or maybe I was just too young to notice it then because she picked up the parenting slack."

One of the thousands of pieces making up Jacob slid into place, everything around it aligning. "So after she was gone, you picked up the parenting slack."

He looked down and studied his hands. Turned them over, as if all of the secrets of the universe could be found there. "For a long time...yes. As the boys grew older, became more self-sufficient, I thought maybe I could start to pull away. Do what I want."

She waited, but he fell silent, lost in past memories. "And then Kati came along," she said softly.

He started. "I realized I couldn't be him. I couldn't just do whatever I wanted. I couldn't be distracted." A corner of his lips kicked up. Not quite a smile, but a rueful acknowledgment. "That day, at the wedding, you walked up to me, and do you know what my first reaction was?"

She rarely hung on to men's words, but she was practically on the edge of her seat with this sincere conversation. Their tones were hushed, though they were guaranteed privacy. "What?"

"I was ready to run out of there with you." He shook his head, a lock of hair falling over his forehead. Her fingers itched to push it aside. "My father was off in his own little world of new love, and I knew he'd once again forgotten he had kids. But I didn't have that luxury. They needed one stable parent."

"But you're not their parent," she pointed out.

Something dark moved in his eyes.

"Jacob," she prompted.

He shook his head. "Yeah," he said, his voice rough. "I'm not. I've been informed my sense of responsibility is maybe overdeveloped. I'm...working on that."

He placed his hand on hers and regarded her steadily. She cocked her head, realizing this was the first time the two of them had gone more than five minutes in each other's company without resorting to taunts, insults, sex, or defensiveness. They were merely conversing. Like adults.

It was strange. But...nice.

"I've gone my whole life trying not to be like my dad. He was addicted to everything, and I knew within the first few minutes of meeting you that I could be addicted to you." He paused. "But I made that your problem. It was mine, and should have stayed mine." He stretched his hand out and grabbed something from her desk. A second later, the rose was in front of her. "I'm sorry. Forgive me."

Slowly, she extended her hand and grasped the rose. She tightened her hand around the stem, the nubs of the stripped thorns digging into her palm. "I don't care what anyone thinks about me. You didn't hurt my feelings."

"I know," his reply was infinitely gentle.

"I was angry, not hurt," she lied.

He dipped his head. "I'm sorry."

He was literally on his knees. The power was in her hands. She could destroy him quickly and send him on his way.

She leaned her head back and thought of the trouble he had gone through to apologize to her, without belittling her feelings or making her out to be the villain. Perhaps it was the sincerity in his voice, or the novelty of such a simple, uncomplicated apology, she could practically envision the tenterhooks of rage releasing their grip on her heart. The rage, but not the bitterness.

"What do you want from me? My forgiveness? Absolution? Because you're talking about years of being made to feel like...nothing." Only Jacob and her mother had had the power to make her feel like shit. To make her care what they thought of her.

He flinched. "I want a chance to earn your forgiveness. Make it up to you."

"With flowers and food?"

"It's a start." He came to his feet and turned to the desk, opening the closest container. The scent of cashews and chicken wafted out to her, making her stomach grumble.

"Why do you care?" she asked, confused. "We could easily never see each other again."

He opened another container. "Because I don't like that option," he said gruffly.

AKIRA'S HAIR WAS PULLED BACK TODAY, THE BLACK SILK tucked neatly in a low bun. On another woman, perhaps the style would only convey professionalism, but the low hum of energy strumming beneath her surface made that an impossibility.

He wanted Akira. Still, always.

Her forgiveness, yes. His words weren't a farce, a lie meant to win points.

But he couldn't help the urge to kiss those full lips, bury himself inside her softness. Again, not her problem. It was his struggle to manage.

He inhaled, suddenly certain his next words would decide the fate of all their future interactions. He needed to make it good, so he ignored his aching dick, cleared his throat, and extended his hand.

"My name's Jacob Campbell. It's a pleasure to meet you."

Akira's fine lashes fluttered, and for a painful moment, he wondered if she would leave his hand hanging in midair. But no, she accepted it, her smaller palm fitting in his as if it had been made to rest there. "Akira Mori."

Something animalistic inside him stretched toward her rough voice. He wanted it to curl around him, keep him calm. For the first time ever, he allowed the pleasure he experienced from her touch to rush over him. It was so much better when he wasn't filtering it through a haze of shame and self-denial.

"Akira," he repeated, his voice gone husky. The pulse at the base of her throat increased.

She studied him for so long, a trickle of sweat gathered at his hairline. She was judging him, weighing his words. Her fingers toyed with the rose he had clipped from his small courtyard garden to deliver his message. The flower had practically screamed Akira's name, it was so lush and fragrant.

She followed his gaze. "I like this rose."

"I'll bring you more." Too hasty, that promise. He would promise her everything, a garden of flowers.

Danger, danger.

He slammed his internal warning system into submission. No more, damn it. He was a grown man, and he needed to start acting like it.

"Honestly," she finally said. "Once someone goes on my

shitlist, they usually stay there forever."

As he'd said, not an option. He glanced away, his brain scrambling. His gaze caught on the puzzle box he had delivered last week. It sat on the corner of her desk.

He cocked his head in the direction of the box. "May I?"

Confusion knit her brows together, but she nodded.

He picked up the box and weighed it in his hand. "I did some research on these after I returned this to you. It's like an old-fashioned lockbox, right?" He touched a panel. It moved slightly. Fascinated, he slid it back and forth. "You have to manipulate those panels in a certain order, each one unlocking the next. Make one wrong move, and the box remains closed." He'd watched a video on YouTube of a man taking one apart.

"Yeah."

"You said you don't know what's inside."

"No."

He glanced up. "Do you want to know?"

Her eyes narrowed. "Yes."

"How many moves?"

She shifted. "Two hundred and twenty-six, for this particular box."

"Have you tried to figure it out?"

Akira shook her head, a strand of her hair coming loose to rest against her cheek, a length of blue black against the cool paleness. "I'm the most impatient person in the world. I'd be tempted to smash it."

"Somehow I don't think that's true." Impatience wouldn't have made her as successful as she was.

"Trust me. I do, however, have some contacts out trying to see if we can track down someone who can open it. Maybe the original manufacturer."

Jacob frowned. So some stranger somewhere would open the box for her? That didn't seem right. Possibly because he could still vividly recall what Akira had looked like, collapsed on her rug, holding the thing to her chest like it was the most precious item in the world.

"Maybe..." He cleared his throat, his idea taking shape. "Maybe I could open it for you."

She scoffed. "You've never even seen a box like this."

"No." He tested a few of the panels, the wood stiff and unyielding at first, finally relaxing enough for him to move. "But I like puzzles. And I am patient."

"You think you can open my box?"

He glanced up, wondering if there was a sly innuendo in her words, but her expression was impassive. "I can try."

"In exchange for what?" She gave a wry smile at the face he made. "I know negotiations when I hear them."

He thought for a moment. "I'm not stupid. You're skeptical of me. Give me two weeks. If I can't open the box in that time, and if you still feel there's no value in our truce at the end of the two weeks, then we go our separate ways."

"The box stays with me. I'm not handing it over to you."

Even better. Jacob had figured the box would buy him at least one more chance to see her, maybe earn him some goodwill if he could crack it.

But this...oh man. Had she realized the gift she'd inadvertently given him?

Normally, he would be polite and circumspect, but screw that. Time to seize the opportunity. "I'll come to you."

Her lips pursed. He could practically see her brain racing. "I'm busy and I work late."

"I'm a night owl," he said easily, prepared to match every argument she launched. He looked around the office, improvising as he went along. "I can come here. Bring dinner. I wouldn't disturb your work."

"What if you do open the box?"

"You forgive me." He shrugged. "That's all I want."

"All?"

He reconsidered the situation. Decided to keep his options open. "No. You stay open to the possibility of us becoming…friends."

That did not seem to impress her. "I have friends."

"You don't have me."

She nodded slowly. "True."

"And," he added, "you buy me dinner."

"Like a date?"

A date between him and Akira. The idea should be laughable. It shouldn't make him want to smile wolfishly at the prospect. He controlled his reaction. "Yes."

She pondered that. "I don't do dates."

The words that fell from his lips were so uncharacteristically arrogant, it was as if someone else were speaking them. "You will."

Her nod was slow, her expression considering. "You'll probably fail."

It took him a second to realize she was agreeing to his asinine proposal. He bit the inside of his cheek so he wouldn't let out a whoop.

"I have confidence in my abilities." He flexed his fingers. "And good hands."

Her eyes lingered on his hands. "One week."

Not long enough. "Two weeks."

She lifted her chin. "Ten days."

Hmm. Ten days would be tight, but he'd made a rookie error in starting negotiations at what he actually wanted. She wouldn't agree to a longer length of time as a matter of pride now. "Ten days. Not counting the days we don't meet up."

"A day counts as any time we're in each other's presence."

"Do we need to have our legal teams draft a contract?" he asked, joking.

For a second, he thought she was going to get her lawyer on the phone. But instead, she gave a slow shake of her head. "I think we can call this a gentleman's agreement."

"So...deal?"

She worried her lower lip between her teeth, a rare sign of indecision. "Deal."

He looked down at the box so he could hide his relief. "We could start tonight. It looks like you have some food here," he said, perusing the desk. "It'll get cold. I haven't had dinner yet."

A smile stretched across her face, and he watched, fascinated. It was a real smile, unlike any she'd ever graced him with before. There and gone in a flash, it didn't last long.

He'd see it again, he vowed grimly.

"Fishing for a dinner invitation?"

"In the most subtle of ways."

"So we can be friends," she said, skeptical.

That sounded right. Comfortable. Not scary or intimidating, for either of them. "Yes."

"Well..."

He waited with bated breath as she considered his proposal.

"I suppose I do have enough food to feed an army," she

said.

Confused, he looked down at the half-a-dozen containers on the desk. This amount of food would barely feed half his family. "I'm sure we can put a dent in it," he replied, in lieu of confessing he was a gluttonous pig who could easily manage to pack away these calories for a moderate-sized lunch.

Her shoulders rose. "There aren't any plates."

He shot her a quick sideways glance. The explanation was out of character for her. Was she nervous? Of him? The situation?

Not right. "Plates for Chinese takeout? Not necessary. What do you like? There's beef and broccoli, chow mein, some stir-fried veggies…"

"I haven't had Chinese in so long, I don't remember what I like," she admitted.

"We order it every week."

She made a scoffing noise. "I'm thirty-four, not twenty anymore. I have to be more careful."

After a comment like that, how could he resist casting an assessing eye over her slim body? He focused back on the cartons, opening the rice. "I think you'll be okay, even with a few indulgences," he said, gruff. "Here, we can share everything." He handed her a pair of chopsticks, which she took warily.

"Thanks."

He didn't blame her for being wary. He would eradicate that. He glanced around and dragged the chair facing the desk closer to the table. He sat down, casual as possible, and picked up the nearest container, uncaring of what it was.

She sat more slowly and did the same. They ate in silence

for long moments, Akira picking at a couple of the containers. "We're going to be spending all this time in each other's company."

"Yes." Torture. Joy. Apprehension.

Worth it.

"There's an elephant in the room, Jacob."

He swallowed the bite he had taken, finding his mouth dry of saliva. He had carefully focused on maneuvering her into accepting his impulsive deal, eyes on the prize of her forgiveness.

Of course there was an elephant in the room. It had taken all his concentration to not let his mind stray to visions of her naked. Pleasured.

He clenched his thighs, fighting his body's natural reaction. "I know."

"Are we going to talk about it?" Her fingers toyed with the chopsticks. "What we did?"

Unbidden, his eyes slid over to the rug. "What we did here?"

"Here. And in that storage room."

Talk about the storage room? He wanted to reenact what they had done in the storage room. Only this time, he would be the one between her thighs, making those cries fall from her sweet, lush mouth, cries he wouldn't stifle, let the whole party hear what he did to her...

Jacob shifted, his cock thickening despite his best efforts. No, no, no. *Too soon.* He wasn't here for this.

Their truce was so fragile. "Probably best not to," he finally said, as matter-of-fact as he was capable of being. "Not yet."

Her beautiful dark eyes gave nothing away. "So when?"

"I'll let you know."

She took another bite from her carton and squinted at him. "So. Now what?"

From one difficult question to the next. It was becoming rapidly apparent he hadn't thought this through. What could he talk about with a woman he'd spent fourteen years alternately avoiding and pining over? "Now we pretend to be normal people."

"Hell." Akira set down the carton. "We're doomed."

CHAPTER 11

*A*kira's doorbell was far too loud.

Or perhaps her home was simply too large, the sound echoing over the massive foyer, up through the unused bedrooms.

She stared at the double doors, her fingers drumming against her knee. She should get up off the stairs where she sat and answer it, but the fact that she wanted so very badly to kept her seated, counting to one hundred.

Jacob would be standing on the other side of the entrance, and though this was the third night in a row they were trying out this tentative peace, it was the first time he was coming to her home. Ever.

Her fingers curled as she slowly counted through the fifties.

There was no possible way she could hide all her personal things here. She'd purposefully laid her stamp on the place, and for good reason—only her closest friends and most vetted confidantes were permitted to visit this house. Business functions were handled in impersonal hotel ballrooms. Not in her home.

She wasn't quite sure how Jacob had managed to invite himself. She'd informed him she would be busy, packing for a quick two-day trip to New York to meet with the head of the Anderson Group, who she feared was getting cold feet about selling his European assets to her. She'd spent too long combing through the due-diligence reports legal counsel had sent her to have this idiot back out now simply because he hadn't warmed to her personally.

She'd told Jacob as much, and the next thing she knew, he was coming over.

He was a wizard. It was the only explanation as to why she was incapable of saying no to this man.

Case in point: this ridiculous agreement. She could find someone else to open the damn box. Tatiana had a lead on the company that had initially crafted the thing. Hell, Akira didn't even particularly care what was inside it. Getting the thing into her possession had been her goal for so long, simply having it was enough for now.

You just wanted to spend more time with him.

Guilty. Though the last two nights had been a bit awkward and strained at times, things were…different. There was a shift in the way he looked at her and talked to her. Like she was the friend he'd said he was looking for.

He had a quiet irresistible charm and surprising hidden depths. Like last night, when he had brought up her work habits. "You always work late like this?"

"No." She could have ended with the short answer, but he'd been looking at her expectantly, as if he was actually curious about her business. "I'm trying to finagle a deal, taking over the European arm of this corporation. They're running the actual businesses into the ground, but they have great locations."

"Sounds important."

"It is. It could instantly almost triple my holdings there." Europe was a market she had long been eager to expand in. That was where the Mori hotels had been particularly robust.

Not that she was competing with her father. But, well…she couldn't deny that it would give her a great deal of satisfaction to rub his face in her success on his home turf.

"So no, I don't always work as late as this, but I probably do work later than most people."

He didn't respond, so she prodded him. "Aren't you going to lecture me on proper work-life balance?" A phrase she rather despised. She had a proper work-life balance, but people either assumed she did nothing but party or she worked herself to death. No one understood her work-life balance was just right for her.

He had cast her a confused look. "I work late sometimes because I enjoy it and I don't want to stop. You should do whatever makes you happy. Even if that's staying here until midnight."

Maybe he was telling her what she wanted to hear. But that made no sense. He got nothing out of winning her over—money, sex, or fame hadn't exactly been a part of his deal.

A shocking thought: perhaps he had no ulterior motives other than getting to know her without the negativity that had contaminated every dealing they'd had before.

She narrowed her eyes. Look at him, not even impatiently ringing the doorbell more than once, though she was taking her sweet time in answering. What kind of a saint was he?

She rose slowly to her feet and made her way to the door,

pulling it open. He gave her his lopsided, rare smile, and she almost slammed the heavy wood in his face.

She wasn't used to this at all. Somehow, it was easier to deal with the man when he was brooding and being silently disapproving. Then she knew what to expect, was able to predict his actions, which in turn dictated her own. This guy...no, she had no idea what he was up to.

"So you answer your own door."

"It's the butler's night off."

He snorted as he walked past her, forcing her to open the door wider to accommodate his large frame. When she didn't respond, he turned, his red sweater clinging to his muscles.

The spurt of lust was almost second nature by now. Almost.

"Oh. You're serious."

She closed the door and shoved her hands into her pockets. "Of course I'm serious. Do you really think I have time to run a house of this size in addition to my business?"

"Hmm." Jacob glanced around, and she had to fight her instinctive urge to blindfold him, perhaps lead him to the most nondescript and boring room in the place. She had a guestroom on the third floor that was in the process of being renovated. He could go there.

No, there was only a bed in that room. He might get the wrong idea. Or the right idea.

"Yeah, I suppose you would need help here."

"It's not such a big deal." She hated the urge to apologize for her wealth. "My mother had a butler."

"Only for parties," Jacob responded absentmindedly, while he studied the crown molding with a heavy fascination. "Not on a regular basis."

Akira rocked back on her heels. "Right."

His eyes softened. "Sorry. Did you not know…?"

"The box is in my library." She covered her slip hastily, not eager to delve into all the ways this man had known her mother better than she had. "Do you want to wait here while I grab it?"

"I'll come with you." He fell into step beside her, adjusting the strap of his ever-present messenger bag.

"You don't have to." Probably best to keep him to safer parts of the house. She'd assumed they would eat in the dining room. Harris had laid out a simple spread for the two of them before heading out for his night off.

She supposed she could have handed Jacob the box, in accordance with their stupid agreement, and left him to it while she attended to her own affairs, but he had provided dinners for the past two nights. If nothing else, she was a good host.

This had nothing to do with her newly discovered fascination for the way he dug into his meals with such relish and gusto, the movement of his strong throat as he swallowed, the unselfconscious way he threw himself into enjoying his meal. Nor did it have anything to do with their still-strained, yet oddly compelling conversations between bites.

"I don't mind," he said mildly.

She slid him a sideways glance as she led him down the hallway. The first floor was made up of her library, kitchen, formal dining room, and three sitting rooms. The library was the only room she actually used when she was alone. "You just want to see my library, don't you?"

"How could you tell?"

"You looked mildly aroused when I used the word 'library'. And I know it wasn't for me, since I don't elicit *mild* arousal." The flirtatious sally wasn't deliberate. It was an automatic reflex. She wanted to recall the words as soon as she'd uttered them.

She flirted with her friends, but Jacob probably didn't. Would he become cold and cutting now? A shaft of sorrow ran through her, but it didn't get far, because he spoke.

"No," he responded, his tone husky. "You don't."

She glanced at him sharply, but his hair hid his eyes. Still, a little fission of awareness ran down her spine.

Well. Well. Well. Was Jacob Campbell flirting with her?

"I like your house. Or what I've seen of it," came his deep voice. Not cold or cutting.

"Yeah?" She quickened her steps. His longer legs automatically matched her stride. "My mother was here once. She declared it all incredibly tacky." Mei had sneered at the huge chandeliers and lavish furnishings. And she had never even made it past the first floor. The second, where Akira did her entertaining, would have given the woman a heart attack.

"I don't think it's tacky. Did you decorate it yourself, or did you buy it like this?"

Her shoulders lifted. "I did it myself."

"It's beautiful. Really."

She gave a single, decisive nod, a tight knot in her chest releasing. "Yes, it is."

"Though I'm probably not qualified to judge. I hardly visit Pacific Heights houses regularly."

"No Specific Whites friends for you?"

He tipped his head, acknowledging her use of the derisive term for the elite, mostly white neighborhood. "No. And I'm okay with that. No offense."

"None taken." She gave him a shark's smile. "The old lady next door still mutters about the 'upstart Oriental' who bought Buffy and Harold's place and turned it into a den of sin." She opened the door to her library.

Jacob stopped. Good. It meant he was properly impressed. "May every den of sin look like this."

"If you're going to sin, darling, you should do it with class."

The ceilings here were as high as the rest of the house, and the massive expanse of walls had been covered by floor-to-ceiling bookcases. A couple of sofas and tables made up a large reading nook in one corner. Her heavy desk and home office setup were arranged nearby.

There was a separate study, but she preferred this area. The scent of the books helped her think. Some of the shelves were empty, but the majority were crammed tight with titles.

Jacob took a few more steps inside and craned his neck up, treating the sight of this room with the kind of reverence most people displayed in her impressive foyer. "This is insane. This is all yours?"

"Well. I inherited about a fifth of the titles from the previous owners, after donating the boring ones I didn't want. The rest, yes. The rest are mine.

"What?" she asked, when he continued to look at her. "Some rich people collect art. I collect books."

"You never told me that."

"I didn't think it was relevant."

"I'm an author. You didn't think I'd find it relevant you have a library the size of a football field?"

"Hardly a football field. Maybe a couple of basketball courts." She couldn't help but savor some satisfaction. Jacob didn't impress easily.

He walked to the closest bookcase and ran his finger along the shelf. "You've had someone alphabetize these?"

"Funny enough, I am capable of putting books in alphabetical order without relying on my serfs."

He shot her an incredulous glance. "When do you sleep?"

She glanced deliberately at her watch. "Sometime between fucking and ruling the world."

The words were a test, and he passed. No flinch or expression of horror at her frank talk, but a snort of laughter that made her want to smile.

She controlled her facial muscles. Really, she was too easily swayed by this man.

She stiffened when he came to an abrupt halt, his shoulders rigid. Abruptly recalling what was in that section, Akira took a quick step toward him, but it was too late.

Fiction. The C's.

He turned and studied her. "You have every one of my books."

She kept her face impassive, though she couldn't help that her fingers had tightened into a fist, her body bracing for a blow. *Never let them see what you like, what you want.* "So?"

"So...why do you have my books?"

Her shoulders lifted in a shrug. "I don't know." Her heartbeat accelerated, a tell that annoyed her, even if he would be unaware of it.

Well, you see, I couldn't stand not having at least the barest connection with you.

She couldn't talk to him. She couldn't bed him. She couldn't befriend him. But for all these years, she could read him.

She tensed, prepared for an interrogation or mocking, and was surprised when he tapped his fingers against the shelf and cocked his head. "Do you want my autograph?"

Her muscles relaxed in a rush, making her legs shaky. Her lips quivered at the corner. "Sure." She strolled closer. Mischief and another, darker emotion had her reaching past him to pull a paperback off the shelf. This book had been released in hardcover later on, she was sure of it, once Jacob became popular, but she still had the original first edition. Her fingers brushed his when she handed it to him. "Here. Do this one."

They both looked down at the glossy cover of *Shield of Sorrows*. Unflinching, he met her gaze. "It wasn't you."

Heat rushed through her, but it wasn't arousal. "I don't know what you're talking about."

He took the book from her and flipped through the pages, a fierce scowl growing on his face. "It came to my attention recently there are those who believe I modeled Lidia after you."

Her laugh was light. Meaningless. "Do you think I've honestly read every book in this library, Jacob? I don't know who Lidia is."

That gave him pause, before a cunning light lit his eyes. "You may not have read every book in here, but you've read all of mine."

She raised an eyebrow. "You're arrogant."

"And you're lying if you deny it. Which is why you aren't denying it."

She leaned against the bookcase, considering him. "I'm an excellent liar."

"Not with me. And I think you know that."

Had he always been this sexily confident? Had his quiet, unruffled demeanor simply concealed it from her? "Okay, hotshot. I've read this book. But I certainly have better things to do than wonder if you used me as inspiration for a self-serving socialite with questionable morals."

She had never been able to read his emotions quite so easily. Remorse deepened the lines around his mouth. "Well, if you had, rest assured, I definitely did not." He pulled a pen out of his shirt pocket and flipped open the book to the title page. Scrawling a couple of lines, he handed it back to her.

Unable to resist, she glanced at the writing. *You're more like the hero.*

She bit her lip to keep from smiling. "Because I'm brilliant, aggressive, and sexually accomplished?"

His face was serious. "Yeah. And because you could probably save the world, if you were wearing the right shoes."

She cleared her throat. It had been a while, but she vaguely recalled the time Agent Talent had freed himself from certain death with a knife concealed in the sole of his wingtips.

As amused as she was, she wouldn't read too much into his words. He was being flip, that was all. Akira placed the book on the nearest shelf, ruining her admittedly obsessive ordering system. "I undoubtedly could."

He shifted his weight. The light from the wall sconces caught the subtle reddish undertones in his hair. "So, what do you think?"

"Think?"

"Of my books."

Her fingers drummed a steady tattoo on the shelf. "You don't want to know."

He winced. "Ouch. Okay. That bad, huh?"

"The intrigue and suspense part is always good," she offered. "You've almost stumped me a couple of times until the middle."

"I'm kind of hoping to stump people until the end."

"Don't worry. Most people aren't as smart as me."

He looked amused. "But?"

"But what?"

"The suspense is always good, but…"

She shrugged. "You need to work on your female characters."

"My…" He drew back, offended. "I've been praised for my female characters."

"You mean the ones you don't brutally murder?"

A dark flush moved up Jacob's face. "*Shield* was my first book, okay? I haven't brutally murdered a woman in…" he flinched, "…at least two books?"

"Hmm."

"I murder men too."

"But never the hero."

He was starting to look annoyed. Perversely, she kind of liked it. "The hero's supposed to live. He's the hero."

"Make him a her every now and again," she replied. "And maybe I might increase the ratings I left you on Amazon."

He opened his mouth. Shut it. Glanced consideringly at the shelf, and then back at her. "I didn't really intend to write one series for this long," he said, with a touch of defensiveness. "I can't just turn James into a her. I'd have to write something new."

"Is that a problem?"

"No. But I'm under contract for at least one more Agent

Talent book."

"One doesn't sound like a lot." She shrugged. "But if you love writing the good Agent's exploits, I can't say much about it."

He rolled his lips inward. "I don't love him much right now. Finishing this last book has been like pulling teeth."

"Ah."

"But *Shield* has been optioned for a mini-series. Sales have never been higher. My agent's pushing for continuing."

She lifted a brow, simultaneously happy for him and dreading the thought of poor, fascinating Lidia coming to an undeserved death on the small screen. "No kidding. Well, what the hell do I know?"

"It would be interesting, though. To write a heroine." His eyes narrowed, and he stared past her. "Someone different."

"If she's cool and very rich, you can use me as inspiration." She shrugged. "I was probably in the minority, but I liked Lidia."

"I can't bring Lidia back..." He stopped, as if realizing he could, indeed, do whatever he wanted.

"Can't you?" She leaned against the shelf. "It's been ages since I read the book. But your Agent Talent never found her body, did he?"

"That would be a cop-out. Raising someone from the dead."

"Why? Seems to me like you ended her story right when she was getting interesting. That's great source material." Her innate business sense rose to the surface. "Killing this series is dumb. If a show is made and takes off, it'll funnel readers your way. A spin-off would be much easier for you or your agent to market."

He nodded, but she doubted he was even peripherally aware she was in the room. His gaze was far away, his long fingers moving over the strap of his bag. "That might work. Maybe," he muttered, half to himself. He grabbed *Shield of Sorrows*. "Do you mind if I jot down some notes?"

He was already moving to the huge wing chair before she could give her assent. Hastily, he sat down and opened his bag, removing a scratched laptop.

"Um. Sure."

He gave her a distracted smile, but it still made her heartbeat accelerate. "Great. Here." He reached into his bag again and pulled out a wrapped sub, holding it out to her. She accepted it gingerly. "I hope you like chicken salad. If not, I also got ham and cheese. I like 'em both." He pulled out another sub, but since his lap was occupied with his laptop, he placed it on the coffee table. Back into his pack he went and withdrew two cans of beer.

Intrigued by his Mary Poppins bag, she drew closer and perched on the armchair opposite him. "What else do you have in there?" she marveled.

He glanced down at the bag between his big feet. "I've had this thing since Kati was four. I don't think either of us wants to know what else is in there."

"Why, Jacob. Is that your mom purse?"

She expected annoyance or defensiveness, but Jacob only nodded. "There's a reason moms need mom purses. My computer bag was the most socially acceptable conveyance I could use for the crap the kids needed." He opened his computer and booted it up. "Now, eat your sandwich."

She thought of the food sitting in the warming dishes in her dining room. Studied the way his hair fell over his

157

forehead, the light in his eyes, the way his strong fingers flew over the keyboard. Slowly, she unwrapped her sandwich.

The room was quiet except for the noise of his typing. When she finished eating, she rose. He paid no attention to her. After throwing her trash away, she retrieved her grand-mother's box from her desk. After a moment's hesitation, she returned to the chair opposite him and curled up in it, hugging the wooden box to her stomach and watching him.

If the weather was cooler, she would lay a fire. So cozy.

Too cozy.

All of it. The conversation they had just had, without a trace of stiltedness or weirdness. The setting. The peace.

The way she absolutely couldn't work up the urge to leave.

I loved your grandfather, but he was a difficult man to simply be with. That's the problem with your mother, Aki-chan. She can't help herself.

Akira jerked, the stray memory startling her. She so rarely recalled discreet conversations with her grandmother any longer.

She had been fourteen, but already taller than the older woman, her knees brushing against the underside of the dining table in her grandmother's home. Mei was a dutiful daughter who offered her mother money time and again, but Hana wasn't ready to leave her comfortable row house.

Akira had discovered later her grandmother had placed the funds her daughter had given her into a trust fund for Akira. When Akira had turned twenty-five, that money had enabled her to buy her first bar.

"What do you mean?" fourteen-year-old Akira had asked her grandmother.

The smaller woman had looked up from her salad and smiled, but it had been tinged with sadness. "Some people will just let you be, even when you're with them."

"Like, leave you alone?"

"No. And stop using the word *like* in every sentence." Born and raised in New York, a faint hint of Long Island clung to her speech.

Akira had ducked her head. She used words way worse than *like*, but never around her grandmother. "Sorry."

"I mean you can be with the person, but still be yourself. You can be happy to be yourself. It's very…nice," her grandmother had said quietly. "When you're with a person who is content to let you be. It's the most peaceful thing in the world."

Akira licked her lips and clutched the box closer to her chest. Such a silly memory. She'd barely understood what her grandma had been saying then, and she still wasn't quite certain what it meant.

Jacob wasn't the kind of person Hana had been talking about. Up to a week ago, Akira would have declared he didn't even like her.

It's the most peaceful thing in the world.

She rested her head against the silk fabric of the chair. So why did this feel so damn peaceful?

His head popped up suddenly, his eyes focusing on her. "Oh, damn. How long have I been ignoring you?"

"Not long," she lied. She should care about that too, since she wasn't accustomed to being ignored. Funny how she didn't. "Did you get your notes down?"

He ducked his head, and she had to steel herself against his cuteness. "Yeah. I planned out some research I'll need to do too."

"Maybe I should tell you more things wrong with your books. It seems to really get your juices flowing."

He gave her a thoughtful look. "I'm not averse to constructive criticism." He closed the laptop and set it on the table, picking up his abandoned sandwich and swallowing a huge bite. He nodded at the box in her hands and spoke when he finished chewing. "Sorry. I almost forgot why I came here."

Her fingers clenched around the wood. That was right. This was why he had come here. Their stupid agreement.

With a bit more force than necessary, she pushed the box across the table. "It's all yours."

AKIRA HELD THE BEER HE HAD BROUGHT BETWEEN TWO fingers. Dressed in jeans and a white button-down, her shiny black hair piled on top of her head, she was about as casual as he had ever seen her.

He would have to do some research on women's clothes. Lidia would have garments of the highest quality, though she had been in hiding for the last decade. His fingers itched to grab his laptop and write the thought down, but he had already played the eccentric author once tonight.

Jacob would, of course, have to finish the James Talent book he was contracted for, but then he'd have the unpleasant conversation with his agent about putting the man on hiatus. Akira was right. A spin-off was smart and would take advantage of the momentum he had built.

It would also let him do something fun and new for a change, let him flex his creative wings. He hadn't realized until he had verbalized his discontent, but the reason this book was so difficult was probably in large part because he was utterly bored. Being in one man's head for this long was exhausting.

With Lidia, everything was wide open. New backstory, new intrigue, new mysteries, new stakes.

A new love interest. Many new love interests.

He almost gasped aloud and cast a longing glance at his messenger bag before he mentally shook his head. Not now.

Jacob cleared his throat and wiped his fingers on a napkin before picking up the box. "I wish I had had a few of these puzzles around when my brothers were younger," Jacob murmured, turning it in his hands. "Anything to keep them out of trouble."

"Ah." Akira shifted in her chair, drawing her legs up. Her feet were bare and small, each dainty toenail painted a deep, vibrant, glossy red. He wanted to nibble on them.

He had never particularly paid much attention to a woman's feet before. But then, he had never seen Akira's feet before.

"How are the Bobbsey Twins?"

His mouth kicked up, thinking of how his brothers would react to being called that by a beautiful woman not much older than them. "They're..." He glanced up, mouth drying when he caught her gaze locked on his lips.

Was it his smile? She probably wasn't used to it. His default setting was solemn, and he had never gone out of his way to grin at her. Testing, he let his face relax, let the grin come. Her eyebrows snapped together, and she looked down at her hands linked together in her lap.

Interesting. His heart beat a tiny bit faster. "They're, uh, great. They opened a landscaping business last year. It works for them. Connor's the brains. Ben's the brawn. And the heart, really."

"I remember them being thick as thieves."

"They're very close."

"I'm glad their business is doing well." She hesitated. "Let me know if I can help."

Most people would kill to get assistance for a fledgling business from Akira Mori, even if that business was as mundane as a landscaping company.

He bit back the instant surge of pride, the automatic denial of help. This wasn't Mei sneaking him a blank check out of whatever lingering emotions she felt for his father. This was a simple, gracious offer.

"Thanks," he said humbly. "If you hear of anyone looking, I'm sure they'd appreciate a referral. You haven't seen it, but they did my backyard."

She wrapped her hand around her knee. "The rose."

"Yeah." He had spotted it sitting in a bud vase in her office yesterday, but he hadn't said anything. Careful. They were both being so careful.

"I'll keep them in mind."

He nodded, beginning his nightly manipulation of the panels of the box. He had done more research on these puzzles since that first night. He'd made progress and logged each successful move in his brain, but since it took two hundred and twenty-six moves to open the thing, it was slow going. He wasn't even a fifth of the way to solving it.

"Kati's going to college in the fall, right?"

His chest swelled, still so proud he could burst. "Stanford," he announced.

She nodded and drank her beer. "I wanted to go there."

"Did you?" He cocked his head. "You went to…"

"Harvard."

"Right."

She shrugged. "It wasn't my scene, but I got my diploma."

"Did your—?" He hesitated, wary of breaking their tentative peace.

"Did I what?"

He cleared his throat. "Did your parents want you to go there?"

A hard gleam entered her eyes. "No. They didn't think I could get in. Well, they didn't think I could get in anywhere." She shrugged. "But I was a legacy at Harvard, thanks to my dad, and we still had hotels with my name on them at the time, so they rolled out the red carpet."

"Ah."

"Still, I always thought Stanford looked like a great place to go. And your sister doesn't have motivation to get as far away from you as possible."

"I don't know," he said ruefully, remembering Kati's frosty goodbye to him that morning when she left for school. "Right now, she's probably wishing she'd applied abroad."

"Oh." Akira brushed a crumb off her shoulder. She had always been slender, but the more time Jacob spent in her company, the more certain he was she had lost weight in the months since her mother had passed.

Not that he cared what she weighed, but his growing suspicion over why the change had occurred did concern him. Grief, though she might deny it. Maybe not grief over the woman her mother had been, but grief over never getting to see the woman the rest of the world saw. Of never gaining closure on their rocky relationship.

She would shut down if he brought it up, and given his own complicated part in her relationship with Mei, he wasn't eager to delve into that Pandora's box. He was also smart enough to know weight wasn't a subject women enjoyed discussing at length. So he would keep his trap shut and merely continue feeding her.

"Trouble with Kati-cat?"

He ignored her use of his nickname for his sister. Kati would kill him if she knew a third party had overheard it. Especially Akira. "There's always something with teenage girls, isn't there?"

Her shoulders lifted. "She's not the type to get in trouble, though, right?"

His eyes narrowed at her subtle emphasis on the word *type*. "She's a good girl," he agreed slowly. "Has great grades, is focused on college."

Akira took a drink from the beer. He had never seen her drink beer at parties, only wine or liquor, but the lager didn't seem to faze her. "Oh, Jacob." Her expression was mildly pitying.

"What?"

"I'm going to clue you in on something you really should be aware of." She leaned closer. "There's no such thing as good girls and bad girls, or the right crowd or the wrong crowd. Life isn't that simple."

"I know," he protested.

"Do you? Or have you put her up on her own mini pedestal? Maybe that's why any problems you have with her throw you for a loop."

"So, what, I'm just supposed to expect the worst from her?"

"No. Expect her to be a human." She pointed her finger at him, stern. "When I was at your cabin and you were calling her? I bet you a thousand dollars Kati was with her boyfriend that weekend."

That was an easy bet to take. He tried to keep his smugness to a minimum. "She doesn't have a boyfriend."

"Maybe she hasn't introduced him to you yet. Because, and I further bet, you and your brothers have successfully scowled and run off any guy she does bring home."

Lies. He was the soul of hospitality to all of Kati's friends. Even the bastard, pimply-faced boys who hovered around, panting after her. "Trust me. She doesn't have a boyfriend."

Akira cocked her head. "She talks to him on the phone a lot. Maybe he's dropped by to study with her. They go silent when you walk in on them."

A tall, skinny kid popped into his head. Quiet, a bit shy, who blushed any time Kati spoke. Their heads had been awfully close together when he'd walked in on them studying at the kitchen table a few weeks ago... "Darren," he growled.

Akira mimed a shooting motion. "Darren's your man. Or rather, Kati's man. Boy. Whatever."

He thought of the hesitancy in Kati's voice when he had called her from the cabin, the way she had quickly switched the subject to Akira. "She's going to get a lot more than her phone taken away if she lied to me and then spent the weekend with some boy," he grumbled.

"Bah." Akira waved her hand. "Give the kid a break. It could have been a lot worse. I won't tell you what I was doing with my weekends at that age."

"She's a young girl…"

"And in a few short months, she won't be under your supervision at all." The words shot through him, burrowing into his heart, but she was relentless. "Soon, she could be shooting crack and having orgies on the weekends, and there won't be a damn thing you can do about it. Let her learn while you're still around."

He subsided, unhappy. "I'm going to ask her."

"Fine. But don't be a dick about it."

"I know you might find this hard to believe, but I am capable of not being a dick," he said wryly.

She pressed her hand against her chest, an action which brought his gaze directly to that expanse of smooth flesh. "Did you…did you just use the D word?"

"I can do a lot more than use it." The words came out unbidden, the sexual entendre surprising them both. It was just that this conversation was coming so easily, so naturally, both of them merely speaking with one another without thinking about their history or consequences or—

Jacob stiffened. He didn't need to rationalize a lapse in decorum, damn it. He was a fully grown man. Let her see he wasn't a type either.

Her lips curved wickedly, and she stretched her legs, drawing his instant attention. God, he loved those legs, displayed to perfection tonight in her clinging skinny jeans. They were long and muscular, her thighs and calves strong.

Strong enough to wrap around a man's waist as he drove into her, trapping her body against a wall in a room lit by a dim bare bulb.

He swallowed, mentally slapping himself from wandering into dangerous storage room territory. Where were they? Oh yes. She was about to make some sort of lewd comment or snarky reply. For the first time ever, he was eager to hear it.

Her gaze lowered, hiding her eyes from him. "What did Kati do to get her phone taken away?"

No sexy remark? Oh. Okay.

He controlled his disappointment and digested her question, hesitating to answer truthfully, that she had been the source of disagreement between him and Kati. Did he want to lose this easy camaraderie, the novelty of sitting in Akira Mori's presence without pride or anger interfering with their conversation?

This was too new. Too fresh. So he merely looked down at the box and started to manipulate the panels. "She was unkind to someone I care about."

CHAPTER 12

A throat cleared from the vicinity of the entrance to the kitchen. Jacob broke off in the middle of whistling "Bad Romance"—the song was too damn catchy—and glanced up from where he was loading the dishwasher. "Oh. Hey."

Kati linked her hands behind her. Dressed in black tights, black shorts, and a tight pink top, her backpack slung over one shoulder, she was ready for school. "Hey."

He straightened. It had been quiet around the house, both of them communicating with each other only when necessary, with stilted, abrupt language.

He hated the strained awkwardness between them, but he wasn't about to give in on such an important principle.

However, this was the first overture Kati had made, and he was prepared to accept it like the gracious adult he was. Jacob nodded at her hair. "You changed your style."

Self-consciously, she fingered the ends of her neon-purple hair. The dye jobs she did at home—when he cleaned later, he was certain to find splashes of purple on the bathroom counter. She must have gone to a salon yesterday, though, because she'd chopped the strands in a shorter, asymmetrical cut.

"You don't like it?"

"No, no," he hurried out. *Anything's better than the puke green.* "It's striking. Very cool."

"Thanks." She continued to watch him, hands shoved into the pockets of her shorts.

He glanced at the watch on his wrist. "You're going to be late for school."

"I'm okay." She wandered into the kitchen. "It's a late-start day."

"Ah." Usually he had Kati's schedule memorized. But it hadn't seemed quite that important in the past couple of weeks.

The kid was capable of knowing when she needed to be somewhere, he told himself, tamping down the spurt of guilt over not paying attention to her the way he always did. "Right."

"I can do the dishes, if you want, when I come home from school," she offered.

He flicked his wet hands. "No problem. I got it."

Kati nodded. "Oh. Okay."

When she lingered, he finally took pity on her. "Something on your mind?"

"Haven't seen you much lately."

"You've had all those play rehearsals." He turned back to the sink. Kati was directing the spring play at school, a rather convenient distraction. It had meant there was no one at home to question why he, the borderline hermit, had spent five nights away from his cave, staying out progressively later. He'd managed to beat Kati home most nights, though a couple of times it had been close, with him flopping on the

169

couch and turning on the TV in time to hear the jingle of her keys.

The previous evening, though, he hadn't been able to manage that trick. He couldn't be blamed. Akira had looked up from her gyro and asked him whether he'd made any progress in plotting his new book. The next thing he knew, they were hotly debating the kind of weapon his heroine would favor. That had led to a discussion on gun control…and somehow, the existence of aliens.

When he reached home well past midnight, he had found the house dark, Kati tucked into her bed fast asleep.

"You weren't here when I got home last night," Kati said, somehow divining his thoughts. She crossed her arms over her chest tightly, as if holding herself back. Her lower lip pushed out. "Where were you?"

He took his time rinsing the pan he had used to make eggs. Meanwhile, his mind raced.

Since his brothers were nosy, they had already asked whether Akira had forgiven him. He had said she was receptive and left it, thanking God they hadn't said anything to Kati and didn't pester him any further.

It wasn't like he had consciously decided to lie to his family about where he was spending his nights. It was just that…Ben and Connor would tease and poke and demand explanations he didn't have. Given Kati's feelings toward Akira and the role the other woman had played in their recent argument, he had a feeling Kati would be hugely displeased, even if he did couch it in terms of a simple agreement.

What could he say? It had started out as a way to get her to forgive him and had evolved into evenings he desperately looked forward to? He had become determined to put that rare smile on her face? The sexual tension between them was nearly palatable, and for the first time in forever, it didn't panic him into running for the door?

"Jacob?"

Jacob shook his head, realizing he was silently standing there with his hands under the running faucet. "Oh, uh. Yeah. I was visiting a friend."

"That late?"

He shot her a glance over his shoulder. "I wasn't aware I had a curfew, Kati."

His sister flushed at the less-than-subtle rebuke. "I'm just saying...you don't usually go out at night. I mean, you don't have friends."

Insulted now, he dried his hands on the towel and faced her. "I have friends."

She wrinkled her nose. "College buddies you meet once a month for poker don't count."

"I have...other friends," he finished lamely, stinging from her accurate assessment. He had a solitary occupation, damn it. He couldn't help that it limited his social interaction.

Dear God, you have no life whatsoever.

"So who's this friend? Is it a girl?"

Able to read his baby sister like a book, Jacob took in her defensive stance and the naked vulnerability in her eyes. His sister wasn't accustomed to having to share him. In the past, when he had the occasional girlfriend, he had gently attempted to correct her possessiveness.

He understood it, but now it rankled a bit. He opened his mouth, ready to inform her of exactly who he had been with, but then he paused.

Really, what was the point in riling Kati up? The clock

was ticking. He and Akira were past the halfway mark in their silly ten-day arrangement. Anything that happened after that would be solely in Akira's court.

No need to have this conversation now. Wait. See.

"Not a girl." Which was not a lie. Akira would laugh if anyone called her a girl. "Really, a friend."

At his confirmation of his asexuality, Kati relaxed. "Oh. Okay."

Inexplicably annoyed, he added, "I might be out again tonight, though. Don't be alarmed."

She was pacified, it seemed. Her frown never rematerialized. "Cool. My friend Darren's coming over after school to study, so we'll be busy 'til play practice. We might go grab some ice cream after."

Darren's name had his ears pricking up. *I bet you a thousand dollars Kati was with her boyfriend that weekend.*

Loath to make matters worse with his sister, Jacob had avoided confronting her about the suspicions Akira had planted in his brain, but now he saw his chance. "You've been seeing this Darren kid a lot," he said, casually leaning back against the counter. "You sure you guys are nothing more than pals?"

"Um." Kati froze. "Well."

Bingo. Jacob winced. Akira was going to gloat. "Kati, I'm fine with you dating. But I think it's important I meet the guy, okay? If you're seeing this Darren kid, tell me."

She cast him a disgruntled look. "Okay fine. We're kinda hooking up."

He reared back. "What...what do you mean by hooking up?" That meant sex, right? Jesus Christ. He'd had The Talk with Kati—possibly the most awkward experience of either of their lives—but that didn't mean he was prepared for his little girl to be sleeping with someone. She was just a baby! Who the fuck did this Darren think he was?

A warning growl built, and she pointed her finger at him. "Jeez, I haven't had sex with him! That means we're dating. Courting. Some smooching. Whatever you old people say."

Subsiding, he relaxed, his blood still running hot. "Choose your words more carefully next time."

"But see?" She jabbed her finger at him again. "This is why I didn't tell you. You scare them. You're going to scare Darren."

Insulted, he crossed his arms over his chest. "I won't scare anyone."

"That's what you do. You terrify, Ben makes fun of them, and Connor goes for passive-aggressive, thinly veiled threats." She held three fingers up. "Eric, Tom, and Abhi. The three of you scared them all off."

"I barely even spoke to Abhi," he protested. He couldn't protest about the other two.

He had been justified, though. One had been shifty-eyed, and the other...well, he couldn't remember what he'd hated about the other, but he was certain there had been a reason for him to treat him with suspicion.

"No. You silently loomed."

He rolled his eyes, ready to have this ridiculous discussion over. "Kati. I don't care if the boys you date are terrified by my looming. You're bringing them home. If I don't meet Darren after school, you aren't staying out late with him after play rehearsal."

"Ugh." Kati shot him a disgusted look and hiked her backpack higher. "Fine. But you can't call him a hipster, or make fun of his skinny jeans or glasses."

"Don't be silly. I'm sure Connor and Ben will handle those comments when they eventually meet him." He held up his hand at her outraged sputter. "Relax. I promise to put all the guns away and remain seated the entire time, lest I scare him by *looming*."

"Make us a snack. Or walk around cleaning. That tends to emasculate you a bit."

He narrowed his eyes at her. "I'll keep that in mind."

A cheeky grin and he was reminded of the mischievous six-year-old who had careened around the house, rarely still. He couldn't help but speak, stopping her as she turned to go. "Kati-cat."

"Yeah?"

"I won't get mad, but..." He hesitated. "That weekend I went to the cabin. Were you spending the weekend with Darren?"

"Jeez, what?" She wrinkled her nose. "No. I spent the weekend at Kristen's. You can call her mom, if you want."

"No. No." He smiled, relieved. "I believe you."

"Although..." A guilty flush. "The reason I hadn't left yet was because I went on a date with Darren that night. We didn't stay here together alone for long, or anything," she hurriedly said, and he didn't miss the qualifier of *for long*. "Kristen picked me up at nine, and I went to her place."

"Okay," he said slowly. He was relieved it had been as simple as that. "Don't keep stuff from me again."

"I won't." She surprised him by skirting the island and walking up to him to wrap her fragile arms around his waist. He immediately returned the hug, not even her thick back-pack keeping him from enveloping her. "I love you."

His heart threatened to burst. "I love you too, Kati-Cat."

"You haven't hugged me in days." The accusation was muffled against his shirt.

The guilt came fast and hard. "I'm sorry, sweetheart. I figured you were too mad…" He trailed off. He hadn't made many overtures toward his sister, that was true. Partially because he was uncertain of his reception, and partially because, well…he was busy.

Busy struggling to write the novel he barely wanted to write any longer, but busier struggling to manage his time with Akira.

Instinctive fear had him tightening his hold on his sister, but the words he had been chanting to himself for the better part of the week intruded. *You're allowed to have a life. You're allowed to see women. You are not your father.*

Kati's voice was muffled. "It was my fault. I don't like when we fight."

He stroked his hand through her hair, not daring to say anything to break this strange spell. Kati was pretty much the only person he regularly embraced, his brothers more prone to do the back-slapping thing with him now that they were grown.

He hugged her tighter and inhaled the scent of vanilla. He had missed this too. Love rushed through him, making his chest expand. He would never forget this little girl just because something or someone shiny came along. *Not like their father.* "Me neither, kiddo."

She turned her head so her words were clearer. "I thought about what you said. It was wrong of me to call Akira a slut. I get super mad if anyone says it to me or my girlfriends. I should be more careful."

He tugged on her hair until she looked up at him. "It's not kind to judge someone like that," he said quietly, as much for himself as for her.

"Yeah. I know. Not even if it's someone I don't like."

Then you're going to hate that I can't quit her. "You barely know her," he protested.

Her nose wrinkled. "Mei told me so many stories."

Damn it, Mei. Once again, Jacob kicked himself for not being more attuned to how poisonous the woman had been when it came to her only daughter. "Mei may not have been the most objective person."

She shook her head. "I guess it doesn't matter."

But it does. If you only knew how relevant this discussion is, kid.

Jacob licked his lips. Later. He could figure this out later.

Unaware, Kati drove the knife of guilt a little deeper. "After all, we're probably never going to see her again."

Unseen by his sister, he raised his eyes to the oven clock. No, he would definitely be seeing Akira again. In less than ten hours, really.

Jacob gave her a final pat on the back and forced a smile as he stepped away. "I'm glad you get it. Here." He stretched up to access the cupboard on top of the fridge, retrieving her phone.

Her face lit up. "Really?"

He slipped the phone into her hand. "I think you've learned your lesson. Yeah, really."

"You used that same trick to hide stuff from me when I was a kid. Putting it away somewhere I couldn't reach."

He ruffled her hair, delighted with the way she faux-scowled and slapped at his hands. "Yeah, well. You haven't grown much since then."

CHAPTER 13

"Oh, shit."

The uncharacteristic curse coming from Jacob had her glancing up from the lease agreement she was perusing. He sat in what had somehow become his chair, long, capable fingers manipulating the puzzle box.

At some undefined point over the past week and a half, she had realized it felt right, his hands on the dark wood.

It keeps him coming back to you, a weak, needy part of her whispered. There it was. If he didn't come back for her, he would at least come back to crack that puzzle. He was too stubborn not to beat it. "What?"

He studied the box, manipulating one panel, then another. "I think…" He glanced up at her and stopped.

"What?"

"Nothing. I thought I had it." He looked down at the box and grimaced. "No. Sorry. False alarm." The chair creaked under his heavy weight as he settled deeper into it and bent again, frowning.

The remains of their dinner were around them. As usual, Jacob had brought a mountain of food. She'd quickly learned

Jacob's huge frame apparently required an equivalently large amount of calories to maintain it.

Also, as he had somewhat sheepishly explained while pouring hot sauce on a monstrous burrito the night before, "Kati is really into healthy stuff. I only get to eat like this when she isn't around."

The image of the manly man choking down alfalfa because his little sister worried over his cholesterol was even cuter than him clipping roses. Curse the man's unexpected adorableness.

A dumb smile curved her lips, a smile she only permitted because his attention was diverted. It was hard to remember how dangerous it was to let down her guard with Jacob when the fire he had laid in her barely used fireplace cracked and popped and the building was silent around them.

She'd forgiven him days ago, though she hadn't said anything to him yet. She was conscious their time together was finite. Jacob had placed the ball firmly in her court on what happened next, and no matter whether he opened the box or not, she couldn't see him much longer.

Oh, she still wanted to jump him. Everything that had so intrigued her before he had set out to win her forgiveness and friendship was multiplied now. His unique combination of kindness, brains, and that humming sex appeal was a potent combination.

The problem was she *liked* him, heaven help her. Liked him far too much to take him for a ride on the crazy train of her life.

What he needed was a quiet, biddable woman who would putter around the house while he worked, bringing him lemonade and freshly baked cookies. They would have loving, pleasurable sex and eventually a couple of spawn running around, messing up a tidy house.

Akira wasn't that woman. She didn't particularly want to be that woman.

Some buried, surprisingly decent part of her had reared its head, making one thing clear: she also didn't want to fuck him up for when that woman came along.

End this. She had chastised herself every night, aware she was dangerously close to infatuation, but then he walked her to her car and told her he would see her again the next evening, and she didn't protest.

The phone rang, shrill and loud, distracting her from her contemplation of the big man taking up so much space. She peered at the display and let it go to voicemail. As soon as her voicemail lit up red, she picked up the phone and deleted the message.

She hung up and turned to find Jacob watching her. He nodded at the phone. "Someone you don't like?"

She gave a casual shrug, the spurt of rage she had experienced upon viewing the number ruthlessly controlled. "The producer for my father's show."

"Oh. Right." Jacob narrowed his eyes. "I remember Mei talking about that. A reality show of some sort?"

How diplomatic. Akira was certain Mei would never have merely talked about her ex-husband's show. She would have passive-aggressively sniped about it. Deservedly.

Akira had been the one to break the news to her mother that her father was going to star on a show with his new wife. Yes, the one he made that sex tape with.

Mei carefully maintained her image as a quiet, soft-spoken woman, except around her daughter. Akira's ears had rung for weeks. As much as she'd usually enjoyed provoking her mother, Akira had empathized on this occasion. It was unfair, the world they lived in, when a man could be amply rewarded for every wrong thing he did. Mistreat your wife? Women will still flock to you. Run your family business poorly? Make billions selling the assets. "Leak" a sex tape? Here. Have a reality show.

"Yeah. Follows the exploits of his crazy new family." She adopted Chloe's valley-girl accent. "Chloe, the aging starlet desperately clinging to her youth. Brandy, the eldest daughter, who finds love in all the wrong places. Brandon and Brendon, the elitist douche poor little rich boys. The vicious twins, Bronwyn and Brad. And of course, Mr. Mori, the aging hotelier money bank who's a handy punch line for every joke."

Jacob eyed her with appalled fascination. "That sounds awful."

"You're probably the only person in America who doesn't know about the Benton-Mori train-wreck happy hour."

"I don't watch a lot of TV," Jacob responded, almost apologetically. "And I don't really understand the concept of reality television. Did you know Kati watches this show which is basically just a bunch of women trying on wedding dresses?" He shook his head, bewilderment stamped on his face. "Why would anyone care what dress a stranger wears to her wedding?"

Oh gosh. So darned cute. Amusement edged out her annoyance. "My father's show isn't nearly so wholesome."

He grimaced. "It does sound like a train wreck."

"The bane of my existence," she heard herself say. Never had she discussed her father's show so frankly, aware her true feelings would only bring the bastard more publicity. But Jacob was safe. Despite their tumultuous past, she could trust him. In this, at least.

"Why is the producer calling you?"

She ran her hand over her hair. She had left it down the past couple of days, having noticed how Jacob seemed to stare at her a bit longer when she did. *Who are you, woman?* "Because I won't talk to my father. I obviously won't talk to the producer either. My assistant fields his calls and deletes his messages during business hours, so I guess he's resorted to trying to catch me at night."

"Are you...involved with the show?"

She snorted a laugh, genuinely amused. "God, no. They'd just like me to be."

His hands continued to idly fidget with the box while he studied her. He saw too much, she was certain. Far more than she intended for him or anyone to see. "I guess your relationship with your dad is as bad as the one you had with your mom."

She took a deep breath. Sure, why not talk about her parents some more? "Worse."

"I only heard snippets about him from Mei. You were a baby when they divorced, right?"

"A year old."

"He got custody?"

She sat back in her chair, resigned to this. For some reason, she wanted to tell him whatever he wanted to know.

Because otherwise this might end.

Again, she brushed the frighteningly needy thought aside. "Technically, it was joint, but my mother didn't want much to do with me. When I wasn't at boarding school, I was with my dad." Her smile was bitter. "Not because he particularly desired me, but his father controlled his purse. And Grandfather Mori believed in appearances."

His brow furrowed. "You didn't live with your mother at all?"

"If I had to come home from school and my father was sick of me, he would send me to her. She couldn't do much about that. It would look bad if she straight up put me on the street."

"Is that when you would spend time with your grandmother?" Jacob lifted the box, as if invoking the woman.

Her gaze drifted to the frame on her desk, the wrinkles on the older woman's face not masking her beauty. Akira had stolen the photo from her mother's house in a fit of righteous anger during a party. She had so few images of her grandmother. "Yes," she replied softly. "She lived nearby. Until I was fifteen or so, if I came to see my mother, I could go see her."

"What happened when you were fifteen?"

"I started flunking out of school. Smoking weed. Doing bad things with boys." Her words were mocking. "Mei was aware I loved her mom. So I was told I couldn't see her unless I shaped up."

"You didn't. Shape up, that is."

"I couldn't," she said, the words torn from her. "I couldn't do anything right to please her. I couldn't change."

Something dark moved across his face. "I would have intervened with Kati if she were smoking weed or cutting class at fifteen. But Mei shouldn't have kept you from someone you love. That's cruel and excessive punishment."

She leaned into his criticism of her mother as if she could

absorb it. "My grandma—Hana—she didn't like it. She tried to sneakily visit me at school, send me presents and cards." Akira's smile was tinged with triumph. "The day I turned eighteen, I came here and used the trust fund my paternal grandfather left me to fly her to Paris. We spent a whole month there." Her smile faded. "She died a year later."

Her chest filled with pressure, and she realized, with a vague sense of horror, her eyes were stinging. What was it about this man that brought out emotions she thought were safely locked away?

Don't look at him.

Her body wasn't hers to control around him. She found his gaze resting on her, those green eyes holding so much compassion she wanted to scream. Panic unfurled inside her, bringing with it deep fear. She shuffled the papers spread out on her desk. "It's, uh…late…"

"Akira. It's okay," he said gently. "You can miss her."

No. No, she couldn't, because that would be a weakness. Weakness was a tool, used to manipulate and control.

"I have to go. I have to."

She expected him to push. But Jacob rarely did anything she expected. He immediately got to his feet and grabbed his jacket. "I'll walk you to your car." His tone brooked no argument.

Not like she would have argued. The street was generally safe, with a coffee shop open late up the street. It was surprisingly comforting, however, to be walked the short distance to the small parking lot on the side of the building, her giant escort watching and waiting to make sure she drove away without incident.

Don't get used to it. This is starting to get a little too cozy, and you know what you need to do.

Too bad what she needed to do and what she wanted to do were such polar opposite things.

She stood and gathered her belongings, accepting the box from him on the way out. That was another thing—he didn't mock her for lugging the thing to and fro from home, hadn't even raised an eyebrow over her weird quirk, making it into her security blanket.

She had lost it for so many years. She didn't want it out of her sight. The only person she could even contemplate handling it was Jacob.

That said something. Something she didn't want to examine too closely.

Conflicted, she walked past him silently, and they made their way downstairs to the side entrance. Jacob's long strides brought him there a second before her, and he opened it, nodding at her.

She took three steps out of the door. And came to a screeching halt, multiple flashes of light going off in her eyes.

"Akira, is it true about Chloe Benton's pregnancy rumors—"

"Ms. Mori, are you excited for your new brother—?"

"Akira, is a reunion in the works—?"

Blinded and disoriented, Akira turned in a half-circle, before a strong hand latched on to her arm and yanked her backward. The door shut, and she was back inside the blessed quiet and peace of the warm hallway of her building.

"What," Jacob said slowly, staring at the door, "the fuck was that?"

She had to take a second to calm her heartbeat before she could speak. "That's what my dear father has saddled me with."

She yanked out her phone and pulled up the browser, muttering, "No wonder his producer was calling me."

"I don't understand."

She only had to load TMZ's homepage to confirm her suspicions. She hissed out a curse. "My dearest stepmother's doctor's office leaked the news about her pregnancy."

"What? Doctor-patient confidentiality—"

"Aw. That's cute of you." Her lips twisted. "Ten bucks says daddy dearest had it leaked, so it would boost ratings for the season premiere."

A pause. "Wait. Your father's having a child? And you're finding out like this?"

Her smile was humorless. "Oh, don't worry. He already informed me of the blessed event during a charming call last week where he demanded I be on the show so the world could catch my reaction."

"Wow." Jacob thrust his hands in his pockets. "He sounds like a dick."

The assessment made her laugh—she wasn't sure why Jacob calling anyone a dick was hilarious, but it was. "He is."

"How do you feel about it?"

"About what?"

"The baby."

She glanced up. "I don't care about it. Doesn't affect me."

If she expected him to be horrified or disgusted by her blunt, non-maternal, non-sisterly assessment of the fetus that was the combination of two people she despised, he didn't let it show. There was no chastisement or assurance she would come to love the thing. He gave a thoughtful nod. "Okay."

Though he didn't ask for explanation, she gave it. "I

mean, if it wants to talk to me or something when it's of age, I won't toss it out. And I feel for any kid raised in that kind of dysfunctional atmosphere, but honestly, what can I do?"

"Not much, I suppose."

"If it's anything like Chloe's kids, it'll grow up to be a rich, entitled jerk."

"You didn't grow up to be a rich, entitled jerk."

She met his gaze. "Ninety-nine point nine percent of people who know me would say that's exactly what I am."

"What about the other point one percent?"

"They consist of my dead grandmother and people who are dumb enough to be my friends." She arched an eyebrow. "Not a very large sample size, I think you can agree."

"And me."

The two words brought her to a halt. She stopped. Swallowed, her throat scratchy. "And you, I guess."

"So…what now?"

"What do you mean?" She tucked her phone in her purse and squared her shoulders. "I need to get to my car."

"Whoa." Jacob blocked her when she made to walk out the exit. "We can't go out there."

She thought about that. "You're absolutely right, or you're going to be photographed. Won't take long for people to figure out your identity and then the gossip will start." She gave a quick nod. "You stay here. I'll go out there, try to dispel the crowds, and then when it's clear, I'll motion you out."

"Uh." He grabbed her arm, halting her again. "You're not going out there either, Akira."

She looked at his hand on her arm, and then back up at him. Annoyance warred with tenderness, but the annoyance won. "There's only one scenario where I take orders from a man, darling. And since we're not naked, that's not happening right now."

If she expected him to blush or stammer, she would have been disappointed. A sizzle of heat flashed across his face, but then his stubborn scowl returned. "There are too many people out there. Can you get the guard…?"

She shook her head before he even finished talking. "I'm not forcing Steve to deal with this. As long as he keeps them out of the building, he's done his job."

"Then you're not going out there. I've seen these paparazzo turn ugly."

"What do you want me to do? Stay here all night? Because I assure you, they have the front and the delivery entrance covered as well."

His eyes narrowed. "What about the other side of the building?"

The other side, which faced a tiny, narrow alley, a patch of land separating this building from the one next to it. "There's no door there. Just a fire escape." At his questioning look, she shook her head. "We are not taking the fire escape."

"DID YOU NOT HEAR ME SAY WE'RE NOT DOING THIS?"

"It'll be fine," he assured her, as he held his hand out. Her pencil skirt wasn't designed for crawling out second-story windows. The fire escape was rickety metal under her feet. She swallowed, looking down from the platform. "There's no stairs leading down from here. It's a drop."

"Yeah, that's how they are on some of these older buildings. Keeps burglars from accessing the windows. It's only ten feet."

Only ten feet. She supposed that wasn't a problem for him because he was roughly nine feet tall. The man was insane.

"I'll jump down, catch you. Then we'll sneak out of the alley. My car is parked about a block away. The reporters are so busy crowding around the door, they probably won't even notice us coming out of the alley."

He glanced over his shoulder, his face flushed. Had she ever seen that particular light in his eyes? Maybe when he had snuck into that storage closet with her, but then it had been overshadowed by shame.

No shame here. He looked young. Full of life and adventure.

It looked good on him. "You're enjoying this," she ventured. "Aren't you?"

He hesitated, but the smile he gave her was tinged with guilty pleasure. "I write about spies for a living. What do you think?" He hauled himself over the railing and got down on his hands and knees to slip off the edge of the platform. He dangled in midair for a moment, holding on to the landing with one hand. Her breath caught when he let go, but then it was over.

He only stumbled a couple of steps when his feet hit the ground, and he rose from his crouch. He lifted his arms. "Come on. Now you."

Jesus Christ. Talk about a trust fall. "Wait." She reached down and removed her shoes. "Take these first."

"Your shoes?"

"I don't want them to fall off my feet when I jump. They might get scratched. They're my favorite."

"Your shoes."

"Do you want me to tell you how much they cost?" she snapped.

"No, let me stay ignorant, please."

Unease roiling in her belly, she gently eased the shoes off the railing, holding her breath as they freefell. He caught them and carefully placed them on the ground. "Okay. Your shoes are fine." He looked up at her expectantly. "Now you."

Akira glanced back at the window, where safety and warmth awaited. Really, was she willing to fling herself off a building so she wouldn't deal with paparazzi? "Maybe I should leave the old-fashioned way," she hedged. "Now that you're outside already, you can easily sneak away."

"Hmm. Sure. If you want to give your father that satisfaction."

She turned to face him sharply. "What?"

Jacob patiently gazed up at her, the light from the street and the halogen bulb mounted on the building giving off enough illumination for her to see him clearly. "I'm sure he'll see you on one of those entertainment news shows. Even if you say *no comment*, he seems like the type of jerk who would be happy you're harassed at all. If people are talking about your reaction, they're talking about him. More ratings, right?"

Akira narrowed her eyes. "You're surprisingly manipulative, Campbell." What was even more surprising was how tickled she was by that manipulation. So perverse.

"I'm only being logical." He looked down, nudged her heels. "Plus, there's the fact you'll be shoeless."

Her snarl was low. "Fine. Fine. Let's get this over with."

She had to work her skirt up almost to her bottom in order to get down on her knees. She cast him a glare over the strangled noise he emitted. "I can't help it," she muttered.

"I don't want you to."

Surprised at his murmur, she glanced over her shoulder, but his eyes were all over the bare expanse of her legs. He met her gaze and grinned, the charm and mischief in it making him appear ten years younger.

Had she thought he was surly and uncommunicative once upon a time? It was hard to remember that when he was looking at her like this. "Come on." He raised his hands. "Jump."

She faced forward, released a deep breath, and let go of the railing, eyes screwed shut. A second of weightlessness, and then he caught her, the hair on his arms scraping her legs.

Her lashes fluttered open to find their faces close together, so close she could see the tiny striations of brown interrupting the pure green of his irises.

"There." His chest rumbled. "That wasn't bad, was it?"

Maybe it was the danger, or the sense that they were compatriots, or the romantic position he was holding her in. Maybe she was simply tired of fighting her attraction to this man. All of the excellent, self-sacrificing reasons to kick him out of her life went flying out the window when she kissed those lips. It didn't help that he responded instantly, parting for the shallow foray of her tongue. She swept in, dominating his mouth, making him hers.

The man was talented with his firm lips and hot tongue. With a low moan of surrender, Akira grasped hold of his shoulders. In a heartbeat, Jacob's grip turned more possessive, his tongue battling with hers for the upper hand.

He gave a little growl, and the air spun around her until a hard surface met her back. His teeth scored her lower lip and she hissed. She loved this, loved the urgency and ferocity he brought with him. All that hunger boiling under his quiet facade.

His hunger may outpace yours. Or it was just right.

Roughly, he pushed her jacket aside and tugged at the sleeveless shell until the stretchy material had pushed below her breasts, the straps tightening around her shoulders uncomfortably. He did the same to her bra. Cool night air wafted over her nipples, tightening them further. Her skirt was already hiked up, but he pushed it higher, making a place for himself between her thighs. She wound her legs around his narrow hips automatically.

"There are people outside the alley," she whispered. It wasn't a protest, though another person might have interpreted it as such.

Not Jacob, though. He drew back, lips wet, eyes glittering feverishly. "With cameras."

Her pussy clenched. It wasn't fair, they were both on the same wavelength. How was she supposed to resist debauching him when he was so willing to play? "They're looking for me."

She was held up by the weight of his body and the brick wall behind her. He'd pushed her into the deepening shadows of the alley, out of the direct light, but it wouldn't take long for an inquisitive photographer to find them.

He stepped closer, cupping her ass in both big hands, and hoisted her up higher, impatiently shoving her panties aside to dip inside her wet folds. His finger grazed the seam of her lips before tentatively pushing inside. "I thought I'd imagined it," he said, so low she had to strain to hear.

"What?"

"How good you feel."

"And did you?"

"No." His lips parted. "It's better. So hot. So wet." He sank his finger deeper, to the knuckle. It wasn't enough. She wanted him to loosen his jeans and cram her full of his thick cock.

"Fuck me," she directed him, uncaring of the danger and risk, or her earlier reservations.

A big hand instantly covered her mouth, his thumb resting right under her nose. When she cried out, his teeth flashed white in the darkness, his excitement over their spy game morphing into a different kind of pleasure. "You like this. You liked it when I did this to you in the storage closet." Her fierce nod dislodged his hand. "Jacob," she gasped. "I need…"

He muted her again and rested his head on her forehead, his hot breaths mingling with hers. She was on fire at every point of contact: his finger stroking inside her pussy, his broad chest against hers, his hand over her mouth. "Shh. I know what you need."

How could he? For the first time in forever, she wasn't sure what she needed.

"They'll hear you." He screwed a second finger in. "Can you hear them?"

She could hear them, faintly, the excited chatter of photographers as they waited for her to emerge from the building. Her body grew wetter, the threat of imminent discovery exciting her even as her brain told her it could ruin her.

He removed his fingers. Before she could protest, the cotton of his T-shirt abraded her exposed nipples as he aligned their bodies so his dick rested against her pussy. He rolled his hips, his jeans rough. "They're going to figure out there's a third exit pretty soon," he murmured. He pressed his hand tighter against her mouth when she moaned. "They'll come see."

Her lips moved under his palm, and he released his hold long enough for her to speak. "They'll see I'm dying to be fucked."

His moan was a whisper of sound. *By who,* he mouthed. He punctuated each word with a thrust, his cock rubbing her clitoris.

"By you," she gasped.

The unappeased sexual tension coiling inside of her since they had ventured forth on their ridiculous agreement coalesced into a giant, frightening thing. His shoulders grew even more tense under her palms, and he began shafting her with short, rough strokes designed to make her come.

She gritted her teeth and cursed the barrier of his jeans. He could be inside of her. She needed him there.

His palm absorbed the small cries she gave as she came all over him. For a second, as he rested against her, that thick bulge riding her sensitive clit, she wondered if he would rip his clothes off and fuck her, any voyeurs be damned.

But no, he pulled away. It took him but a second to readjust her top and help her put on her shoes, tugging her skirt down to its proper length.

A tendril of fear curled around her. Would this be like last time? *Oops, I tripped and started grinding into your pussy,* she thought with some bitterness. *So sorry. Let's erase this from our collective memories.*

But when she forced herself to confront him and search

his face, there was no shame or regret, only the same light that had been there before, mixed with a heavy dose of arousal. "The crowd in the front is growing," he whispered, gesturing to the north end of the alley. "We need to move."

He was right, judging from the noise, and it was a sign of how badly she had wanted him between her legs that she hadn't realized that herself.

She took his outstretched arm as he started to lead her in the opposite direction. They only went a few steps before he stopped and looked at her shoes. "Your heels are too loud." He knelt and quickly unlaced his boots. "Wear my shoes."

Oh, Jesus. There was a strange, undefined melting sensation going on in her chest. "I don't think yours will fit me," she managed. "I'll be even louder, clomping around."

A frown came and went on his face. "Okay. Here." He pulled his socks off, somehow balancing to keep his bare feet from touching the ground, and put his shoes back on. He knelt again and tapped her knee.

Confused, she lifted her feet for him to slip the socks over her heels, creating rather large cotton booties. He rolled the sock down, tucking it in behind her heel to keep the material from slipping.

"There." He glanced up from underneath his lashes and grinned. "That should help."

She examined the odd footwear. "I really hope the photographers don't see me now," she said dryly, struggling to hide her emotions behind sass. "This would be hell to explain when I land on the worst-dressed list."

He surged to his feet and took her arm again. "You'll start a trend."

∽

"Did you see that guy's face when we drove right past him?"

Akira chuckled, thinking of the paparazzo who had scrambled for his camera when he caught sight of her sitting in the passenger seat of Jacob's car. Luckily, it had taken him too long to start his car. Akira hadn't been keen on a car chase.

Jacob coasted to a stop in front of her house. "There's no reporters here, at least."

"No." She shrugged. "They don't usually come up here. Hedges are too big, and the more famous neighbors get cranky."

"Maybe this thing with your dad will blow over by tomorrow."

She quieted. In all the excitement, she had forgotten about her father and the headlines he had caused, simply because he was an attention whore. The TMZ headlines flashed across her mind. She didn't want to know what other sources were saying. She gave a harsh laugh. "Yeah. Maybe."

"If not, I can drive you to work tomorrow, if you want. I worked out about two more ways into and out of your building on the way home."

Yeah, he really had enjoyed himself tonight. She suppressed her smile. "I'm guessing I'd have to wear a catsuit?"

"No. Well. You could wear a catsuit, but—Actually, yes, yes, it is vitally important you wear a catsuit."

She chuckled, cutting herself off when she caught his odd look. "What?"

"Nothing. I've, uh, never heard you genuinely laugh, is all."

"Never?"

His gaze darkened. The streetlamp glinted over his hair as he shook his head. "After I... In your office, on the floor. After...you laughed. But not like this."

After she had come. When she'd been breathless and satisfied at finally getting what she'd wanted for so many years. The brief moment of joy he'd quickly crushed.

"Well." She studied her hands. "Anyway, I don't need a ride in. I have a driver. I'll have to retrieve my car anyway." She used the word *driver* deliberately, an attempt to distance them, but he only nodded, his gaze far away.

"I'll see you tomorrow night, then." He leaned in and kissed her.

Not on the lips. On the cheek. His lips glanced over her skin, a dry kiss somehow far more intimate than another man's tongue inside her.

Her hand wrapped around the car door handle, the cold metal chilling her. "I can't see you again."

There was silence for a moment after her blurted-out words.

"Bullshit," came his soft reply.

Surprised at the succinct disagreement from a man who had proven to be more than agreeable, she forced herself to meet his eyes. "I mean it."

He studied her face in the dim light of the streetlamp from outside. Far below them, the city lights twinkled, but this was the enclave for the wealthiest in the city. Privacy was guaranteed.

She wished she had chosen to do this in one of her busy nightclubs. Amidst a thousand people. That might have made things easier.

Liar.

"Oh, I'm sure you mean it," he said, his words even. "What are you scared of?"

"Nothing," she responded too quickly. "I just don't want to see you anymore."

"I think I deserve a reason," he said, skepticism written all over his face. "Because it didn't sound like you didn't want to see me when I was making you come all over me in that alleyway."

He certainly didn't have much of a problem with frank speaking now, did he? She swallowed, the click of his seat belt releasing loud in the small Toyota. He leaned over and curved his hand around her cheek, his eyes seeing far too much. "Do you know how hard it was for me to stop and pull away from you?" he said, his voice thick. "I could feel your wetness through my jeans."

Jesus, no problem with frank speaking at all. He had come a long way from not being able to look at her for fear of illicit thoughts. Unable to resist, she dropped her hand down to his crotch, his mouth opening when she massaged the thick bulge she found there. Not for the first time, she wondered what he looked like.

"I know exactly how hard it was," she murmured, caught up in the heated need pulsing through the small space. Her belt unbuckling was loud in the silence of the car. "Or rather, is."

"Akira…"

Walk away from him. You were about to do it. Don't make this messier.

She couldn't. Let her steal this one more thing for herself. It was unfair they had done so much, yet she hadn't even seen him. "You've made me come three times so far. You haven't come once."

"I'm not keeping score."

His breath rushed out of him when her hands deftly worked the buttons closing his fly, finding him encased in snug black cotton. "Shut up, Jacob. Stop being so saintly for a couple of minutes, would you?"

Unable to wait to have him naked, she leaned down and mouthed his erection through the snug material, rewarded by his groan.

With one fingertip, she edged open the fly of his boxer briefs, reaching inside to release his hard cock from captivity. Fully erect, it jumped into her palm. She inhaled, the scent of hot, aroused male and the perfect shape of his erection making her dizzy with delight. She wished she had more light so she could inspect every inch of his cock, from the engorged veins to the fat mushroom-tip head, wet with his need.

"You've been hiding this big cock all these years from me." It wasn't an empty compliment. His cock was in proportion to the rest of his body. She ran her palm over the head, slicking it down his shaft. "I don't know how I'll fit it in my mouth."

His hand slid under her hair, gripping her neck. "Try," he said, obviously beyond all social niceties.

So much for saintliness.

He didn't shove her face into his lap, merely ran his fingers over her nape in a coaxing motion. When she didn't immediately go down on him, he shifted, his hips slightly arching, as if to tempt her.

Jacob wooing her into sucking his cock was about the sexiest thing she'd ever experienced. She encircled his shaft, rubbing it against her cheek before licking it up one side and down the next.

"Jesus, Akira." He gathered her hair in his fist, pushing it back so he could see her face. "Suck me."

"What's the magic word?" she teased.

He growled, his fist tightening in her hair, sending a bolt of arousal through her belly. "Now."

Good enough. She opened her mouth and sucked him in, his salty taste an addiction she would be hard-pressed to deny. There were certain things in life Akira felt she was very good at—sucking a cock was one of them, a point of pride Jacob agreed with, judging from his choked cry when she swallowed most of him down her throat, letting it constrict around him.

She pulled off and did it again, and again, until he was writhing beneath her hands and mouth. She glanced up, but his head was tilted back, his eyes shut, face twisted in almost agony, curses and moans falling from his lips.

She knew when he was about to come by the way his hips rose and fell in a sloppier rhythm. He grasped her hair tighter. "Akira, wait, I'm going…"

She shook her head and sucked him deeper, until the hairs at the base of his cock tickled her nose. He gave a loud, torturous groan and flooded her mouth.

When he was finished, she swallowed and rose from her position. His cock was still semi-erect, lying wet and heavy on his thigh. Her mouth still watered, and her cunt wasn't much better.

Reality came back to her in a rush. *You've had your fun. Now you know what you need to do.* "We're even," she choked out. "And now we're done."

That should have been the final line of her glorious exit, but a click preceded her trying the door handle. The lock had engaged, a lock that didn't open even when she clicked the button. She turned a murderous glare on the driver who was casually buttoning up his pants, hiding his glorious dick.

Mind out of his pants, damn it.

"Child locks," he explained kindly.

Oh no he didn't. "Open. The. Door."

"In a second."

"I will break the window."

"I don't doubt you will."

"Eager to explain that to your insurance company?"

"Eager to explain something to you." He held up his fingers, the fingers that had been buried in her hair as she sucked him. "That was fabulous."

She couldn't resist preening. "I know."

"Second, we are not done."

There went the temptation of wallowing in her blowjob skills. "We are."

"Fine. Tell me why."

"Because…" Why were words so difficult around this man? "You and I aren't compatible."

"I know I've been an ass—"

"This isn't about that." She shook her head impatiently. "You're forgiven, okay? We're fine. We can be done now."

"I don't want to be done."

His wide shoulders were so damned tempting. Why was she being reasonable, again? She could have all of this. Even if it was for a night, they could work themselves out of each other's systems. That was the simplest route to take.

But as they'd discussed already, for some reason a single orgasm wasn't quite enough for either of them. No, it would be messy and complicated, and her life was messy and complicated enough. Sex was what she used to escape that mess. Not compound it.

"Dinner's been fun, and sure, some quick hook-ups in an alley or a car are sexy, but you don't know me. Not really."

"Is this the part where you tell me you're too dirty and bad for me?"

She liked it too much when he said those words. "I make no secret of what I am."

"What makes you think I don't like bad, dirty things too, Akira?"

Her thighs clenched. "Because you're not that kind of man."

"Who's sorting people into types now?" He leaned in, the scent of sex and him forming a heady combination. "The day I don't want to have sex with you is the day I'm declared dead."

He looked up at her, the banked fire in his eyes pulling her in. "I can't take a breath without remembering what your skin smells like, and I'll never get the image of what you look like when you're coming, when you're being fucked, out of my head as long as I live."

Dear Lord. That was it. That was her hot button.

Because nothing in recent memory had turned her on as much as proper, straight-laced Jacob Campbell using the word *fuck* in that low, even tone.

Her heart beat faster as he shifted closer, creating an intimate bubble around them. "Should I tell you?" he asked with devastating softness. "Should I tell you how I think about those house parties you allegedly throw? Yeah, I've heard of them. Should I tell you what I thought when I watched you have sex with another man?"

She was frozen. When had he wrested the control from her? She struggled to speak, to be her sassy self. "At those parties, I don't limit myself to men," she managed.

Hot arousal flared in his eyes. Heat poured off his body. For a moment, she despised him for coming back into her life, letting her see the fire running underneath his proper surface. She'd be so cold when he left.

"You should never have to limit yourself."

Her eyes slitted in pleasure at the frank approval of his words. Oh, but if he only knew how gluttonous her appetites could be, he would never give her free rein.

She breathed in deep, struggling to regain the upper hand. "I don't think wanting me was ever your problem. Your problem is hating yourself for it."

"Ask me if I feel disgusted with myself right now. After grinding you to an orgasm in an alley. After coming in your mouth in my car. After imagining taking you up to your bedroom."

She could barely get the words out. "Do you feel disgusted?"

His smile was so bright it hurt her. The lines around his eyes and mouth deepened. "Not in the slightest."

"That's it? Your issues are gone?" She snorted. "Wow. I'm better than a psychiatrist."

"They aren't gone. But my desire to be with you is trumping my stupid issues."

"I thought you didn't want to be obsessed with me."

"Yeah, that was a dumb thing to say, huh? Turns out, I don't know how to be anything but obsessed with you. So, please...let me."

She'd never found a man pleading sexy, but somehow

Jacob pulled it off, so much so she had to look away. "I'm happy this weird aversion therapy has worked for you. But it changes nothing. You don't want me."

"Why would you say that?"

"Some people are amazing when you scratch away that first layer." These words were difficult, a betrayal of the proud, confident woman she portrayed to the world. "Like you. But not me. I'm not better."

His lips compressed. "You know what, why don't you let me make that decision?"

"Because somehow I've ended up liking you," she said gently.

His mouth opened. "I...like you too. That's all the more reason for us to—"

"I like you too much to fuck with you. So, no." She injected every ounce of finality she could into her voice. "I'm sorry. But no. Please unlock the door."

He blinked. Looked down at his console and disengaged the lock. "You know what I think?"

There was such coldness in his voice, she paused in opening her door. "I don't care."

"I'll tell you anyway. I believe you're running scared."

She stilled, her back to him, before slowly coming to her feet, hand resting on the door. "I've destroyed men who have dared to call me a coward, darling."

"Yeah? I'd rather you destroy me than shut me out for my own good. We're not done, Akira." His smile flashed. She could have frozen him out if it had been a threat, but she was unable to respond to that seductive promise. She closed the door on his final words. "You owe me one more night."

CHAPTER 14

The black envelope came at noon the next day. Jacob murmured his thanks to the private courier who handed it to him and closed his front door, turning the mysterious card over in his hand.

Made of thick vellum, it was heavy and slick, the paper too glossy to be from anything but a specialty stationery store.

He inserted his finger under the flap and opened it as he walked back to his kitchen. Tossing the envelope on the counter, he peered at the words printed in embossed gold font on the single-page invitation.

It stated only today's date and a time, seven p.m. Certain he was missing something given his bleary, sleep-deprived eyes, Jacob flipped the single page over, but there was nothing else there.

There could only be one person behind this. He pulled his phone out of his pocket and dialed a number he had stolen off his sister's phone weeks ago.

It was answered on the first ring. "Yes."

Tenderness, irritation, and annoyance warred within him at the sound of her voice. Since she hadn't bothered with pleasantries, he didn't either. "What is this?"

A pause. "What is what?"

He didn't buy her light response. "This card I got. What is it?"

"How did you know I sent it?"

Because it was very much in her style. Bold. Dramatic. Confusing as hell. "Kati likes to tell me I don't have many friends. The list of potential senders wasn't long."

"Hmm. Maybe you should try being more charming."

He resisted amusement. "What is it, Akira?"

She paused, as if gauging his tone. "It's an invitation."

"An invitation to what?"

Another pause before she spoke, the words uttered in a soft purr which reached through the phone and stroked up his spine. "You said you've heard of my house parties."

He almost bit his tongue. His heart stopped before starting up again, clipping away at a too-fast rate. "I have."

"Then you have your explanation."

He stared at the date on the thick stock paper. "Tonight?"

"That's what the date says."

He hesitated. "The things I've heard…are they accurate?"

"What have you heard, Jacob?"

He glanced around, but the house was silent. He was alone. They were alone. "That you sponsor orgies."

"Sponsor," she repeated slowly. "Like one sponsors a marathon runner. Or a starving child."

"Host, then."

"Yes, Jacob. This is one of the orgies I host."

She was cool and calm, but he had seen so many of her moods over the past week and a half, he couldn't quite buy the act. He tapped the invitation on the counter. "What changed your mind?"

"Maybe you're not the only one who's obsessed." Before he could process that bombshell, she continued. "You wanted your last night. You're getting it." She paused, and he could picture the smirk on her face. "You can come tonight or not at all."

A power play. If he didn't go, he would sacrifice his last night with her. If he did go, he would be throwing himself into the deep end of the pool, as Ben had called it.

She didn't play around.

He smiled, and he didn't need a mirror to know it wasn't a friendly one. Well, hell. Neither did he. "Is this a test? You think I won't call your bluff?"

"I'm hoping you will."

Maybe she was. She probably thought he would...what? See something kinky and slink away so he could go nurse his hang-ups?

He allowed himself to imagine being there, with her. Heat rushed through him. Nope. No shame. No guilt. Those emotions had left him paralyzed for far too long. It was time to fucking live his life.

But that didn't mean he could forget the people who depended on him. "Hang on one second."

Switching lines, he called Ben. His brother picked up on the second ring. "Manscapers."

Jacob's eye twitched. God, he hated the name of their business. "I need you to stay with Kati tonight." His words tumbled over each other.

"Uh...why?"

"You know how you and Connor were talking about clearing my plate for me? I need you to do that. Come over and spend the night. One of you. Both of you. I don't care."

"Okay," Ben said slowly. "Sure. No problem."

"Great. I have to leave at six. Kati and her boyfriend will be here about eight. Her bedroom door needs to be open, and don't let the boy stay past her curfew. Lights out at eleven."

"Wait, what boyfrie—?"

"Bye." Jacob switched lines. "Hey."

"Generally when I invite guests to orgies, they don't put me on hold."

"Generally when you invite guests to orgies, they probably don't need to procure a babysitter for the night."

She clucked her tongue, suddenly sounding more like the woman who had sat across from him in her office for the past couple of weeks, and less the femme fatale. "You're getting a seventeen-year-old a babysitter? Ugh. Give that kid a break."

"Her new boyfriend's coming over to study. There's a reasonable amount of freedom, and then there's being a wholly irresponsible guardian, and I'm not the latter." A swell of relief sank over him at the accuracy of the words, the truth in them. "I'm not."

She was silent for a moment, her words quiet when she spoke. "No, you're not."

Jacob took a deep breath. "And to answer your question, yes. I'll be there tonight."

She cleared her throat. "Good. That's…great."

"I'm not so easily scared off," he told her gently. "I can see why you might think that, but you don't know what's in my brain. In my fantasies."

"In those fantasies of yours," she asked with devastating bluntness, "do you fuck in front of other people? Because that's what tonight entails."

His chest expanded. He stared at the invitation until the embossed lettering blurred. "Would it be you?"

Silence. "Would it be me what?"

"Would it be you I would be...?" He trailed off. Not because he was ashamed of the word, but because he might combust if he allowed himself to complete the thought.

She whispered the directive to him, like the devil on his shoulder she was. "Say it."

He breathed the word. "Fucking."

Her husky reply told him he wasn't the only one affected. "Maybe. Or maybe it would be others. Or maybe it would be me and others."

"Any of it." He closed his eyes. "I want all of it. And none of it will change the way I think of you."

"Come to my party," she finally replied. "And we'll see what thoughts you have left by morning."

CHAPTER 15

$\mathcal{J}$acob pulled up outside Akira's mansion a little before seven that night. The winding driveway along the side of the home was already filled with luxury cars, his Toyota looking sadly practical amidst the glitz. In all the years he had lived in this city, he had never been to Billionaires Row quite so many times in the space of a couple weeks.

A valet came jogging up to his car the second he placed it in park and opened his door. "Sir."

"Thanks." He handed the other man his keys and got out, stomach jumping.

It wasn't the wealth he was intimidated by. Thanks to Akira's mother, he had hovered on the fringes of wealthy society for most of his adult life. It didn't matter how many bedrooms or libraries or kitchens Akira had in this palatial home. It didn't matter that there was an incredibly long driveway along the side of the house or a five car garage visible from the street, tucked under the house—in a city where a single reserved parking spot could be sold for a premium price, that was pretty much the height of luxury.

No, what had his palms sweating was what lay on the

other side of that door.

Talk about the deep end.

Jacob's shoulders squared. *You wanted this. You want her. Let her see what you're really like.*

He strode up the pathway to the front door, but it opened before he could knock. Jacob lowered his fist, faced with a small elderly man decked out in a full suit. With tails and everything. Had Akira found this guy rattling around in a European castle somewhere? "Good evening, sir," he intoned.

The murderer. That's who Jacob would cast this guy as. Predictable, perhaps, but his stern visage and perfectly pressed appearance didn't really permit anything else. Jacob cleared his throat, realizing he had been eyeing the man for far too long. "Hello, I'm…"

"Mr. Campbell. We have been expecting you." The little man stepped aside, his bald head gleaming.

Definitely the killer. He'd take care of unwitting guests with a slow-acting poison. In the library, which Jacob knew from his past visit was delightfully soundproofed.

Quit being weird. "Thank you." He stepped inside the massive foyer. If Akira's office was elegant, understated wealth, here she had gone for ostentatious, in-your-face filthy money. The chandelier hanging from the high ceiling dripped crystal, twin stairways spiraling up to the second floor. Paintings in ornate gold frames lined the hallways leading away from the foyer.

It was loud and unapologetic and brash, without a hint of subdued elegance. It suited Akira.

"You had no trouble finding the place, sir?"

"No, not at all."

"I suppose not. You have been here before, have you

not?"

"Yes. Ah, last week."

"Of course. And then that time when you were skulking about in the middle of the night."

Jacob turned slowly and eyed the older man, who stared back at him impassively. Still, Jacob made a mental note to watch his back. And sniff his drinks. "I'm sorry, I didn't catch your name."

"Harris." The man gave a little bow.

"You're Akira's butler?"

"Her butler, her valet, her security, if the police need to be called." A thin smile emerged. "You understand."

"Yeah. I think I do. Rest assured, my nocturnal skulking days are over."

"I'm sure we're both pleased to hear that. May I take your coat, sir?"

"Sure. Yes." He shrugged out of his jacket and handed it to the man. He had been unsure what to wear to this, so he'd opted for a suit, without the tie. Googling *what to wear to an orgy* had resulted in little assistance. Many interesting images. Little assistance.

Harris draped the jacket over his arm. "I do welcome you, of course, on behalf of Ms. Mori. Since this is your first time attending one of Ms. Mori's gatherings, I thought I would take the liberty of going over some general guidelines."

Mystified, Jacob dipped his head. "Okay."

"Alcohol will be served tonight. We hope you drink responsibly, but you will be cut off if you appear, in Ms. Mori or the staff's discretion, overly intoxicated. We require all guests when leaving to submit to a Breathalyzer test before retrieving their car. If you choose not to submit to the test, or if you are incompetent to drive, Ms. Akira will be happy to ensure you get home safely in her personal car." Harris spoke as if he had recited this particular speech a hundred times.

Jacob wanted to smile, but the seriousness of Harris's demeanor told him it wouldn't be appreciated. "That's reasonable."

"Wonderful." Harris cleared his throat. "The safe word this evening is 'spy'. If any guest so much as utters it, the expectation is that all parties shall immediately cease their actions. This is a hard-and-fast rule—Ms. Akira demands consent from all parties at all times. Anything less is unacceptable."

From a ride home to safe words. Where was he?

Oh yeah. At an orgy.

Spy. Had Akira picked that one? A nod to him?

"Ahem."

Realizing Harris was awaiting his reply, he snapped to attention. "Yes. Certainly."

The butler gave him an arch look, unimpressed with him. "If you have any hard limits, you ought to make them clear. Everyone here is accustomed to frank speaking. Do you understand?"

"Hard...limits? Like, pain, you mean?"

"If you like." Harris smoothed Jacob's coat. "We normally test guests for any sexually transmitted diseases prior to their attendance, but Ms. Akira informed me we were making a special exception for you." The butler pursed his lips, clearly unhappy with this directive. "Regardless, all guests are required to wear protection. If there is something you wish to have but do not see, simply ask, and someone will provide it for you. The only exception to this rule is if you and your partner or partners agree to forgo protection. That's generally only done by those guests in a relationship."

Jacob nodded. "Sounds fair."

"You are not in a committed relationship?"

A certain hostess flashed in front of his mind. "No."

Harris rocked back on his heels. "Finally, and this goes without saying, but Ms. Mori does require absolute secrecy regarding any events that transpire over the course of the evening."

"Not going to make me sign a nondisclosure agreement?" He was half-joking.

"Unnecessary." Harris's grin was hard but tinged with pride. "Would you cross Ms. Mori?"

"I already have." Jacob rubbed his neck. "It wasn't an enjoyable experience."

"Then you'll know better than to do it again." Harris pinned him with a stern glare. "This is not part of my usual spiel. If I ever see you skulking around this house in the middle of the night, I or an associate will shoot first and ask questions later."

No. Not a poison. A gun, a quick and clean shot to the head. At the edge of a cliff, so cleanup would be painless. That's what this man would use.

He should be offended, but oddly he wasn't. He had spent years considering Akira to be a solitary creature, so it was good to see the depth of this man's loyalty. Akira needed a pit bull in her corner. Preferably, many pit bulls. "Understood," he responded.

"Excellent," Harris said, brisk and professional now. "I will show you up to the salon so you may join the other guests."

"That's unnecessary, Harris. I can take Mr. Campbell everywhere he would like to go tonight."

At the dulcet tones, his attention shifted to the woman standing midway down the stairs. He struggled not to gawk, but he was certain it was a wasted effort. Akira regularly took his breath away wearing those damn pencil skirts. This was...beyond anything he could have imagined.

She wore a dress tonight, but one he'd never seen a woman wear in public. The orange corset-like top cinched her waist so it was tiny enough he could probably span it with two hands. Red and orange swirled together in her long skirt, which draped over the stairs like a waterfall of flames. One slender hand rested on the balustrade. She took a step down, and her leg appeared out of a slit in the skirt, revealing her strong thigh.

She took another step down and smiled at him, her dark eyes flashing. This smile was practiced and smooth, different from the ones he had painstakingly coaxed from her over the past couple of weeks. It was a smile she could give any man.

He had filthy dreams of sharing her body with other people, but oddly, he wanted a smile from her meant only for him.

He didn't hear what the butler said, but he was aware of the other man leaving them. Jacob moved closer until he was standing at the base of the stairs. They were separated by four steps, but her perfume, some dark blend of roses and honeysuckle, twined around him.

"Tell me something," he murmured.

She cocked her head. Her long hair had been pulled up at the top to create a voluminous poof, and then curled and draped over one shoulder. Glamorous. Unattainable.

He wanted that smile, damn it.

"Anything you'd like."

"Did you have to hold this pose for long, waiting for me to walk through the door?"

Ah, yes. The grin slipped. Surprise followed by irritation quickly chased across her face before she donned her mask again. "I don't know what you're talking about."

He waved a hand up and down. "You know. This. Don't get me wrong, you look amazing. Did you have a couple of serfs arrange your skirt so perfectly?"

"Serfs are notoriously unreliable. I've stopped employing them entirely."

"Peasants then."

"They have to earn their keep somehow." Her mask cracked, softened. "So you came."

"I came."

A dark and vulnerable shadow lit her eyes, a direct contrast to the power and strength of her pose. "It is our last night. You understand that."

He placed a foot on the stair. "Whether it is or isn't is up to you."

"You say that now."

"I'll say that twelve hours from now."

She inclined her head. "Come along, then. Let's go upstairs."

He climbed the stairs, staying one step behind her, partially so he could stare at her luscious ass outlined in the clinging skirt. Her back was bare but for the criss-cross of her bodice's ribbons, and he mentally traced the hollow at the base of her spine with his tongue.

"I trust Harris gave you the rundown."

"Yeah. He's, uh, very thorough."

She stopped at the top of the stairs and cast him a sharp look over her shoulder. "Thorough?"

"Yes. He's got his orgy spiel down pat."

"Orgy spiel? Usually he just explains which areas of the home are off-limits and where the restrooms are."

He cast a glance in the direction the butler had gone. "Oh."

"What did he discuss with you?"

"Breathalyzers. Safe words. Condoms." He grimaced. "Hard limits. All the things I'd want to talk to an elderly butler about."

Akira's peal of laughter washed over him. Something deep within him stretched toward the sound, delight filling him, even though her amusement was directed at him. "He might be holding a grudge. He wasn't happy I didn't press charges against you for trespassing when you delivered those flowers," she confessed.

"Obviously," he mock grumbled, any annoyance dissipated by the brightness of her grin. *That smile. That's what I wanted.*

"So what is your hard limit?"

He let out a soft sigh. "I don't know. Severe pain, I guess."

She nodded, thoughtful. "I can work with that." Still smiling, she lifted a shoulder. "If it helps, I'm very serious about drinking responsibly and safe sex. Those are sort of make-or-breaks for attending. However, I carefully vet the people who attend my parties and personally explain the rules." She continued walking, taking a left down the hall. "Sorry about Harris, especially if it made you uncomfortable.

Consider it a friendly hazing."

Jacob would do just that, but he'd be on his guard around the man anyway. A knife to incapacitate. Then the gun. Then the cliff. Yes. That was how the butler would do it.

He was distracted from his murderous plotting by the sleek, strong expanse of Akira's back. Entranced by the two delicious dimples right above her ass winking at him, he was barely conscious of sliding his hands around her waist, pulling her to a halt in the abandoned hallway.

He knew she was leading him to a hedonistic adventure, but he wasn't sure if he could make it if he didn't have one taste of this woman. A sip to tide him over. As if they had a will of their own, his hands tightened on either side of her narrow hips. She froze, standing still. Neither protesting nor demanding an explanation. Leaving him free to indulge his instincts.

Dropping to his knees, he leaned forward and settled his lips over those dimples. Distantly, he heard her gasp, but all he could do was lick her, nuzzle her, kiss her. Easing his hands under her skirt, he pushed the voluminous fabric up until her small, firm ass was visible, lit by the low wall sconces every couple of feet.

Anyone could come upon them, but he didn't care. And judging by the way she widened her thighs, neither did she.

He ran his hands up her smooth legs, the powerful muscles of her calves inviting him to linger. He had no time for that, though. His index finger pushed the thin fabric of her lacy black thong aside, and he inhaled, dragging in the scent of her wet body. He extended his tongue and gave her one, long, slow lick along her vulva. His taste buds demanded more immediately, but he slammed a lid over his instincts, not allowing himself to linger at the button of her clitoris.

One sip. He swallowed, savoring her taste. Licked his lips, in case a trace of her clung there. He lowered her skirt and rose to his feet. Her hair was so shiny and perfect, he was loath to disturb it, so he nudged it aside only the barest amount to kiss her neck, his hands tightening on her hips as she gave a breathy moan. Her head turned, her lips seeking his. Her breath was coming fast, pupils dilated.

"No matter what happens the rest of the night," he growled, a stranger having gained control of his mouth. A stranger he liked, one he had buried long ago. "Remember the first tongue you had on you tonight was mine."

Since he wasn't capable of stopping, he pulled her close and pressed a kiss on her lips. He meant for it to be sweet and gentle, but he couldn't control his pent-up need. It quickly turned blisteringly sexual, especially once she tugged at his lip with her teeth.

He cradled her neck and tilted her head, angling her so he could fuck her mouth with his. And that's what this was, the darkest, basest approximation of sex. He wanted to rip off her dress and pull her to her knees and sink inside of her right here and right now.

Wait.

Yes. If he waited, it could only be better.

They separated, both breathing hard. He studied Akira's face, her cheeks flushed, her red lips slick. "Will you remember?"

"I will." Her smile came, quick, fleeting, and oddly, painfully sad. But genuine, not one of her practiced deals. "Who are you?" The question was wondering and a little frightened.

He gave her a blinding smile, his chest expanding. "I don't know anymore. Let's find out."

CHAPTER 16

*J*acob wasn't sure what he expected when he entered a hedonistic den of sin, but a nice, sophisticated cocktail party wasn't at the top of his list.

There was a chandelier in the salon, but no one was swinging from it. The Oriental rug was lush, but naked bodies weren't rolling around on it. No one was wearing a mask and advancing on him menacingly with a butt plug as soon as he entered.

Anticlimactic.

Roughly twenty people were gathered in a sitting room which was larger than the entire first floor of his house. He patted himself on the back when he realized most of the men were dressed as he was, though a few had also donned ties.

The women, for the most part, wore cocktail dresses, a couple on the risqué side. He might be biased, but none of them were as beautiful as Akira. None of them, not even the ones who cast him curious, hungry looks, made him want to shove them into a dark corner and inhale them.

Jacob took a sip of his beer and leaned against the bar, instinctively seeking Akira out in the crowd. In here, her vibrancy was dialed up to blinding. The air around her crackled, and guests turned and looked when she laughed or spoke.

She'd been drawn into a conversation by a group of women as soon as they had entered. She had nodded to the bar and told him to grab a drink. He had gratefully retreated.

Your usual M.O. Stop observing. Start participating.

A man came to stand next to him. "Scotch," he said to the bartender, his voice smooth. And familiar.

Jacob cast him a glance, and then did a double take. Jesus. He shouldn't have been surprised, he supposed, but a part of him hadn't really expected to see the man from that charity dinner, the man who had screwed Akira while he watched. Silly assumption. If the guy was okay with Jacob watching him fuck Akira at a party for a nonprofit organization, why wouldn't he be here tonight?

Remy was even better looking out of the fluorescent lights of that storage closet. Great. Jacob rubbed his jaw, thankful he had, at least, shaved for tonight.

As if he was used to perusals from men and women, the other man grinned at him and accepted the drink from the bartender, his blue eyes dancing. "Hello, Jacob."

Jacob tipped his head. "Hi. Remy, right?"

"Yeah." His grin broadening, the man stuck out his hand. "Thought I recognized you, standing over here by yourself. First time at Akira's, huh?"

Jacob accepted it, raising an eyebrow at the pressure Remy exerted on his fingers. Damn it, he hated when men played this particular game. "You don't want to do that."

"Do what?" Remy asked, still smiling. But now Jacob caught the sharp edge to his smile.

Internally sighing, Jacob returned the squeeze at only a fraction of what he was capable of. Still, Remy winced, his hand immediately loosening its grasp.

"That's what," Jacob said apologetically. "I'm kind of strong, and if I'm not wrong, you're a model of some sort and probably need your appendages intact."

"Uh, yeah." Remy surreptitiously massaged his hand with the other. "I'm not exactly a model, but I do work with my hands. Thanks."

Jacob shrugged, resigned to feeling like a large, lumbering oaf around the lean and elegant man. "No problem."

Remy watched him, but this time with cautiousness, as he sipped his scotch. "We don't get a lot of newbies. Most of us here…" he nodded to the party, "…know each other well."

"I bet."

A dimple appeared in the man's cheek. "You'll get to know us too. Don't you worry."

"Oh, I'm not worried."

"It's natural to be nervous the first time." The man leaned in close. "Just remember, if the butt plugs are too large and scary looking, you can request something smaller."

Jacob took a long pull from his beer and placed it on the bar with a definitive click. "So you know, I've raised three teenagers. If they haven't been able to fuck with my head yet, neither will you."

"But I can fuck you otherwise, right?" Remy purred. "That's why you're here."

Jacob thought back to his conversation with Akira. He could have put men on his list of hard limits. But he hadn't. He met Remy's eyes squarely. "I'm here for lots of reasons."

Remy's lips thinned, unimpressed. "Akira doesn't usually

announce parties on the fly like this."

"No?"

"No. And she doesn't invite a new guy and make excep-
tions for him. And she doesn't call me out of the blue and tell
me she's going to be my guest at a charity function. And she
doesn't bang me in a closet after making sure some guy is
certain to follow." Remy's amicable mask slipped. "So tell me,
Jacob. Who the hell are you?"

Akira had manipulated it so she would be at that charity
dinner? Perhaps Jacob should be annoyed by that, but he was
relieved. Thank God she had. Or he wouldn't have had the
balls to crawl back to her.

A laugh danced over the party, pulling Jacob's attention
away from the man in front of him. His shoulders tensed as
he watched Akira throw back her head and chuckle. The
noise was loud and rich and boisterous, and without his
volition, his body leaned forward as if he could absorb it.

He had attended numerous parties where Akira had also
been a guest. He'd never heard her laugh like that. Thinking
back without the filter of fear and guilt, he recalled Akira
would always spend the evening smiling her shark's smile,
coolly calculating her effect on everyone.

There was none of that here. These guests were her
friends, not just people who happened to love a bit of kink.
Akira wasn't a loner. Harris wasn't the only one in her corner.
In the dark of night, she had her own inner circle.

Warmth coursed through him. Good, he thought savage-
ly. She needed a line of defense. He could be in her inner
circle, eventually, once she learned to trust him.

Patience. It took time and effort to storm a princess's castle. He couldn't run in, waving his mighty staff about.

Remy cleared his throat, and Jacob blinked, yanked out of contemplation. "I'm her..." he trailed off, "...friend."

Remy's expression was skeptical. "How did you meet her?"

Jacob attempted to focus. "Her mother married my father."

"Her mom passed away a few months ago," Remy said flatly.

"Yes." Jacob couldn't begin to explain their complicated history in a nutshell. "They were married a long time ago. Mei and my dad divorced."

"I didn't hear about this."

"It's common knowledge." He cocked his head. "Unless...unless maybe you haven't known Akira as long as I have."

Remy's nostrils flared at the subtle rebuke, but Jacob caught the glimmer of respect buried in his ice-blue eyes. Still, the man jabbed, his voice silken. "So you're...stepsiblings."

That sounded...wrong. "No. I mean—technically, yes, but it was only for a year, fourteen years ago." He paused. Frowned. "And we were both grown, it's not like we grew up together—"

"Jacob, stop talking. You're making us sound utterly depraved." Akira appeared at his elbow and smiled at Remy. "Remy. So glad you could make it."

The warmth between the two was palpable as they kissed European style. "Thanks for inviting me, as always." Remy turned laughing eyes on him. Jacob wasn't fooled now, though. He was quite aware Remy would destroy him if he so much as lifted a finger against Akira. "I was just talking to your brother here," he said smoothly.

"Behave, Remy," Akira cautioned. "Or we both know I could call up *your* brother and have a chat with him."

The other man's eyes widened comically. "You would break my heart like that, love?"

"In a heartbeat." Akira threaded her arm through Jacob's. It felt right. So right, he covered her hand with his and looked down at her, only to find her studying him somberly. "Lay off the new guy. The Brother Jacob schtick is reserved solely for me." Her face softened. "Or it was."

Was? Why the past tense? Because the subtext, that he was a boring, sober monk, no longer applied?

Good. He gave her a wicked smile.

Remy wasn't important any longer. Showing Akira how un-monk-like he could be was.

"Your wish is my command," Remy said lightly.

Akira snorted and tore her gaze away to look at her friend. "If only it were that easy."

Jacob realized then the room had quieted. He lifted his head, noting at least half the participants had departed. The ones remaining were occupied nuzzling with a partner or two. "Where is everyone?"

Remy answered, "There are two smaller salons Akira sets up for people who wish to participate in scenes. Who's playing tonight?"

"Zoe, to start."

The other man gave a low whistle. "Taking Jacob's training wheels off on the first night, huh?"

"We both know I'm only easy when I want to be."

"A scene...like, a show?" Jacob interrupted the banter.

Akira tipped her head. "Something like that."

"As in control as Akira is, she's remarkably hands-off on our little parties," Remy responded, seeming to realize Akira's answer told Jacob nothing. "Some of the guests like to put on a show." He regarded Akira fondly. "Akira made sure they have a place to do it."

Jacob snagged his beer bottle and drained it, a lot intrigued and a little apprehensive. "Sounds interesting." He placed the bottle on the bar. "Shall we?"

Remy waved at them, his attention on a man across the room. "You guys go on. I'll catch up with you."

Jacob tightened his fingers on hers as Akira led him away. "If you wanted me to mingle, I'm afraid the only person I met was Remy."

"I didn't expect you to mingle. I expected you to go get a drink and then survey the crowd like you were watching a play. It's what you do anytime there's any kind of gathering."

He glanced at her, surprised.

"What?" she asked. "I've been to dozens of parties with you."

"I didn't realize you were observing me at all those parties." But why not? There hadn't been a get-together he had been to where he wasn't acutely aware of every action Akira made.

A flush crept up her chest. Jacob hid his smile. The woman could speak blithely about group sex, but point out that she may have surreptitiously studied his habits, and she blushed.

"I didn't need to watch you like a hawk to catch a pattern," she said defensively.

"Sure. And I do mingle, you know. You make me sound like a creepy shut-in."

"Not creepy. Just brooding. Introverted."

He squinted. "Brooding introverts build bombs in cabins in the Midwest."

"They also write books."

He surveyed the rest of the people remaining in the room they were leaving and dropped his voice. "Will these people have sex in here?"

"Some of them," she responded, blasé. "I keep four rooms open on this floor, though the other three are generally for scenes. Everyone is free to use the space as they wish."

They stepped inside the adjoining room. The low track lighting in the ceiling was focused on the raised dais in the middle.

"You've built a stage," he said with some surprise.

"When people like to have pool parties, they install a pool," Akira said matter-of-factly.

Half-a-dozen comfortable leather couches surrounded the stage. All but one was occupied. Akira sank onto the empty one and crossed her legs, the slit in her skirt revealing her silky smooth leg up to her thigh.

He settled next to her, his gaze drawn to that pale expanse of flesh. "What happens now?"

She shushed him as a dark-haired woman strode into the room, instantly capturing everyone's attention. "Now you get to meet Zoe. Guests love her. She encourages audience participation." She pursed her lips. "Let me know when you want to tap out."

CHAPTER 17

$\mathcal{J}$acob narrowed his eyes at his hostess. Akira was so cute when she was treating him like a naïve virgin. Cute and maddening.

Practical-experience wise, this might very well all be new for him, but he possessed a more fertile imagination than most normal people. Intellectually, his depravity ran deep.

The room was dead silent now, however, and he was too polite to loudly argue with his woman and interfere with everyone's enjoyment. Unable to completely let her snarky comment go, he settled his hand on her thigh and gave her a warning squeeze.

Deliberately, she placed her hand over his and dragged it up her inner thigh until it was almost at her groin. Then she gave him a smirk and mouthed, *Watch.*

Akira's skin burning against his palm, he turned to the stage and the Hispanic beauty mounting it. Zoe's tall, curvy body was displayed to perfection in a lacy green negligee that did little to hide her large nipples and shaved mound.

Another woman neared the stage, fingers working the knot of the robe she wore. Before she climbed the steps, she slipped it off her shoulders, baring her naked body to the crowd. Her ass was round, her big breasts jiggling with her fidgeting as she came to rest, standing in profile to them. A sigh rose from one viewer, while another growled appreciatively.

"The naked woman is Tess," Akira whispered. "Pretty, yes?"

No doubt, the blonde was sexy, but... "Not as pretty as you," he whispered back, and caught her fleeting smile out of his peripheral vision.

Zoe stalked around Tess in a circle, teasing her by stroking her flanks, her hair, her back. She paused, standing behind Tess, fingertips on that full ass. Her hand snapped back, the loud noise cracking through the silence. The blonde gave a choked-off cry, her ample flesh jiggling from the blow.

Akira shifted. "Is this too much pain for you?"

"What?"

"You said your hard limit was..."

"Severe pain." Not this, the slap of flesh against flesh. Would she spank her again? His fingers curled, pressing into Akira's resilient thigh.

Zoe tapped Tess's hip and the girl obediently shifted, turning so her soft body was facing him and Akira directly. For a brief second, he made eye contact with Tess before her lashes fluttered down. A well-built, good-looking man melted out of the shadows to join the duo. He was already naked, his cock hard. He stood passively beside Tess, but there was no mistaking the expression on his face when he looked at the taller woman. Love. Heat. Worship.

"That's Zoe's husband," Akira confirmed.

The man stroked Tess's nipples while Zoe tugged on her

hair, arching her neck. She placed her lips close to the younger woman's ear, but her voice carried through the room. "If you're not quiet," she said, as if she were explaining something to a small child, "I will make this painful. Do you want it to be painful?"

"No, ma'am."

"Smart girl." She turned her narrow gaze to her husband. "Do you have the clamps, David?"

"Of course."

"Good." Zoe pressed a kiss on Tess's shoulder and nodded at the plain wooden chair set in the center of the stage. Head bowed, the girl walked to the chair and sat down.

Zoe tilted her head, a sly smile on her face as she stared at her husband. "Put them on her."

David sank to his knees, his mouth honing in on one nipple and then the other, using his teeth to pull the tiny nubs out so they stood farther away from the girl's body.

Tess cried out when the first clamp closed around her nipple. She squealed with the second.

Zoe closed her hands over the girl's shoulders, holding her steady, or perhaps comforting her, Jacob wasn't sure. "The third one, David."

Tess opened her eyes, and they gleamed. A single tear worked its way down her cheek, which would have concerned Jacob if not for the frustration and excitement obviously visible on the young woman's face. "Where does the third one go?"

Zoe's laugh was low and a little mean. "I know this is your first time playing with us, Tess, but you're no innocent. Open your legs."

"Oh, but..." Her long lashes lowered, her flesh quivering.

"I don't know if I'll like that. Won't it hurt?"

"In the best possible way. Come now." Tess nodded to David, who wasted no time in spreading the girl's legs, exposing her pink, wet pussy to everyone in the room.

A breathy moan drifted over from the couch to his left. Attention diverted, Jacob glanced over to find the couple there locked in a passionate kiss. The woman was straddling her partner's lap, her back to his front, legs arranged over his. His hand cupped her cheek, turning her head so he could claim her lips. The woman's legs were bare, her lover having shoved her dress up, his other hand moving between her legs.

"I told you—Zoe loves audience participation. Even if the people are only participating with each other."

Jacob jerked his head back around, the sudden movement and the voyeuristic excitement making his head spin. Akira smiled her shark's smile. "Had enough yet?" she asked, her low voice taunting him.

Dick aching, he leaned in, her flowery scent twining around him. "Not even close."

"Her clit isn't hard enough," David complained on stage.

Zoe ran her finger over the other woman's cheek lovingly. "So make it hard."

David stuck his tongue out and prodded the little nubbin. "Like this?"

"You can do better than that."

He raised his hand and lightly slapped at Tess's pussy, wringing a wild cry from her. David spanked her clit again. Then again. Tess writhed in the chair, restrained by Zoe's grip on her shoulders.

"Do it now," Zoe said sternly.

David landed a final blow and lowered his head, drawing

her erect clitoris into his mouth for a quick suck. When he drew away to attach the metal clamp, Tess screamed.

On an academic level, Jacob understood clamps and the purpose behind restricting blood flow to increase pleasure, but the metal glinting at the woman's nipples and clit seemed torturous. "Do you use those?" he asked Akira.

"No," she responded.

He nodded, but she continued. "Mine are gold. With little diamonds on them."

There went his heart again, galloping off. He knew the question would feed into her impression that he was an innocent, but he had to know. "What do they feel like?"

She cast him an amused glance, turned, and picked something up off the side of the table. "Do you want to find out?"

He could barely talk, he was so aroused. "You keep nipple clamps lying around?"

"On nights like these…yes."

"You are an excellent hostess."

"So I've been told." Her hand smoothed down his chest, and she nodded to the tableau in front of them. Tess was still crying, but she didn't look miserable. Her color was high, her passion palpable. Zoe knelt next to her, stroking her hair, her arms, her breasts, while David remained between her legs, his head cushioned by her plump thighs, running his hands over her skin and rubbing his face against the light curls covering her pussy as if he were incapable of getting enough.

Akira shifted beside him, and her fingers coasted over the upper slope of her breasts, which were overflowing from the tight corset. "Answer me. Do you want to find out?"

He cast the clamps a dubious look. "You want to put those on me?"

"If you're curious, I can."

"Does it hurt?"

"Yes. But I like it." With one tug of her bodice, her breasts popped out in all their round glory, her light brown nipples puckered. She wasn't large, but she was firm. He could easily spend hours mapping her softness and roundness. She teased the hard tip with her fingers, tightening and compressing the tip so it was hard and long. Matter-of-factly, she snapped the clamp closed, her slight gasp his only clue that it affected her.

Black eyes met his. "Now you?" The words were rich with challenge.

He wet his lower lip and leaned back against the couch. She moved over him so she straddled one of his splayed legs, not blocking his view of the performance. "Keep watching," she breathed.

As if he could look away. David gave a teasing lick to Tess's pussy before he stood. "She was very good," he said to Zoe in his gravelly voice.

Akira popped open the first button of his shirt. Then the second. The third.

Zoe petted Tess's hair, like she was a fond pet. "Indeed. Shall we reward her?"

"Yes. Please," Tess sobbed. "I'll do anything."

"She talks a lot," Zoe said consideringly. "I think we can find a better use for that mouth, don't you?" She grabbed Tess by the hair, the controlled strength in her grip a marked contrast to the gentleness of her previous touch and tone. "On your knees."

Jacob jerked when Akira's hot mouth latched on to his nipple. She bit, sucked, flicked her rough tongue against him.

His head fell back, and he stared at the vaulted ceiling. He slid a hand around her neck and tried to hold her there, his hips arching up when she scraped her teeth over the sensitive tip.

She pulled away. Before he could protest her departure, cold metal kissed his nipple. There was a second of sharp pain as the clamp shut, and he groaned, forgetting to modulate his voice. "Holy shit."

A low male chuckle from the couch next to them told him his outburst had not gone unnoticed. He would've minded, except his head was swimming with pain and pleasure. "God damn it, Akira."

"Shh," she soothed. "It's getting better, isn't it?"

It was. The pain had lessened to a dull throb. He glanced down at his body, now adorned in gold and diamonds. More arousing than the sensation was the sight of the coordinating clamps compressing their flesh.

Her breasts rose and fell. "What do you think?"

"It's…interesting." Testing her, he rubbed his thumb over her clamped nipple, delighting in the way her lids fell to half-mast and she stretched toward him.

"That feels good."

"Does it?"

"Mm-hmm." She matched his motions, gently tugging at the clamp. His thighs tightened as pleasure and pain shot through him. "See?"

She leaned forward so they were chest to chest, and kissed him. Their lips turned carnal, both of them too aroused for anything but the basest of kisses. Her clamped nipple brushed against his, and they moaned into each other's mouths.

She pulled away, her eyes having lost the watchful, challenging expression she'd gifted him with most of the night, replaced by pure need.

Something uneasy within him calmed at the sight of her obvious lust. He had craved this like he craved that special smile from her. Confidence bloomed within him, and he crushed the wispy fabric of her skirt, pulling it out of his way until his hand could wrap around her ass.

He used his grip to grind her pussy against his thigh, her wetness hot even through his slacks. She gasped and clung to him, her eyes shutting before they snapped open. "Wait. No. You keep doing this."

Her words were so low he had to lean forward to hear her. His thigh muscle inadvertently jumped, and she clutched his unbuttoned shirt. "Doing what?"

Akira shook her head, a determined glint replacing some of the lust. "Nothing."

It didn't sound like nothing. But all thoughts flew out of his brain when Akira scooted closer and pressed her chest against him again. Her tongue slicked up his neck. "What are they doing on the stage?"

"Akira…"

"Talk." Her tone brooked no disobedience.

Jacob struggled to focus. His hands were filled with a woman he'd wanted for too long, his body in sweet agony, so it was—no pun intended—hard. "She, Tess…she's on her knees."

Akira traced his ear. "What's she doing on her knees?"

"Trying to suck…" He hesitated.

Akira's slender fingers flicked his clamped nipple, and he bit off a curse before finishing his sentence. "Trying to suck David's cock."

"What's stopping her?"

"Jesus, Akira."

"Tell me."

"Zoe's holding her by her hair. She can't move."

David slapped his cock against the girl's lower lip, teasing her. Zoe leaned over the woman. "If you suck him very well, I will let you be fucked. And you can come," she said to Tess sternly. "But if you do not, then I will send you home unsatisfied. Do you understand?"

"Yes, ma'am," Tess whimpered.

Zoe wrapped her hand around her husband's dick and jacked it until a drop of precome appeared on the tip. She guided Zoe's head closer until her lips enclosed the thick girth. Zoe was the one who controlled the motions and the depth of the action. With one hand she played with David's saliva-slick cock, the other was still gripping Tess's hair.

"How is she, darling?" Zoe crooned.

"Not as good as you," David rasped.

"Did you hear that?" she asked Tess. She fondled her husband's balls. "Deeper. Choke on it." She urged the woman's face farther until she gagged, gave her a respite, and did it again.

A thought popped into Jacob's brain. He shifted and opened his mouth to speak, but then hesitated.

"What?" Akira asked quietly.

She was studying him as intently as he watched the action on the stage. "How long have they been married? David and Zoe?"

She pushed his shirt aside so her teeth could worry his shoulder. "High school sweethearts."

They were in their late thirties, at least. A long time. "He seems as comfortable up there as she does."

"They're well suited to each other."

Was that a trace of wistfulness he heard? He tightened his hold on her, but her head remained bent, tasting the skin of his neck and chest. "Do you think they ever get jealous?"

She froze and glanced up, her eyes wary. "No."

His blood was pounding so hard his head ached in concert with his dick, but he was intrigued by the forceful response. "You're that certain?"

"Maybe he'd be jealous if she secretly went out to dinner with another person. Not here, darling. Not with this. Pleasure is fluid and meant to be shared." She paused. "But, that's an attitude most people don't have. I can't imagine you, for instance, would be okay with your girlfriend or wife having sex with other people."

His heart stopped and then galloped at the words "girlfriend or wife."

He thought what life would be like if Akira was his girlfriend.

Dear Lord. It would be loud and dramatic and frequently annoying, but never boring. They would fight all the time. Laugh all the time.

Fuck all the time. Whenever he wanted.

Could he share her sexually? If she was his partner?

His gaze shifted to the debauchery over her shoulder. Zoe stood behind Tess now, her legs straddling the girl's as she bobbed the woman over her husband's cock. David groaned, his gaze drifting back and forth between the woman on her knees and the woman he was married to. As Tess bottomed out, he leaned forward and grabbed Zoe by the neck, bringing her in so he could kiss her. As their lips parted, Jacob caught a tangle of lips and tongue and teeth.

Jacob pulled Akira closer. "I might."

"Might what?"

He tugged at her earlobe with his teeth. Let it go when she sighed. "Might be okay with sharing my girlfriend or my wife. If I was there. If I was a part of it. If she was sharing with me."

A tremor went through her, so slight he would have missed it if he weren't hugging her close.

"You're just saying that."

He nodded at the scene on the stage. "I've fantasized about that. About two women…"

"Worshipping your cock?" She gave a soft snort. "What man hasn't?"

Despite her dismissive words, her hand wedged between them, right on his fly. He breathed a sigh of relief when his dick was released from its prison, the air-conditioned coolness of the room a welcome relief on his heated flesh.

She leaned back and was silent for a few heartbeats, staring at his cock, her hand barely encircling its thickness. She moved her hand up to the flared head and then down to the base. "I didn't get a good look at you in your car."

He had never given his size or the appearance of his cock much attention. It was a part of his body, one he had occasionally resented and cursed over the years when it wanted something his brain objected to.

But the way she was looking at him, the way she sounded as she held him, made him glad for whatever it was about him that pleased her.

"You're so big." She traced the veins. "So gorgeous."

He raised an eyebrow, vaguely discomfited by any part of

him being called gorgeous. But hey, if she liked his cock, he was more than happy.

"Poor baby," she crooned, and squeezed him. "You should have said something earlier. I bet this hurts."

"It does."

A triumphant, challenging smile lit her face. "Let's see what we can do about it." She turned her head in the direction of the couch next to them, where the couple had been kissing, and nodded once, regal command infusing her. "Jessie, can you come here for a second? I need a hand." Her lips lifted. "And your mouth."

A beat later, the pretty redhead crawled over. Her pupils were dilated with lust, a flush covering her skin. "Gladly."

"Akira…" He said her name because he was too excited to verbalize anything else.

She misinterpreted his utterance, however, as protest. "You said you might be okay with sharing. Don't you want to find out?" Her smile was tinged with resignation. "Or say the word, and we can opt for something a little less extreme."

He could say it, and she would back off. He glanced at the redhead, and at her date watching from the sofa, massaging the bulge in his pants, barely visible in the glow of the lighting illuminating the stage.

He turned back to Akira. Sweat collected at his hairline. Coming here had been a big step for him, but this…this was the pivotal moment, the second he either folded or went all-in.

Jacob nipped her lower lip, and then laved it. "I want to find out. Give me my fantasy."

Akira's narrow nostrils flared. In a flurry of red and orange chiffon, she came to kneel on the couch next to him.

There were no introductions made. Akira merely held his cock up for the other woman and nodded. Without another word, Jessie's lips closed around his cock and she swallowed him, her throat working. His hands fisted as he tried not to shout, to pull the audience's attention away from the stage. Though it would be difficult for them to even notice him, he realized with a single glance around the room. Everyone was making their share of noise, the scene on the stage proving far too inspiring to most of the viewers.

Akira slipped off the couch and pushed at his legs to make room. He spread them wider to accommodate both women, his mind spinning. This was overstimulation of a kind he had never before experienced.

He loved it.

Akira stroked Jessie's hair, and the girl eased up so Akira could also play, and then he had two tongues lapping his cock. A hand—he wasn't sure whose—fondled his balls, pulling and teasing them.

A motion out of the corner of his eye alerted him that Jessie's date had risen from their sofa and made his way over. He had his cock out, his hand slicking over the lubed surface as he watched the two women going down on him.

Their tongues tangled and rubbed against each other, occasionally sharing a kiss while they toyed with him.

His hands fisted on the couch next to him, unable to hold back the rough words. "I'm going to come."

"Good," Akira said, and cast the woman a glance that was both mischievous and competitive. "Whoever gets him there gets the prize."

The impish guest grinned. "The usual?"

"Mmm-hmm."

"What's the prize?" he managed to mumble, though how he was able to marshal any thoughts, he wasn't certain. His dick was wet with saliva, and two plump lips weren't far away.

"You'll see." Akira gripped his cock and swallowed it deep, prompting a helpless moan from deep in his chest. Jessie took her place the instant she withdrew. They alternated, the two of them, until he had no choice but to touch them, one hand buried in black hair, the other in red.

His balls drew up tight to his body, his spine tingling. When Akira's warm, wet lips surrounded him, he shut his eyes and blew, his thighs tensing as he flooded her mouth.

She withdrew, one finger swiping at the corner of her mouth and then licking it.

"You win." Jessie smirked and turned, leaning back against the couch, her legs spread.

"I did." Akira turned her hot eyes to the other woman and gave his spent cock a final pet, her blood-red nails a marked contrast to his skin.

She crawled between the other woman's legs, shoving her dress up, revealing strong, tanned legs. Nice legs. Still, Jacob wouldn't have hardened as quickly as he did for a pair of nice legs. No, it was Akira's lips and hands on those legs that turned him inside out.

Jessie moaned as Akira kissed her way up her leg. The girl's escort moved closer to their couch, his gaze locked on the two women, one hand around his thick cock. With the other, he pulled Jessie's hair out of her face. "You good, babe?"

"Mmm-hmm," she moaned, her voice rising when Akira found her pussy.

There was absolutely no need for quiet any longer. The three people were fucking on the stage now, Zoe holding Tess's face against her pussy while David fucked her from behind. Her muffled shrieks were silenced against the other woman's flesh.

Around the room, moans and gasps and cries rent the air. Jacob squinted, part of him wishing he could see the specifics of what each occupant was doing, but the stage lights illuminating the room only afforded him general impressions of locked arms and writhing bodies.

You'd implode if you could see everything.

This was true. His cock was already hard and ready to play again, thrusting obscenely out of the fly of his pants, still wet from the women's saliva and his own come.

Jessie's date fisted his hand in Jessie's hair. On her next moan, he took advantage of her open mouth to push his cock inside.

Instinct guiding him, Jacob slid off the couch so he could get on his knees next to Akira. The old Jacob might have asked for permission—hell, the old Jacob would have never been here—but this Jacob thought nothing of working Jessie's dress higher so he could have an unobstructed view of Akira's mouth on her pussy.

Akira's head came up for a second, and he caught confusion and arousal in her face before Jessie groaned and Akira returned to her place, running her tongue between the woman's plump pussy lips. She was so wet, Akira's face was covered in her juices. Her painted-red lips covered the woman's clit and she sucked, and Jacob had to squeeze his cock tight not to come right there.

Jessie squealed, and the vibration must have been enough

to send her lover right over the edge. He grunted and held her head still while he came.

Akira redoubled her efforts, and his vision became startlingly clear. He tracked every detail of this scene and the way she looked—the high flush on her cheeks, the way her breasts dangled below her, her utter absorption.

Not daring to think, he drew his hand over the elegant line of her back and over her ass, clutching the fabric of her dress.

She cast him another glance, and he saw surprise this time too. That he was taking any initiative, maybe? That he was still there? That he was embracing her desires?

He shifted her G-string aside with one crooked finger and found her pussy waiting for him, so hot and wet he almost died when he dipped inside.

This was his. The thought rooted in his brain with the kind of certainty he couldn't shake. The pussy he had stamped his mark on when he'd walked through the door. It was his, no matter who fucked it.

His hand came up, and he smacked the resilient flesh of her ass, indulging a long-held dark fantasy. Christ, how many times had he shamefully watched a porno where a woman was spanked until her ass was red, the flesh jiggling with every strike? How many times had he jerked off, imagining Akira in the place of those nameless actresses?

He smacked Akira again. A moan and a squeal. Again. Same response. Again and again, his heartbeat pounding, his poor, blood-deprived brain logging each movement she made that told him she liked what he was doing.

Hungry, he moved his hand lower, sinking his middle finger inside her. She was hot and wet, and she clamped down on his digit so hard he thought he might come from that alone.

She wiggled her ass, and he took the cue, slowly fucking her with the single finger before adding another. And another, until her ass was bobbing in the air as she fucked back for more.

Her moans and breaths were muffled against the other woman's pussy, but Jacob had pulled orgasms from her before. He could read her. She was so hot for it, so eager, it wouldn't be long.

For either of the women, it appeared. Jessie clutched her man's hand and came with a loud scream, rivaling the noises anywhere in the room.

Akira lifted her head, black eyes flashing and meeting his. "Don't...stop," she breathed.

"I couldn't."

A shriek brought his gaze to the stage. Zoe had released the clamp around the girl's nipples, and she was massaging her breasts. David's hand traveled between the girls' legs as he continued to fuck her from behind.

"Not that one," she sobbed.

"Tess," Zoe soothed, and captured her head between her hands. "You want to come, don't you?"

"Yes," she cried out.

"Then let us take it off."

Tess nodded reluctantly but let out a scream when David did just that, pain and pleasure mixing in the noise until Jacob couldn't tell what she was experiencing.

There was no mistaking, however, the pleasure racking her as she began to orgasm, or the way she bore back against the cock fucking her as if she would die without it.

He met Akira's eyes, and with one hand he removed the clamp on his nipple. There was pain as blood rushed to the previously constricted tip, but it was the kind of pain that made his balls tighten.

He reached below Akira and did the same to her breast, loving the way her eyes darkened before closing, the way her body shuddered as she grasped his thigh and Jessie's calf. He shoved his fingers deep inside her and ground his palm upward, agitating her clit. He held it there as she came and came.

"Perfect," he murmured.

CHAPTER 18

$\mathcal{J}$acob didn't look intimidated, or scared, or frightened, or remotely close to running away.

He looked hungry. Like a starving man facing a buffet.

Not for the first time since she had planned this night in a spurt of rash impulse, Akira wondered if she had done the right thing. She'd been so certain he'd be chased off within the first hour, either by disgust or intimidation. It was one thing for him to catch isolated glimpses of her sex drive. It was quite another to see the extent of her depravity firsthand.

But he seemed to be…loving this? He hadn't shied away from her hunger. He had embraced it. Gotten off on it.

Rough fingers drifted over her nape, and she shivered. They were leaning against the wall in the adjoining room, where a man worked a woman over with a whip. Still not severe pain, in her opinion, and since Jacob had yet to call it quits, she figured he agreed.

He was watching the scene, intent on the players but not furiously, violently engaged as he had been when Zoe was running the show. No surprise. Zoe was a master at crafting arousal with everyone in the room.

His pants were done up again, but his shirt was only half buttoned, resulting in a disheveled and slightly used appearance.

They hadn't exchanged much conversation after she had come, her face still wet with Jessie's pussy. Steve and Jessie had retreated to their couch to canoodle. The couple had met at her last party and become romantically involved. They were still in the cooing stage of new love.

Their lovey-doveyness wouldn't have been so annoying if every fiber of Akira's being hadn't urged her to also snuggle into Jacob's lap. That sort of behavior was out of the question when her emotions were so riotous.

So instead she had quickly tidied herself up and led him out of the room while the stars on the stage shrieked in orgasmic bliss.

Akira bent her head so his fingers could trail along her neck, and shivered before she caught herself.

Out of control. That was what he made her feel. Unable to command the world as she normally did. She'd lusted after many a man before, but never one like this. He gave her an indication of lust and she forgot everything in the world except getting him as close to her as possible.

She'd wrestled herself back in the other room, though. She had been the one controlling the show.

I might be okay with sharing my girlfriend or my wife. If I was there. If I was a part of it. If she was sharing with me.

Mentally, she snorted. Lies. Jacob would never be okay with such a thing.

He didn't look too upset when your head was between another woman's thighs.

'Cause it was girl on girl. Men's brains short-circuited

when breasts were rubbing together.

That must be why he looked so disgusted when Remy was fucking you inside a storage closet.

She blew out a breath and tossed her hair over her shoulder. This was dumb. She was neither his wife nor his girlfriend, so whatever they had been muttering about in that room would never apply to her.

His breath made the fine hairs on her neck perk up as he leaned down and whispered in her ear. "Have you ever been one of these people?"

What did that mean? She bristled, ready to defend her friends. "I am one of these people, darling."

"No." He nodded to the center of the room. "The show. Have you ever done that?"

"Been whipped?"

"No."

"Held the whip?"

His mouth quirked up. "As believable as you would be as a dominatrix, no. Have you ever been a part of the scene?"

She took a deep breath. "No."

"Why not?"

"I don't know. I've never found the right incentive." She lifted a shoulder. "Not that I haven't given a show or two. Just not on the stage."

"Hmm." His consideration was punctuated by the ecstatic cries of the woman. The noise filled something inside of Akira.

Depraved. The word was often tossed her way, and though she scoffed at it in public, internally she knew they were right.

Her life would be so much easier if she were different. If

only she were the quiet, biddable female her mother had craved. If she were the silent, malleable doll her father had attempted to browbeat her into.

Sweat gathered at her hairline, the smell of sex and the heat generated by multiple bodies suddenly overwhelming her. She needed air. "Excuse me," she choked out. "I have some hostess duties calling my name."

He straightened. "Right now?"

"Mm-hmm. Feel free to stay." She slipped out of his grasp, his fingers snagging on her hair as she bolted. She didn't stop to savor that bite of pain.

She should have known he wouldn't listen. His heavy footsteps sounded a few seconds behind her in the deserted hallway. "Akira."

Perversely, she hated how quiet his voice was. Nothing rattled him, did it? He had to be perfect at everything.

Including being perfect for you.

Terror shot through her. No. Nobody was perfect for her. Certainly not Jacob.

If only you could be the woman for him.

She whirled around to confront him, her skirt flaring with the movement. "Why aren't you done yet?"

His brow furrowed. She had to keep her gaze on his face because it was too tempting to glance down and stare at his chest, which was exposed by the sloppily fastened buttons of his shirt.

"Done with what?"

Done with me. "Done trying to prove to me that you can play in my league, Campbell."

"Akira…"

"No. Don't you do that. Don't you say my name like

that." She took a step closer. "Finish this. Drop the other shoe. Call me whatever names you want and get out." He would leave eventually, right? Better it be now. He didn't belong here. He couldn't be one of her regulars, her friend.

How would she be able to get enough of him if she could see him whenever she commissioned those elegant black invitations? She had been obsessed with him for years, and that was when she had been certain he hated her. If he came whenever she called, literally...

She would never be safe. Control would be gone, forever, because she would be in a continuous state of losing her head over him.

His mouth dropped open. "I would never call you..."

She made a sharp motion with her hand, cutting him off. "Go away. Go anywhere. I need a drink."

She swiveled and marched away from him, back through the main salon. The vibe had changed in here, as it always did when the night wore on. Skin flashed. Tongues tangled. Hands groped. Carnality replaced flirtation and lust reigned supreme.

Akira was so inexplicably mad, she couldn't even savor it.

A few feet from the bar, Akira was pulled up short by two large hands on her waist. She didn't have to look behind her to know who had captured her. Those paws could only belong to one person.

"Let me go," she said between her teeth.

His reply was immediate. "No. I don't think so."

If she didn't know stamping her foot would make her look like a child, she'd do it. "I mean it."

"Say the safe word then," he replied, matter-of-fact. "That's how it works, isn't it? You say the safe word, and I have to stop?"

Spy. She tried to force her mouth to say the word, but she couldn't. Just couldn't. "Go home."

"Nope." His hands slipped around her waist to meet in the front, clasping her tight. The sighs and moans and gasps around her were like a soundtrack. Her own personal orchestra of need.

Jacob's cock was thick where it nestled against her ass. He made no apologies for it. "I know shutting up is a challenge for you, but you're going to do it."

She snorted, unable to sputter anything else out.

"I'll take that as an agreement," he said. "Now, I get our history makes it difficult for us to have any kind of relationship. I've apologized, in every way I know how, short of cutting open my veins and bleeding for you. I told you I want you, and I understand you may be wary of that too. But you need to listen to me now." He brought his lips directly to her ear, so only she could hear. "There is nothing you could do that would make me want you less. Nothing you could do that would kill this desire for you."

"You don't even know…" she wheezed. "You don't know me."

He laughed. The bastard laughed! All low and amused. "Akira. I do know you. I'll wager I've known you longer than anyone else here."

"Length of time doesn't mean anything."

"You're right." He nudged her hair aside so he could kiss her neck. "But you noted how good my observational skills are."

"And what have you observed?"

"You seem to think I'm some sort of scared boy who's

going to run when I discover something about you I don't like. Which is stupid."

"Is it?"

"Yes. Let's get one thing straight. Nothing you do with your body would shock me. And nothing could disgust me."

She choked out the words, though a small, dangerous kernel of hope bloomed in her chest. "You say that now, but when…"

"No." His hand clenched over her stomach. "There is no *but when.*"

"You're a decent guy…"

"Decency doesn't equal a lack of a filthy imagination, Akira." His breath coasted over her shoulder. "Look around. Tell me what you see."

She glanced around her. They had drawn some attention, though she suspected friends were respectfully pretending not to listen in on their furiously whispered conversation. "I see sex."

"Yes. And love. And trust. You're not running from them. Why are you running from me?"

Because these people didn't love her as anything more than a friend, a fun hostess. Their bond might be deep, but it wasn't all-consuming.

Like it could be with Jacob.

"It's just…not the same," she said stubbornly. "I don't have to defend myself to you."

There was silence. "Perhaps I'm being unfair. I have to prove myself to you, right? That's the whole point of to-night?" Jacob's forefinger hooked under the laces on her corset. "Maybe you need to let me show you how bad I can be."

"What are you doing?"

Dumb question. His fingers too blunt and clumsy to figure out the knot on her corset, Jacob merely grabbed ahold of the lace and tugged. Hard. The material tightened uncomfortably over her breasts before loosening with a snap, becoming more lax when he yanked the ties through the eyelets.

They stood in the center of the room. The young bartender she'd hired more for his discretion and open-mindedness than his drink-mixing capabilities was slowly polishing a glass, but watching her. One by one, as more of her skin was revealed, heads turned their way.

Jacob pushed the corset down, taking her skirt with it, until the clothing pooled around her feet and she stood naked in front of the crowd. She closed her eyes, but she could feel gazes flicking over her as she stood there in nothing but a thong.

"I wish the stage was in here," he murmured. "You should always be the center of attention."

She said the only words she could manage. "This isn't like you."

Rough hands ran over her ass, petting her and parting her, stroking her flesh. "I'm just learning who I am, but I think this is exactly like me."

"So you'll what? Have sex in front of a crowd? I may not set myself up as the main attraction, but I've done it before. Have you?"

"No." His face rubbed against her hair, as if he were trying to absorb her through his skin. "But I think it should be fine. I'd be self-conscious, but I've been told I have a first-class ass."

The tug of lusty humor was frightening. A Jacob ready to embrace her desires wholeheartedly was a dangerous Jacob. She'd never recover when he slipped out of her grasp.

"Besides. These are your people. They're safe. Right?"

She inhaled, her resistance wearing thin. "Yes. They're safe."

His palms shaped her hips and stroked over her breasts, lifting them as if offering them to the crowd. "Should we let them have a taste?"

Debauch him. Stain his soul. Her greatest dream. All hers for the taking. Her fragile wall of resistance crumbled. Her head fell back against his shoulder, and she gave a helpless nod.

"Too bad," he said. "There are too many of them, and I don't want to wait that long."

"So pick a couple," she whispered, seduced by him and the sexuality thick in the air.

He paused, and she realized for all his posturing, he was still a newbie at this. She waved her hand at the men sitting on the closest sofa. Out of the corner of her eye, she caught the grin that split Remy's face as he grabbed his friend Ty's hand and strode toward them.

Jacob's chest touched her naked back, fine cotton brushing against her shoulder blades. "What do you want them to do?"

"I thought you were in charge," she said archly.

She felt him smile. "Why can't we both be in charge? Division of power."

Share the power? She shared a lot of things, but power wasn't one of them. Being top dog was easy.

Sharing was…uncharted territory. Scary. But so tempting, she couldn't resist playing with fire. She stretched her hand up behind her, scratching her fingernails over his cheek. "I want to be stuffed full, every inch of me filled with cock," she murmured. "There. That's my command. Now you decide how to get us there."

His exhalation ended in a groan. "I think I can do that." He gripped her neck. "On your knees."

Oh, yes. Yes, yes, yes, she wanted his quiet, stern, powerful voice. The voice she had fantasized over for years, the one that made her wonder if he'd play naughty professor or conquering knight with her.

She gave in to the pressure on her neck and sank to her knees. Whispers and rustles came from their audience, which was growing, murmurs of her participation spreading through the other rooms.

Jacob knelt next to her, beckoning Ty and Remy closer, until they were standing near enough for her to touch. He smoothed a strand of her hair away and pressed a tender kiss on her cheek. "Take out their cocks."

A month ago, she couldn't have imagined Jacob knowing what a cock was, let alone saying the word. Dear Lord, he had changed.

Or maybe he had stayed the same. Her perception had changed.

With shaking hands, she undid Remy's pants first, pulling out his erection and stroking it until he hissed a curse. He was already hard, but that was no surprise. The man was always ready to go. It was part of what made him so in demand in his profession.

"Now the other one."

He was objectifying the two men, turning them into tools

for her pleasure. Tools he could direct.

Desire made her lightheaded. How had such a relatively inexperienced man looked inside her and pinpointed her favorite fantasy?

The answer buzzed around her brain, but she swatted it away, not eager to confront anything deeper than physical pleasure. She glanced up at Ty. Of average height, the third man was built like a boxer, compact and muscular. He was a sweet guy, someone Remy had brought as a guest a few years ago and who had made enough of a favorable impression that she remembered to include him afterward. His smile was sweetly seductive, teeth flashing white against his black skin as he watched her, dark eyes hot.

She didn't let go of Remy's cock while she undid Ty's fly, her hand delving inside his trousers to find him hot and hard. His cock wasn't as long as Remy's, but it was nice and thick. He hissed out a breath when she stroked him.

"Suck him," Jacob directed.

"Which one?"

He paused, as if considering her question. "Either. Both."

Her thighs tightened, and she glanced between the two men. She held her hand up to Jacob's face. "Lick this for me. I need lube."

Holding her gaze, he licked her palm, his tongue rough. She enclosed her wet palm around Remy's cock, while using her other hand to steady Ty. He groaned as she swallowed him down, almost to the back of her throat, sucking him deeper with every stroke.

Remy's hand settled in her hair, his familiar fingers tangling as he directed her to take his friend harder, his growls of approval spurring her to her best performance.

Jacob's calloused hands slipped over her shoulders and her chest, weighing and cupping her breasts. She gave a muffled shriek when he pinched her nipple hard, the sound pulling a groan from Ty.

She was disappointed when Jacob eased her off Ty by holding her neck, but she couldn't resist the surge of arousal at his hand pressing against her vulnerable windpipe.

"He's going to come," he chastised her, his louder voice a sign of his growing confidence. "How will you be stuffed full of cock then?"

Akira licked her lips. "There's no shortage of men here."

She felt him smile. "You are such a greedy woman."

She was greedy. She always had been. It was one of her many shortcomings.

His hold gentled, until he was stroking her throat with his thumb. He pulled her around so she was facing him. Green eyes clashed with hers, filled with excitement and need.

"Remy," he said, his voice guttural. "On the floor."

She didn't look to see whether Remy obeyed. Who wouldn't obey that sharp bite of command?

She knew people were watching her, and that only drove her arousal higher. Fuck yeah. She should be the center of attention.

"I want you to ride him," Jacob instructed her.

Her breath caught. "What about you?"

His smile was sinful. "I'll be inside you too."

Weak, she turned and clambered on top of Remy, not concerned that her movements lacked grace. His cock was already encased in a rubber, ready for her. She straddled his hips, his face tightening when she sank down. He didn't move, well accustomed to the mechanics of a three-way, but pulled her tight to his chest.

Akira rested her forehead against Remy's collarbone and inhaled the scent of his expensive cologne. Foil crinkled. Remy slid his hands down her spine and opened her ass cheeks, and lube trickled between them. She hid her face in Remy's neck, relaxing as Jacob worked his thick dick inside her ass.

A whimper escaped her as he seated himself deep, until he could lay over her, his sweaty chest plastered against her back. "Good?" he rasped.

"Yes. Dear God, yes."

"I've never done this before." His confession was for her ears alone, wondering and hot. "How have I never done this before?"

Good. Possessiveness roared through her. She wanted as many firsts as she could take from him. "Do you like it?"

"Like isn't a strong enough word." His hips pulsed, as if he were unable to hold still. "Are you full yet?"

She moaned when he ground a little deeper. "My mouth's empty."

He gave a wheezing laugh against her shoulder at her plaintive tone. "So fill it."

Ty's cock was right there, bobbing next to her face. She turned her head, and he eagerly stepped forward, holding himself steady so she could swallow him.

Now she was filled. Completely surrounded by pleasure and thickness and desire.

Jacob and Remy started to move, their motions so in sync, they could have been doing this for years. The pleasure of them filling her overwhelmed her so much that she had to break away from Ty's cock, unable to maintain coordination.

The man fisted his erection and jacked it, her saliva making the surface slippery. With his other hand, he pushed back the hair that had fallen into her face, stroking her cheek.

Love. Trust.

Acceptance?

No. She stiffened.

Jacob mistook her, halting, Remy following his lead. "Problem?" Jacob wheezed.

"No." There was no problem. No problem at all. This was easy, and simple, and basic.

His hips resumed their motion. He used his grasp on her hair to jerk her head back, her neck arching. "You like this?"

The bite of pain made her pussy clench. Dear God. He was a natural. "Yes."

"Say it louder."

"Yes!"

"You like being stuffed with cock."

She whimpered as both men powered deep, their cocks hitting all the right spots. "Yes."

"Akira…" There was a depth of meaning in her name. He leaned in, until he could whisper in her ear. "I can feel him against me."

The words were all she needed to explode, her pussy tightening and releasing in hard contractions. Remy stiffened underneath her, his hands going to her hips and grinding her down as he ejaculated.

Jacob withdrew from her gently, but her fingers still curled when he slipped out of that muscular ring. In marked contrast to his gentleness, his fingers were rough and hard when they wrapped around her arms.

She was so boneless, it was an easy matter for him to pull

her off Remy and turn her around to face him. His jaw was set, eyes intense.

He tugged his condom off and gripped his cock, shiny streams of precome weeping from the slit at the tip. He pumped his erection, eyes at half-mast. "Where do you want it on you?" he asked, his deep, gravelly voice unrecognizable.

A no-brainer, when his eyes were tracking certain parts of her body like there were bull's-eyes on them. "Tits."

His face tightened, jaw flexing. One jerk, two, and he granted her wish, his streams of come dripping over her breasts and down her belly. White teeth flashed as he bit his lip to hold back his shout.

He sat back, his muscular chest rising and falling. The sharp bite of passion in his gaze had been replaced by hazy satisfaction, his face relaxed and open. His palm settled on her waist, and he tugged her closer to him, so he could run his fingers through the mess he'd left on her chest. He swirled his come around before grasping her breast, roughly massaging it into her skin.

The cries and ecstatic sighs of their audience filled the room. Ty contributed to the din, probably because Remy had recovered enough to tend to him. Akira didn't look. She was too busy staring at Jacob.

"You didn't need to be quiet. When you came, I mean," she finally spoke, uttering the first thing in her head. She hadn't thought much of it in the moment, but he had restrained himself when she and Jessie had gone down on him as well.

He hadn't muffled himself when she'd gotten him off in his sensible Toyota last night, though. She'd heard every noise he made as his semen filled her mouth, from his muttered dirty curses and directives to his manly sighs and groans and grunts.

He bent his head to her breast and licked the tip that he'd just come on. She shivered. "Yeah I did. That's personal."

"More personal than fucking me in front of an audience?"

A vertical line appeared between his eyebrows. "Yeah. Weirdly, yeah." Two fingers tilted her head up, so she could look him in the eyes. "Do you want that? To hear me?"

Now that she had considered it, yes. She wanted it more than anything. Her nod was perhaps too enthusiastic, which prompted a smirk she'd never seen him wear.

"Then let's get out of here. Take me up to your place."

CHAPTER 19

The party was in full swing downstairs. They should be staying and availing themselves of all the skin and flesh they could handle, gorging themselves on every hedonistic delight.

Instead, Akira was climbing the stairs to the third floor, which housed her personal suite of rooms, with Jacob trailing behind her, the silence between them heavy with sensuality. Because he wanted her alone.

Pleasure was meant to be shared, but she couldn't deny when he'd uttered those words her first reaction had been...yes. Absolutely. Please.

She shivered when his fingers curled around her hip, the touch steadying her. She was aware this action, taking him upstairs, meant she had succumbed entirely, her resistance and good sense crumbling in the face of short-term gratification.

Her impulsive nature wouldn't allow her to do anything else. That voice in her brain was whispering words of false comfort, that she'd be okay, that this was just for one night, that she'd be able to work him out of her system by tomorrow.

That voice was a liar. Yet she clung to it like a monkey.

They entered her bedroom, and she turned on the lights, suddenly nervous. Observant as always, his sharp eyes missed nothing, taking in the sparse furnishings and decor. Her living space wasn't fussy or opulent like the rest of the home, a conscious decision made to satisfy her various moods. Her bed was a well-made but functional king-sized four-poster, flanked by matching nightstands. Bookcases lined two of the walls, filled with her favorite titles, the ones she didn't want to bother going downstairs to hunt when she was sleepy. The only indulgence was the silk pillows and sheets. She did like the kiss of the cool fabric when she was in bed.

This wasn't something she'd share with him, but no other person had climbed into that bed with her. Not that she hadn't invited lovers into her home. They'd remained downstairs. Where they belonged.

Jacob took it all in in a single glance, and his gaze came back to her. She expected him to say something about the room, but he had other things on his mind. He dropped his jacket and shirt on the floor, and his hands went to work on the fastenings of his hastily donned pants.

"I want a shower," he said, his voice rough.

"Bathroom's right over…here." Her breath hitched when his pants hit the floor. She hadn't had a chance, as of yet, to fully appreciate his cock. It was thick and large, rising out of a nest of dark brown curls, each vein making her eager to follow those trails with her mouth.

She wanted to devour him whole, worship him with her body.

His mouth curled, as if he could read her mind. "You

need a shower too," he crooned.

An uninhibited Jacob was a potent Jacob. Her body grew wet anew at his heavy-lidded gaze sweeping over her loosely tied dress. "You think I'm dirty?"

"I know you're dirty. I want you in the shower so I can make you filthy."

Don't mind her. That was just her knees going weak.

He gestured for her to turn around. It only took a couple of tugs for the dress to fall to the floor. He held her elbow in an oddly protective gesture. "The shoes too."

She obeyed, stepping out of her high heels.

His thumb caressed her palm as he led her to the bathroom, courteously allowing her to pass before he entered. Her bathroom was the largest in the house, but it suddenly felt too small when he came inside and closed the door behind him.

"Into the shower," he directed softly.

Dumbly, she obeyed, shivering from the quiet command in his voice. She had known he would be wonderful at growling out orders. Her fantasies hadn't been able to comprehend how good he would be.

He stepped in behind her and turned both showerheads on. He winced at the initial coldness of the water, but didn't move away. Only a few frigid droplets landed on her skin. He was shielding her with his body.

Too good for you.

The night. That was all she wanted.

It's all you need, came that sly voice in her head. Was this what addicts heard when they were staring at temptation?

Jacob didn't have to stretch far to adjust the showerheads, and hot water hit her front and her back. He grabbed the bar of soap from the shelf and brought it to his nose. "Is this what makes you smell so good?"

"Maybe. I don't know what I smell like."

"It's close, but…" A frown crossed his face, and he lathered up the soap, running his hands over her breasts and belly and back. As the water sluiced the suds off, he leaned down and buried his nose in her neck, not budging when she gave an uncharacteristic giggle and shoved at him.

He inhaled deeply before straightening, his hands tracing a lazy pattern over her stomach. "Ah. Yeah, that's it. It's the soap and…you."

His fingers traveled lower to delve between her thighs. She flinched, and his touch instantly gentled.

"Sore?" he questioned.

"In the best possible way."

He gave her that cute, lopsided smile and continued, his hands running over her skin quickly and methodically. When she was sparkling clean, she took the bar of soap from him, using it on his front first.

Like him, she was efficient and brisk, though he gasped when she ran her lathered hand over his cock and balls. She pushed at his side, having him turn around so she could work on his back.

Akira sank to her knees, the better to appreciate the view. "I love your ass," she murmured, focused on her chore. These sorts of compliments could be uttered tonight.

He huffed out a laugh. "So you've said. Um. Thanks."

She ran her hand over the swell of his firm buttocks. "Hasn't anyone but me ever told you how glorious your ass is? I assure you, you were being checked out tonight."

"No. It's never come up in polite conversation."

She tapped him with the flat of her palm, loving the way

the tight muscle didn't budge. He made a muffled sound but didn't stop her.

Unable to resist, she leaned forward and bit one cheek. This time, the noise he made was louder, half aroused and half disbelieving. "What the hell are you doing?"

"Your ass is so bitable."

She did it again, her hand smoothing over his hip to find his cock thick and hungry. She wrapped her fist around him and jacked him lazily until he was fully erect, nipping at him when he attempted to get away.

He gave a groan and pivoted. She looked up the expanse of his body, loving the massive muscles of his belly and chest. His eyes were dark as he studied her. A trickle of water ran over her cheek, and she licked it away.

He shook his head, reaching past her to turn off the shower. "Bed."

Her hair lay wet on her back. The steam kept them warm for the moment, but that would fade. Still, she was too impatient for the short walk back to her bed. "Or here."

Large hands grasped her arms. She wasn't accustomed to being manhandled, but Jacob lifted her easily until her toes dangled off the tile. He touched his nose to hers. "The next time I get inside of you," he said deliberately, "I plan on being there for a long, long time."

She licked her lips. "Bed it is then."

Though he had her agreement, he clearly wasn't taking chances. She gave a shrieked laugh as he hauled her up in his arms and over his shoulder in a fireman's carry. "What are you doing?"

"Making sure you don't get away."

"I'm not going anywhere."

"So you say." Wet skin slid across wet skin. He grabbed a towel from the towel rack and rubbed it over himself half-heartedly before running it over her ass. He dropped the towel on the bathroom floor as he walked out, and slipped his palm over her bottom.

"And you say my butt is spectacular." His hand came down on her ass, not hard enough to hurt, but enough to warm. She gave a yelp that was abruptly cut off when his hand lingered, stroking the red mark he had left behind. "You like that?"

She wanted to smile but controlled it, fearful he would see it and think she was laughing at him. There was a hint of pleading in his question. He was hoping beyond hope that she liked his palm smacking her, because he clearly liked it very much.

She stretched her hands down over his back and scraped her fingernails over his ass, which clenched in reaction. "I adore it," she purred.

The room spun around her as he tossed her on the bed, and then he was there, a couple hundred pounds of aroused male bending over her, bracketing her smaller body. "Really?"

"Really." She drew her leg up, sliding it over his muscular thigh. "Would you like to do it again?"

Small white lines formed around his mouth. "Yes."

She craned up, touching her nose to his. "How many times have you jerked off, thinking of spanking my ass?"

A shudder ran through him. "Too many."

"Was I a bad little slut in these fantasies?"

He closed his eyes and inhaled, deep and slow. "I don't like that word."

"What word?"

He licked his lips, his shoulders tensing. "Slut."

"You seem to. In this context."

He opened his eyes, confusion darkening them. "I do."

She could tease him, but there wasn't a single bone in her body eager to send him into a shame spiral. "Doesn't make you a hypocrite. You like it because it makes me horny." She rubbed her nose against his. "There's no shame in being turned on by what turns your partner on."

He didn't respond for a long moment, during which she wondered if she'd made a critical misstep. Finally, his muscles relaxed, enough for her to feel safe about slipping back into the eroticism of the moment. "You didn't answer me. Was I a bad little slut in those fantasies?"

His smile was tight, but genuine. "You're always a bad little slut in my fantasies."

A dark thrill shot through her. She wanted those lips to form every dirty word in every language.

Can he do that in a night?

She shook off the depressing reminder of their fleeting engagement. "And in reality?"

"In reality..." He ran his hand down her side, tucked it under her back, and easily flipped her over, onto her stomach. "You're more than I could have ever imagined."

She arched her bottom so it was high in the air and stretched her arms out like a lazy cat. His hands coasted down her spine and over the curve of her buttocks. He hesitated there, his palms weighing her flesh. She pressed back against him, eager. "You've already fucked my ass. Don't be shy about spanking it."

"Not shy," he murmured, his full attention on her bottom. "Savoring."

The first blow made her rock forward and cry out, her head swimming with the heat of his touch. She glanced over her shoulder and found him staring at his hand, as if he didn't know whose it was.

"Again," she said, low.

His gaze met hers, and it was filled with such fierce exultation, she wanted to cry. Yes. This. This was what had hummed below his quiet facade all those years. He landed another, harder blow, and her head jerked forward and dipped, her breath catching in her throat.

Again and again, he slapped her, until her bottom was surely cherry red, and then his hand smoothed over her ass, easing below to find her pussy wet and inviting. He growled at the feel of her, grasped her legs, and pushed her onto her back.

His cock drove inside her, and she gasped. He paused, droplets of sweat making their way down his tense face. "Does it hurt?"

"Yeah." He started to ease out, but stopped when she continued speaking. "I like it when it hurts a little."

Dark excitement flared in his eyes as he slipped into their fluid give and take of power, his tone turning his next words into a tease instead of concern. "Is your ass sore?"

She arched her hips, eager for him to continue thrusting. He complied, albeit slowly. Far too slowly. "Inside and out. Thanks to you."

His lips opened, a rush of air escaping. His cock grew harder, the muscles in his arms flexing as his hips picked up speed. She spread her legs wider so she could take him deeper. He angled his body so he could see more of her face and body, alternating between her eyes, her lips, the jiggle of her breasts as he fucked her, the place where they were joined.

"You love to observe everything, don't you," she purred.

"I want to make sure none of this ever leaves my memory."

She ignored the shot of exultation those words brought and palmed his ass. He pulled back farther, made his thrusts slower, more explicit, allowing her to savor the sight of his thick cock, the condom wet from her juices, the tangle of his pubic hair scraping her shaved mound when he went balls-deep.

His hand slipped between them, his fingers unerringly finding her clit. "That first time, in your office," he spoke, his words almost soundless. "Do you remember when my mouth was between your legs?"

Like she could ever forget. But she couldn't lose a prime opportunity for pushing him. "Where between my legs? Be specific."

His cock hit a spot that made her whole body clench. Ridiculously attuned to her reactions, he dragged his hips back and forth in short strokes. "When I was eating this sweet pussy, licking every inch. Tongue fucking it. Sucking on your clit."

Oh. Yes. He had the makings of an excellent dirty talker.

His strokes shortened even more, so he was barely moving, simply agitating that bundle of nerves deep inside her. "Do you remember?"

She bit her lip and whimpered. "Yeah."

"I thought there couldn't be anything better than tasting you right here." He punctuated every word with a thrust.

"And now?"

He gave her a fierce, half-crazed smile. "There's nothing

better than fucking you."

"Am I the best you've ever had?"

His thrusts grew faster, less coordinated. "You know you are."

"Have I ruined you for all women?" Her greatest fear. Her greatest desire.

His eyes were unfocused as he slammed into her, his slippery fingers rubbing her clit so hard she couldn't make sense of anything. She was concentrating so intensely on her rushing orgasm she barely made out his response, hissed through set teeth as he fucked her.

"Yes."

WHEN JACOB ROLLED OFF HER BODY, AKIRA WANTED TO protest, but she bit her lip, keeping the weak words inside. Muscles too lax to move, she lay there, eyes closed, and listened to him stagger away to the bathroom. A jolt of satisfaction ran through her at his unsteady steps.

He was only gone for a few minutes before returning, his large, competent hands shifting her so he could pull the comforter over them both. She smiled sleepily when he cursed at the number of pillows on her bed, shoving most of them to the floor before wrapping himself around her. His heat seeped through her skin, and she gravitated toward it.

He pressed a chaste kiss against her temple and sighed, his chest moving up and down under her cheek. "Akira…"

Her toes curled at the deep tone, the way he dragged out the syllables, caressing every one with intimate knowledge.

His palm lifted her wet hair and fanned it out on his chest to dry. "Akira," he repeated, this time with a wondering air.

Perhaps it was the curious bubble of privacy they were in, in a house with revelers barely a floor away, but when she opened her mouth, the unguarded admission spilled out. "I love the way you say my name."

"I love your name." He kissed her shoulder, tightening his hold on her. The wiry hairs on his legs scraped her skin as he tangled them together. "I always thought it was the prettiest thing I'd ever heard."

"I hate it." She stiffened, waiting for him to pounce with a demand for further clarification.

He nuzzled his cheek against her hair. "Why?"

She shut her eyes. His voice was curious but not badgering. That was his trick, wasn't it? That patient stoicism. Never overtly demanding she reveal her secrets, but making it clear he would be there if she wanted to.

So damn seductive.

Her inner struggle didn't last long. Sighing, she gave him the shortened version. "My father—or really, my father's father—wanted two offspring, a boy and a girl. Allegedly, the story goes, after I was born my mother handed me to him and said, 'You better be satisfied with this one, because you aren't getting another one out of me.' All she had to do was win her father-in-law over to naming me 'Akira', and she turned me into a tidy little inside joke."

"I don't get the joke."

"Akira is traditionally a boy's name. Considered fairly unisex now, luckily for me." She smiled without mirth. "I think my mom knew when I was born I wouldn't satisfy him as a daughter, let alone a daughter and a son. Like, oh, you made me have a kid? Here. Have a useless one."

A fine thread of tension had invaded his limbs, but his

voice was measured when he spoke. "Mei should never have told you that."

As it always did, her soul soaked up his disapproval of her mother like grass soaking up rain after a drought. "It was the truth, I have no doubt."

"Doesn't matter."

Akira tugged the blanket higher. "Eh. It's not like I had some crazy illusion about how much either of them wanted me for me."

"How come you never changed it? If you hate it?"

Because I wanted to make it mine. Aware this was a frighteningly serious post-coital conversation but unable to shut it down, Akira lifted a bare shoulder. "I should have. My father's turned my last name into a joke too. But…I don't know. I wanted it to mean something more than what they intended for me."

She felt rather than saw him nod. His chest vibrated as he spoke. "I understand wanting to rise above your parents." Low and soft, the respect and validation in his words twined around her.

People respected her, but she didn't crave it from most. Not the way she craved it from Jacob. The way she had always secretly craved it from Jacob.

Never let people see what you want. Fear made her pull away, her hair leaving a damp trail on his chest. "That's right. Your parental baggage."

"Yeah. My parental baggage."

She crossed her arms over her chest, edging farther away so they were no longer touching. "Never would have pegged Harvey for being a little neglectful."

He rolled to his side and propped his head on his hand,

watching her far too closely. "More than a little. Why do you keep moving away from me, Akira?"

She froze. "I'm not." Lies.

"You are." Deliberately, he placed his hand on her belly. She flinched. "How many people know that story about your name?"

"My parents. Me." She forced herself to meet his eyes, hating every second of this vulnerable experience. Stupid, but in relating that anecdote, she'd felt like she'd cut herself open and laid herself bare. "You."

He stared at her, unblinking, for so long she was about to roll over and feign sleep. Then he opened his mouth, and she knew sleep wouldn't be happening anytime soon. "Until she was nine years old, I thought Kati was my daughter."

Akira stilled, her mouth half open. Jacob's eyes had darkened until they were almost black.

Was he even aware he had spoken? His gaze was unfocused. "What?"

A muscle clenched in his granite-hard jaw. His words were pulled from him as if against his will. "When I was nineteen, I slept with my dad's girlfriend." He flicked a glance at her. "I didn't use a condom."

Akira drew in a deep breath. "How could your dad's girlfriend…"

"Don't blame her. She wasn't much older than me. Twenty-two or twenty-three, maybe. And she hadn't had the easiest of lives." His smile was harsh. "I told you, my dad didn't think much. Just acted. She came in for an appointment, and the next week he was introducing us to the love of his life and moving her in."

Akira shook her head, flabbergasted. "How did you…how

did it happen?" Because there were few things in life she was certain about, but Jacob's belief in honor and decency was one of them. Sleeping with anyone's girlfriend would be an anathema to him.

"I don't really remember how. I was on break from college, we were home alone, we started drinking..." He was the one who cut physical contact with her now, sitting up and tucking the sheet around himself, as if to cover up his sins. "I fucked my father's girlfriend."

Her eyes widened. Dear Lord. Knowing how decent he was, she was certain the guilt from that single act of betrayal must have nearly destroyed him. She could still hear it, dripping from every disgusted word.

"To her credit, Jane broke it off with my dad that night, moved out of the house. But then a month later..." Jacob shook his head, a haunted look in his eyes. "She told my dad she was pregnant.

"I called her right away, as soon as I heard, and asked if it could be mine. She started crying. Said she didn't know, she didn't want a baby anyway. I told her she didn't have to worry, I would take care of my kid."

Akira's fingers tightened around his, imagining the overwhelmed nineteen-year-old boy Jacob had been. Hurting for him.

"She said my father had given her the same speech. And then begged me not to tell the man anything." Jacob's chest rose and fell with his deep breath. "She said she was considering giving up her parental rights and letting my dad raise the baby. That we could have a paternity test, but she would rather have a respectable middle-aged doctor raising her child than a nineteen-year-old kid."

"What did you do?" she asked, her voice hushed, matching his.

His eyes were filled with remembered pain when they met hers. "I went to him. I told him I had slept with his girlfriend and the kid might be mine."

"He was angry," she guessed.

"No." Jacob's laugh was short. "No. He chuckled. Said he would have done the same. Boys will be boys. How could I have been expected to resist a girl who looked like that?" He shook his head in disbelief. "How could anyone think that what I had done was right? I was wrong. We were wrong."

Akira's heart twisted. Fucking asshole. Jacob might have betrayed his father, but the man had betrayed him right back by showing his son that he was a shallow, pleasure-seeking jerk.

"My dad told me he didn't care who the biological father was, he had always wanted more kids. He was better equipped to take care of a child than I was. I should forget about my little slip. I was dumb. Young. So I played along. Thought I really could forget."

"But you couldn't, could you?" Akira possessed a healthy amount of heartlessness, but even she would have had trouble cheerfully burying the knowledge of her child's parentage when she saw the kid every day.

"How could I? Every time I looked at her, from the moment she was born...I made sure I lived close by, so I could be there for my brothers, yes, but mostly so I could be there for her." He shook his head. "When my dad divorced Mei, I'd about had it. I was somewhat financially stable. I was going to demand a paternity test. Take him to court if I had to. Anything to bring some stability to her life."

"Then he died."

Misery moved over his face. "Then he died."

She was silent for a minute. "What happened when she was nine?"

He wrapped his arms around his knees. "She came home from school one day, crying. It was close to Mother's Day." He motioned his hand in the air. "When kids make dumb little tin can pencil holders. She was sad she had no one to make anything for."

"God, I hated those days." Akira mimicked his pose. Decades later, she could well remember sitting in a corner on the days when other kids had been making crafts. Neither of her parents would have welcomed a gift.

"Me too." Jacob ran his hands through his hair, messing up the brown waves. "Jane, she kept in touch after she left. She would call on Kati's birthday and Christmas—still does. But they weren't close. Kati wouldn't have thought to make her something and send it to her.

"So I called her and told her it wasn't fair to Kati, if I was her dad, that she not know. I told her I was going to have a DNA test. She wasn't thrilled, but she didn't put up much of a fuss."

Instinctively, Akira knew why Jacob hadn't just broken the news without proof. The little girl who had been sobbing at Harvey Campbell's funeral had loved their father. Jacob wouldn't have wanted to mess with her memories based on a hunch and bad timing.

Jacob's voice was shaking as he spoke. "I got one of those kits off the Internet. Swabbed her mouth. Told her it was a little game."

She knew the answer already, but she spoke it out loud.

"You weren't her dad."

His lips turned white at the corners. "No. I wasn't. I'm not."

She stroked her hand up his back, knowing exactly how he had felt. Some men might have been thrilled to be told they weren't a baby's father. Not Jacob. "You were devastated."

He looked at her, his eyes swimming with unshed tears. "It was like someone took her away from me. In the back of my head, I assumed, you know? And then that was gone. I was just a sibling. A half-sibling. She wasn't mine."

Akira didn't often find herself in the role of comforting anyone. So it felt a bit awkward for her to tug him down until she reclined on her pillow, his head lying on her chest. Her fingers tangled in the cool silk of his hair. "She's still yours."

He gave a shuddery breath and pressed a kiss against her nipple. Not in a sexual manner, but she couldn't resist the tingle that ran through her.

"Who knows about this?" she asked.

"Jane. Me. Now you."

"Why would you tell me?"

"Because I wanted to. Because you made yourself vulnerable to me."

She shifted. "This isn't on the same level as my telling you about my name."

"That's not the only time you've made yourself vulnerable," he replied quietly.

Intuitively, she knew he wasn't just talking about these past few weeks, but the fact he'd always been a weakness in her otherwise impenetrable armor.

That he was so obviously aware of this dynamic made her

want to crawl out of her skin.

"Maybe also because I wanted you to understand better why I was the way I was," he continued, his words raw. "Why I've been so careful, all my adult life. I couldn't be like him. Selfish. Hedonistic. Impulsive. Do you see?"

She didn't respond, but she ran her fingernails up his back, soothing him as best she knew how. By his shuddery sigh, she could tell he liked that, so she did it again.

She did see. She understood why he was a little fucked up and broken inside. She saw why he had walled himself away from her, from anyone who jeopardized his responsibility to his family. She understood why he had hated himself for being so attracted to her.

She saw all of those things, including the sure knowledge she was in big, big trouble. Because she wanted this man, in her bed and in her life. And she couldn't have that, couldn't risk hurting him as much as his asshole of a father had.

Selfish…check.

Hedonistic…check.

Impulsive….check, check, check.

How was she any different than Harvey Campbell?

His lips closed around her nipple, and she shut her eyes, biting her lip. A few hours. She would be selfish for just a few more hours.

And then she would end this.

CHAPTER 20

$\mathcal{J}$acob woke up to the sound of clothes rustling. His body was spent—he was fairly certain his cock wouldn't be able to rise for another forty-eight hours, given the exertions of the previous night—but he nonetheless turned toward the noise with a welcoming smile, his eyes blinking open.

Only to scramble upright, clutching the blanket over his lap like a scandalized virgin. "Jesus."

Harris turned from where he was draping something onto the subtly patterned burgundy armchair in the corner of the room and peered at him. "Mr. Campbell. Good morning."

"Morning." Jacob cleared his throat. "Uh. Can I help you?"

"No, sir, I am here to help you." Harris nodded at the neatly folded garments on the chair. "Your clothes, pressed. Breakfast is waiting for you downstairs. Your car will be brought to the front when you are ready to leave."

As subservient as Harris's words were, there was a hard purpose in his eyes that told Jacob he wouldn't hesitate to help him along if Jacob dallied.

"Where's Akira?"

Harris linked his hands in front of him. Was he wearing gloves? Yes. Those were definitely gloves. What casting department had sent this man over, anyway? "Ms. Akira had to leave."

Jacob frowned. It was Sunday. Though Akira might happily go into the office on the weekends, workaholic that she was, he didn't think she would do it when they were lying in bed together. "Was there an emergency?"

"No. She had to leave on a business trip. She told me to convey her gratitude for the evening and ensure you had all you needed before you left."

Jacob stared at him, a fission of temper igniting in his chest. "A business trip." One she hadn't told him about last night or before she left.

Yeah. Right.

He was getting the bum's rush, and she didn't even have the balls to do it to his face.

Harris inclined his head ever so slightly. "Yes, sir."

Had last night meant nothing? Didn't she get that he had bared his soul to her? Hell, he had never told anyone the stuff he had said to her. About Kati, and her mother, and his father. They were things his brothers didn't even know.

It doesn't matter. She doesn't think you're in her league.

Was that it? Did it really come down to sex? Maybe last night hadn't been up to her standards…

He squashed the demon of insecurity the second it hatched. He had felt her coming around him, had ridden her to exhaustion. The hell he hadn't made it great for her.

He thought of the way she had curled away from him after talking about her name, the naked vulnerability in her eyes when he had kissed her cheek and her forehead afterward.

No, this wasn't about him. This was about her. And normally he'd be sympathetic and understanding, but damn it, she hadn't even stuck around to hash this out properly. That rankled. A lot.

He wanted to growl, but the man watching him impassively had nothing to do with him and Akira. Harris was merely doing his job. So Jacob nodded and choked out between gritted teeth, "I don't need breakfast. Give me ten to dress and I'll be out of your hair."

Harris hesitated, and in that moment, Jacob caught something terrible on his face: Pity.

"Ten minutes," Harris repeated.

Nostrils flaring, Jacob launched out of bed as soon as the other man departed, and threw his clothes on, his anger insulating him from his true, more depressing emotions. He was about to turn and leave when he caught sight of the box on Akira's nightstand.

His jaw set. She carried the thing with her from work to her home and back again each day, like a toddler with a security blanket. There wasn't a chance in hell she wouldn't take it with her on a business trip, even if it was a last-minute deal.

Trip, my bitable ass.

Jacob glanced at his watch. He still had six of his ten minutes left. Plenty of time.

Five minutes later, he set the box on the nightstand, its lid removed and pushed to the side. He didn't glance inside. That wasn't his business. He did, however, find a notepad and a pen in her nightstand next to a box of condoms that was nearly empty, thanks to him.

A minute later, he left the room, not looking back.

CHAPTER 21

*A*kira was miserable.

She wasn't accustomed to being miserable, so it was particularly worrisome. Friends didn't help. Work was a chore. She could throw another house party, but the thought made her feel nauseous. It would only remind her of Jacob.

Too many things did. In the past month, she'd been certain she could get over him, but then she'd see someone with messy hair or hear a particular intonation in a stranger's voice or look into a pair of green eyes, and she fell in the vortex of her memories.

She touched her purse, as if to reassure herself that the note Jacob had left her the morning after she had hid from him like a coward was still there, nestled in a place of honor next to the precious contents of her grandmother's puzzle box.

You might be able to forget about him quicker if you didn't haul his damn letter around.

How could she not, though? She had read it so many times, the paper was becoming dangerously fragile. She could recite it from memory.

I figured out how to unlock this the last time we were in your office. Sorry, I just didn't want my time with you to end. I suppose you've decided differently.

I won't chase you again. But if you decide to take a risk and come to me, I won't turn you away.

I like you. If you let me, I could love you. All of you.

She jerked her hand from her purse as the elevator doors opened. She climbed inside with a throng of other people and pressed to the back. Since that morning, when she had sat silently curled up on the bed in a guestroom until Harris told her Jacob had left, she no longer had any desire to be the center of attention. Let someone else be the party girl, the star. Let someone else shut the club down. Let her be lost in a sea of people.

Manhattan was a good place to let that happen. She was here to meet with the Anderson Group for what would hopefully be the final time. The due diligence was completed, the sales and purchase agreement vetted. All the CEO had to do was accept her final bid, damn it, and sign on the line.

She could have sent her attorneys. The man had taken a strong dislike to her, so he might respond better to someone else wooing him. However, she'd never hidden behind a bunch of old white men before, and she was hardly going to start now.

Even if she was miserable. The corners of her mouth turned down.

The elevator doors opened, and the other passengers milled about her, disembarking. Preoccupied, she was about to step out, when a booming voice filled her ears. "Hello, Akira."

She froze. She would know that upper-crust English accent anywhere. No, no, no. Not now. Not ever, but especially not now. Bracing herself, she lifted her head and looked up into her father's face. "You."

"Me."

In a move that had become instinctive, she glanced around for cameras. No one else was in the elevator. Probably for the first time since she had seen him after his damn show had started, he was alone.

He accurately interpreted her look. "No, no cameras today." He leaned in, prompting her to take a step back. He was always doing that, forcing himself into places where he wasn't welcome.

Guilt flashed through her. Like she had always done to Jacob, barging in to his space?

No. He had stormed her castle that last time. She'd told him to stay away. Then she'd let him ride her to blissful exhaustion, but she'd warned him, hadn't she?

Hiro hit the ground-floor button.

Her hand tightened around her purse. *Ignore him.* "Excuse me, I have an appointment."

"You'll find it's been canceled."

She halted and turned on her heel, barely noticing when the door closed behind her. "What?"

"It's been canceled." Her father gave her a thin smile. Hiro was a handsome man, she supposed, tall and slender and elegant. Everyone, particularly Mei, claimed Akira resembled him.

Only in looks, she assured herself. The thought of favoring **him in** anything else sent a chill down her spine.

"Who canceled it?" Though she knew she was off her game, she slipped into the persona that dealt with her father the best. Rich bitch.

"Anderson decided it was unnecessary. He and I have come to a gentlemen's agreement regarding the sale of his European division."

The blood rushed in Akira's ears. The business she had spent months vetting and studying and courting had been purchased out from under her? By her own father? Rage guiding her actions, she slammed her fist on the emergency-stop button. The car came to a swift, jerking halt.

"You're bluffing," she said, attempting to modulate her voice. *Don't let him see what this is doing to you.* "Anderson wouldn't do that. That's bad faith."

Hiro shrugged. "This CEO has a surprisingly rigid moral code for someone who owns bars." The man said the word *bars* like he might *crack dens,* showcasing the strange morality that made his show and family acceptable but her legitimate business an embarrassment.

"What does that have to do with me?" Akira demanded.

"He doesn't like you. Thinks you're too wild."

Akira's nostrils flared. "You released a *sex tape*."

Her father lifted a shoulder. "Yes. We discussed that. A regrettable mistake, on my part, but it was a private moment with my future wife never meant for public consumption."

Fucker. She wondered how the bastard managed to bleat any of that with a straight face. Her breaths were coming faster than she'd like, but there was little she could do about that. "How did you know?"

"Know what?"

"That I was going after Anderson? It was kept under wraps."

He clucked his tongue, rocking back on his heels, clearly

enjoying this moment. "You really shouldn't talk business in front of your driver, Akira."

A stab of sorrow hit her heart. Kevin? One of her own had betrayed her?

She pushed her hurt aside to deal with the shark standing in front of her. "Why did you do this? You hated being a hotelier. You don't know anything about this industry."

Her father cast a measuring glance at her hand. Carefully, she uncurled her fist and flexed her fingers. "You know why."

Of course she knew why. Ever so slightly, her shoulders slumped. "You want something from me."

"You could have answered my phone calls," the man pointed out gently. "And we wouldn't have to play this ridiculous game."

"This seems like a high price to pay to get me to guest star on your show."

Self-satisfaction oozed out of him. And why not? He had the upper hand. "Oh, no. Not guest star. We're thinking semi-regular. I've even negotiated an opening credit for you."

He sounded like she should be happy. Was he delusional? She linked her hands together to stop their trembling. "Are ratings that bad?"

"I prefer to be proactive. They've offered Brandy," he said, referring to Chloe's daughter, "her own spin-off. She's a big part of the ratings grab. I can't chance the new baby will be enough to pull viewers in."

Akira experienced a momentary pang of sympathy for her unborn half-sibling. She couldn't say much for her childhood, but at least she hadn't been a tool to score big with Nielsen. "But I will?"

His lips twisted. "People find you fascinating. For whatever reason. You only need to come in a few times a season. You barely have to think. The producers manage most of the scenes."

So much for reality television. "Oh, is that all?"

"This will benefit you as well. We can discuss compensation. Plus, there's no price you can put on this kind of publicity."

"I assume," she bit off, "you will also immediately back off this gentlemen's agreement you have with Anderson."

"And recommend he close the deal with you." Her father spread his hands. "We all win, Akira."

"This is an expensive risk you took," she remarked. "If I tell you to go fuck yourself in the ass, you're stuck with a hundred underperforming bars in Europe."

He looked unbothered by that thought. "I have the money to burn, and it won't be the first time I've jettisoned some establishments. Hell, maybe it could even be a nice inheritance for your little brother and sister."

For a second, she considered his offer. She could open her own places in every market where Anderson was doing business, but that would take her years, and she'd be competing with this chain for market share.

This purchase would rocket her to the next level. Finally, the Mori name could mean something great again, not the punch line of a semi-scripted TV show. She would be able to stand for something.

All she had to do was bend to her father's will.

The silence ticked around them, the air in the enclosed elevator quickly growing hot.

A thin trickle of sweat ran down Akira's back. *Bend. What does it matter?* Everything came with a condition. Love was a weakness, used to exploit, used as a carrot and a whip to force compliance. There wasn't a single thing in life that came without strings.

Her fingers closed on the supple leather of her purse. *If you let me, I could love you.*

I won't turn you away.

There had been no strings in Jacob's note. No strings on his friendship, or his body. He had simply opened himself up to her, leaving the choice of grabbing him in her hands.

Can't care about him, can't let him see, because...

Because why?

Because someone will use him to manipulate you.

Like Jacob's rock-solid strength would ever permit anyone to use him as a pawn.

Because he could use your feelings to manipulate you.

Like his honor would ever let him dangle the promise of his love out of her reach while she grasped for it.

She inhaled, her world coming into laser-sharp focus, every priority slotting into place. So she was going to lose the business she had hoped to purchase. There were more bars in the world, and if her father wanted to fight her on every damn one, so be it. She was on guard now.

There was only one Jacob, and the only one stopping her from having him was herself.

Strength filled her, shoring up the parts she hadn't known had weakened at some inexplicable point. *I could love you.*

"Keep the bars," she enunciated every word. "I'm not playing this game."

Confusion spread over her father's face. Had he expected her to fall apart and take his ridiculous deal?

He clearly hadn't bargained with her in a long, long time.

"You think I'm bluffing."

"On the contrary, I'm hoping you're not. I remember how much you despised running a business. The constant demands on your time, the millions of boring minute details?" She gave him a nasty grin. "Buy the damn things. I give it maybe three months before you're looking to unload them."

"Not to you, I won't."

She lifted her shoulder. "I have more money and power than you could imagine, because I earned it. Because I know how to work my ass off." She flicked her fingers at him. "Seriously. Keep them. I can easily crush you."

"This isn't over—"

"It is over. Because if you pull a stunt like this again, I swear I will call every reporter I know and tell them that delightful little story of how you forced my mother to give birth to me. That would be some lovely publicity when you're gearing up for the birth of your new child, hmm?"

He stilled. "What?" His thin lips barely moved.

She smiled, but there was no amusement in the gesture. "Oh, yeah. She told me, about a year before she died."

"You don't know what you're talking about. Mei—"

"Mei didn't want children. But your clock was ticking, so you lied and told her she wouldn't get pregnant. Then came me. Surprise."

Her father made a visible effort to bring himself under control. "I hardly locked her in a dungeon."

"No," she said, a strange sort of calm settling over her as she cut this cancer out. There was no room for anything but complete control. "But she was nineteen. You were thirty-two. You knew exactly how to emotionally browbeat her, didn't you?"

He fiddled with the cuffs of his sleeves, straightening the suit. "You have no proof of any of this."

"Maybe not. But you'd be surprised how ready the media would be to believe someone who has literally nothing to gain." She paused. "I may also have a couple of Mei's diaries. I haven't read them yet. But how much do you want to bet they chronicle the life she had to live with you." Her smile wasn't pretty. "You could say a lot about Mei, but people respected the hell out of her."

His face mottled with color. His next words were the equivalent of waving a white flag. "I should have let her get rid of you. If my father hadn't been harassing me for an heir—"

"You didn't want an heir. You wanted a brainless puppet."

"Better a puppet than a slut."

"Oooh." Akira tilted her head and smiled. "Are we resorting to your pet names already? Frankly, Daddy, I'd rather be a slut for sex than a whore for fame."

Quick as a flash, his hand wrapped around her upper arm. His grip was too hard, the fingers digging into her flesh. "You listen to me, you little…"

Blocking the pain, she glanced up at the unobtrusive camera in the corner of the elevator. "Careful, Daddy. Your cameras may not be in here, but that doesn't mean we aren't being watched. How would manhandling your daughter play to your viewers?"

He released her immediately and took three steps back, until he was plastered against the opposite wall. She looked at him, really looked.

He was old. Old and pathetic. He thought her business was at the center of her heart, so he had attacked it. Dumb. She loved her work, but if she lost it tomorrow, she would recover. Rebuild her empire.

The same couldn't be said of Jacob.

No, her father would never be able to hurt her, ever. He couldn't know what was in her heart because he had no idea how to have a heart.

Hiro breathed deep, his face mottled. "You're an idiot. This is going to set your business plan back."

It probably would, but she could manage that. Contrary to what so many people believed, she was no stranger to rolling up her sleeves. "So it gets set back." She pushed the emergency button to resume the elevator operation.

"You think I don't know how hard you've tried to prove yourself to me?"

"Yeah. I'm done with that. We're done," she said, her voice so cold and stiff her father made no response. "You never contact me again. Never look at me again."

He was silent until they reached the ground floor. As the door opened, she heard his bitter words. "So self-righteous. You are no better than me. You can try for the rest of your life, but you'll never be better than me."

Her fingers slipped over her purse. "That's where you're wrong." As she spoke, the truth washed over her, filling her with confidence. "Listen up, Pops. You got lucky today, but for future reference... I won't strike first, but I will strike back. Hard. Probably best for you to keep that in mind."

She dropped her sunglasses over her face. Her feet picked up speed, until she was running as fast as her heels would allow by the time she cleared the huge glass double doors and spilled onto the crowded sidewalk. Yes, she was better than that man.

And she deserved the best.

CHAPTER 22

"*What* do you mean, he's not here?"

Ben stared at Akira from inside the door to Jacob's home. "Ah. I'm sorry. He's not here right now."

Akira closed her eyes. This was not a part of the script. Jacob was supposed to be home when she came to her senses, like a steadfast rock. Rocks didn't roam.

"Well, where is he?" Her voice rose higher on the last syllable, despite her best effort to appear her normal, unflappable self.

To be fair, that was probably already a lost cause. She'd hopped on a plane from New York to San Francisco, rented a car since Harris was now investigating her driver, and driven straight here. Her hair was disheveled, falling out of the bun she'd hastily tucked it into, and her clothes had definitely been far more crisp at eight a.m. eastern time. She supposed she could have freshened up, but all she'd managed to do for the past however many hours was repeatedly call Jacob's phone—which went straight to voicemail.

Ben cocked his head and studied her. "Do you want to come in for a minute?" he asked, not answering her extremely

293

important question.

No. She didn't want to come in. She wanted Jacob. "Is he at his cabin?"

"Nope." He stood away from the door and gestured. "I think you should come in."

God, did she look like such a mess that the kid had to use that coaxing tone on her?

Man, not a kid, she corrected herself. Her relationship with the other Campbells was different from her relationship with Jacob, simply because she didn't see them as often. In her head, Ben would forever be thirteen, a pimply teenager she had been peripherally aware of.

She'd always thought he was the easiest of the Campbells to like, an impression reinforced by the stories Jacob had recently shared with her about his siblings. A little less intimidating than either of his brothers, Ben was shorter and more muscular, with a ready gentleness in his eyes. The brawn, Jacob had called him, but it was brawn combined with a mischievous kindness.

She scrubbed her eyes, prepared to throw herself on that kindness. "Ben—"

"It's cold outside, and you aren't even wearing a jacket." A heavily calloused hand closed over her elbow and guided her inside before she could protest further.

She automatically looked down at her thin blouse and skirt, her suit jacket having been misplaced at some point during her frantic cross country return trip. It was chilly, but she'd been chilly since she'd left Jacob lying in her bed, so really, what difference did it make? "I was on the East Coast this morning."

"Ah, that explains it. Are they experiencing that spring I

hear so much about?"

"Yeah, I..." She trailed off, realizing Ben had led her through the foyer and into the kitchen so quickly she had barely processed where she was going or what the interior of the house looked like. She eyed him, reconsidering her initial impression of his smarts.

Ben's smile was innocent. "The others are right out back. Here." He shrugged off his hoodie and draped it around her shoulders, before opening the back door.

Others? She balked at the doorstep and clutched Ben's well-worn sweatshirt, not eager to have to deal with Jacob's entire family. "Ben, if you could..."

"They might know where Jacob is."

"*Do* they know where he is?" she snapped.

"They might."

She gritted her teeth at the stubbornness she could suddenly see underlying the man's genial kindness. Ben wouldn't tell her anything until he was good and ready.

Sure, she could hop in her car and try the cabin, but what if Jacob wasn't there? A wild-goose chase was the last thing she needed right now. "Awesome," she muttered.

He didn't comment on the sarcasm in her tone, merely gestured for her to precede him.

Like most houses in this neighborhood, the first floor was a full story up from street level. At the landing outside, she stopped, looking down at one of the most beautiful gardens she had ever seen. Small but lush, it was so riotous with color she was startled out of her one-track search for Jacob. "You did this?"

Ben's grin was pleased. "Yup. Me and Connor. Well, I did the heavy lifting, of course." He leaned over the railing.

"Hey, guys, look who's here!"

Left with little choice, movement restricted by her narrow skirt, Akira followed Ben down the metal staircase.

The rest of Jacob's family was sitting around a sturdy but inexpensive patio table tucked under the overhang of the stairs. Kati stared at her, her pretty round face slack with surprise and curiosity. Connor's reaction was more restrained. He sat back in his chair and crossed his ankle over his knee, watching her with an assessing look.

There was a third person sitting there, a skinny, young kid wearing a bow tie. The boyfriend. Damon? Darrell?

She dismissed him. He wouldn't know where Jacob was, so he could officially be classified as Not Important.

Lemonade sat in a pitcher on the center of the table, a tray of cookies next to it. Akira had no doubt this was a common event at this cozy home, the family gathering around a table in the beautiful backyard as they ate and chatted.

"What are you doing here?"

Kati's borderline-rude question startled Akira out of her introspection. The query arrowed into her, making her wonder. What the hell was she doing here? This sort of domestic familial bliss was not her thing.

But Jacob is your thing.

That was right. Still, her voice was more subdued than she hoped when she answered. "I'm looking for Jacob."

Kati's eyes narrowed. "Well, he's not here."

Steel in your backbone. Ice in your veins. Just for now, until she found Jacob. She straightened and gazed down at Kati.

"So I hear. Where is he?"

"I'm not telling you. And I know your tricks now, so

don't think you'll be able to figure it out on your own."

"Kati," Ben said, a gentle sting in his voice. "Relax."

"Why do you want Jacob anyway? He already gave you my jewelry box."

Akira raised an eyebrow at that. "Your box?"

Kati had the grace to flush, but she lifted her chin. "It was Mei's. She gave it to me. It was mine."

The kid had potential as a worthy adversary. Her words contained a good deal of sense, pricking the part of Akira's conscience bothered by the fact that the girl did have a valid claim to Hana's box. So she nodded. "You can come over next week and pick something out of Mei's jewelry collection. I was going to sell it and give the money to charity, but a piece or two won't make much of a difference."

Kati blinked. "Uh—"

"That won't compensate you entirely," Akira continued smoothly. The box was worth more to her than any single piece of Mei's jewelry. Hell, it was worth more to her than all of Mei's jewelry. "But it'll be a stopgap measure until I can work something else out."

Connor linked his hands over his flat belly. "That's not necessary." He shot Kati a stern look when she stirred. "None of it. We were happy to return it to you."

Ugh, these men. Why wouldn't they just let the women deal amongst themselves? Everything would be so much easier. "Excuse me," she said coolly. "My business is with Kati."

"Kati's only seventeen."

"I can contract with a minor." She paused, not looking away from Connor. "But if that's really a problem, when do you turn eighteen, child?"

"In two months."

"There." She gave Connor a thin smile. "In two months, she and I can deal with each other as adults."

Connor returned her smile. The brain, Jacob had called him, and Akira didn't doubt it. There was something calculating in his gaze that none of his siblings shared. "Hey. Darren."

Darren. That was right. The boyfriend.

"We have some family business to take care of. You mind excusing us?"

"Darren can stay," Kati protested.

"Nah, it's cool, Kati," Darren said, shooting wary looks at Connor. "I gotta go home. I'll pick you up for ice cream later?"

Connor broke their gaze to turn narrowed eyes on the boy. "Are you asking us, or are you asking her?"

"Um. Both of you, sir."

"They don't have any say in whether I go out or not." Kati glowered. "Pick me up at seven."

"Where are you going for ice cream?" Ben asked mildly.

Darren swallowed, shifting his gaze between each brother as if he were unsure which one might attack. "Mabel's?"

"Hmm." Ben clucked his tongue. "Really? Are you sure about that?"

"Uh—that is…"

Kati let out a low growl, sounding so much like Jacob, Akira hurt. "Oh my God. Stop teasing him. Come on, Darren. I'll show you out."

"Okay." Darren folded his hands together and inclined his head slightly. "Namaste."

Ben gave an audible groan. Though Akira had just found

herself annoyed by the brothers, she couldn't help her smirk when Connor crossed his hands over his chest, stared at Kati's boyfriend, and shook his head once. "No."

Ben coughed. "See you later…Darren."

It could have been a cheerful sendoff, if it weren't for the silky menace in his voice. Darren looked more than a little worried as Kati dragged him out, giving Ben and Akira a wide berth.

"Aren't one of you going to follow them?" Akira asked dryly. "He could be trying to take advantage of your sister right on the front stoop."

"I would, but Kati's still cranky I sat between them during the movie last night." Ben wiggled his eyebrows.

Akira pounced on the kernel of information. "So Jacob's been gone since yesterday?"

Ben rubbed the back of his neck. "Jacob's been gone for a couple of weeks, Akira."

Akira froze. Jacob wouldn't have up and left his family on a whim, not for that length of time. Unless he had desperately needed to be alone. Maybe because he was in pain?

Had she hurt him so badly?

When she had sat in the guestroom that morning, she'd stared at the bedspread as she waited for Jacob to leave and told herself she was letting him go for his own good. So he could be happier, so he could have what he deserved.

Of course you hurt him. If you felt like you'd ripped your arm off, imagine how he felt, writing you a note telling you he could love you.

Akira clutched her purse, lead weighing in her belly. "Please tell me where he is." Unaccustomed as she was to pleading, her words were halting, unsteady.

Connor was silent, but Ben fixed her with a sympathetic look. "Akira, see…I don't know if we can. He's in a strange mood—"

"Strange how?"

Ben shrugged. "Grim. I mean, he's always serious. But this is extra dark. Even for him."

"Dark?" she asked faintly. Jacob only appeared taciturn at first glance. When he brought a person into his world, he was warm and funny and clever… He brought her dinner and perfect roses and gave her his socks.

Darkness had no place in his soul.

Connor was studying her with an intensity that would disturb her if she weren't already so disturbed. "We know you guys had a run-in a while ago when he came to you about Mei giving Kati that thing." He cocked his head. "Do you know anything about why Jacob's acting this way?"

Unable to say anything, Akira looked away. She couldn't lie to Jacob's brother, but whatever was between them felt far too new and unsettled for her to open up to the man either.

Jacob had kept their unusual relationship from his family. She had suspected he would, and she didn't fault him for it. But it didn't feel right to come clean to them without him here.

"See, the reason I ask is because it's really out of character for him to call us with no warning and tell us to come stay with Kati for an extended period of time like this. So if you did have something to do with him running off…"

"Connor, this isn't our business," Ben interjected.

"It's absolutely our business," Connor shot back. "We're the ones who had to put our life on hold to take care of Kati."

Satisfaction mixed with anger. Satisfaction Jacob was putting himself first for once, even if she was the reason he had to take some time away. Anger at these dumb, thickheaded oafs. "Really?"

"Really what?"

"Really. You had to put your life on hold for a couple of weeks?"

Connor set his jaw. "Yeah, we did."

"That must have been hard." She nodded so furiously, her hair bounced. "So hard for you to do that."

"Your tone is conveying sarcasm, but it *was* hard. We have a business, and personal lives and—"

Oh. No. He. Didn't. Akira stepped right up into Connor's face, crowding into his personal space, exposing him to her most ferocious glare, the one that made grown men run for their lives. This young pup didn't stand a chance. "Jacob has put his life on hold for you since you were born," she hissed. "For you and your brother and your sister. He has a career, and he could have a personal life, if he were able to have some fucking time to himself, if he weren't always worried about his precious babies at home. So shut your goddamned whiny mouth. If he needs you to pull some duty at home on short notice, you do it. Hell, if he needs a kidney, you rip it out with your bare hands and hand it to him. It's the least you owe that man."

Shock chased across Connor's face. He folded his arms over his broad chest. The resemblance between all the brothers was strong, but Connor's features were more refined than Jacob and Ben, his full lips and long lashes making him almost pretty. "I know exactly what Jacob's done for me. Us," Connor responded defensively.

You're overreacting. This is not your place. It wasn't her family, after all. Her ire was controlling her mouth, however, and there was no stopping her now. She sneered. "So put on your fucking big-girl panties and act like it. It won't kill you to help him out now and again."

Connor grew silent and studied her for a long moment before glancing over her head at Ben and exhaling. "Damn you. You were right."

"I told you so," came Ben's mild response.

"I didn't think he would actually jump in the deep end."

Realization dawning, Akira slowly took a step back. "You were playing me. Trying to get me to tip my hand."

"No." When she lifted an eyebrow, Connor had the grace to look shamefaced. "Not entirely."

"We don't haze Kati's dates because we're chauvinist pigs and she's the baby girl," Ben explained. "We're all protective of each other."

She curled her fingers, trembling from leftover adrenaline. "Fuck you both. That's what this was, hazing Jacob's date? What are you trying to do, get me to prove myself?"

"Wait, Jacob's dating *that woman*?"

They all turned at the feminine yelp to find Kati standing at the bottom of the stairs, hands in her back pockets.

That woman. That Akira. Akira was pissed to begin with, and the girl's words only exacerbated her temper. "Don't call me that." Her voice was low but clear.

"What?"

"Don't refer to me as *that woman*," she clarified. "You sound like my mother. I hate it. Call me by name or not at all."

Kati paled, but to Akira's surprise, nodded. "You're right. I'm sorry. I know better."

Akira was tempted to smack her down further, but Kati lifted her chin, and there was something in the curve of her jaw, the downturn of her lips, that resembled Jacob so closely Akira didn't have the stomach to swat the girl away.

A bit more subdued, Kati frowned at her brothers. "Did you guys know they were dating?"

"No."

"Yes." When everyone looked at Ben, he shrugged. "Jacob was crushed when he was an ass to you, Akira, and then a couple days later he says it's cool and forget it? He couldn't even look me in the eyes. I knew something was up, especially when he started to disappear at night."

Kati's frown became more pronounced. "No one ever tells me anything."

Akira would have loved to throw up her hands and storm out of this awkward three-ring circus. Unfortunately, she didn't know where she would go. "We're not... It's not like that," Akira interjected.

"Then what is it like?" Kati asked, hostility slipping back into her voice. "Are you the reason he ran off?"

Akira's lips tightened. "Maybe."

"What the hell did you to do to him?"

"That's between me and him," Akira replied.

Kati snorted in obvious disbelief. "So why do you want to see him now?"

Akira could manipulate them. She could outsmart them. She could verbally reduce them to ashes.

Instinctively, she knew that would get her nowhere. "I need him," she said softly. Humbly. Truthfully.

The Campbell siblings were silent for a moment, making Akira wonder whether they would close loyal ranks against her, keeping her out.

To her surprise, Kati was the first to speak. "Will you hurt him?"

A no might get her the answer she sought, but it wouldn't be honest. "I won't intentionally hurt him." She couldn't promise anything else.

The only person who had ever loved her the way these people loved each other was her grandmother. She was out of practice and out of her depth with Jacob, and she feared she would probably fuck up more before all of the dust settled. Generating chaos had always been something she excelled at.

But she would try.

Ben looked at Connor, who eyed Kati. She was the one who piped up. "He's at the cabin."

Connor stepped past Akira and picked up the pitcher from the center of the table, pouring a glass. "Have a drink, if you're driving there now. Your lips are dry."

Because she hadn't drunk or eaten anything since the previous night. She accepted the glass, nearly lightheaded with relief. That was it? They weren't going to torture her some more? "Why did you tell me?"

Connor stared meaningfully at the glass, and she quickly took a large gulp of the sweet, tart drink. "Because he's already in rough shape," Connor responded matter-of-factly. "Our main concern is not making him worse. But I don't think you'll do that."

"How do you know?"

"'Cause you don't look so hot either, Akira," Ben said sympathetically. "Go see him. Work things out, please. We'll hold down the fort as long as he wants, but we do miss him."

Akira drained her glass. She looked at Kati, who merely

shrugged. "I owe you."

"For what?"

Kati's lips firmed, and she glanced down at the ground. "You must be eager to get going. I'll walk you out."

Akira nodded. "I am, yes. Thanks." She shrugged off Ben's sweatshirt and handed it to him. "Bye. Maybe I'll…see you?" Only if things worked out with Jacob.

Please let them work out with Jacob.

Connor murmured his goodbye, and Ben gave her a bright smile. Kati followed Akira up the steep staircase, her flip-flops squeaking on the metal. They were silent until they left the earshot of the men, and then Kati spoke. "That was nice of you, trying to pay me for the box."

Was that what the girl felt she owed Akira for? "You did have a claim to it, and I'll give you fair value."

Kati bit her lip, her steps slow as they walked through the kitchen to the foyer. The colors Jacob had chosen for his home were soothing blues and creams. Akira caught a glimpse of warm wooden antique furniture in the dining room and living room. "Mei used to wear a necklace a lot," Kati murmured. "It was a delicate gold chain with a starfish on it."

Akira knew immediately the necklace Kati was referring to. Once Akira had become an adult, she rarely saw Mei outside of parties or gatherings, where she wore flashier though still tasteful jewelry.

But when Akira had been a child, Mei had often worn that simple piece.

"I know it," Akira replied. "I'll put it aside for you."

"Thanks. I'd really like that."

The suppressed emotion had Akira glancing sharply at the girl. "You loved her."

"Yeah." Kati's lips twisted. "I mean, I don't think she loved me like a daughter or anything. I don't think I even loved her like my mother. But she taught me how to put on makeup one day, and we would watch soaps together, and…I don't know. She could be really awesome. We were kind of close by the end there."

Akira stopped at the front door. She studied the heavy frames that had been arranged on the walls. No original Monets in them, but the prints were serene watercolors that urged her to curl up in the comfortable home.

"At the end…" Akira said, hating herself for asking, but something within her desperately needing to know. "She was a little softer? Less guarded?"

"She was."

"Did she talk about me at all?"

Kati flushed to the roots of her hair. This time, it was her turn to study the walls. "Ah, she did but—"

It was nothing Akira would want to hear. Probably things Akira had heard for years when the woman was alive.

There would be no deathbed declaration of love for her. "Never mind. Forget I asked." The polished brass doorknob turned easily in her hand.

"I called you a slut, you know."

That brought her to a halt. She cast a glance over her shoulder at the teenager. "Excuse me?"

The girl's fair skin must have been scalding hot, she was blushing so hard. "I still feel bad. That's what I owe you for. Don't worry," she said hurriedly. "Jacob punished me. I didn't know you two were involved, so maybe he was extra mad."

Warmth chased through her, singeing away the cold.

That day, in her library, when she had questioned Jacob as to why he and Kati were on the outs, he hadn't been able to look her in the eye. No wonder. *She was unkind to someone I care about.*

Akira turned to face the younger girl. "That was before we were…involved."

"Oh."

"I'm sorry you were punished. I don't much mind being called a bitch, or a whore, or a slut," she informed Kati gently. "Those words usually mean the person saying them thinks I'm too rich or too smart or I'm having too much fun. But I think your brother has a moral streak that doesn't allow him to see things the way I do sometimes."

"Yeah." Kati looked down at her feet. "Whether you mind or not, I think he'd like me to apologize to you. I shouldn't have said it. I guess I was with Mei so much, and—"

"Apology accepted," Akira cut her off, not eager to dwell on all the names her parent called her.

Still staring at her feet, Kati mumbled, "He's like my dad, you know. Those other two idiots, they're my brothers. But Jacob's basically my dad. I hate that he's hurting."

Akira wasn't adept at handling children. She could safely say there wasn't a maternal bone in her svelte body.

But even she couldn't remain unaffected by that pronouncement. She cleared her throat, filing the moment away so she could recount it for Jacob. If and when he took her back. "Yeah. I know."

"So if you guys get together and he's happy…" Kati shrugged. "I don't think we'll be best friends, probably, but I'll try not to be jealous and mean. Because you're right. He deserves more than taking care of us for the rest of his life."

The lukewarm acceptance was more than she could have expected, especially since Mei had most likely poisoned the girl for years against her. Akira opened the door. "Thanks. I appreciate that."

Kati bit her lip, suddenly looking very young. "Jacob calls me every night. But when you see him, could you maybe remind him opening night for my school play is this Friday? I didn't want to pressure him, but I want him to be there."

Akira murmured her agreement. She had made it down the stairs to the street when she heard her name behind her.

She turned, her hand on the railing. "Yes?"

Kati's smile was bright, the first genuine grin Akira had seen out of the girl since she was a child. "I remembered something. You asked if Mei mentioned you at the end."

Akira immediately shook her head. The last thing she needed to take with her to Jacob was the demoralizing memory of her mother telling Kati she was a slut.

She'd told Kati the truth—the names generally didn't bother her much. Her mother simply had a unique ability to be the exception to that rule, always. Her opinion, Akira had cared about. Hers and Jacob's. "That's—"

"Once Mei was talking about your dad, and she said there was nothing more wonderful then the fact that you were more successful than he was."

Something clenched in her chest, making it difficult to breathe. "Really?"

"Yup."

It wasn't a deathbed declaration of love.

But it was something.

CHAPTER 23

By the time Akira pulled her car to a stop at the cabin, she sorely wished that it hadn't been her driver who had betrayed her. This second leg of Operation Find the Brooding Author had been particularly tiring. The sun was starting to set, and her emotional and physical exhaustion was making itself known.

She turned the car off and stared at the small house, half-fearing the Campbell siblings had lied or alerted Jacob to her imminent arrival. Jacob's car wasn't anywhere to be seen. The clearing was quiet and abandoned.

He could have parked around the side of the place, she told herself, and clambered out of the car. Her heels sank immediately into the earth, which was damp from recent rain. She glanced down, idly noting they were the same pair she'd tossed to Jacob when they were ducking paparazzi and escaping from her second-story office window.

Not even her favorite shoes were safe from the memory of the man.

Dismissing the mud clinging to the narrow heel with a never-before-seen blithe disregard for her precious footwear, she reached into the backseat to grab the paper bag she'd stowed there. Shifting the weight to one arm, she took a deep breath before making her way to the front door, her shoes sticking in the dirt.

Akira opened the screen door and tapped lightly on the wood.

Nothing. She rapped harder.

Nope.

Akira hesitated, torn between returning to the relatively safe haven of her car and barging in.

Barging in was her M.O., right? No reason to stop now, when she'd come so far.

The knob turned easily in her hand when she tried it. She stepped inside cautiously. "Hello?" she called out, hating the note of uncertainty in her voice. "Jacob?"

The cabin was silent.

Gaining confidence, Akira stepped inside the home, balancing the bag in her arms, and closed the door behind her. "Jacob? It's me." The open door meant he was home, right? Or was he so trusting he left the damn thing unlocked all the time?

If so, they really would need to have a serious talk about his lack of security.

She stepped into the tiny kitchen and dropped the bulging bag filled with food on the chipped countertop, casting a glance at the coffeepot, which was filled with black, sludge-like liquid. She placed her hand against the pot. Still warm. He couldn't have gotten far.

A noise reached her ears, muted by the thickness of the cabin walls, and she briefly closed her eyes. Well, why wouldn't he be chopping wood? Full circle. Maybe it was her fate to always be forced to face him when she was fatigued and he was dripping sweat and engaging in an appropriately sexy activity.

After she stowed her purse carefully in the cabinet next to the bookshelves—she adored the expensive handbag itself to pieces, but between her grandmother's treasures and Jacob's note, it now contained her most precious possessions—she followed the noise to the clearing she had found Jacob in the first time she had come to this place.

Sweaty palms were not a regular experience for her. Neither was uncertainty. Yet Akira had to battle both as she caught sight of the man she was seeking. Stripped to the waist, his bronzed skin glistening, he brought the ax down ferociously on a helpless log. Hastily, she wiped her hands on her hopelessly wrinkled skirt.

Her heart pounded, her breath coming faster. Thirty feet separated them, then twenty. Then fifteen. She halted, shifting her weight from one foot to the other, her shoes ruined beyond all repair. *Say something.*

Fear strangled her, stealing her voice.

Another faltering foot and he looked her way. Dark hair fell into his eyes, and he gave an impatient shake of his head, as if to both clear his eyes and express disbelief at what he was seeing.

They stared at each other across the distance separating them for a long minute.

Akira wasn't sure how expensive Jacob's ax was, but she bet he was a man who took care of his tools. He barely paid attention to where he dropped the thing on the ground. In the cool air, steam rose from his sweaty shoulders. His hands opened and closed at his sides, his chest pumping with the force of his breaths.

His first step was slow, as was his second, but his stride increased with every move, until he was standing directly in front of her, close enough she could trace the individual lashes on his eyes.

"What the hell," he shouted, startling both her and probably every bird within earshot, "took you so fucking long?"

She was aware her mouth had fallen half open. Jacob was capable of yelling? Automatic defensiveness made her stand up straight. "It hasn't been that long."

"Not that long?" The muscle in his jaw jumped. "One more day, Akira. One more day, and I would have hunted you down."

Hunting didn't sound terrible. She had a feeling Jacob could have made it a sexy hunt. "You said you wouldn't chase me."

"I lied, okay?" He raked his hands through his disheveled hair and took a deep breath, making a visible effort to bring himself under control. "I fucking lied. Of course I would chase you. Of course I would beg you to give us a chance. How am I...what am I supposed to do when I can't *function* without you?"

Like butter, she melted. He couldn't function without her? "I—"

"I can't eat. I can't sleep. My dick is raw from my stroking it, thinking of you."

Her belly tightened. How on earth did he make that last sentence sound so damn romantic? "I had to figure some stuff out."

His lips firmed. "And did you figure it out?"

"Yes. Jacob..." That was all she managed to say before

huge hands closed over her upper arms, and she was yanked forward for a soul-searing kiss. His palms slid down her back as his tongue fucked her mouth, his fingers tracing the individual bumps of her spine and settling over her ass. His fingers squeezed, pulling her closer to him.

He growled when she ripped her mouth away. His eyes were hot, dark with need. His hand wrapped around her neck, his thumb settling at the vulnerable hollow of her throat. "I need to fuck you," he said, distinct and deliberate. "That clear?"

Oookay. Her knees weakened, both at the words and the hint of pleading in them. She gave him a slow smile, designed to maintain his impressive level of lust. "Then do it already."

He made a rough noise and took her mouth again, ferocious in his hunger. It took him seconds to shred her shirt and her bra, his hands running over her breasts and stomach. Her back came up against something hard, and he released her long enough to flip her around. Her hands automatically rose to protect her face from the tree bark. Calloused fingertips caught on the fine fabric of her skirt as he worked it over her ass.

She closed her eyes tight, listening to the sound of foil wrinkling as he donned a condom. "Been carrying a condom with me all the time," he said, his voice almost soundless. "I knew I'd need to be inside you the second I saw you."

What could she say to that? Bless his practical brain.

His body layered over hers, his sweat binding their flesh together. His first thrust made her teeth rattle. She dug her fingers into the tree, uncaring about the hell she was putting her manicure through.

She wasn't wet enough to take him easily, but the bite of

pain was delicious. He worked his thick cock inside her cunt, forcing her open, followed by the drag of flesh on flesh as he withdrew.

Jacob wrapped one hand in her hair, twisting the strands around his fist until he had a solid grip. He tilted her head back, his breath tickling her ear. "What do you want?"

She whimpered as he flexed his hips, sinking back into her. "More."

"More of this?" He thrust hard and fast a number of times, making her body tremble and her hands scramble against the tree for purchase before he returned to his slow, shallow thrusts. "Or this?"

"Yes. Harder," she breathed.

"Want to tie you up to this tree. Come out and fuck you whenever I want," he panted. "Would you like that?"

Her pussy clenched over the cock shafting her. "Yes."

"You'd be my fuck-toy."

Shameless. That's what she'd made him. "God, Jacob." She reached behind her to grab his hip, her fingers glancing over his slick skin before her wrist was grasped. He slammed her hand over her head, against the tree, and manacled both of her wrists in his unforgiving hold.

"I give it to you," he growled. "You take it. Understand?"

"I'm sorry," she babbled. "Give it to me, please."

He shoved himself deep, the fat head of his cock bumping a sweet spot inside her. When she cried out, he kept himself there, grinding his hips in slow circles. "Have you ever fucked a man bare?"

She couldn't respond. Not when he was working her G-spot as if his cock had been made for her pussy. She shook her head.

"I've only gone without that one time, when I was a kid. I don't even remember it, too much bad shit came after." His breath came in gusts against her shoulder. "Will you let me, one day? Fuck you without anything between us?"

How was he capable of speaking? She arched back against him, but he was already as deep as he could go. If only he would thrust...

"Answer me."

"Yes," she gasped.

"Yes, what?" Another tight circle, his cock bumping high inside her.

She struggled to marshal whatever brain cells she had left so she could drive him as crazy as he made her. *Share the power.* "Yes, you can be my first."

He stilled.

"You can fill me up with your come," she breathed. "Until it's dripping out of me. Until you've marked every inch of me. You can spend days coming on me. In me."

His moan was helpless in her ear. He pulled out almost all the way before slamming back in. His fingers interlocked with hers, and he finally, finally gave her exactly what she wanted, until they were both groaning, their bodies straining together in the forest, the filthiest of animals.

He yanked her blouse aside, the bristle of his light beard scratching her skin a second before his teeth sank into her shoulder. Her body bucked, and her climax roared through her, the sharp bite of pain mixing with the unbearable pleasure of his cock.

His shout was unrestrained and wild as he strained against her, his fingers digging into the flesh of her hipbone, his cock jerking. The condom muted the heat of his semen, and she

315

was annoyed he wasn't naked inside her, filling her up the way she had described.

Soon. They would be smart, and careful, of course, because she couldn't be anything less. Yet…soon. There was no one else she trusted to pluck that particular cherry of hers.

The truth rushed over her, making her dizzier than her orgasm could have. There was no one else she trusted like Jacob.

When he withdrew from her, she gave a cry in protest. His fingers skimmed over her back in a soothing gesture. "I'll be back inside you soon." The words were a threat and a promise all rolled into one.

She heard a rustle and a zipper before his arms came around her and he sank to the ground, arranging her on his lap so they could catch their breaths—a good thing, since her legs wouldn't hold her. She buried her head against him, inhaling the scent of sex and Jacob, combined with the rich loaminess of the soil and the fresh scent of the grass.

Suddenly, being one with nature wasn't quite so terrible. She would trade glamping for camping if it meant she got fucked like this. By this man.

She closed her eyes, attempting to regain some semblance of rational thought.

His chest rumbled. "Are you okay?"

Okay? What a tepid word. She might never be okay, thanks to him.

At her silence, his fingers trailed over her shoulder, over the tender spot where he'd nipped her. "I bit you."

"It's fine." It was perfect.

"You're scraped up. I've been shaving every day, in the hopes you might show up. Of course you pick the day I don't."

"I like your beard," she said, too bemused to utter anything else.

His rough palm slid lower over her arm, moving her ruined shirt. In a flash, he stiffened against her. "Akira."

She sighed, resigned to not having the opportunity to quietly contemplate the momentous fact her entire world had shifted. "What?"

"Did I do this to you?"

She leaned into his touch, somewhat hating her instinctive need to absorb his warmth but loving the fact he was there for her to leach it off. He'd always been a part of her life, but now he had twined himself through her soul.

"Akira. Answer me."

Already conditioned to respond to the stern demand in that sexy voice, she blinked at him, some of her orgasm-induced dreaminess fading. Too sated to move, Akira barely managed to glance at her upper arm, where Jacob's fingers were delicately tracing the skin. A dark bruise had formed there, in the shape of a man's hand.

Her father, when he had grabbed her. It didn't hurt much. She always had been prone to bruising easily. "Not a big deal."

But he wasn't listening, having discovered her hands, which were scraped from the bark of the tree, some of her nails broken and ragged. His lips pinched together, and he launched to his feet, gathering her up in his arms.

Startled, she stiffened. "What are you doing? Put me down," she demanded.

That only garnered her a severe frown.

"My hands are scraped, not my legs," Akira said dryly.

"Shut. Up."

She was about to argue further when she realized she was cradled against a more than fine, naked, muscular chest, and why the fuck was she protesting that?

She'd never been carried like this. She was too tall, too sharp, too intimidating for any man to ever attempt it. She supposed she could have ordered one to do it, but that wouldn't be the same.

So she shut up. She laid her head against his shoulder, pressing her cheek to his skin. She twined her arms around his neck and scratched her fingernail through the fine hairs there, appreciating the slight shudder he gave.

He glanced at her, eyes narrowed, as he shouldered through the front door of his cabin. "Quit that. You'll hurt your hands more."

Always eager to misbehave, Akira traced a lazy pattern over his neck.

Jacob didn't bother to close the door behind them. He placed her gently in one of the mismatched chairs in the kitchen and leaned over her, bracing one hand on the table. Her shirt was in pieces, her breasts still exposed, but he was far more concerned with the hands he held in his, with frequent worried glances at her upper arm and shoulder.

She would be insulted on behalf of her breasts, but she was too busy melting into a puddle of tenderness over the fierce, protective frown he was bestowing upon her.

"Stay here." He paced to the sink and removed an old first-aid kit, coming back to crouch in front of her a second later. As abrupt as his manner was, his touch was infinitely gentle as he cleaned her palms with antiseptic. She winced from the sting, and his lips turned white at the corners.

"There are a couple of splinters. Hang on."

His dark head bent over her as he worked patiently with a pair of tiny tweezers which should have been too small for his hands.

When he was finished, he brushed his thumb lightly over the mark his teeth had left. "I'm so sorry. I shouldn't have been so rough."

"It's fine," she assured him. "It doesn't even hurt. Neither do my hands, actually. I wanted you to be as rough with me as you were. It felt good. Felt right."

Despite her words, his frown remained as he grabbed a roll of gauze from the kit. After dabbing a bit of ointment on her palms, he began to wrap it around her hand. "That bruise on your arm…"

She gave a rough sigh. "That's from my dad."

He didn't explode or rail or scream, but merely paused for a second. When he spoke, the lack of emotion in his voice was chilling. "I'm going to kill him."

She peered down at him, a wee bit alarmed. "Don't. He's not worth it."

"He doesn't get to put his hands on you. No one does."

"You do. I mean, you can," she assured him, so hastily she might find it comical if her potentially stupendous future sex life wasn't on the line. God forbid Jacob regressed into his shyness over enjoying the rough and tumble treatment they both needed. She was already thoroughly addicted to his gentleman-in-the-streets-freak-in-the-sheets vibe.

Akira had a feeling they'd barely scratched the surface of his freakiness. She suppressed a shudder.

He didn't acknowledge her words, his gaze hard. "Do you want to kill him? I can help you plan it out. That's kind of my thing."

"I can't tell if you're serious or not, but it's turning me on a little," she admitted.

A glimpse of humor flitted across his face, but he sobered quickly. "I'm dead serious."

"I don't want to kill him." She paused. "Unless he crosses me again. Then I will destroy him. Financially, at least. Which is probably worse, in his eyes, than actually killing him."

"Good."

"You think I can do it?"

"I know you can. He's no match for you." His quiet confidence in her made her chest hurt. "But if you need me...I'm still happy to kill him."

Her smile was wobbly.

"Akira, I—"

"I'm sorry I left you that morning."

He huffed out a breath and looked down, securing the gauze on one hand, then the other. The old cuckoo clock on the wall ticked. "That's okay."

"No, it's not. I shouldn't have."

His lips softened. "Really. It's okay."

She flexed her bandaged hand, all her thoughts swirling in her brain. Their past, their present, their future. If they had a future. They had to have one, right?

That was what the signs were pointing to, but she was a business woman first, and she trusted nothing until the deal was formally closed, every single potential vulnerability addressed. "The note you left... Could you really love me?"

He froze. His hands went to the arms of her chair, as if to steady himself.

When he didn't speak for a long moment, butterflies danced in her belly. "Are you going to make me beg?"

His mouth worked. "You would beg?"

"Yeah. I'd really be pissed off about it." She scowled, her ire already building at the thought of compromising her pride. This was a small price to pay, though. "But I'd do it."

He swallowed, his Adam's apple bobbing. "Yes."

Oh. Well. She took a deep breath, unaccustomed to pleading with anyone for anything. "Please—"

"No." His fingertips covered her mouth, silencing her. His eyes had warmed. "I didn't tell you to come find me because I wanted to see you humbled, but because I wanted us both to be certain of your decision. I don't want you to beg. You should never beg. Yes. Yes, I could love you."

"Ah." Some women might appreciate a lengthy declaration, but not her. Not now, when she'd waited so long. Relief made her lightheaded. "I—Why?"

"Why would I love you?"

"Yes."

"What kind of question is that?" His thumb brushed under her eye, collecting moisture she hadn't wanted to escape.

She sniffed, mildly horrified at how pitiful she probably appeared. More pitiful when she bleated out her next words. "People don't love me."

"Bullshit," came his instantaneous, mild response. Another pass beneath her eye to catch a stray tear. "All those people at that party? Your employees? What about them?"

"They're friends."

"They're friends who would jump off a cliff if you asked it of them."

"It's not the same." Unable to meet his gaze, she looked

down at her hands, which were bandaged far more extensively than a couple of scrapes warranted. "It's not the way you love your family completely, entirely. No one's ever loved me like that, except my grandma."

"Because your parents were sociopaths," he stated. "Not your fault."

Happiness threatened to explode within her, but she couldn't let his blind defense of her stand. "My father might be a sociopath, but my mother wasn't. She loved people. She was capable of it. She loved you and your father and your siblings." She bit her lip. "A couple of years ago, she told me my dad manipulated her into having me, that she didn't want me at all."

His hands framed her face, cradling it. "Then you understand that it was nothing you did."

"No!" Akira shook her head, no longer able to stop the tears from actively coursing down her face. She brushed them aside impatiently. "She'd tried to feel something for me, and it was impossible. I could have tried harder. Don't you understand? I could have behaved, and she would have given me—" She hiccupped, completing her utterly pathetic image. "And now she's dead. She won't ever love me."

"She would never have loved you. No matter what you did." His words were brutal, making her lurch forward in pain. "Let me tell you about your mother. Yes, she could love people, and yes, she could be kind. She could be overwhelmingly kind. But she was also the most stubborn, inflexible, and occasionally cruel person I have ever met in my life. I don't know what sick game she was playing with you—maybe she really did convince herself that you were at fault—but I guarantee you that it was just that, a game. You could have worn the right clothes and said the right things and done everything she ever wanted you to do, and if she decided from the moment you were conceived she despised you, then there was nothing that would change her mind." Jacob took a deep breath. "She was wrong. I'm ashamed I didn't realize before how wrong she was. I'm sorry I made it worse. I will spend the rest of my life telling you that. She was wrong. And ultimately..." His lips pressed against hers in a featherlight kiss. "You know what?"

"What?"

"It's her fucking loss."

Maybe it was her watery vision, but in that moment, with the setting sun casting a halo around him and his stern expression, he looked like an avenging warrior. Or an angel. Or a warrior angel.

"I don't want to hurt you," she whispered. "I'm not the type of woman you should have."

His laugh was low and deep. "Ah, Akira. You really need to stop separating women into types."

"I'm serious. You should have someone sweet and kind and gentle."

"Whereas you're mean and abrasive and sarcastic."

"I am."

"Yeah, you are," he agreed, slightly offending her with the quickness of his reply. "But that doesn't mean you can't be sweet and kind and gentle. One quality doesn't cancel out the rest." He settled his forehead against hers. "I want you, not some faceless ideal. I want you in my family."

The words both thrilled and terrified her. "I don't know how to be a part of a family."

"Yeah, and all I have is my family." His eyes were patient.

"I'd say we're pretty perfect for each other, then, don't you think? Lots of things we could teach each other."

Her limbs were shaking. She had come this far with the intention of reclaiming what she had thrown away, but she hadn't really been convinced it would happen. Now that it was…

"I'm tired of being a father and a brother, Akira. Help me be a man."

Her mind calmed, everything sharpening into crystal-clear focus. Silly man. Didn't he get it? He didn't need to plead. He'd titillated her from the second he'd frowned at her, ruined her the moment he'd wrapped his arms around her, and devastated her by handing her a perfectly formed rose.

She was already his.

And maybe…he was already hers.

Her bandaged hands found their way to his face, and then her lips met his. The kiss was long and slow and sweet, her mouth clinging to his even as he rose to his feet and helped her to stand.

His hands moved over her skirt, shoving it to the floor, removing the remnants of her shirt and bra. The chilly air blowing in from the open door made goose bumps rise along her skin, but she couldn't care when his hot chest pressed against hers.

Her fingers worked the fastening of his jeans. When they were both naked, he picked her up, her legs automatically winding around his narrow hips.

"Fuck me," she murmured.

A slow, evil smile spread over Jacob's face. "Oh no, my greedy girl. First we make love."

"I HATE MAKING LOVE," AKIRA GASPED.

Jacob chuckled, so happy he could burst. His heart hadn't felt so light in weeks, not since he had woken up and discovered Akira missing from her massive bed.

Now she was back though, in *his* massive bed, and damn it, this time he meant to make her so damn blissful she stopped fretting over silly things like whether she was good enough for him.

He needed a sweet, kind, gentle woman? Maybe. Sometimes. But he had found that in Akira. He wanted her.

He wasn't entirely certain she believed him yet. He would make her see. He would make her see they were perfect for each other.

Perfect in every way. His toes dug into the mattress. He was buried completely inside her, ass tight, sweat pouring off him, every muscle clenched. All of those were great things, but at some crazy point, he had decided that the best thing he could do was not move.

She thumped his shoulder. She didn't have much upper-body strength, but her small fist was bony, so it did make him wince. Unwilling to give in so easily to his hungry woman—his woman, that was absurd and exciting all at once—Jacob only readjusted his palms on either side of her head and looked down at her, his lips curved. "I finished my contracted book, you know. The last couple of weeks, I've been working nonstop on my new series. Lidia's shaping up nicely."

"Great," she gritted out between her teeth. "Can we talk about this later?"

"She's lusty, my heroine," he said brightly, deliberately ignoring her. "I was toying with this idea of a scene where she's experimenting with tantric sex."

"Does she love it?"

"Yes."

She panted. "Well, I can already see she's not modeled after me. Quit it now."

"Patience," he soothed. He ducked his head, capturing her lips, licking the seam and mimicking the thrusts she wanted him to replicate with his lower body.

She ripped her mouth away, her chest moving up and down with the force of her need. "I'm not patient."

"I know." He made his smile deliberately sweet. "But I am. I could stay like this forever."

The words weren't a lie. It might kill him, but he would die happy.

Her groan was tortured.

His head lowered. "I could be persuaded to move."

"What do you want? A blowjob? A threesome? A four-some? So many sexual partners it would be absurd to count?" she asked hopefully.

"No." Wait. *You idiot. Don't turn down those things.* "I mean, yes. But what I really want, more than anything in the world…" his whisper was so soft, she had to strain up to hear it, "…is for you to tell me what an amazing person you are. Worthy of everything. Especially love."

The lines around her mouth deepened. "Don't be cheesy, Campbell. It doesn't become you."

"Okay. I suppose I could stay here and never move."

She dropped her head to the pillow. "You patient, ma-nipulative asshole."

Smug satisfaction made him grin. "Yeah, I am." He gave a subtle roll of his hips, and she gasped. "You made me admit I deserve a life of my own. You need to admit you deserve love."

Akira swallowed hard, her throat working. "You make me come, and I'll tell you."

He raised his eyebrow. "You're mistaken as to who's in charge here."

"Am I?" Cunning replaced some of the lust in her gaze, and his eyes almost rolled back in his head when she tightened her pussy on him. She clenched again, and again, pushing her hips up so he could sink a tiny bit deeper. "Maybe you're mistaken."

She worked her hand between them so she could fondle her breast. His eyes tracked her fingers on her nipple, the way she toyed with the brown nubbin. "Do you like that?" she crooned. "How hot and tight you've made me?"

He watched her through slitted eyes, aware his control was slipping right out of his fingers. "You know I do."

"Only you can do that. I don't get this wet for anyone else."

A shudder ran through him, a shudder that made her smile triumphantly.

"Make me come, Jacob. I'll give you anything you want."

The words were so seductive, he couldn't resist any longer. With a low groan, he succumbed, thrusting into her hard, until her cries echoed throughout the cabin.

He collapsed on top of her. Ragged nails scratched up his back, the gauze on her hands tickling him. Her lips pressed against his ear. "I guess... I'm worthy of love."

He closed his eyes, exultation shooting through him. He felt only a twinge of guilt over the small lie he'd told in that note.

I could love you.

Such a tiny lie. One extra, unnecessary word he'd forced himself to write because he was worried he'd scare her off otherwise.

Soon, he assured himself, he would come clean soon.

He brushed a kiss against her lips. "Thank you," he whispered.

CHAPTER 24

"We're going to be late."

Jacob smiled and leaned his head against the railing of the porch, not taking his eyes off the sun setting over the treetops. "We won't be late. Why don't you come sit here for a minute?"

Akira gave a sigh and came to stand next to him. "I will not have your sister hate me because you don't get to her play on time. Well. Hate me more than she already hates me."

"She doesn't hate you. She told you where I was."

"Let's not read too much into that."

"We'll be on time. These are our last few minutes before we have to go back to civilization. Enjoy them."

Just like that, she softened. They'd been spoiled by the last three days of total isolation, and neither of them was particularly looking forward to returning to the city. Too bad they both had unavoidable obligations there.

She stared at him meaningfully until he glanced up and rolled his eyes. "It's my last clean shirt, Akira."

She folded her arms over her chest. His lips twisted, and he grasped his white T-shirt, pulling it over his head in a smooth motion. He arranged the cotton material on the stoop next to him.

Instead of plopping herself down, she gingerly placed her Birkin bag on the makeshift blanket. His exasperated sigh turned into an amused laugh when she landed in his lap. His arms automatically encircled her and tugged her closer.

She pressed her head against his strong shoulder. A part of her realized she ought to be a little concerned over how second nature hugging Jacob had become. *Where's the steel in your spine? The ice in your veins?*

Eh. It was still there. Ready to be used when she needed it.

She didn't need it when Jacob had his arms wrapped around her. When it was clear he was as mushy for her as she was for him.

"It's probably a good thing we have to go back to the city tonight for Kati's show," he said drowsily. "We're running out of food. Then we'd really be roughing it."

"The food I brought with me would have lasted two normal people over a week."

"You know better than that."

That she did. Akira ran her hand over his flat belly. The fact that it was flat was a miracle. "Glutton."

"The only reason it lasted this long is because we had other things to occupy us."

Many glorious things. Akira had only pushed Jacob off her occasionally, to check in with her office and make sure her business was functioning without her. Anderson had sent her multiple apologetic emails, and according to Tammy, had been calling nonstop, ready to finalize their deal.

Akira suspected someone had sent the pompous asshole a

fat dossier of her father's greatest moments, aside from his notorious sex tape. A hard smile crossed her face. On a related note, Tammy deserved a bonus.

However, Anderson, that old bastard, could sweat it out until Monday. She was busy. Delightfully busy.

Jacob was her match in bed, maybe more insatiable than she was, but it was their conversations that made her realize they were perfect for one another. Like last night, when she had announced that she would pay for Kati's outstanding tuition as recompense for her grandmother's box.

"The hell you will," Jacob had calmly responded.

"I will." Akira licked a stray crumb off his chest. The dangers of eating in bed, but they hadn't managed to leave the lumpy king-sized mattress much.

"I told you I'm not taking your money, and you said—"

"I promised not to write you a check."

"You're splitting hairs."

"If it makes you feel better, I'm also establishing a need-based scholarship in my grandmother's name to go to another incoming freshman. That one will be a full ride."

His lips had pursed. "Yeah?"

"Yeah. If and only if you let me pay for Kati." She batted her eyes at him, loving the irritation on his face. "How do you feel about yanking a scholarship away from someone who might not be able to go to college otherwise, Mr. Softy?"

"You wouldn't do that to some poor kid."

"Of course I would. Like I care about some stranger I don't even know."

Irritation was replaced by craftiness, which should have warned her. "I'll accept this deal, but I want you to pay for two additional incoming freshmen, not one."

She snorted. "What do I look like, I'm made of money? We're talking a private school."

"I realize your shoe budget might take a hit, but you'll manage," he said ruthlessly. "One more thing. That second scholarship is offered under *your* name."

She recoiled. Her name on a scholarship? She donated plenty to charity, but never in ways that traced back to her. It would utterly ruin her image. "Ew. No."

"Mmm-hmm." He stacked his hands under his head. "Or no deal."

She fumed for a brief moment. "I was a little too cartoon villainy, wasn't I?"

"Yeah. Plus there's the fact that you really, obviously want to pay my sister back. And you would never start negotiations at the number you were actually going to settle on. How many kid's educations were you planning on funding?"

"At least three," she admitted grudgingly.

"Hmm. Three it is, then. Two will be under your name."

When she opened her mouth to protest—the name part, not the number—he raised a single eyebrow. "Or the deal's off the table."

She smiled now. Never would she have imagined she'd have to negotiate to get someone to *take* her money.

Her phone buzzed in her purse. Akira ignored it. When they returned to the real world, they would have to deal with their work and families, but not now. Akira ran her finger over Jacob's nipple, which was tight from the chill in the spring air. He pressed an absentminded kiss on top of her head. Right now, in this moment, the world was theirs.

"Where are you going to take me for dinner when we get back?" he asked, his mind obviously still on food.

"Dinner?" Akira tugged at his chest hair. "It's your job to bring me dinner, peasant."

"Nope. You have to take me to dinner. That was the deal."

"What deal?"

"I open the box in the allotted time, you take me out on a date."

"I bought all the groceries that have kept us fed for days," she pointed out.

"What do I look, cheap? I want a real dinner, woman."

"Ugh. Fine. I'll take you somewhere fancy. With big portions."

His smile was sleepy. He rubbed his cheek against her hair. "I never asked. What was inside of it, anyway? Your grandmother's puzzle box."

"Oh." She leaned back so she could see his face better. "I thought you knew. After all that work you did, you didn't peek?"

"No. What was inside wasn't as important as the chance that puzzle gave me to spend time with you. Plus, I couldn't look before you did." He gave her a look as if he was surprised she would even think he would be sneaky. That honor of his.

She wriggled her finger at him. "This. It's much easier to lug around than the box."

He took her hand to touch the ring she had donned after her shower. "Wow. I can see how this would be worth a couple of college tuitions."

While the gold setting was real, the sparkling pink and clear jewels were paste, something she had noticed right away. Then again, not everyone grew up learning skills like jewelry valuation. She opened her mouth to correct him, but stopped when she replayed his words in her head.

Huh. Maybe it wouldn't hurt him to think the stones were real. It wasn't lying, Akira reassured herself. She was merely delaying providing clarification. Like, after she'd cut the check for Kati. Then she could point out he had made a deal, damn it, and the sentimental value of the box was definitely worth a few scholarships even if the ring was a fake.

She was already looking forward to the argument.

"Only the ring was inside?"

"No. There was also this." Loath to move from her comfortable seat, she stretched to reach into her bag, her hand brushing against his note. It wasn't necessary since she now had the real thing, but she would keep it. Maybe she would tuck it into her grandmother's box, since she had so few sentimental items to fill it with.

Then when she wanted to get to it, she would push the puzzle into Jacob's hands, sit back, and watch his capable, patient fingers manipulate every panel. Foreplay.

Akira pulled out a small card case from her purse, flipping the engraved silver lid open to reveal a photo of her grandmother, young and beautiful, her arms thrown around a man who was staring down at her with undisguised adoration.

He took the case and studied the photo, his face softening. "You look like her."

Delight filled her. "Really?"

"Don't you see it?"

"I thought there was a slight resemblance, but…" Akira lifted a shoulder. "People say I take after my father."

"You're tall like him, but that's about it. Look. The eyes, the chin. Her mouth. Her hands. Her legs, except yours are longer."

She stared at the photo. She'd never seen her grandmother at this age, and as he pointed out each individual feature, the likeness became more apparent. Such a silly thing, but it calmed her soul to be able to put more distance between herself and her father. *I don't even look like you.* "She always said it was a shame I inherited the shape of her legs."

"I love your legs. They're strong." His fingers measured her calf. "There isn't a force in the world that could knock you over."

She cuddled closer to reward him for those fierce words.

"Is that man your grandfather?"

"No." *I loved your grandfather, but he was a difficult man to simply be with.* Akira accepted the photo from Jacob and caressed the silver case.

"Ah. An old lover?"

"Maybe." *It's very...nice. When you're with a person who is content to let you be. It's the most peaceful thing in the world.*

"It looks like someone she loved very much. Someone who loved her."

"I hope so. Someone she could be with."

His face was gravely serious when he tipped her chin up. "Am I that someone for you?"

She pressed a kiss in the warm hollow of his throat and curled her hand over Jacob's chest, right above his heart. The muscle thudded softly against her palm. "Yes. I could... I could love you."

He didn't say anything, but the tightening of his arms around her told her she'd pleased him. Innate honesty forced her to continue speaking, even when she knew she might be better served by shutting up. "I'm not... I was taught love was a weakness. Something to be used against you. I may not be able to tell you I love you. Not often, at least. Not at first."

He considered her words with his usual seriousness. "Can I tell you I love you? Maybe not today, right this minute. But eventually?"

Deep, endless hunger flashed inside her, warring with fear and trepidation. The hunger edged the fear out, like a glowing sun forcing darkness away. She nodded, mute.

His face softened, and he gave her a slow, solemn smile. "Good." He squeezed her, sharing his solid strength. "You know, I'm not much for talking anyway. I'd rather you show me."

DEAR READERS

Thank you so much for reading *A Gentleman in the Street*! I hope you enjoyed it. This novel is the first book in my Campbell Siblings series, so this isn't the last you'll see of Jacob and Akira.

If you're looking for other books of mine that are similar in heat level and genre to A Gentleman in the Street, I recommend trying the Bedroom Games Series or the Pleasure Series. In fact, before falling for Jacob, Akira (and Remy!) made a brief—and dirty, of course—appearance in Bet On Me, Book 3 of the Bedroom Games Series.

If you would like to know when my next book is available or just want to chat, please visit me at www.alisharai.com, follow me on twitter @AlishaRai or find me on facebook.com/alisharai.

Happy Reading!

AN EXCERPT FROM PLAY WITH ME

BOOK ONE OF THE BEDROOM GAMES SERIES

I want to keep you bound to my bed forever. Black leather ties encircling those dainty wrists, those slender ankles. Stretched wide for me. You'd never be able to escape.

Inhale.

Even if I make a fortune some day, it won't compare to how rich I feel every time you open your thighs for me.

Exhale.

I love you. Always.

"Ma'am?"

Tatiana Belikov snapped the manila folder in her hands shut, hiding the pile of old and tattered letters she'd made the mistake of skimming—though the words weren't new to her—while waiting for the receptionist to finish her phone call. She was all too aware of the slight sheen of sweat on her upper lip. She stuffed the folder in her oversized bag as she rose to her feet, her trembling hands making the job more awkward. "Yes. Hi."

The woman gave her a warm smile. Tatiana didn't have a vast working knowledge of the hiring practices of rich and powerful men, but television had taught her the waiting area would be guarded by a sexy, slinky shark of a woman. Wyatt's assistant looked like she should be playing bridge somewhere.

"I'm so sorry about that. Now, what can I help you with?"

Your boss and I popped each other's cherries years ago. Can you please tell him I'm here? She cleared her throat. "I was hoping I could see Mr. Caine."

"Do you have an appointment?"

"No, I don't."

The other woman—Esme Schmidt, her desk tag read—turned away from her computer, her frown genuinely regretful. "I apologize, dear. But Mr. Caine doesn't see anyone without an appointment. If you'd like to leave a message, I can see that he receives it."

The waiting room wasn't packed—only one other person was present, a frowning, shifty-eyed baby boomer clutching two briefcases bulging with documents. Still, Tatiana couldn't imagine how much work went into running an operation of this size. Showing up with no notice wasn't the best tactic, but alas, she hadn't really thought about it until it was too late to call off this crazy venture.

"Can you please give him my name? I know he'll see me." She didn't know that he would listen to her, or even speak with her for very long. But curiosity alone should get her a couple of minutes. A couple of minutes was all she needed.

Maybe not all she *wanted.* But all she needed.

When the older woman hesitated, Tatiana pushed, injecting equal amounts of charm and confidence into her plea. "We're friends. He'll be so disappointed if he knows I left without seeing him. Please." She clutched the strap of her bag, the letters weighing it down. "Tatiana Belikov."

The older woman pursed her lips. As she reached for the phone, Tatiana heard her mutter something that sounded like, "It's your funeral."

"What now, Esme?"

The low, annoyed voice came through the receiver, too deep and booming to be contained by a small piece of plastic. A small chill ran down her spine. It had been roughly a decade since she'd heard that voice, and it still managed to make her sit up and take notice.

He sounded harder. Tougher. And not happy.

He was about to get even more unhappy.

"There's a young lady here to see you."

"Is she on my schedule?"

"No, sir."

"Then she doesn't exist."

Esme cast her a reproachful glance, and Tatiana winced, mouthing, *Sorry.* She was sorry. She also wasn't budging.

Esme continued. "She says to tell you her name is Tatiana Belikov."

Tatiana didn't know what she expected. A laugh. A guffaw. Or worst of all, a "Who?"

Instead, resounding silence greeted the announcement. Tatiana's breath caught as she waited for…something. Anything.

A creak brought her gaze from the phone to the mahogany double doors leading to what was assuredly the lion's den.

Back straight, head up. Oh, but her hands. What to do with her stupid, restless hands? Worry urged her to link them together. The stirring of her girlish heart had her longing to twirl her hair.

Her pride took over. She clenched those hands into militant fists.

The door opened wider, revealing a man she barely knew, yet at the same time, knew all too well. He was larger now, a full-grown male instead of the gangly youth she'd known. He wore a solid black suit, harsh against his very white shirt. His tie was bright red, a splash of color that should have been garish but instead added a dash of charm and whimsy to his otherwise stark appearance. He wore the suit well—but then, was there anything he wouldn't wear well? He still had the physique of the common laborer he'd been, not the executive he was.

Had he been any other man, she would have accused him of posing for her. But he'd never had much vanity about his body, using it as other people did a tool. He moved, placing his large hands on his hips and pushing back his suit jacket, as if to display the trimness of his waist and stomach.

Dear eyeballs, anytime you want to stop eating this guy up with a spoon, that would be good. But it was so damn hard. The man had aged well, and she had never been immune to his appearance. As a bumbling, awkward freshman in high school, she'd drooled every time she'd looked at the hottest senior. Even when they'd broken up, she'd had to battle that tug of attraction.

He could have at least gotten a bald spot. But, no, he had a full head of hair. He'd worn it long when they'd been lovers, as suited a young rebel. Now, the coal-dark strands were cut short. She tightened her fists until her nails cut into the skin of her palms, the better to resist the temptation to see if he still liked a woman running her fingers through that cool silk.

His eyes were as dark as his hair, framed by a fringe of lashes so thick he'd been teased into more than one fistfight over whether he wore eyeliner. Those eyes were trained on her, piercing through her thin armor, right into her soul.

"Tatiana Belikov." His voice was emotionless, as if they

were acquaintances meeting at a dinner party, not standing face-to-face for the first time since the finale of their tumultuous relationship.

She raised her chin. She might look delicate, but she was no pansy. "Wyatt."

He cocked his head. "What a…surprise."

"Mr. Caine? The young lady said you were friends. Do I need to call someone?"

Her boss's reaction was disturbing Esme. Tatiana wondered if women frequently had to be bodily removed from Wyatt's office.

"That won't be necessary, Esme. I do know her." His smile was a flash of white in his swarthy skin. "And yes. We're old friends."

She shivered, though she wasn't sure why. The lush, climate-controlled office wasn't cold. "I apologize for barging in like this so unexpectedly." He didn't speak, didn't rush to reassure her that she wasn't barging in. She wasn't sure she expected him to. "I need to speak with you about an important matter."

Wyatt's only reaction was a raised black eyebrow. His expression was closed, remote, sardonic. Déjà vu. He'd worn this same face countless times as a teenager. Wyatt had perfected the careless-rebel role back then, which she had sworn, in her dreamy, girlish way, she could see beneath to his squishy, warm heart.

Not that she was fooling herself into thinking she could see anything now. A lot of time had passed, and they were both different people.

"How curious. Of course. Far be it from me to deny a lady."

Was she the only one who noticed the emphasis on that last word? Wyatt glanced idly around the waiting area, and she followed his gaze to the other occupant in the room. The man sitting on the sofa made no secret of his avid interest in their exchange. "Esme, reschedule this gentleman's appointment to tomorrow."

The man scowled, transferring his gaze to Wyatt. "What? No. I need to see you today!"

Wyatt gave him a cold look. "You'll reschedule to tomorrow."

A pang of guilt made Tatiana turn around and peer at the man. "I really am sorry—"

"Well I don't care if you're sorry—"

"I think you're forgetting," Wyatt cut him off cleanly, with the precision of a surgeon wielding a blade, "who's here begging a favor from whom, hmm? You want to help dull the memory of how you screwed me over last time we did business? You'll reschedule. To tomorrow."

The man opened his mouth, but something he saw in Wyatt's face made him shut up. Paling, he shook his head, muttering as he fished out a handkerchief and mopped his forehead.

"Come into my office," Wyatt said to her, his voice smoother, lower.

Will you walk into my parlour? said the Spider to the Fly. She bit her lip. Nerves were making her belly jump.

At least, she hoped it was just nerves. A low-level buzz of caution around this particular shark was a good thing. It would keep her on her toes. Lust would be far more troublesome.

Damn it, Wyatt. If not a bald spot, maybe some chub. Real-

ly, is a paunch too much to ask for?

"Tatiana."

Uttering her name should not make the fine hairs on her arm stand up and salute. It was the way he said it that was magic, all cool command and expectant.

Goddamn it. It wasn't just nerves.

She resisted the urge to fan herself and took a step toward Wyatt. He shifted and held the door open, waiting for her to precede him.

She walked inside the office, unable to stop herself from adding a twitch of attitude to her ass. A glance over her shoulder proved it was wasted—he was closing the door, his back to her. Her lips compressed. Fine. She would give him some other opportunity to slaver over her still-pert body.

He wasn't the only one who had aged well. And any minute now, she would stop sounding so freakin' defensive.

To occupy herself, she glanced around the luxurious office. The cherry desk was huge and uncluttered, save for a sheaf of papers piled on the surface. The chair was plush black leather, and its price tag alone could pay her bills for a month. A wet bar graced one corner of the room; probably de rigueur for a man who owned a casino. The floor-to-ceiling windows that made up the fourth wall showcased a glorious view of Las Vegas.

The walls were a creamy off-white, and while a few tasteful paintings decorated them, there wasn't a single picture of family or friends. Which made sense, since she knew his mother was dead, his father had barely been more than a sperm donor, and he'd had no other real family growing up. Her quick research of the low-key CEO of Quest Casino had turned up the news he had never married nor had children.

According to Wikipedia, at least. A private detective she wasn't.

"You have a nice office," she said, in order to break the heavy silence. She turned to find him standing at the door, one hand on the wood as if he were barring others who might try to enter.

Or to keep her from leaving.

He dropped his hand. "Thank you." Still expressionless.

"The whole place is nice." Tatiana waved, to encompass the large building she stood in. She supposed, compared to the Mirage or Caesars, Quest was a small entity. However, what the hotel and casino lacked in size, it made up for in exclusivity and class. In the five years since it had been established, it had hosted politicians, heads of state, and millionaires—all of whom were guaranteed discretion and the opportunity to indulge their vices with no commoners about to carry tales. One article she'd read had written, *What happens in Vegas stays in Vegas, but what happens at Quest...no, nothing ever happens at Quest.*

Wikipedia was a freaking *fountain* of information.

"You've played here?"

The question was posed innocently enough, but she thought there was a bite of mockery in it. *You have the means to play in my sandbox?*

Her spine stiffened. "No. I've never been here before today. I meant it seems nice."

"Thank you. You don't live here, I take it."

"I live in San Francisco now."

"San Francisco? That's far from New England."

"So's Las Vegas."

His lip curled. "Touché. But I had no real ties to the East

Coast. I'm surprised you were able to leave your beloved family behind."

The knot between her shoulders seized up. "I see them on the holidays."

"That's enough for them? Hmm."

The rush of defensive words beat in her head, dying to pour out of her mouth. The girl she'd been would have let them spew. The woman she was now had learned some semblance of self-control. "Yes. We miss each other, but I like living out here." Plus, she had some newly discovered family within a day's drive, or a short plane ride. Right here in Vegas, even. *Coincidence, you're a cruel bitch.*

He stared at her, those black eyes unsettling. "You're looking well." His glance was a quick one, up and down her body. Her skin still felt seared.

"Thank you." She fought the urge to fidget with her clothes. The simple grey sheath dress paired with a dark blazer was her go-to classy outfit for when she needed to disguise her normally artsy style and meet with a client or a gallery owner. She'd needed confidence, though, so she'd added one of her favorite necklaces, multiple strands of coiled, interconnected hammered gold that hung between her breasts. "You are as well. Have to say, I never saw you as a businessman. And running a casino, of all things."

When they'd broken up, he'd been taking college classes part-time, so though he was three years older, academically he'd still been around her level. Every other spare minute he'd had had been spent working: a bookstore, so he could learn during his breaks; construction, so he could fall back on a trade; a waiter, for the free meals. Not to mention anything else he could get his hands on.

Her physicist parents hadn't been able to stand that. *Tatiana, you need a boy who will put his education first.*

"You know how much I like to be unpredictable."

"How did you get into it?"

He just looked at her.

She tucked her hair behind her ear. "If you don't mind my asking." She should probably get down to the purpose of her visit, but small talk wasn't a bad thing. Plus...she was curious. Wildly curious.

Wyatt shrugged. "I came to Vegas with some guys and won a shitload of cash in a poker game."

She raised her eyebrows, not expecting that.

He tapped the side of his head. "Turns out I have a knack for cards. Used the money to buy into bigger and bigger games. Ended up meeting some people who had more money than me and an interest in investing in a place here in town. It worked out."

"Yeah, it did. What luck." And what a deliberate downplay, she was certain, of the amount of work and energy Wyatt had poured into this venture.

"You make your own luck. This city is good for that sort of thing."

She sure hoped so.

"And what is it you do?"

The question was no doubt a polite response to her own inquiry. Still, she perked up at his interest. "An artist. I design jewelry."

He cocked his head. "Really? Last I heard you were a bio major. Big change."

It had been a big change—and Wyatt knew very well she had only been a bio major to please her adoptive parents. "I dropped out of college during the last semester of my senior year," she said, keeping her voice even. She refused to fall back into that need to prove him wrong about her so-called slavish devotion to her family.

Even if he had been right all those years ago. No nineteen- or twenty-year-old wanted to be told their parents controlled them.

He turned away from her and walked to the wet bar. He poured a glass of amber liquid and swallowed it back in a single gulp. He immediately helped himself to another serving. Well. Maybe he wasn't quite as cool as he looked.

He faced her and raised the glass. "Sorry. Drink?"

"No. Thank you."

Wyatt took another sip, slower this time. "My surprise over what you do for a living is surpassed by the fact that you're here at all."

"I know." She hesitated before launching into the speech she'd carefully prepared on the plane ride over. "Thank you for seeing me. I know we didn't part on the best of terms, but I want—"

"Sit."

"Um."

He gestured to the brown leather sofas arranged on the far side of the room. "If you like. You can sit."

"Yes. Okay." So civilized. They were so very civilized. She crossed to the little seating arrangement and perched on the edge of the loveseat. He strode over, and she tried to not notice how the fabric of his pants clung to his thighs. Tried. And failed.

Hold steady, girl.

She breathed in and then out. The material of the couch

was warm against the backs of her thighs. Her skirt had ridden up when she sat down. She shifted, wishing she could stand and adjust the fabric but not wanting to call attention to the length of bare leg that was exposed.

Too late. The attention had been garnered. His gaze dipped over her legs before gliding up over her chest.

She could easily clear her throat and put him in his place. *You wanted him to see you still had it...*

So she didn't.

He glanced up from his leisurely perusal. Not a trace of shame crossed his face when he realized he'd been caught ogling her. He sat back in his seat. "You were saying?"

What had she been saying?

"You want..." he prompted, his voice caressing the two words.

Yes. She wanted. A hazard of her fair complexion: blushes were too obvious. "I wanted to speak with you. I have a proposition for you."

"Is that right?" A slow smile crossed his thin, slightly cruel lips. "That sounds...interesting."

"Not that kind of proposition."

The smirk spread. "I don't know what you're talking about."

Her, on her knees. Hands bound. Him, holding her head steady.

That kind of proposition.

She tried to banish the images—the memories—from her mind by focusing on something else. But all she could see was *him*. His wide shoulders, his powerful legs, the masculine beauty of his face.

"I found my birth family," she blurted out in an effort to

say something, anything that wasn't *Can I feel your biceps?*

If the abrupt words startled him, he didn't show it. His gaze turned to his glass. The ice in the drink clinked together.

"Did you now? Congratulations."

"Thank you."

"That must have been a big deal for you." He rolled his glass between his hands. "You spoke of it a lot as a teenager."

A lot was an understatement. Her parents, who had adopted her when she'd been a few days old, were as kind and loving as they were infuriating and meddling, but she'd always felt vaguely out of place with them. She was petite; they were sturdy and tall. She was a dreamy, impulsive artist; they were practical scientists. Discovering her roots had been a frequent fantasy.

"It happened recently. About a year ago. My brother— my biological half-brother—he was the one who found me."

"What's it like to be a sister?"

The easy conversation, too, was familiar. Tatiana's stiff posture relaxed as she settled into the luscious couch. "Weird. Normal."

"That makes sense."

She gave a half laugh and struggled to clarify her answer. "I've always been an only child. And then there's someone in your life who looks like you and automatically cares about you on that basis alone, before they even know you." Still bemused by it all, she shrugged. "He's just...family. It was right. New, but right. Know what I mean?"

"Maybe. I've felt that way a time or two." He studiously avoided looking at her. "Never about blood relatives."

Tatiana sobered. The place they'd grown up in was small enough to have a designated town drunk, and Wyatt's father had been it. After his wife had died, he'd abused his son emotionally until the day Wyatt turned eighteen and moved into his own apartment.

Talk about his home life had been high on the list of taboo topics. Their fights over him not allowing her to meet or even talk about his dad? Epic.

All you could freak out about was your hurt over him not sharing. You barely gave a thought to why he would keep something like the pain he'd endured private. Ugh. Relationship hindsight was brutal. Sympathy and regret made her voice scratchy. "Yeah."

"So. No other new relatives?"

Her lips twisted. "None that matter. My brother was raised mostly by his father, which from what I understand was a good thing. His—our—mother lives in L.A. She...she wasn't interested in meeting with me." Or, really, even speaking to her. Her childish dreams of becoming biffles with her birth mom had died a swift and nasty death. She'd shaken it off, helped by her brother's delight in getting to know her.

"I'm sorry." Wyatt took a sip of his drink. The slight jiggle of his knee caught her attention, unusual for such a controlled guy.

Now that she thought about it, his shoulders did look tense. That was strange. She was the one who should be anxious.

She spoke a little faster, some of her ease vanishing. "It's her loss. But my brother. He's a sweet boy. He's got a really big heart and a loving personality. He has a wife and a small baby, and they've invited me for Thanksgiving and driven to San Francisco to see me—" She shook her head, unable to express the wonder of this blessing that had unexpectedly come into her life. "They've been—are—wonderful."

"That's good. I'm happy for you." He glanced at his watch. The move was discreet, but Tatiana caught it.

She needed to get to the point. The poor guy was probably wondering what, if anything, all her bleating had to do with him, and rightly so. Tatiana bit her lip. "Well, you see. It turns out that my little brother—and you're going to laugh about what a small world this is—his name is Ronald West. I understand he used to work for you."

Oh. His fingers tightening around the glass until the knuckles turned white was not a good sign. "Indeed." His voice was soft. "He not only worked for me. He stole from me."

"I know." She licked her lips. "But if you only knew…his wife's mother was sick, and they went into debt. He was desperate." She didn't understand the level of desperation it would require to commit embezzlement, but despair had been obvious in Caitlin's voice when the younger woman had called her yesterday, hysterical. *It's all my fault, Tatiana. He did it for me. I don't know what I'll do if he goes to jail.*

"I don't know if you remember this, Tatiana, but I had a few desperate times in my past. Yet I never stole."

Tatiana flinched. "I remember. I know. But you have to understand, Ronald's not like you." Ronald was actually frighteningly similar to her, with her tendency toward dreaminess and impulsiveness, but magnified about tenfold. Not for the first time, Tatiana was grateful she'd had her strong, pragmatic parents as role models. "He's not a criminal, not at heart. He knows he made a mistake." Or at least Tatiana assumed he knew that. It had been hard to understand what he was saying on the phone. His tears kept getting in the way.

Except his boss's name. That had come through loud and clear. She'd been disbelieving at first, but a Google search had turned up the fact that yes, her Wyatt Caine was indeed *the* Wyatt Caine.

After her third glass of wine, she'd booked her flight to Vegas. Had it been two in the morning? Three? It was a little blurry.

"He sent you to plead his case." Wyatt shook his head. "Hiding behind a woman's skirts? That doesn't convince me he's a paragon."

"He doesn't know I'm here. Or that we knew each other." She'd come straight from the airport to see the man Ron had stolen from. The man she oh so coincidentally had slept with once upon a time.

"So, what? He told you he was in trouble, so you decided you should use the fact that we've fucked before to your advantage—"

Sorry, had he said something past the word *fucked*? 'Cause if he had, she hadn't processed it. The word sounded harsh and vulgar on his lips, the way it should be. The way she liked it.

Her hands fluttered, and she grasped them together, stilling their motion. "I was surprised to discover who you were. I didn't know until yesterday."

"I wasn't hiding."

"Neither was I," Tatiana snapped, suddenly annoyed. "Yes, I may have come here instead of going through a lawyer because of our past relationship, but it's not so crazy that this is the first time we've spoken after all these years. It's not like you ever came looking for me after we broke up either."

They froze, and Tatiana wished she could recall the words. Needy, grasping words, just lying between them. Wyatt captured her gaze, his black eyes boring into her soul. "I didn't realize you wanted me to contact you."

Her face felt stiff and frozen. "I didn't. That is. I never thought about it." She lifted her chin, determined to get through this. "And I know you never thought about me after we broke up. I moved on. You moved on."

"Until now."

"Yes. Until now."

"So tell me. How exactly were you going to use my nostalgic memories of you to get me to drop the charges against your brother? Was I supposed to be overcome with lust at the sight of your body? Remember the way it felt to sink my cock inside your virgin cunt?"

She trembled. With outrage. It was totally outrage.

He leaned closer, placing his glass on the table between them. The clink was too loud, making her flinch. "I do remember that, sweetheart. You were so tight. Your eighteenth birthday, right? I don't know how I waited that long."

No. She wasn't going to stand here mute while he ripped into her. "You waited that long because my father would have killed you for touching me before that."

"It might have been worth it." He inched forward, farther into her space. "So what's in the script, Tatiana? Aren't you supposed to be begging prettily for your brother's life?"

She eyed him, trying to draw the tattered remnants of her cool around her. "I came here because I thought you might be reasonable. All I want to do is work out some sort of payment plan. I have savings. I can loan that to Ron, and he can repay his debt. If, in return, you agree to not press criminal charges."

"He *stole* from me. I can't abide thieves. And fifty thousand dollars is hardly chump change."

Oh. My. God. Neither Caitlin nor Ron had gone into the details, beyond saying thousands. Perhaps naively, Tatiana had assumed they had meant, at the most, ten thousand. Ron was a blackjack dealer who would be hard-pressed to find any kind of job if word of this got out. Caitlin stayed at home with the baby. How could he have ever thought he could replace this kind of money? Did he honestly think no one would notice it?

Anger at her brother overwhelmed her, but she tried to focus. She'd rip the kid a new one later.

She looked Wyatt in the eye and reached into her bag. Her fingers brushed against those damn letters, but she dug past them to her checkbook. "Fine." She pulled it out, slid her pen free, and looked up at him. "Give me the exact amount, and we'll make this right."

Oh, she loved the way he eyed her in that superior way. He named a figure, obviously expecting to call her bluff.

She briskly filled in the blanks, trying not to think of the fact that she'd never put so many zeros on a check. Years of living the life of a starving artist, unwilling to take a dime from her parents after she'd bucked them and left college, had made her appreciate her success when she had achieved it. She'd saved like a squirrel hiding nuts for a cold, hard winter.

Wintertime was here, she supposed. Family above all. Plus she would get it back, if slowly, from Ron. It was worth it to save her stupid, loveable brother from prison. She made a mental note to transfer the necessary funds from her savings account that evening.

Wyatt watched her tear the check off and lay it on the coffee table. "You don't have that kind of money."

She capped the pen, tucking it back into her checkbook. "What makes you say that?"

"Your dress and shoes. If they even came from a department store instead of a supercenter, I'd be surprised." His gaze dipped to her neck. "The gold in your necklace is real, I'll grant you, but it's hardly a liquid asset you can tap into."

"Since when did you get so good at women's fashion?" He *was* good, too. She'd bought her dress and shoes at Target. On clearance.

Oh she loved shopping. But not for boring, conservative clothes like these. Floaty fabrics, slinky dresses, impractical shoes, unnecessary accessories. If she splurged, those were her weaknesses.

"Since my job consists of assessing the depth of my opponent's pockets."

"Is that how you see everyone playing downstairs? Your opponents?"

"They're betting against the house, aren't they? I *am* the house. And I always win."

"Well, you're wrong this time. The fact that I'm not wearing expensive clothes right now doesn't mean I don't have money." She hooked the necklace in her finger and lifted it. "This *is* real. Wearable, precious art. And people pay dearly for my creations, Caine."

His black eyes glinted with an avaricious gleam as he studied the necklace, as if he was cataloging its weight and price tag. "You're talented."

The small compliment smoothed some of her ruffled feathers. "I know." She allowed the necklace to drop, to lay against her breasts. "I may not be as wealthy as you, but I've been as successful in my field as you've been in yours."

His lashes dipped. "Apparently."

She placed her fingers on the check and slid it across the table. "So I can afford to pay back my brother's debt. I'll speak with Ron. There's no need to bring legal pressure against him."

"This feels like hush money."

"It's not. It's restitution."

"And if I don't take it? What then?"

She met his gaze evenly. "Then maybe I do beg prettily a little."

He stilled. She didn't know how long they were locked in a staring contest. Frankly, she didn't care. Part of her, a frighteningly large part of her, was enjoying it too much.

She'd handed him everything, all the power, and he knew it. She could pull out those letters she had as well. Remind him of the things he'd said to her, in his own words. Really strip them both bare.

Wyatt leaned back on the sofa. "What if I said I would promise not to press charges against your brother…" he spread his legs slightly, putting his palms on his powerful thighs, "…if you spent a night in my bed?"

Does Wyatt honestly think it'll be that easy? Grab PLAY WITH ME, the first title in the Bedroom Games Trilogy, and fall in love with Wyatt and Tatiana one page at a time!

AN EXCERPT FROM
GLUTTON FOR PLEASURE

BOOK ONE OF THE PLEASURE SERIES

*T*hick, firm and curved just right, the shiny red skin stretched taut over hot seed and juice. Devi Malik squeezed the turgid flesh. *Perfect.*

The kitchen door burst open. "He's back!"

"That's nice." Devi tossed the whole red chili pepper into the pan of sizzling shrimp and vegetables. She'd need to put in a larger order of the little buggers next week. When had spicy become the new black?

"You're not even listening to me."

Accustomed to her eldest sister's dramatics, she took her time to stir the pepper evenly into the entrée before looking up. Rana stood in front of the commercial range, one fist propped on a curvy hip and a Cheshire-cat smile on her beautiful face. The Saturday dinner crowd would be piling in soon, and Devi needed to get in her groove, but long experience told her she wouldn't get any peace until Rana vented whatever news she carried. "Sorry. What did you say?"

"He's back. Mr. Tuesday Special."

Devi's hand jerked and hot oil splashed the inside of her wrist. "Damn it!" She dropped the spatula, yanked on the cold water at the faucet next to the stove and thrust her hand under the stream.

"Oh my God, are you okay?"

The icy water brought the painful throb down to a bearable sting. "Yeah, it's fine."

"You should be more careful. If I'd known the news would startle you that much, I would have warned you."

Devi cast a sharp glance at Rana's face. For just a second, she thought she caught a glimpse of shrewd cunning in her sister's eyes, but it vanished into simple concern. She withdrew her hand from under the water and dried it with studied casualness on the towel tucked into the front of her apron. "I'm sorry, I don't know what you're talking about."

With a flourish, Rana placed her orders on the board and lowered her voice to a whisper. Devi didn't know why she bothered. They were alone but for the two other chefs hard at work at the opposite end of the kitchen. "Jace is here."

Jace Callahan. Middle initial R. She knew that because she had gotten tired of Rana's silly nickname for the man and looked up his credit card receipt one night. Talk about stupid and pathetic.

In the face of her silence, Rana huffed an impatient breath. "Tall, dark and delicious? I know, I'm surprised too. He's not usually here on Saturdays."

Devi opened her mouth to deliver a blithe reply but the steam in front of her caught her attention. "Oh crap." She turned off the burner and fanned at the smoke. "Look what you made me do. You know the Jacobs send their plates back if everything isn't perfect."

Rana barely spared a glance at the pan. "It still looks fine to me."

"Shrimp isn't like other meat. It's not something you can overcook and have it still taste the same." *A distraction, please God.* Her mind raced. There was no way she could discuss her secret crush with either of her sisters—they could read her like a book.

She speared a shrimp, stuck it into her mouth and grimaced. Too chewy. She took too much pride in her craft to serve customers of The Palace chewy shrimp. Devi grabbed the pan and scraped the rest of the dish into a plate. She didn't believe in waste, so it would be her dinner later. The Jacobs would have to wait a little longer. Devi turned to the small dark woman at the far end of the room and raised her voice. "Asha, can you take the incoming? Redo table six. My sister," she continued, lowering her tone so only Rana would hear, "won't let me do my job. Don't you have customers to wait on?"

"All my tables are covered. Leena's gone for the night, and I need to get some paperwork done for her. And guess what? You're covering one of the tables for me."

No, no, no. Of course Rana hadn't brought up Jace for kicks and giggles. Devi's stomach sank under the suspicion of where her sister was going with this. "The Jacobs?" she stalled, and tried to look mildly curious. "You're right, they are so difficult, let me handle them."

Rana shook her head. "Jace said he wanted to meet his chef. So you need to serve him tonight."

In their small, family-owned restaurant, it wasn't unusual for the regulars to meet the chef. Hell, sometimes she even ended up waiting tables while she mingled if they were short on staff. How could she hand her secret object of lust his dinner, stand close enough to touch him and act as if he were just any other customer? She needed time to think about this, needed time to work this out. "Ummm..."

"Awesome, table eight."

Time up. "*Wait.*"

Rana turned with one hand on the door.

Damn it. "What's the order?"

Rana beamed. "Jace gave me the cutest little smile and asked if we could give him his usual even though it was Saturday. How could I say no?"

How, indeed. Though orders off menu always created a hassle for her, she couldn't blame her sister. If it had been her, she probably would have offered to feed him whatever he wanted by hand. Naked. Or by any other body part he preferred. Naked.

Rana sighed, as if reading her mind. "Aren't those black Irish types perfect? Brooding and charming, without even trying."

"I don't care how brooding he is. I'm just handing him his dinner."

Rana rolled her eyes. "Jeez, I'm kidding. Though it wouldn't kill you to flirt a bit. I swear, getting you a love life is a full-time job."

"I don't want to hear it." Lately Rana had been hinting, in her usual heavy-handed manner, that Devi needed to get out more. Ironic, really, since her overprotective big sisters had a well-known history of finding massive faults with the men she did finally bring home.

"Just be nice to him. I'm not telling you to strip naked. You save that for a date you're not cooking."

She wished.

"Oh, and by the way, he's got a guest. Double the order."

A guest? What? He always ate alone. Jealousy fired through her veins. After all, it was a Saturday night. He probably had a date.

It could be his mother, his friend, anyone.

Or a date.

Rana had already left and it wasn't like she could ask, anyway, without launching the Spanish Inquisition. She wiped her hands on her apron and pulled out onions. The specials were hers and hers alone, one for every day of the week, some of her favorite meals. When one was ordered, she did all of the prep and the cooking. The customers didn't know how small the kitchen was—they got a kick out of ordering something *prepared exclusively by the head chef,* as her middle sister and the restaurant's manager, Leena, had written on the menu.

Devi minced the garlic and ginger in a bowl of ice water to put aside while the onion turned transparent in the oil. Naturally, she had noticed when table eight had ordered her special twist on a thick lamb curry, her personal favorite, four weeks in a row. Noticing turned to curiosity when Rana had gushed over his attractiveness, tipping habits and overall perfection. One peep outside the little window turned her curiosity into full-blown lust. How could she have not snuck outside the kitchen to get a better look?

She added fresh tomato paste, yogurt and her secret spices to the onion and left it to simmer while she cut up chunks of lamb and dropped it in a separate pan.

Tall and broad-shouldered, he carried his arrogant good looks well—short dark hair, eyes the color of melted chocolate framed by thick lashes and a face that could have been chiseled by a master sculptor. He wore expensive suits, which wasn't unusual in and of itself, thanks to all of the office buildings surrounding their restaurant in downtown Lewiston. Unlike the rest of the after-work crowd, though, he didn't look at all tired or rumpled from the day's work or the Florida summer heat. Oh, and his butt always looked awesome. Devi made sure she caught at least one glimpse of the spectacular view during each visit.

His solitary status also set him apart and gave her foolish heart another tug. Sure, people ate by themselves, but when he did it, he appeared incomplete. Not sad or lonely, but alone. All the same, he shrugged off any of the feminine attention he received, even Rana's teasing. Men made giant fools of themselves over Rana when she scowled at them—no one resisted her once she entered flirtatious mode. Jace seemed immune to her sister's charms though, focusing on his meal, and later, on the music and entertainment they provided.

Devi poured the curry and the ginger-garlic infusion over the now-golden lamb and tossed in diced potatoes. She left it to simmer while she plated two steaming bowls of white rice and pulled hot loaves of *naan* from the oven, automatically doubling their usual portion for two. After his first couple of visits, Devi had taken to sneaking a few extra pieces of the leavened bread into the cloth-covered basket. Jace always polished it off, using it until the end to soak up any remaining sauce on his plate. The chef within her appreciated his enjoyment of her food—he ate her favorite dish with a delicacy and tidiness at odds in such a big man.

As a woman, she loved the way his mouth looked closing over the bread.

She shivered, poured the curry into two earthenware

bowls and added a garnish of cilantro to each. With a deep breath, she stood in front of the swinging doors, the large tray balanced on her hand.

No big deal. You're not an agoraphobic, you've served people before. Hand him his meal, wish him a good dinner. Nice and professional. And maybe even mildly flirtatious. She could use the practice, futile as it may be. She couldn't remember the last time she had batted her eyes at a man. No wait, she had never batted her eyes at a man. Maybe she should ask Rana for eyelash-batting lessons before she met Jace.

No. Open the door, idiot. His dinner's going to get cold and then you'll have to deal with an irate, gorgeous man. Before she could dream up any more procrastination, she shoved the door open with her hip and walked out. And then she stopped short, certain for a minute her vision had blurred by the steam in the kitchen. Two gorgeous Jaces sat at table eight, their faces presented in perfect profile. After a second look, she picked out subtle differences. Jace sat on the left, dressed in his requisite suit and indolently relaxed in his seat. The man on the right had the same dark, curling hair, but longer and shaggier, not shaped into a ruthless cut. Lines were etched around a slightly cruel mouth, and his gaze shifted constantly, his body tensed and coiled to spring at a moment's notice. His shoulders spanned an even wider width than Jace's, and the T-shirt and jeans he wore revealed a body as perfect as his brother's.

She had often thought it unfair she had been dropped into a family of gorgeous daughters, so she hoped this delicious pair of twins didn't have any siblings. No one could possibly compete with those two.

Jace smiled at something his doppelganger said and the

identical man grinned back. Her breath caught at their masculine beauty.

Well, that proves it. God has to be a woman.

Hungry yet? Devour GLUTTON FOR PLEASURE, the first novel in The Pleasure Series!

ALSO BY ALISHA RAI

Campbell Siblings Series
A Gentleman in the Street

Pleasure Series
Glutton For Pleasure
Serving Pleasure
Managing Pleasure

Bedroom Games Series
Play With Me
Risk & Reward
Bet On Me

Karimi Siblings Series
Falling For Him
Waiting For Her

Single Title
Night Whispers
Hot as Hades
Never Have I Ever
Cabin Fever

Made in the USA
Middletown, DE
27 October 2015